WILD DESIRE

"I'm going to kiss you, Miss Kincade."

Her eyes locked on his lips. "You can't."

"I have to," he said as he lowered his head slowly toward hers.

"You promised that our relationship would be a business relationship, Mr. Steele," she insisted weakly, unaware that she leaned toward him as she spoke.

"This *is* business, Miss Kincade. Important business," he assured her quietly, his lips so close to hers that she could feel the heat of his kiss even though their mouths were not touching.

"We shouldn't," Temerity whispered, bringing her mouth closer to his.

"Don't you think I know that?" he asked with a groan as he slanted his mouth over hers.

Forgetting all the sensible reasons why she shouldn't become involved with an employee, she surrendered to Steele's kiss. She only knew she couldn't ignore the pleasant throbbing coiling deep within her, the wild desire to wrap her arms around him and press herself against him . . .

If you enjoyed this book we have a special offer for you. Become a charter member of the ZEBRA HISTORICAL ROMANCE HOME SUBSCRIPTION SERVICE and...

Get a FREE
Zebra Historical Romance
(A $3.95 value) No Obligation

Now that you have read a Zebra Historical Romance we're sure you'll want more of the passion and sensuality. the desire and dreams and fascinating historical settings that make these novels the favorites of so many women. So we have made arrangements for you to receive a *FREE* book ($3.95 value) and preview 4 brand new Zebra Historical Romances each month.

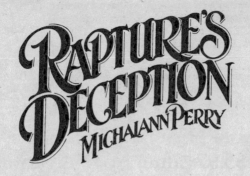

RAPTURE'S DECEPTION

MICHALANN PERRY

ZEBRA BOOKS
KENSINGTON PUBLISHING CORP.

ZEBRA BOOKS

are published by

Kensington Publishing Corp.
475 Park Avenue South
New York, NY 10016

First printing: November 1987

Printed in the United States of America

I read somewhere that sisters are caused by chance, but friends can be only the result of love. How truly blessed I've been to have known them both in one person. To my dearest friend, my sister, Beth Maxie, who will always be my little "Bethie."

And to Maureen, Barbara, and Janey, who have been my encouraging "fans" from the very beginning.

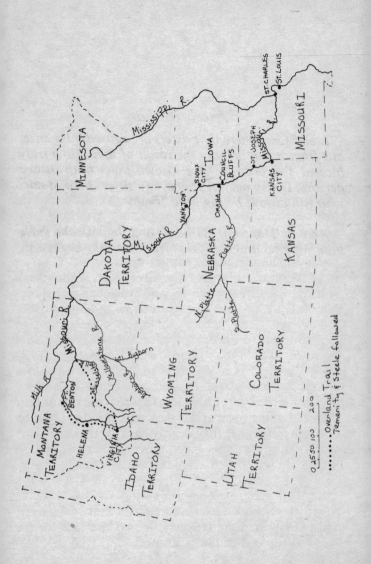

Introduction

The Missouri River's broad current was a stream of flowing mud filled with dead tree trunks that waited ominously beneath the churning brown surface to rip the bottom from any unsuspecting riverboat that passed by. Yet each spring during the last half of the nineteenth century hundreds of steamboats ran the watery 3000-mile-long gauntlet west.

In the years following the Civil War, if the river's constantly shifting sandbars and ever-changing shoreline did not ground the steamer; if Indians did not attack and burn the vessel; if the boilers did not explode when pushed beyond endurance as they built up steam to fight the current that at times ran as fast as ten miles per hour; if they had been able to find a constant supply of wood for the greedy fuel-consuming engines; if they were able to make it past the rapids near the head of the river; and if they were not destroyed by any one of another fifty deadly hazards that were part of every day life on the river, they could expect to earn profits on one trip that might easily repay the entire cost of the boat.

So with unequaled determination and pride, brave rivermen continued to fight their way west on the river, and each year more steamers joined the race for the "gold at the end of the rainbow."

Chapter One

Oblivious to the fact that she dragged the hem of her stylish ankle-length gray dress through a puddle of dirty water on the sidewalk, the raven-haired girl stepped off the curb. Her high-heeled patent leather half-boots beating a rapid tattoo of determined steps on the brick pavement, she started across the street.

"If I can't hire someone before the day is out, I'll take the *Intrepid* upriver myself! I'm not going to let anyone steal his boat! Not while I have a breath in my body," she grumbled indignantly, the light in her blue-gray eyes already hard with steely perseverance as all the arrangements to be made stormed through her mind.

"Watch out!" a loud male voice suddenly shouted, but the girl was too lost in her own thoughts to notice. She didn't slow her step.

"She's going to be killed!" a high-pitched voice shrilled through the air. "Somebody do something!" the same woman screeched hysterically, finally cutting into the girl's mind-consuming speculations.

Never occurring to her that she might be the person in danger, Temerity Kincade stopped and anxiously turned her gaze in the direction from which the warnings had come. Perhaps she could help whoever was in trouble. But before she could determine which of the awestruck spectators on the sidewalk had called out for help, she was hit in the side with a force that knocked the breath from her lungs and propelled her to the other side of the street—a split second before a spooked team of horses pulled a driverless wagon over the spot where she had been standing.

Frighteningly aware that she had barely escaped being trampled to death by the runaway horses, Temerity was even more conscious of the constricting weight on her chest. She warily opened her eyes to see what was holding her pinned to the pavement.

"Are you all right?" the deep voice breathed heavily into Temerity's ear before the man raised his head to look into wide questioning eyes—stunned gray eyes fringed with the thickest, blackest lashes he'd ever seen.

Relieved to find that she was not under a wagonload of freight, Temerity laughed nervously. "I think so," she assured her rescuer, the quiver in her voice surprising evidence of the strange feelings she was experiencing with the man's unfamiliar weight over her upper body. His handsome tanned face only inches from hers, the stranger's clean-smelling breath sent disturbing chills rippling throughout her body.

"Why didn't you get out of the way?" he scolded, lumbering uneasily to his feet and offering large, well-shaped hands down to her. Not unaccustomed to physical exertion, the large man was more affected by the experience than he would have expected to be, and his broad chest continued to rise and fall rapidly while he waited for her answer.

"I don't know," she replied. Temerity glanced at the crowd of witnesses they had drawn, uncomfortably aware of the spectacle she had made of herself. She blushed self-consciously and hurriedly took his hand, allowing herself to be drawn to her feet in the hope that the gawking onlookers would leave once they saw that she was all right. "I didn't realize I was the one in danger until I heard the wagon wheels clatter past."

His worried hazel eyes anxiously roved over the disheveled girl for signs of injury but saw none. "You could've been killed," he said, his words wafting gently over her and sounding more like a tender endearment than the stern chastisement he had obviously meant it to be.

"I know," she sighed, her expression confused. The fact that she didn't have the strength to remove her hands from the man's warm grasp was even more disturbing and real than her near escape from death. "I'm in your debt, sir," she said with a shaky smile, forgetting the bystanders, who were already beginning to disperse. She was conscious only of the concerned eyes that observed her, and she returned the enraptured gaze with her own honest appraisal of his rugged, mustached features.

Though he was dressed in the manner of a Westerner, not a man from the city, he had the ambiance of one who would no doubt be equally comfortable in the finest drawing rooms in the East or in the most primitive wilds of the West. Neither his unpomaded chestnut hair—which was entirely too long and unruly to be stylish—nor the look in his captivating brown-gold eyes—which were definitely too bold to be considered genteel—took away from the man's attractiveness. In fact, if anything, his rough exterior enhanced his masculine charm.

Appearing to be in his late twenties and at least a foot taller than Temerity's five-foot-four-inch height, the man wore a brown woolen sack coat that strained to contain the obvious power in his broad back and

11

shoulders, together with a white linen shirt that contrasted sharply with his dark good looks. A bright red neckerchief tied at his throat called her attention to the open collar of his shirt, which exposed a hint of the thick mat of curling hair that covered his chest. She flushed as the wish to see more of his body skidded across her mind.

Horrified by her thoughts, she quickly averted her gaze away from the man's neck, unwisely moving on to his snug nankeen trousers tucked into tall leather boots. Unintentionally, her eyes came to rest on slim hips and strong legs that shaped the buff-colored pants perfectly to his muscular contours, leaving little to the imagination and no doubt at all as to his sex.

The man was first to force himself to break the dazzling, debilitating physical contact. Making no effort to hide his regret, he released her hands and retrieved his wide-brimmed tan hat, replacing it on his head after absently finger-combing his thick hair. "May I see you home?" he asked in a low, husky voice.

Embarrassed by her blatant appraisal of the man, Temerity glanced downward and brushed nervously at the mauve satin piping on her alpaca walking dress. Keeping her eyes downcast to give herself a moment longer to regain her composure, she reached up to resecure the hatpin in her smart black silk Tyrolese hat and check the silver hairpins in the large netted chignon at the back of her head. She finally managed to answer in a low even voice which gathered strength with each word. "That won't be necessary, but thank you for offering. I have some business to conduct and must be on my way."

The man wiped a thumb and forefinger down his upper lip to neaten his full mustache, a nervous habit he had developed when at a loss as to what he should do next—as he was now. He knew he should accept her

12

refusal and leave it at that. Be done with her. But for some reason, he didn't want the moment to end. Not yet.

"Are you certain you're all right? Shouldn't we go somewhere and sit down until you feel less shaky? You look a little pale. Perhaps a cup of tea?" he suggested hopefully.

"Really, I'm fine," she laughed breathlessly, finally gathering the courage to look him in the eye again. She was certain the hot color she could feel rising in her cheeks, the weakness in her legs, and the painful pounding in her chest were the result of her close call with tragedy and would pass momentarily. "I do appreciate your concern, though, and I wish there was some way I could repay you for risking your life to save mine. You deserve a reward, but I have no money with me."

"Then let me escort you to your appointment. My reward will be seeing you safely to your destination, Miss uh—"

"Kincade," she answered automatically. Although it was terribly improper for her to give her name to a stranger in the street, it seemed the only thing to do in this case. After all, the man *had* saved her life! The least she could do was be civil. "Temerity Kincade. And your name, sir?"

Though she hadn't noticed the odd quirk of his eyebrow when she first said her name, she did think it rather odd that he hesitated a moment before telling her his. "Steele," he finally said.

"Well, again, Mr. Steele, I am in your debt. Thank you for your kindness," she said, offering her hand, as one man would to another.

Surprised at the unusual gesture from a lady, Steele took the slender gloved hand in his and returned her handshake, finding her grip assured and strong, and he was overcome with a need to know more about the

13

was overcome with a need to know more about the young woman. Most females would have fainted if they had experienced what Temerity Kincade had. *Or at least they would have suffered a case of vapors,* he thought disparagingly. Yet she was not only standing confidently on her own two feet, but she was planning to go on about her business, completely unconcerned with the smudges of dirt and small rips in her expensive dress.

"Are you certain you won't let me take you somewhere?" he asked again, continuing to hold her hand and search her upturned face for the answer to what made this girl so different from any he'd ever met.

She smiled politely, deliberately removing her hand from his warm grasp and ignoring the pang of regret she experienced at finding it necessary to step away from the circle of well-being she had felt from the moment of his first touch. "No, thank you. This is something I must do myself." Without further words, she smiled and turned to go.

"Miss Kincade," he called after her, stopping her anxious departure.

An expression of annoyance shadowed her oval face. She had so much to do and couldn't afford to waste any more time. But she couldn't be rude, could she? Temerity turned to face him again, a polite smile on her face once more. "Yes, Mr. Steele?"

"I would like to call on you sometime. Would that be permissible?" His deep voice was shy and hesitant, bringing a tone of sincere sympathy and regret to Temerity's when she answered.

"I'm afraid that will be impossible, Mr. Steele. I will only be in St. Louis a few days longer, and I already have commitments. Again, thank you for all of your help, but I really must be on my way." She smiled and left him, this time making certain her manner and tone would convince him that their encounter was at an end.

14

A few minutes later, having put the man from her mind, Temerity made a final check of her hair and gloves, drew herself to her full height, took a deep breath, and walked with determination through the doors of the waterfront tavern that had been her destination. Ignoring the curious stares of the rough-looking customers inside the Rooster's Roost, she allowed herself a moment to adjust her eyes to the dark, smoke-filled room. Then holding her proud head high, she fixed her unwavering sights on the surprised bartender and marched confidently across the saloon, looking neither left nor right, until she found herself facing the astounded man behind the scarred, wooden bar.

"You shouldn't be in here, miss," the baldheaded man stammered, continuing to dry the beer mug in his hand with a cloth that was far from clean. "This ain't no place for a lady."

"Then let me state my business, and I'll be gone." Her voice was low and even, and she was amazed to realize that it revealed no sign of the trembling fear ravaging through her. Suddenly, it didn't seem like a very good idea to be here. But what could she do? This was her last resort. The *Intrepid* had to have a crew, a pilot! She couldn't back down now. "If you will kindly let me make an announcement to your customers, I will leave as soon as I am through."

"I guess that'll be all right," the bartender conceded, looking around the saloon hesitantly. He took a shotgun from under the bar and pounded it on the wooden counter to call the throng of drinkers to attention. "Lady here's got somethin' to say. Listen to her. Go ahead, miss."

"I—" she started, but found her mouth dry, her tongue thick and useless. "I—" she tried again, but had to stop once more.

"Spit it out, honey!" a man shouted.

"Yeah, we got some serious drinkin' to take care of!"

There was a roar of agreeing laughter and Temerity closed her eyes for an instant before beginning again. She forced herself to swallow a few times to wet her mouth, reminding herself that people were like animals. They sensed fear and weakness and would never come to work for her if they realized she was afraid.

"I'm hiring a crew to take the *Intrepid* upriver day after tomorrow," she finally said in a hurried gush of words that miraculously managed to break through the constricting dam in her parched throat. "I have positions available for one pilot, several firemen, a mud clerk, two engineers, and a number of roosters." She chose to use common river slang when speaking of the roustabouts she needed to work at the lowly deck hand jobs, thinking to seem more knowledgeable. But her plan failed. None of the belligerent faces looking at her were in the least interested in her ability. All they saw was that she was a female—therefore a voice to ignore.

"I ain't goin' upriver with no woman captain!" one rough voice guffawed, drawing shouts of boisterous agreement from his confederates.

Judging from the looks on the surly faces, she realized her cause was useless. But just as she turned to go, a last saving idea suddenly occurred to her and she smiled with renewed hope. "I do understand your misgivings, sir. But believe me, I'm willing to make it worth the while of the right men. Not only do I plan to pay top wages, but I expect to give each member of the crew a bonus at the end of our trip—the amount to be determined by the amount of our profit."

"What's that mean in dollars 'n' cents?" one sarcastic voice bellowed hostilely.

"It means that after all of the trip's expenses are paid,

16

you will earn a share of the profits—in addition to your regular salary."

"It ain't worth the risk to go with no female at the helm. 'Sides, how do we know we're gonna git our money at the end?"

"Yeah," other voices grumbled as they all turned their backs on the distraught girl standing helplessly at the bar. She looked back at the bartender, who shrugged his shoulders and returned the shotgun to its place on the shelf. Temerity Kincade would not be finding a solution to her problems at the Rooster's Roost. That was certain.

Realizing the futility of saying anything more, Temerity bit the inside of her lip in an effort to stop the tears she felt welling in her throat and started forlornly for the door. Where else could she go? This had been her last hope, and now it was gone.

"Hey, sugar," a gravelly voice cooed, as a long hairy arm shot out and pulled Temerity onto the lap of a barrel-chested riverman who reeked of alcohol and filth. "What ya wanna go'n' do a man's work fer? A sweet little thing like you oughtn't be a worryin' her pretty head 'bout takin' no boat upriver." He wrapped his large arm around her waist and pulled her even closer against his perspiring torso. "Indians might git ya, an' ya know what they do to their women, don't ya?"

"Take your hands off me!" Temerity ordered the burly man, whose stubbled face was already nuzzling her neck and ear, sending chills of revulsion and consummate fear jerking through her.

"Ah, come on, sweetie. Ya know it feels good!" he laughed at the encouraging cheers of his mates as he slid a grimy paw up from her waist and roughly clamped her breast.

Temerity gasped in shock and tried to pull the man's

17

hand away from her. Why didn't someone help her? How could they all stand by and let this happen?

"Give us a little kiss, honey," the man begged, gripping her face and turning it toward his offensive features. To her horror, the hand on her breast continued to painfully fondle and squeeze.

"No!" she shrieked, turning her head as she managed to work her elbow into the position where she could jab it into his rounded belly. But despite the look of the gigantic man, he was as hard as granite and her assault had absolutely no effect on him, except that he was able to pull her closer to him and trap the attacking arm between his body and hers, rendering her even more helpless.

Suddenly, she felt herself lifted into the air and slapped down on her back in the middle of a large wooden table, which had been cleared of bottles and glasses with one great sweep of the huge man's arm across the rough surface. Her head reeled with the impact, and for a moment she lay stunned and unmoving.

"Come on, boys," Temerity heard the bartender beg as she stared wide-eyed at the circle of leering faces that surrounded her where she lay sprawled on the table, her arms held in viselike grips by two men, her legs dangling helplessly over the edge. "You've had your fun. I don't want no trouble. Let her go!"

"Jest shut yer trap, barkeep—if ya know what's good fer ya!" the large man looming above Temerity ordered. He reached for the struggling girl's bodice. "This little lady needs to learn what females was meant for. She oughta know her place. Gals got no business tryin' to run no riverboats." He gave the waist of her bodice a yank, pulling it free of her skirt and exposing her corset. Lewd cheers of admiration rose from the excited crowd.

18

Screaming wildly for help, Temerity squirmed and twisted, kicking out at the man's shins as she did. She was certain there was nothing she could do to protect herself, but she had no intention of lying there and being raped without putting up a fight.

"Ooeee, we got us a little hellcat, boys!" the man chuckled eagerly, taking the opportunity to raise her skirt and separate her moving legs to step between them at the table edge. Only inches from the junction of Temerity's legs, which was protected by nothing more than thin white drawers, his bulging arousal stretched his trousers tight.

The man concentrated all of his attention on the fly of his dirty cotton trousers as his thick stubby fingers fumbled with the buttons, and Temerity took up her struggles with a renewed strength that surprised the two who held her arms. Unmindful of modesty now, she managed to draw her knees up to her chest and kick her preoccupied attacker in the groin with a force that took him off balance.

Before he could regain his equilibrium, he was lifted off the ground by his shirt collar and pants waistband. The expression on the man's lubricious face, one minute leering purposefully, became one of bewildered surprise as he was hurled head first toward the wall. He landed in an unconscious mound in the corner of the dark room, no longer a danger to Temerity.

"Anyone else?" Temerity heard the familiar voice ask as she felt the pressure on her arms let up and saw the surrounding wall of would-be rapists back away from the table where she struggled to sit up. Looking frantically from face to face, she tried to understand what had happened. But now instead of lust in the drunken eyes, she saw only fear. "Cover yourself up, Temerity."

Aglow with relief and gratitude, her eyes flew in the

19

direction from which the blessed voice had come, and Temerity tried to right herself, clutching her bodice and smoothing her skirts down over her exposed drawers as she did.

"If I ever hear of any one of you doing something like this again, I'll personally hunt you down and kill you," Steele said through clenched teeth, his angry hazel eyes deliberately touching each of the rivermen in a way that left them with no doubt he would not hesitate to follow through on his deadly promise.

Never losing control of the men frozen in their tracks by his aura of authority, Steele swept Temerity into his arms, ignoring her protests that she was fine and could certainly walk.

"Don't forget what I said," he reminded the men, who would probably never be able to put the deadly gold glint of Steele's eyes from their minds as long as they lived.

"Are you all right?" he asked the girl in his arms when they were safely outside. It was the same concerned voice she remembered from earlier—nothing like the frightening tone with which he had spoken to the rough men in the saloon.

Temerity's first inclination was to nod contentedly, relax her head against the hard muscular wall of his broad chest, and continue to luxuriate in the warmth and security of his strong, protective possession. But, of course, she couldn't do that.

"I'm fine," she whispered, not really certain she was. "It appears that you have now saved me not only from death, but also from a fate *worse* than death!" she said, her tremulous smile and attempt at levity failing dreadfully. He wasn't laughing or even smiling. In fact, her words seemed to make him angry, and she shivered involuntarily as his golden eyes imprisoned her silvery blue gaze, making it impossible for her to look away.

20

"Do you find what just occurred amusing, Miss Kincade?" he growled.

"No, I didn't find it amusing at all," she admitted shamefacedly. "I was very frightened and don't know what I would have done if you hadn't come to my rescue when you did."

"What possessed you to go into such a place?"

"I was desperate."

"Desperate?" he repeated, certain he couldn't believe what he was hearing. Surely this proud young woman's situation could not be so serious that she would consider prostitution. But why else would a female enter such a place as the Rooster's Roost? And it wouldn't be the first time a young woman of good family had joined the ranks of the world's oldest profession. If anyone knew that, he did. "I can't believe the only answer to your problems could be this!" he said, his lip curled distastefully with painful memories.

He carried her effortlessly across the street, giving no indication that he planned to put her down until they had put Rooster's Roost far behind them.

Totally unaware of the thoughts raging through Steele's mind, Temerity tried to explain. "But you don't understand! My father stands to lose everything if I don't do something to help him!"

"Are you saying your father sent you in there?" Steele's square jaw tensed and relaxed alternately as he waited for her answer.

"Of course not! It was my own idea!" she confessed, already knowing what her father would say if he found out what had happened. He had told her he didn't think she'd be able to hire a crew by herself. And evidently he'd been right.

"Well, thank God for that," Steele muttered, entering a tiny café, unmindful of the stares they were drawing. He finally released his proprietary hold on the

21

disheveled girl and set her in a wooden chair at a red-gingham-covered table. "Does your father know what you were willing to do to help him?"

"Of course, he does, but I don't imagine he thought I would have such a difficult time going about it."

"What!?!" Steele blurted out, pounding his fist on the tiny round table with such force that the flatware and dishes on its surface actually bounced into the air. "And you're willing to sacrifice yourself for a man who cares no more for you than that? What kind of father is he?"

"He's a wonderful father," Temerity defended, not caring that the other customers in the small eating place were staring at them. "And of course I'm willing to make any sacrifice for him. He's my father, and I'll do whatever it takes to help him."

"But selling yourself," Steele groaned. "Did you really think you could go through with it? And if you'd been successful, how much money do you suppose you could earn?"

Temerity's eyes widened in horror. "Sell myself!" she shrieked loudly without thinking. The only sound in the room was a united gasp of shock from the restaurant's other customers. Hearing her words echoing in her ears, Temerity looked around, embarrassed and suddenly conscious of the overwhelming silence in the room and the scandalized expressions of outrage on the faces of the other people, who couldn't avoid overhearing the strange conversation. But she couldn't stop now. Not when he had made such a vile accusation.

Temerity leaned across the table and glared unflinchingly at Steele. "What are you talking about? How dare you suggest such a thing to me! Do you actually believe I went into that place expecting what happened?"

He leaned forward on his forearms and returned her

angry glare. "Then why were you in there?" he ground through gritted teeth.

"I was there to hire a crew for my father's riverboat, Mr. Steele!" she announced, feeling little satisfaction at seeing the look of surprise in his golden brown eyes.

"Do you expect me to believe that?" he asked, a flicker of realization beginning to nag at his conscience.

"Do you expect me to care what you believe, Mr. Steele?" she countered, standing up as if to leave. "Again, thank you for your assistance today. But we have nothing further to discuss."

Steele reached out and grabbed Temerity's wrist and pulled her back to the table. "Where do you think you're going?" he asked angrily. "You're in no condition to be walking anywhere, and certainly not alone."

"Such concern for a woman of my low morals, Mr. Steele?" she snarled, but allowed herself to be returned to her seat. She was feeling more unsteady than she had realized and wasn't absolutely sure she could make it to the door, much less to her buggy, without fainting.

"Perhaps I misjudged the situation," he admitted begrudgingly, his intense face asking for forgiveness.

"Perhaps?" Her posture remained stiff and unrelenting.

"I was wrong. I can see that now. But what on earth ever possessed you to do such a stupid thing?"

"I need a crew. And Rooster's Roost was the only place left I could think of to look for one." She realized now how foolish her plan had been and how it could have seemed that she had another purpose in mind.

"Couldn't your father do his own hiring? Or perhaps his pilot? Why did you think you had to be the one?"

"My father was seriously injured a few weeks ago, and the pilot who had been with him for years was killed in the same accident. So there is no one but me,"

23

she said defiantly.

Steele had been out of the city and hadn't heard about Kincade's misfortune, but he would make a point to look into it right away. In the meantime, his admiration continued to mount. He couldn't help being impressed with the brave girl who had walked alone into the Rooster's Roost, who still held herself so proudly, despite all that had happened to her. In the span of an hour, she had narrowly missed being killed and raped. Her lovely dress was dirty and torn, and her beautiful black hair was totally disarranged, its luxurious strands falling around her pale face to her shoulders, but she was not the least concerned with herself. Instead, this remarkable woman was only worried about her father and his problems.

"Surely the trip can wait until your father regains his strength."

"He may never fully heal, Mr. Steele. His back was hurt and he's partially paralyzed. No, it's up to me."

"Then why not sell the boat?"

"Because I can't let him give up hope! If I were to sell the *Intrepid,* it would mean I didn't believe he'd ever get well. Besides, he owes money on it, and we'll lose it to his creditors if we don't make the upper river trip this season."

"Oh?"

"He made an arrangement with the Cameron Line that if they would lend him forty thousand dollars he would not only pay them back in the fall plus a percentage of his profit, but that if for some reason he was unable to pay the debt, they would assume ownership of the *Intrepid.* So you can see I must make that trip. I can earn enough profit from one upstream venture to not only pay my father's debts, but also enough to take care of him for several years to come."

"How did your father find himself in such dire

24

circumstances? I always thought Tim Kincade did pretty well for himself," Steele said, realizing too late that Temerity Kincade hadn't told him her father's name.

But she was too engrossed in her problems to notice his slip. "A year ago he formed a company with other investors to take goods upriver. They planned to sell at big profits in the mining camps. But when one of his partners took the firm's goods to Wolf Valley, he was so appalled by the rough life in the gold camps, he couldn't get back to St. Louis fast enough. He foolishly entrusted all the merchandise to another man, who was to sell it for him. Unfortunately, after the man sold the goods, he ran off with the profits. The company ultimately collapsed, leaving my father seventy-five thousand dollars poorer. This year, he scraped together enough to purchase more goods by mortgaging the boat to the Cameron Line. Then he had his accident. So you can see if I don't get those supplies upstream, it will all be for nothing. Not to mention the fact that I will owe all the booked passengers a refund. And a lot of their money has already been spent on supplies!"

Suddenly remembering how the men in the tavern had backed off when Steele had entered, a new idea struck Temerity like a bolt of lightning. "Would you like a job, Mr. Steele? I realize you aren't a riverman, but I'm prepared to pay you top wages to act as my hiring agent and first mate. Plus a generous percentage of the profits upon our safe return to St. Louis!"

Chapter Two

Steele's eyes widened with disbelief. "You want *me* to work for *you?*" he choked. In frustration, he wiped his thumb and forefinger downward over his full brown mustache.

"Yes, I do. Don't you see? You're the answer to my problem! Will you do it?"

When she looked at him with those huge, crystal clear eyes of blue-gray fire, so trusting, so hopeful, how could he deny her anything? But, of course, what she was suggesting was not only ridiculous, but out of the question. Impossible!

"I can't work for you." His voice was gruff and impatient, showing his anger with himself for even letting the possibility enter his mind.

"Why not?" she returned, her tone calm and reasonable, revealing none of the desperate internal turmoil she was feeling.

"In the first place, I already have a job. And in the second place, how do you know I can be trusted?"

Temerity searched his gold-flecked eyes, and she was convinced that she had nothing to fear from this man named Steele. The corners of her sensuous mouth curved upward in a satisfied, knowing smile. "But I can trust you, can't I, Mr. Steele?"

Steele attempted another argument. "What if I don't know anything about riverboats?"

"You don't need to know anything, Mr. Steele. I have all the knowledge we need to take the *Intrepid* to Fort Benton and back."

Steele raised a suspicious brow and narrowed his eyes. "I find that rather difficult to believe, Miss Kincade," he answered quickly, his respect for the girl's determination growing by the minute, his own good judgment crumbling at the same mercurial rate in the face of her audaciousness. The comprehension that she would really try to take a riverboat upstream, with or without help from him, slowly dawned on him; and he was stunned by the realization that she might just be able to carry out her ridiculous plan. In fact, he decided, she could probably do just about anything she set her mind to. Steele's sudden insight set his emotions roiling with anger—and respect, which except for his grandmother, he'd accorded to very few females in his life.

"Well, you'd best believe it, Mr. Steele. I was born on a Missouri riverboat in the middle of an Indian attack, and I've spent eighteen of my twenty years at my father's side learning about sternwheelers and the eccentricities of the Missouri River."

Temerity paused for a moment, waiting for Steele to react to what she had said. But he remained silent, his expression an odd combination of disbelief and admiration. She went on, certain now that the only way she would be able to save her father's boat would be if Steele could be convinced to assist her. The terrible, frightening experiences of the afternoon were shoved to the back of her mind, and all her energies were concentrated on one goal.

"I give you my word, Mr. Steele, I know everything

28

we need to know to carry out the actual operations of the boat; but unfortunately, I can't do it alone. I have the knowledge"—she smiled fatefully and tapped her temple with a graceful index finger—"but not the muscle. I need someone physically strong enough to command the crew's respect." Stopping to think for a minute, she modified her statement. "I believe I can eventually earn their respect—once they've seen that I know what I'm doing. But in the meantime, until they see me in action, they won't consider coming to work for me—simply because I'm a woman. They're willing to work for drunkards, total incompetents, and notorious cheats, but they don't want to work for a female. If you act as my proxy and hire my crew for me, they won't know who they're actually working for until we're already on the river. By the time they realize who's in charge, I will have proved myself to them. What do you think, Mr. Steele? Will you do it? Will you help me one more time?"

She leaned across the table to place a slender, beseeching hand on his arm and looked into his eyes, deliberately playing upon the desperate situation he would leave her in should he refuse. As long as fate had cast her in the role of helpless female—a role she had resented for as long as she could remember—she would use it to her advantage. "There is nowhere else I can turn, Mr. Steele. You're my last hope."

Steele studied the delicate hand resting on his arm. Why did it make him so angry? A woman's hand was a woman's hand. But this one was different, touching him in a way he couldn't understand—didn't *want* to understand! Milk white against his coarse brown sleeve, the young woman's light touch seemed to burn through the cloth of his coat, searing its way up his arm where it tugged ruthlessly at his heart. How could he be falling for such an obvious feminine ploy? He who had learned at a painfully early age that women couldn't be trusted and that they would resort to any means to get what they wanted!

Yet he could not look away from the small fingers gripping his arm, though they threatened to make him forget all reason and every hard lesson he'd ever learned where the opposite sex was concerned. Still, it took every ounce of restraint he could muster not to cover the small hand assuringly with his own larger version and actually agree to her crazy scheme. His anger grew—anger at the girl, anger at himself for wanting to be . . . to be what?

What are you doing listening to this foolishness? he chided himself silently. *No one in his right mind would ever consider such an absurd plan. No woman is capable of taking a riverboat three thousand miles west. Not even one who was raised on the river.*

Steele removed the scorching hand from his arm with determination and gingerly placed it on the table—where he was certain it could do no further damage to his equilibrium and good sense. But even though it was no longer touching him, he could still feel its heat coursing through his veins, burning its way into his heart, marking him a condemned man. His anger rose to inferno heights. "You know nothing about me," he stressed adamantly.

"I know all I need to know, Mr. Steele. I know men listen to what you say. I saw the look of fear you instilled in the eyes of those ruffians in the tavern, and I know you would command the same respect from a crew—no matter how little you know about steamboats. Please, Mr. Steele," she begged, inwardly cursing the tears she felt pooling in her eyes. She couldn't cry. Not now. Not when she'd seen a glimmer of respect in his intense hazel eyes. If she cried, he would see her vulnerability and, like all the others, refuse to help.

Of course, Temerity had no way of knowing that her watery blue-gray look of desperation was more potent than any words she could have spoken, or that it would dissolve the last chink in Steele's armor with the deadly certainty of hot acid spilling on metal, leaving him helpless to deny her his assistance.

"I might be able to help you find a capable crew," he acquiesced, even as he told himself that he was crazier than she was if he went along with her. However, if he could hire a dependable captain, a knowledgeable pilot, and a trustworthy bully boy to keep the crew in line, things might work out. He hated to see a good man like Tim Kincade go under because of a run of bad luck. Besides, if he helped Kincade, he'd be helping himself, and it was probably the only way Kincade's daughter could be persuaded to give up the foolish idea of taking the *Intrepid* upriver herself. What it all boiled down to was that he really had no other choice in the matter. He couldn't stand by and allow her to destroy her father's boat. And he certainly couldn't let her go into any more saloons searching for workers, which he knew without a doubt was exactly what she would do if he turned her down. He had to help her.

"And you'll go with me to oversee them—especially the roosters?" she said, her eyes open wide in anticipation of his affirmative answer.

"We'll see," he replied to his balled fists on the table. He couldn't look her in the eye. He knew this was not the right time to tell her that he had no intention of going upriver on the *Intrepid*—or the fact that she would not be going either. Besides, if he took one more glance into those misty blue eyes of hers, now so full of renewed hope, still glistening with unshed tears, he would be tempted to agree to almost anything—even something that went against every bit of common sense

31

he possessed. So he kept his gaze carefully directed downward while he nervously flicked the edge of his large tanned hand over a nonexistent speck on the immaculate gingham tablecloth.

"Oh, Mr. Steele, I don't know how to thank you," she exclaimed, energetically jumping to her feet to leave, the earlier horrors of the afternoon completely behind her. "We must start right away. The *Intrepid* is scheduled for departure day after tomorrow."

Steele shot up out of his own chair in protest. "Day after tomorrow? How am I going to round up a crew by then? I'll need at least a week!"

"You can do it, Mr. Steele. I have great faith in your ability," she smiled.

How the hell did I get myself talked into this mess? Steele asked himself, but aloud he said, "I'm afraid you're going to be very disappointed, Miss Kincade. There are only so many things one man can do in forty-eight hours."

"We don't really have *forty-eight* hours," she announced. "Actually, we only have forty-two. We depart at eight in the morning."

She can't be serious. But another look at the unwavering expression on Temerity Kincade's expectant face told Steele not only that she was completely serious, but that she would not be deterred from her goal by anything he said. Still, he had to try.

"You will have to put off the departure time," he insisted sternly, deliberately fixing his most intimidating glare on her.

"I'm not delaying my departure, Mr. Steele," she said pleasantly, her smile meeting his glare with equal determination. "I'm leaving as scheduled—full crew or not!"

"Great," Steele grunted, slapping money down on the table, even though no one had taken their order or served them—no one had been brave enough to approach the table. "I'll see you home, then I'll get to work and see what I can do," he conceded, not noticing the look of relief that swept over the café owner's face as they left the restaurant. After all, he couldn't let the *Intrepid* leave St. Louis without a capable crew. *Crazy woman won't just destroy her father's boat, but she'll kill herself and anyone unfortunate enough to go with her.*

"There's no need to see me home. I have my buggy. Don't worry about me. Just worry about finding a crew. Have them report to the *Intrepid* as early as possible tomorrow. I'll trust your judgment as to which men are the best for the job."

Which men are the best for the job! She sounds like there'll be a choice at this late date. Doesn't she realize all the best men are already hired?

"Then I'll see you to your buggy," he said with resignation, his mind racing for a way to stop the girl from attempting to carry out her insane scheme without spoiling his own chances to get to know her more intimately—which he had every intention of doing.

Though why he would want anything more to do with her, he didn't know. Granted she was lovely and intelligent, but so were a hundred other available young women in St. Louis. What was so special about this particular one? The last thing he needed was to get entangled with a woman who lived up to the ridiculous name *Temerity* in every sense of the word.

Rash, foolhardy, reckless were only a few of the words hammering at Steele's thoughts as he remembered the brief moments shared with Tim Kincade's daughter. He mentally kicked himself for getting involved and for letting her take over his thoughts. *She's stubborn, willful, careless.* Steele smiled and

33

shook his head. *But I've got to admit, she's sure got more than her share of spunk! More than I've seen in all the women I've ever known in my twenty-eight years on this earth!* he acknowledged with a begrudging grin as he walked north along the levee, heading toward a large gray building that dominated the area surrounding it. He shook his head in an attempt to forget the lovely face, but it did no good. *She's got to be the most bull-headed female in Missouri! Maybe in the whole damn country!*

If there was no way to stop her, and Steele began to suspect there was not—short of hog-tying her, *which might not be such a bad idea*—he would make certain she had the best crew available to look out for her and the *Intrepid*. Then he would be able to wash his hands of the whole affair—and Miss Temerity Kincade, riverboat operator, and concentrate on Temerity Kincade, desirable woman.

"I'm truly sorry that you disapprove, Mr. Yeager, but until September thirtieth, the *Intrepid* still belongs to my father, and it is leaving the levee tomorrow morning at eight o'clock—as planned," Temerity told the representative from the Cameron Line who had come to talk to her.

The young man, taller than Temerity by no more than two inches, wiped a handkerchief across his perspiring forehead, ran a finger along the inside of his shirt collar in a futile effort to loosen it, and began again. He was no longer able to disguise his frustration. "Please try to understand, Miss Kincade."

"Oh, I understand, all right," Temerity said, nodding her head astutely as she took a step toward Harold Yeager, drawing so close that the cloying scent of his hair pomade and the stale tobacco and coffee on his breath made her slightly ill. But she did not give in to her nausea. Instead, her fists balled angrily on her hips, she planted her feet squarely on the *Intrepid*'s wooden deck, and pushed her face up to his to make her accusation through a tight smile. "The Cameron Line can't wait to step in and take over, can they? Tell me, Mr. Yeager, is this how the Camerons have gotten the rest of the riverboats on their line? Well, go steal someone else's boat. The only way you're going to get this one is over my dead body!"

"The Cameron Line doesn't want to take the *Intrepid* away from you, Miss Kincade," the man said. "We only want you to put off your departure time until we can find a suitable crew for you."

"I don't need your 'suitable crew,' Mr. Yeager," Temerity sneered as she whirled away from the obviously exasperated man to check over a cargo list a lanky young cabin boy was holding for her approval. "That's fine, Jimmy," she smiled at the red-headed fifteen-year-old before returning her attention to Yeager. "Now, if you don't mind, sir, I have no more time to waste on this conversation. So, I will bid you good day," she said, dismissing the man with a polite but definite nod of her head.

"But, Miss Kincade," the flustered man protested. He attempted to follow her toward the gangplank, but Temerity continued to ignore him, her attention now focused on the large man walking down the levee toward the *Intrepid*.

"Mr. Steele! I'm so glad to see you," she shouted, waving eagerly to the man who approached. Subconsciously aware of the way the early afternoon sun highlighted the rugged planes of his handsome face, and the way it brought out the red in his mustache and sideburns, she couldn't help wondering if the hair on the rest of his body had that same rich auburn cast to it.

Blushing at the highly personal turn her thinking had taken, she scolded herself silently. *A lady doesn't think about things like that!*

"Where have you been?" she asked irritably as he came on board, more annoyed with her own thoughts than with his absence. Still she was unable to shift her attention away from the vee of chest hair that showed at his collar. In the bright sunshine it was red too.

"I've been hiring a crew, Miss Kincade," Steele answered curtly, his frown masking the unexpected pleasure he felt at seeing her again. However, as he reached the spot where she was standing, he noticed Harold Yeager for the first time, and his expression changed to one of wariness. But he managed to hide his concern so that neither Temerity nor the man from the Cameron Line noticed. "Is there a problem?"

"Mr. uh . . . ," Yeager started, nervously wiping his perspiring hand on his jacket before offering it to Steele.

"Steele," Temerity offered smugly, taking Steele's arm and turning back to face Harold Yeager. "Mr. Steele, allow me to introduce Mr. Yeager of the Cameron Line. Mr. Yeager, this is my first mate, Mr. Steele," she said, smiling with satisfaction at the smaller man's look of dismay.

"F-first m-mate?" Yeager stuttered, looking up the long length of Steele's frame. "I d-don't und—"

Steele's eyes narrowed dangerously. "It's good to meet you, Mr.—was it Yeager?" he returned quickly, not allowing the man to finish his statement.

"Mr. Steele, will you please explain to Mr. Yeager that the Cameron Line has no say in the *Intrepid's* affairs before September thirtieth, and then, only if my father fails to pay his debt to them?"

"I'm afraid she's got you there, Yeager," Steele drawled easily, but the smile on his lips and the hard glint in his hazel eyes shot an obvious warning to the shorter man—though Yeager failed to recognize it.

"But I thought—" he persisted.

"Whatever you thought, Yeager," Steele cut him off again, "the law's on her side. If she wants to hire a crew to take this boat upriver with her cargo, you can't stop her."

"But what if she loses the boat?"

"Then the Cameron Line loses its money. It happens all the time. But you knew you were taking a gamble when you lent her father the money, didn't you? However, to set your mind at ease, Mr. Yeager, I promise you that I'll do everything in my power to protect the *Intrepid*—and Cameron's investment. Now, you go on about your business, and let us get back to ours," he said, firmly gripping the man's arm and guiding him toward the gangplank. "Miss Kincade will see you in three months when she comes to pay her father's debt. In the meantime, she wants nothing further to do with *anyone* from your company. Is that clear?" he asked, his tight smile a grim threat of reprisal if Mr. Yeager chose to misunderstand his meaning.

"I understand perfectly, Steele," Yeager said, vowing to find a way to repay the arrogant man for treating him so rudely in front of Temerity Kincade. When he had heard about her father's plight, his mind had quickly formulated a plan to be the one to step in and save the *Intrepid*. But he hadn't expected to run into Steele. Now that plan would have to be altered, but he would still find a way to get something for himself out of this situation. *One way or the other!* he vowed as he rushed down the gangway.

Without thinking, Temerity threw her arms around Steele's neck in an exuberant display of gratitude. "You were wonderful, Mr. Steele!" she laughed gleefully as she watched Harold Yeager make his hurried departure. "I knew you were the right man for the job the minute I saw you!" she said happily.

The realization of what she had done hit her full force, and a wave of embarrassment swept over Temerity. Her jubilant expression quickly changed to one of shock and then to one of confusion as she became uncomfortably aware of an unfamiliar heat raging through her. Her hands slid from around his neck to rest against his chest.

But before she could pull away, Steele placed his hands lightly at her waist and examined her face with a look of amusement on his own, but he said nothing. He just watched her with a knowing smile. It was then she noticed the mischievous dimples in each of his cheeks. And her heart did a flip in her chest.

Painfully conscious of his touch on her waist, burning its way through her bodice and corset as if he had put hot irons to her bare skin, Temerity was suddenly afraid. Afraid of Steele, yes, but even more afraid of her own tumultuous feelings.

For the briefest instant, Temerity searched his face, her own expression asking a million confused questions. But at last, she managed to drop her arms and attempt to take a step back. However, Steele's hands, their heat radiating exquisitely through her every pore, stayed where they were, and it was impossible for her to move away.

"I'm sorry," she apologized hesitantly, not at all certain she was, not even certain that she wanted the physical contact to end. Yet she knew she had to say something. And she had to put some space between herself and the man—though she was positive her knees would surely buckle if he released her.

"I'm not," he murmured softly, his dimples deepening as his warm breath wafted over her face, weakening her resistance even further. "I find it rather pleasant," he told her, setting another storm of erratic confusion reeling in Temerity's brain.

She placed her hands on his and deliberately removed them from her waist, forcing herself not to surrender to the desire to hold them longer than necessary.

"Mr. Steele," she said as firmly as she could manage, knowing she was failing miserably in her attempt to disguise the tremble in her voice. "We must have a definite understanding from the very beginning." With stubborn determination, she concentrated on regathering her assurance once the incapacitating physical contact was ended. But she couldn't escape the knowing look in his eyes, or that impish dimpled grin.

He knew! He knew how he had affected her and he was pleased with himself. Well, she would wipe that self-satisfied smile off his face before long. If she didn't need him so desperately, she'd do it right this minute. But she couldn't afford to lose him. Look at the way he had handled Yeager so easily—when she'd been unable to make the least bit of headway with the Cameron employee after thirty minutes of discussion.

Telling Mr. Steele what she thought of his arrogant manner would have to wait, she realized with frustration. Saving the *Intrepid* was too important. "Ours will be a business relationship only. Nothing more. Is that agreed?" she ground out through a stiff smile, carefully restraining her need to scream at him.

"The thought of anything else never crossed my mind, Miss Kincade," Steele said, his open smile wide and guileless.

But something in his gold-flecked hazel eyes, though they were opened innocently wide, told her this was not the last time their relationship would teeter precariously on the tightrope between business and personal. And she was surprised to realize that the knowledge thrilled her at the same time it frightened her—even though she vowed to fight him every step of the way.

"My behavior was inexcusable, and I do apologize for throwing myself at you in my excitement, Mr. Steele. But you can be assured I won't forget myself again," she continued curtly, determined to put their arrangement back on a proper footing.

"*Now* I'm sorry," Steele said, the gleam in his eyes telling Temerity the business relationship she was hoping for had met only the first of many tests.

"Mr. Steele, a gentleman would accept a lady's apology without going out of his way to remind her of her error."

"I didn't know being a gentleman was one of the requirements for this job, Miss Kincade."

Temerity opened her mouth to speak. But good sense stopped her automatic reply. Though every natural instinct she possessed told her she would be smart to send Steele packing, she couldn't. She still needed him and couldn't let him go. She would just have to be on her guard every minute if she expected to keep him at bay for the next three months!

Deciding it would be best to ignore his last words, she glanced around to see that things were still moving smoothly with the loading of the *Intrepid*. "The men you've sent so far seem to be doing an excellent job, Mr. Steele. I do appreciate your efforts on this short notice, and I give you my word that your bonus at the end of our trip will reflect that appreciation," she said in an even voice. There, that should remind him that he was the employee and she the employer. If he wanted his money at the end of the trip, he would remember his manners.

"Oh, I definitely plan on collecting that bonus, Miss Kincade—though what it will be is yet to be determined," he answered, turning to walk away from her before she could come back with the scathing reply on the tip of her tongue.

"Uriah!" he shouted, forgetting Temerity entirely as he hurried to greet a white-haired giant of a man who was just coming on board. "I was wondering if you'd checked in yet," he asked the pipe-smoking man.

"Good to see ya, boy," the old man said, his gravelly voice sounding angry, in direct contradiction to the cheerful twinkle in the clear blue eyes that peered out from beneath bushy white eyebrows. "Is that her?" he grumbled, taking the worn pipe from between his teeth and pointing the stem toward Temerity. "Is that Tim's kid?"

"I'm Tim Kincade's daughter," Temerity said stiffly as she stepped forward.

"Pretty little thing, ain't she?" Uriah said to Steele.

"She kind of grows on you," Steele said, winking conspiratorially at Uriah.

Temerity shot Steele a look of annoyance and asked, "Are you going to introduce me to this man, Mr. Steele?" Her voice displayed a forced pleasantness she was not feeling at the moment.

"Spunky too," the old riverman laughed, scratching his white-mustached upper lip before clamping his pipe back between his teeth.

"Definitely spunky," Steele agreed, enjoying Temerity's irritation. "But I guess we'd better get the introductions over and get you settled. Miss Kincade, allow me to introduce you to the best master pilot to ever run a steamer up the Missouri. This is Uriah Gunther."

Temerity smiled and held out her hand. "Mr. Gunther, it's my pleasure."

"Is that how t' greet a fella who was fightin' off the Injuns while you was gittin' borned?" Uriah snarled.

Without warning, he pulled Temerity against his burly frame and lifted her feet off the deck to swing her around before setting her back down.

"You worked for my father?" she gasped, not noticing that in her shock she automatically reached for Steele's arm to steady herself when her feet touched solid wood again. But he noticed and so did Uriah Gunther.

"Sure did. Course you wouldn't 'member me 'cause the last trip me an' your pa made together was 'bout fourteen years ago in 'fifty-four. That's b'fore the gold fever took holt o' me. But I sure do 'member you. Runnin' round and givin' out orders like you was the captain, 'stead o' your pa!" The older man laughed. "Course, you always had the whole crew wrapped 'round your little finger, so no one minded your bossy ways too much." Suddenly, the master's tone changed. "Sorry to hear 'bout your ma. She was one o' the sweetest ladies I ever knowed—an' one o' the prettiest." He winked a bright blue eye. "You look like 'er, you know."

"Oh, Mr. Gunther, I'm so glad you came," Temerity said, gripping the man's arm affectionately, not even worried that it had been fourteen years since he had piloted a riverboat on the ever-changing and unpredictable Missouri River. She felt no need to hide the emotion forming a lump in her throat. "I had begun to be afraid there would be no one I could really trust," she said without thinking, quickly amending her statement when she became aware of the strange look that passed between the two men. "Except for Mr. Steele, of course," she added hesitantly, looking up at Steele to bashfully smile her appreciation for bringing Uriah Gunther to her.

"And she hasn't made up her mind about me yet!" Steele laughed, the teasing light in his hazel eyes

42

warming her all over and telling her that she had only begun to know him. "But I'm going to keep after her until she does."

"'Pears t' me you've got your work cut out for you, boy," Uriah warned in his rough voice. "'Cause I 'spect this here little gal's gonna be a tough one to fool."

"Gentlemen, if we're going to be together the three thousand miles to Fort Benton and back again," Temerity interrupted, "you're both going to have to stop talking about me as if I'm not here!" Her laugh was gay as she walked with the two men up to the wheelhouse to show Uriah where he would be working the next three months.

"And if we're goin' t' work together, Miss Temerity," Uriah Gunther returned in his voice that always sounded angry. "You're gonna have t' understand that there's one thing rivermen ain't. That's *gentlemen*. An' you ain't likely t' be changin' none o' us neither."

"We'll see about that, Uriah," Temerity laughed, stealing a sidelong glimpse of Steele, who caught her glance with his own amused gaze and held hers captive for a brief moment. She shook her head as if to rid herself of the confusion Steele's merest look brought to mind and returned her attention to Uriah. *There's nothing to worry about,* she assured herself. *As long as Uriah is here, I can certainly handle Mr. Steele!*

Chapter Three

Temerity's gaze swept proudly over the main deck of the *Intrepid* one last time as she prepared to give the order to pull up the gangplank. The *Intrepid* was loaded to capacity with thirty cabin passengers, a number of deck passengers, a full crew, and three hundred tons of freight. Though anyone could see that the ungainly Missouri River steamboat had none of the grace and grandeur of its Mississippi and Ohio River counterparts, to Temerity it was beautiful.

Specially designed for upper river voyages, where the current sometimes reached speeds of ten miles per hour and the water level could often be measured in inches rather than feet, the ugly little Missouri River sternwheelers were unequaled.

To draw the least amount of water, they had to be much lighter than the steamers that ran on the deeper Mississippi. Consequently, flimsy pine or poplar was used for the decks, bulkheads, and upper works rather than sturdier, but heavier oak, and they were often patched up with parts salvaged from wrecks. Designed to slide over the water rather than move through it, their ingenious flat-bottomed, tiered-wedding-cake shape, and lightweight construction enabled the homely little sternwheelers to sit with eighty percent of the boat's bulk above the water line. That was the main thing that separated them from the luxurious Mississippi River sidewheelers: how deep they sat in the water or how much *draw* they needed.

Fully loaded, as the *Intrepid* was now, a Missouri River steamer could easily navigate through waist-deep water if necessary, and unloaded would draw as little as twenty inches of water, using its spoon-shaped bow to actually climb sandbars, which were scattered along the river. No Mississippi sidewheeler could make such a boast!

Finally satisfied that she hadn't overlooked anything, Temerity turned to order the gangplank up. It was then she saw Steele running down the levee. A flood of relief surged through her. She had given up hope that he would be going with her. After all, he had never actually said he would help beyond hiring the crew. She had just assumed. But now, seeing him hurry up the gangplank, she knew one more worry was behind her.

"Mr. Steele!" she called out, and rushed to meet him. "We were about to leave without you! I thought you weren't coming. Where have you been?"

"I've been on dry land—where you should be right now!" he said angrily as he reached the small girl who carried herself as if she were six feet tall rather than only five feet four. *God, she's gorgeous,* he groaned inwardly as he took in her smiling, upturned face. He noticed the wisps of her almost-black hair were already curling out of her neat chignon to frame her face, and he was torn with the desire to snatch the pins from her hair so that he could see all that glorious dark mane fall around her shoulders.

Mentally berating himself for the turn his thoughts had taken, Steele grabbed Temerity's upper arms and pulled her to him. "What the hell are you doing here?"

46

His face was so close to her that she could see a tiny pockmark on his left jaw, could even pick out the different shades of brown and auburn in his mustache.

The open, smiling expression on Temerity's face went from excited pleasure to stunned surprise to boiling anger in a matter of seconds. "Take your hands off me!" she ordered as sternly as her trembling voice would allow. She told herself the quiver she felt running through her body was anger, not the uncomfortably wonderful awareness of Steele. "What is the meaning of this?"

"I'll take my hands off you as soon as this boat takes off without you on it!"

"You're crazy!"

"I'm crazy? I'm not the one who has a crew of trustworthy men to take care of her business, yet still thinks she can do a man's work. Come on, let the men do what you hired them for, and you go home and take care of your father—where you belong!" He took a step toward the gangplank, dragging her with him before she could comprehend what was happening.

"I'm not going anywhere," she shouted, taking him by surprise and jerking her arm free of his grip. "No place except to the Montana Territory! So if you aren't going with me, Mr. Steele, I suggest you remove yourself from my boat because we're leaving right now," Temerity hissed at the man who stood glaring down at her with anger and frustration distorting his rugged features.

"Look, Temerity," he returned, his voice a controlled groan as he wiped his fingers nervously down his mustache. "I'm sorry I came on so strong. It's just that when I heard a female was actually going to take a boat up the Missouri, I knew it was you. I never thought you'd really do it! I thought once you had a crew . . . Why the hell are you insisting on this foolishness? I've

47

hired men that are perfectly qualified to take the *Intrepid* to Fort Benton and back. There's no need for you to go along. The helm of the *Intrepid* is no place for a lady. It's too dangerous."

"Do I really impress you as being so stupid that I would entrust my father's entire future to strangers? After what happened to him last year, I don't trust *anyone!* Now, if you're through, we're going to get under way. Are you going with me or staying here?" she asked one last time, still hoping the stubborn man would change his mind. She had reasonable confidence in the crew he had hired and was certain she could make the trip without Steele's assistance, but she also knew that she would feel a lot more secure if he were with her. "Well?"

"Well, good luck, Miss Kincade! I tried to help you, but now I'm washing my hands of the whole crazy business!" he threw back at her.

Without further delay, he turned away from the stunned riverboat owner and took the few long steps necessary to make it down the gangplank. As far as he was concerned, he had done all he could to ensure a successful venture for Tim Kincade's boat. If the man's fool daughter insisted on getting herself into more trouble than she could handle, then let it be. He wanted no more to do with her!

Temerity watched as the broad-shouldered man disappeared up the levee, his long angry stride carrying him up the brick incline in a matter of seconds. "Well, let him go," she mumbled to herself, fighting the tears she felt stinging in her blue eyes as she turned to make certain Uriah was ready to get under way. "Who needs him?" But a strange wave of fear and uncertainty rippled through Temerity as she took one more look over her shoulder, praying in spite of herself that he had changed his mind. But Steele was nowhere to be seen.

Forcing herself to face what lay ahead without his support, Temerity gave the order to lift the gangplank and stepped over and around the boxes of cargo that covered the main deck, working her way toward the stairway that would take her up to the boiler deck.

Uriah Gunther sounded his whistle, the engines grew louder, the paddle wheel began to churn the water, and Temerity reached for the support of a sturdy packing crate as the boat lurched forward. The *Intrepid* was on its way west, and it was due solely to her determination.

It should have been a thrilling moment, knowing she had done what no one had believed she could do. But the feeling of excitement she should have felt wasn't there. She knew this moment would not be happening if it had not been for Steele, yet he wasn't there to share it with her, wouldn't be with her in her moment of triumph over the Cameron Line. She didn't know why it mattered, but it did. It shouldn't make any difference to her, but darn it, it did!

Temerity shook her head in what she knew was a useless attempt to drive further thoughts of Steele from her mind. She cursed herself silently, even as she indulged in one final, wishful look at the receding St. Louis levee before she turned away.

But there was no more time to think of what might have been, for her attention was abruptly brought to the excited crowd gathered at the rail on the port side of the boat. The way several deck passengers were shouting their encouragement to someone off the boat, her immediate thought was that a passenger had fallen overboard.

Steele was mercifully forgotten as Temerity rushed to join the gathered crowd to learn what the trouble was. All she needed was for one of the *Intrepid*'s travelers to fall overboard and drown before they were even out of sight of the levee. There was no doubt in her mind that the accident would be blamed on the fact that there was a woman at the helm of the riverboat—no matter where the real responsibility belonged.

Elbowing her way between the people at the rail, Temerity managed to get there just as a man on the levee dove into the water and started swimming toward the *Intrepid*. The cheers of the crowd rose, and no one in the boiler room could hear Temerity when she called out for the engines to be cut. But from his vantage point in the little wheelhouse on the hurricane deck atop the *Intrepid*, Uriah had seen the man dive into the water and had called down the order through the speaking tube from the wheelhouse to the boiler room.

With strong, sure strokes, the swimmer quickly covered the distance from the levee, drawing alongside the *Intrepid* in only a few minutes and grabbing hold of the open-sided main deck at Temerity's feet.

Stooping down, she gripped the man's hand with both of hers and tried to drag him on board, but she couldn't do it alone. Fortunately, she didn't have to. The passengers on either side of her were already reaching under the bottom rail to catch the swimmer under the arms and hoist his upper half out of the water before dragging his entire body onto the deck, which sat only a few inches above the water level.

His breathing labored, the man lay face down on the deck for a long reviving moment while he regained his breath. Still holding his hand in hers, Temerity knelt at his side, the expression on her face concerned as well as puzzled. Something about him was familiar.

With the force of a gale wind at the peak of a storm, she realized who the man was. She couldn't imagine why she hadn't known immediately. But it was only in the brief instant before the man lifted his head, his wet chestnut hair now appearing as dark as her own, that Temerity recognized the man's clothing and build. She couldn't stop herself from gasping aloud as he raised up and looked at her.

"Steele!" she accused, attempting to drop his hand as if it were hot, but she found her own imprisoned in Steele's sure grip, just as her gaze was trapped in the golden depths of his hazel eyes. "What are you doing here?"

"What's it look like I'm doing?" he asked with a sheepish grin. "I decided to take you up on your offer," he admitted, the expression on his face impish as he dragged himself to his feet with the aid of the nearby passengers. "Do I still have a job?"

Temerity glanced nervously at the sea of faces that surrounded the two of them. Each passenger seemed to sense the electricity that ran between the wet man and the owner of the *Intrepid,* and they waited expectantly for her answer.

"Of course you do," Temerity returned, blushing profusely at the thought that everyone around them had seen the pleasure on her face when she recognized the swimmer as Steele, and annoyed by the fact that every time she and Steele had a meeting, they drew a crowd. He seemed destined to cause her to make a spectacle of herself over and over again. The relief she felt at having him on board was quickly matched by her mounting anger.

"The job is still yours," she added angrily, snatching her hand from his warm grip and averting her gaze so she wouldn't have to look at his cocky grin. Or at those smug dimples. How could he look so sure of himself when he was standing there dripping wet and looking like a drowned river rat? He should be the one who was embarrassed, not her. He was the one who had made a fool of himself. So why was she the one blushing? Temerity's temper rose another notch.

"However, you will have to sleep on the main deck with the roosters. Unfortunately, when you didn't arrive on time this morning, we booked a passenger in the cabin we had reserved for you," she added spitefully, and walked away from him, pushing her way through the crowd to hurry up the stairs to the boiler deck and to the protection of her own cabin.

How dare he do that to her? For two cents she would have him thrown back in the river. *But there's a lot more than two cents at stake here, isn't there?* she grumbled silently. *Face it, Temerity, if he hadn't come, you're not sure you could have carried out this trip! Admit it, you need him.*

"That may be, but I'm certainly not going to let him know it!" she told the reflection in the mirror as she patted the coarse net that supposedly kept her chignon neat at the back of her neck. Screwing her face into a look of disgust, she smoothed back the stray wisps that stubbornly curled around her face—though she didn't know why she even tried. They would work their way loose before she even got to the cabin door. They always did.

Having finally regathered a facsimile of her composure, Temerity straightened her shoulders and stepped out of her cabin into the bright sunlight. But no sooner had she accustomed her eyes to the morning glare than all of her resolve was totally destroyed. The first person she encountered was a grinning Steele at the bottom of the stairs leading up to the hurricane deck—the third deck where the wheelhouse was located.

"Feeling better now?" he asked her, his eyes raking appreciatively over her from head to foot, taking care not to ignore a single detail of her appearance.

"I'm glad to see you found some dry clothing, Mr.

52

Steele," she managed stiffly, unable to look into his strange, gold-flecked eyes. Instead, she concentrated on the rough garments he wore—which turned out to be a mistake. Everywhere she looked she was unerringly reminded of his glaring masculinity and power—yet she couldn't avert her gaze.

Steele had borrowed a gray pullover shirt, no doubt white at one time, from one of the larger passengers. But it was quite obvious that the Good Samaritan had not been as broad in the chest and shoulders as the man before her, and Temerity gaped incredulously. The shirt was stretched tightly over well-defined chest muscles as it strained to enclose Steele's bulging biceps—to the point that Temerity wondered how long the shirt's seams could contain all that strength. An unexpected shiver ran through her as she remembered the security she had felt being held in those same arms and against that hard chest when Steele had rescued her from the tavern two days before.

Flustered by the sudden memory, Temerity tried to focus her eyes elsewhere. But to her dismay, she realized the deep vee in the shirt's open collar was exactly at eye level and that it blatantly displayed the curling reddish-brown chest hair she had found so fascinating the day before. Again, she felt the desire to reach out and touch it.

Embarrassed beyond reason by her curiosity about the feel of the springy mat of fur and the memory of his arms around her, she blushed at her scandalous thoughts and nervously directed her glance downward— thinking to escape the mesmerizing sight. But she quickly discovered that her visual senses were to receive no relief as her gaze was drawn helplessly to the man's pants.

Temerity's blue eyes opened wide in shock, for it was apparent that the well-worn denim work pants belonged to a much thinner man. They fit Steele's long muscular legs and narrow hips like a second skin—a fact that Temerity found not only embarrassing but uncomfortably exciting. She felt a strange sense of panic pulsate deep in her belly, in her most private parts, but still she could not look away.

"See anything that doesn't meet with your approval?" Steele asked, just as Temerity's gaze inadvertently came to rest on the disturbing way the snug pants stretched tight across the undeniably masculine bulge at the top of his legs.

Temerity's startled blue gaze flew up to meet his amused grin. "What?" she choked, almost as shocked by her own open appraisal of the man's body as she was at the thought of being caught at it. Surely she had misunderstood him. A gentleman wouldn't . . . But he had told her he wasn't a gentleman, hadn't he? "What did you say?" she repeated, her voice not much more than a raspy whisper.

"I asked if my clothes meet with your approval," he clarified nonchalantly.

Temerity couldn't escape the nagging notion that his question was in no way related to his clothing. She studied his face carefully, not certain if she should slap it or take his explanation at face value. Finally, her natural common sense made her opt for the latter. After all, if she accused him, he would only deny it and she would be the one to look foolish—again.

"They're fine, Mr. Steele," she said stiffly. "Though I've no doubt you will want to purchase things of your own when we tie up for the night at St. Charles. If you have no money, I will give you an advance on your salary," she offered in a businesslike manner—as businesslike as she could muster when her heart was pounding so painfully against the walls of her chest that she was certain Steele would notice it moving the bodice of her dress. How could one man cause such a storm of reaction?

Without waiting for his reply, she turned away from him abruptly and pretended to be interested in the antics of two hounds she could see bounding after a rabbit on the Illinois bank of the river.

"Temerity," he said softly as he approached the girl who stood at the rail with her back to him. "I don't need your money."

Her heart leapt into her throat, strangling her with its ferocious hammering.

"Then why are you here?" she asked, finding it necessary to clear her throat to make the words come out. He was standing directly behind her now. She didn't dare look at him, so she continued to gaze out over the water, straining to concentrate on the dogs in the distance rather than the possible answers to her question.

"Don't you know?" Steele answered. He gently put his hands on her shoulders and turned her to face him again. "Don't you know why I couldn't let the *Intrepid* leave without me?"

"No, I don't," she murmured, her own confused blue-gray eyes drinking in the handsome face that loomed above hers. Her mouth became dry and her knees grew weak. Somewhere in the back of her mind she told herself she should have eaten breakfast; but even as the thought occurred to her, she knew that lack of food was not her problem.

It was Steele. Steele was the reason for her growing light-headedness. Steele and his devil's grin. Steele with his gold eyes and rugged mustached features. Steele and his way of looking at her as if he could read her every thought. Steele and what he did to her when he touched her. Even now she could feel his hands on her

55

upper arms burning their fire through her entire body.

"I came because I wouldn't be able to live with myself if something happened to you and your boat and I hadn't done all I could to prevent it," he said, searching her silvery eyes to see if he could find the answer to what it was about this woman that kept calling out to a protective instinct in him he hadn't known he possessed.

Temerity slowly let out the breath she had unconsciously been holding while he spoke. For some foolish reason, for only the briefest moment, she had let herself believe he had come for no other reason than to be with her. She had actually thought he might be feeling the same strange attraction she was feeling. But it hadn't been that at all. It had been some distorted masculine sense of duty and importance. Nothing more. She silently laughed at her disappointment.

"I see. Well, let us hope that all the workers feel the same loyalty you do, Mr. Steele," she said, forcing herself to smile at him. "If they do, I'm sure we will have a very successful voyage. Now, if you will excuse me, while you talk to Uriah I will check with Gus on the noon meal preparations. You were going to the wheelhouse when we met, were you not?"

"I was," he returned, trying to determine what it was he could have said that had caused her eyes to change so quickly from the bright blue of a warm summer sky to the cold gray of winter. Maybe he had misread an expression of gratitude for one of interest. Steele shook his head doubtfully. He had known too many women in his life not to recognize that look. He had affected her. He was certain he had. "Temerity," he said to her back as she started to walk away.

"Mr. Steele," Temerity interrupted, turning slowly to face him as she did. "I must insist that you give me the proper respect and call me Miss Kincade as my other employees do. Now, what is it you want to say?"

"Nothing, *Miss Kincade*," he answered, brushing past her to take the steps two at a time up to the hurricane deck.

It was not until a few hours later, after Temerity had joined the cabin passengers at the long dining tables in the main cabin for lunch, that she was able to look at her encounter with Steele in the correct perspective. What had she expected? A shipboard romance? With an employee no less? *You've read too many dime novel romances,* she scolded herself, remembering how she and the other young women at Lindenwood Female College in St. Charles had eagerly read and exchanged the romantic adventure stories Professor and Mrs. Strother had so heartily disapproved of.

"Miss Kincade, I must commend you," a smooth masculine voice interrupted Temerity's mental chiding.

Temerity looked up from her plate of sliced ham and lima beans into a pair of clear blue eyes. "Whatever for, Mr. Rawson?" she asked the tall blond man who had been seated next to her for the first meal. She studied the man's handsome face, determining the gallant man to be in his mid-to-late forties, though there was only a touch of gray in his golden hair and sideburns. Despite his age and slender build, Charles Rawson still appeared to be in excellent physical condition, and his friendly open smile was a panacea to Temerity's despondent mood.

"Why, for the excellent food and the efficient way the *Intrepid* seems to be run. Not only is this one of the best meals I've had on a Missouri River steamer, but the *Intrepid* is one of the cleanest boats I've seen."

"Thank you, Mr. Rawson," Temerity smiled, glad to see that some of the immediate changes she had insisted on had paid off.

Rawson turned to the other passengers who seemed interested in their conversation and explained, "I've been on riverboats where the passengers were forced to bring their own food, and the only water available had to be dipped out of the river with a pail tied to a rope."

Temerity laughed at the horrified look on the faces of the two matrons at her table. "And the river has pulled more than a few incautious people overboard when they tossed that bucket into the water beside a moving steamer."

"No!" Mrs. Fisher, a plump woman at the table, gasped in shock.

Seeing the look of fear that covered the woman's face as she shot her husband an accusatory glance across the table, Temerity was ashamed that she had added to the woman's fears.

Mr. Fisher looked helplessly at Temerity for assistance.

"You don't have to worry about that on the *Intrepid*, Mrs. Fisher," she assured. "Whenever we can, we bring fresh water for drinking and bathing on board. But when we do use the river water, the roosters fill the barrels for your use. You won't have to get your own water on the *Intrepid*."

"But the river water is muddy!" Mrs. Fisher insisted nervously.

"We put prickly pears in it to settle the mud," Temerity said, returning her attention to her meal. "This really is quite good. I will have to tell the cook he has done an excellent job."

"It's delicious," Rawson offered, popping a bite of ham and cornbread soaked in lima bean juice into his mouth. "Seems a shame to put the leftovers, if there are any, in the grubpile," he said, wiping his mouth before taking a swallow of water to wash down his food.

"Grubpile?" Mrs. Street, another woman at the table, asked, continuing to eye her own water suspiciously, as if trying to determine if it was safe for

58

drinking. "What is a grubpile?"

"We don't have one on the *Intrepid,* Mrs. Street, but on most steamers, the grubpile is what the deckhands eat. The food leftover from the passengers' meals is thrown into a huge container, and the workers scoop out their portions with their hands."

"Oh," Mrs. Fisher groaned, fanning herself with her hand as she reached for her water.

"No grubpile?" Mr. Rawson asked incredulously. "What do they eat?"

"We have tables set up on the main deck with food on them for the deck passengers and the deckhands to serve themselves," Temerity explained. "The roosters work hard and deserve a decent meal, the same as any other man. After all, without them we'd still be sitting at the levee in St. Louis."

"You have a point, Miss Kincade. Unconventional though it may be," Rawson conceded, his respect for the young woman growing by the instant. How many females would have the intelligence to outfit a steamer and take it upriver? Much less have the daring to treat her workers with respect. Everyone knew that the roustabouts who worked on riverboats were the scum of the river, only responding to force to keep them in line. But Miss Kincade would learn, and perhaps he would just hang around to help her when she discovered the old ways were sometimes the best.

"Tell me, Mr. Rawson, what is your line of business that you seem to know so much about river travel?" Mr. Street asked, thinking to turn the conversation to something other than the running of a steamboat. As far as he was concerned, all he needed to know was that the *Intrepid* would take him to his destination safely. He didn't care what the roustabouts, or *roosters,* as Miss Kincade called them, ate.

"I own a chain of mercantile stores along the river,

Mr. Street," Rawson answered, tearing his gaze away from Temerity to look at the other man.

"A chain? How many is that, Mr. Rawson?" Mrs. Street asked.

"Well, let me see, good lady. I believe at last count there were fourteen," he said, feigning modesty as he did. "That is the purpose of this trip. To check on my investments and to consider some new locations for my establishments."

"Fourteen? That's a very impressive number, Mr. Rawson," Temerity said. "Tell me, do you see the coming of the railroad as a threat to the steamboat as a means of getting your merchandise delivered?"

"I believe that eventually the rail will completely replace the water as a mode of transporting people and cargo across the country."

"Surely you can't think the riverboat will become extinct!" Temerity laughed.

"Just last month the first train reached Sioux City, Miss Kincade. Merchandise out of Chicago can now reach my Sioux City store in as little as ten days. Is there any way a Missouri River steamboat can get its cargo eleven hundred miles upriver in ten days—not to mention the time it takes the freight to get to St. Louis by rail?"

"But the cargo will have to go by river the remaining eighteen hundred miles to Fort Benton, Mr. Rawson. I'm certain you will agree with that," Temerity said with a confident smile in his direction. She refused to believe that the end of the steamboat era would ever come about because one train had gotten to Sioux City, Iowa.

"It's just a matter of time until the railroad reaches the river in any number of places, Miss Kincade. In no time at all, the railroads will bridge the river at various points and continue west, eventually putting the

Missouri River packet out of business altogether."

"Well, Mr. Rawson, I'm certain you're convinced you speak the truth, but until that day you talk of comes about, I'm going to continue to put my trust in the steamboats." Turning to the others at her table, she smiled her best hostess smile. "Now, if you'll excuse me, I have work to attend to. As soon as the tables are cleared, the main cabin will be divided so that we can provide a bar and gaming room in this half for you gentlemen, and a sewing room will be available on the other side for the ladies' comfort and socialization."

Temerity left the table and hurried down to the main deck to be certain the deck passengers and crewmen had eaten.

"How was your dinner, Miss Kincade?" a familiar voice asked from behind her as she crossed the main deck to where the workers were clearing away the remains of the noonday meal.

"It was fine, Mr. Steele. And yours?" she asked, turning to look him in the eyes. She was determined she was not going to quake and tremble with excitement every time she encountered the man. "I had expected you to eat in the main cabin."

"Is that an order, *Miss Kincade?* Because if it's not, I prefer to eat down here with my men," he answered.

Just then two young women, not much younger than Temerity, ran over to Steele and grabbed his arms. Steele looked at Temerity and gave a helpless grin as he allowed himself to be pulled over to the rail.

"Are we on the Missouri River now, Mr. Steele?" the blonde squealed as she pointed to the banks.

"Why do they call it Big Muddy, Mr. Steele?" the redhead asked.

"We just feel so safe knowing you're in charge, Mr. Steele," the blonde cooed, looking up at Steele and shamelessly batting her blue eyes.

Wheeling away from the sight of the two girls clinging to Steele's arms, Temerity didn't wait to hear his answers to the silly questions. Obviously, he was enjoying their flirting. Far be it from her to interfere with his pleasure.

"We just feel so safe knowing you're in charge, Mr. Steele," she mimicked sarcastically as she hurried to the top deck to visit with Uriah in the wheelhouse.

Chapter Four

Temerity set out at a brisk pace that quickly took her up the natural rock levee at St. Charles. Having overseen the off-loading of an order of general merchandise for Mrs. Machat's dry goods store, another for Mr. Heye's general store, as well as six iron stoves for Mr. Tuttle to sell, she had waited until the men on the *Intrepid* had completed the task of taking on a large consignment of grain before heading up Clay Street to the business district.

"Miss Kincade," Mr. Rawson's friendly voice called. "Would you like some company on your trip into town?" he asked, drawing alongside the young woman.

"Why, Mr. Rawson, that will be quite pleasant." Temerity smiled, taking his offered arm. "Though you may regret it before we're through. I must go to Cunningham's to order fresh meat for tomorrow's meals, then to the Farmer's Market for fresh vegetables. After that, I'm going to the brewery to see if I can convince Mr. Shaffer to give me some barrels of his beer on consignment to sell when we arrive in Fort Benton."

"I doubt that any man would ever regret being allowed to accompany such a lovely young woman, no matter how industrious her undertaking," Rawson responded warmly. He placed his free hand over hers, where it rested lightly at the bend of his elbow, and smiled down into her upturned face.

"That's very thoughtful of you, Rawson, but it won't be necessary," Steele's hard voice cut into the pleasant exchange.

Temerity and Rawson turned their heads in unison to see Steele bearing down on them. "I'll accompany Miss Kincade," he said, his smile cold as he glanced from Temerity's stunned face to Rawson's surprised expression. "It's part of my job," he added, the ring of sarcasm in his voice as he said *job* grating across Temerity's tightly drawn nerves like a rusty saw on a finely tuned violin.

"Mr. Steele," Temerity started, irritated that the man seemed to be deliberately set on ruining what had promised to be a pleasant outing. But Steele didn't allow her to finish what she was saying.

"You promised you would help me purchase my new clothing," he said pleasantly, deliberately intending to give Rawson the idea that he and the lady steamboat owner had more than a business relationship—and succeeding.

Looking helplessly at Charles Rawson, she stammered, "I did n—"

"Of course you did, Temerity," Steele interrupted again, laughing as he took her hand and put it in the crook of his own arm. "Don't you remember?" He patted her hand patiently and explained to Rawson, "We were in such a rush to get away that my things were left in St. Louis. But when Temerity found out about it, she felt it was her fault and gave me her word she would personally make up for my loss. You do understand, don't you, Rawson, old friend," he added, beginning to enjoy the look of confusion on the older man's face.

Despite his seemingly friendly expression, Steele's smile didn't reach the hard coldness in his golden eyes, as his piercing gaze bore into the other man's puzzled countenance. *Just make one move to stop her and I'll rearrange your face, you oily-talking son-of-a-bitch,* he threatened silently, forcing his features to disguise what he was thinking, a talent it had taken him years to perfect. Glancing down at Temerity, his self-satisfied grin cocky, Steele asked for confirmation, deliberately making his expression one that would give Rawson the wrong idea. "Isn't that right, Temerity?"

However, Temerity didn't return Steele's adoring expression, and a glimpse of the fury he could see burning in her large blue-gray eyes, now narrowed threateningly, told Steele he'd better get her away from Rawson before he lost the advantage the element of surprise had given him. He could feel her nails cutting into the taut muscles of his bent arm, and he knew Temerity Kincade was already recovering from her shock. Another minute and she wouldn't care who was watching. In fact, he'd be lucky if he could get her out of Rawson's earshot before she burst into the tirade he knew awaited him.

"Come on, Tem, let's go," Steele coaxed cheerfully as he began to walk Temerity away from Charles Rawson.

Without thinking, Temerity followed Steele's lead for a few steps before she realized what she was doing. She stopped her progress immediately, planted her feet on the levee, and glared at the mustached man who actually had the audacity to look surprised that she didn't want to go with him.

"What's the matter, love? Have you got a pebble in your boot?" Steele asked, the obviously artificial concern on his brow inciting Temerity's temper to explosive proportions. How dare he do this to her?

The fire in her eyes darkened the irises to pools of molten lava. "No, I don't have a pebble in my shoe, and you know it!" she fumed. "Just who do you th—"

"Is there some misunderstanding, Miss Kincade?" Charles Rawson interrupted, stepping forward and placing his hand on her left arm—as if he meant to challenge Steele. "Did you make arrangements to have this man accompany you into town or not?"

"Did you or did you not suggest that I would want to purchase new clothing while we were in St. Charles?" Steele interjected at the same time.

"Yes, but—" she answered the glowering man on her right, immediately provoking a startled look of surprise and irritation from Rawson, which he immediately disguised as he dropped his grasp on her left arm and took a step back.

Realizing that Rawson thought her affirmative answer was to *his* question, and horrified by what he must be thinking, Temerity tried to right the situation. "No, I didn't!"

"No?" Steele came back quickly in answer to the reply meant for Rawson as the other man moved toward the flustered young woman again. "Don't you remember our discussing it just this morning when we—I mean *you*—came out of your cabin?"

Temerity's eyes widened so that the white was visible all around the bulging orbs, and the sound of her sucking in a wheezing gasp of shock and anger was the only reply she could manage. She looked frantically at Mr. Rawson, hoping—praying for all she was worth—that he hadn't noticed Mr. Steele's slip. Or had it been a slip? She threw a suspicious glare at Steele but could tell nothing from the innocent expression on his handsome face.

"Well, Miss Kincade?" Rawson said, the tone of his

voice telling Temerity he hadn't missed a single one of Steele's words and that he expected an explanation.

Her gaze shifted to Rawson again, then to Steele, then back to Rawson. What was she going to do? The poor man was waiting for her answer. She had to say something. She couldn't let him believe the vicious innuendos Steele had made. She opened her mouth to deny the ugly words, then closed it again and nervously glanced back at Steele.

On the other hand, he hadn't actually said anything that wasn't true—innocent but true. It was the way he had said it; and being a real gentleman, Rawson would feel he had no choice but to defend her honor should she accuse Steele of lying. A man like Charles Rawson wouldn't have a chance against an ill-bred clod like Steele!

Though the two men were the same height, both at least four inches over six feet, she knew blond-haired Rawson would be no match against Steele's hard determination. Not only did Steele have a twenty-year advantage, the slim Rawson was not in the least muscular and would be beaten to a pulp if Steele's anger was ever unleashed on him. Look what had happened to the man in the Rooster's Roost! Temerity cringed involuntarily at the thought.

Remembering the fate of the would-be rapist, who was a good deal larger than Charles Rawson, Temerity realized she had no choice. She couldn't allow Rawson to be injured because of her. Looking helplessly at the older man, she apologized. "I'm sorry, Mr. Rawson. Since this is to be a business trip, it will be best if Mr. Steele accompanies me," she said bitterly, hoping Rawson didn't think her anger was directed toward him, but unable to keep it from her voice. "Perhaps another time," she offered lamely over her shoulder, no longer resisting as Steele hurried her up the levee toward the business district of St. Charles.

However, the instant she was certain they were out of Rawson's hearing, Temerity stopped in midstep, forcing Steele to an abrupt halt. "How dare you do that to me!" she blustered indignantly. "Just exactly who do you think you are?"

"I'll make it up to you," he promised, the glint in his eyes smug as he tightened his grip on her arm and prodded her forward again, giving her anger no more importance than he would have given to a gnat buzzing around his face. "Come along, Temerity," he ordered paternally.

"It's Miss Kincade to you, *Mr. Steele!* And I don't want to come with you!" she protested vehemently, jerking her arm free of his hold and stopping dead in her tracks. Balled fists on her hips and feet planted squarely on the ground, her stance dared him to touch her again.

"Then why did you?" The grin on his face was insufferable. And those damned dimples! They ought to be outlawed.

"Because I didn't want poor *Charles* to feel he had to protect me from you!" She took particular pleasure in the fact that Steele's jaw knotted and the right side of his mustache twitched involuntarily when she deliberately used Rawson's given name instead of his surname. "I was afraid *he* would be hurt!"

"Do you really think that smooth-talking dandy would dirty his hands in a fight?"

"I most certainly do. Mr. Rawson is a gentleman, and he would feel compelled to defend a lady's honor even though he had no chance of winning!"

"Gentleman, huh?"

"Something you would know nothing about, I'm certain!"

"For a female who wanders the riverfront alone and

frequents saloons, you're awfully concerned with propriety, Miss Kincade!" Steele hurled back as he turned away from her and continued ascending the levee without a backward glance.

With those cruel words of reminder ringing in her ears, Temerity was left standing alone and sputtering furiously. Well, they weren't through with this discussion yet. Steele was going to have to learn that she was the boss, his employer, and what she did was of no concern to him. He was going to have to change his behavior toward her or she would be forced to fire him—no matter how good he was with the men! She had no intention of putting up with his disrespectful conduct another five minutes—much less another three months. They were going to settle this matter now! Once and for all!

Disregarding *propriety,* Temerity ran after Steele, catching him by the sleeve and trying to stop him at the top of the levee. However, he obviously had no intention of acknowledging her and didn't slow his stride in the least. She was forced to run alongside him to keep pace.

"Mr. Steele! If you want to keep your job, we're going to have to get a few things straight right now! You were deliberately rude to a man who is a perfect gentleman and ruined my chances of enjoying his company while I carry out my business."

Steele stopped and turned to face her. "There you go again. Do you really think that, because a man dresses in fancy clothes and knows all the right things to say, it makes him a gentleman? It's obvious you haven't met too many *gentlemen,* Temerity."

"I've told you to call me Miss Kincade!"

"As I was saying, it's obvious you haven't met too many gentlemen, *Temerity,* or you'd be able to see that Rawson's a smooth-talking lecher. Nothing more!"

"Lecher!?!" she squealed. "Isn't that the pot calling the kettle black? If you'll recall, it isn't Mr. Rawson who speaks in rude innuendos and suggestive dialogue!"

Rude innuendos and suggestive dialogue, indeed! Steele opened his mouth to rebut her accusation, but suddenly realized he couldn't and clamped it shut again. He wiped his thumb and forefinger over his mustache. She was right. He'd gone about this entire situation in the wrong way, from trying to manhandle her off the boat in St. Louis to literally snatching her off Charles Rawson's arm. Only a blind fool wouldn't be able to see that brute force wasn't the way to control an infuriating, strong-willed female like Temerity Kincade. A female like her couldn't know she was being handled or she would balk every time. He should have known that.

An idea swiftly took shape in Steele's mind. *Handling a special woman like Temerity requires subtlety. That's it. Subtlety's the answer.* And he had to admit he'd been anything but subtle. That was for damn sure. He had literally thrown himself into her life two days ago and had been trying to tell her what to do ever since—none of which she'd done! Well, that could change—would have to change. From now on, he would be subtle. In fact, he'd be the subtlest human being ever put on this earth! He would have to be, if he didn't want her to fire him, and she was mad enough right now to do just that. He didn't want to be fired. More than ever, he didn't want that—not now.

"You're right, Miss Kincade," Steele agreed suddenly. "My behavior has been abominable. I have no excuse. I can only hope you will accept my apologies and give me a chance to make amends. I give you my word I will make every effort to remember *my place* from now on," he promised glibly. *Of course, you may find that our ideas of "my place" are slightly different,*

Temerity! "Would you like for me to locate Mr. Rawson so that he can accompany you as planned?" he offered, glancing around as if eager to find the other man and be rid of her.

Taken back by Steele's change of attitude and obvious attempt at gentlemánly behavior, Temerity gaped openly at him. She hadn't expected him to back down so easily and couldn't decide what to make of the surprising turn of events. Had it been her threat of dismissal? Surely not. He had made it clear that he didn't need, or even want, this job. Why had he changed so suddenly? Well, whatever the reason, he had. That was all that mattered.

"Well, Miss Kincade?" he asked, fighting the desire to smile at the stunned expression on Temerity's lovely face.

"Well, what, Mr. Steele?"

"Shall I look for Mr. Rawson?"

"Oh," Temerity breathed indecisively as she nervously looked around for the other man. "He seems to have already disappeared. And I suppose it really does make more sense for you to go with me when it pertains to business—if you will remember . . ."

"My place?"

"Yes," Temerity returned anxiously, suddenly flooded with uneasiness. Something in the challenging gleam that emitted from the golden-brown eyes that watched her, awaiting her next words, told her she hadn't gained the least bit of control over Steele. The knowing eyes even hinted that she had played directly into his hands and had taken several steps backward! And the astonishing fact was that she realized she didn't even mind! "Then, since that's settled, shall we be on our way?" she suggested pleasantly, moving to take Steele's arm.

Steele looked down at the small gloved hand resting

on his sleeve and asked, "Are you certain 'my place' isn't walking five paces behind you, Miss Kincade?"

Temerity's gaze shot upward to burn angrily into Steele's amused eyes. But there was no sarcasm in his expression, only affectionate teasing, and Temerity realized with a crashing jolt that beside her was exactly where she wanted Steele to be. Not ahead of her, and certainly not behind her. "Even I don't demand that much 'respect,' Mr. Steele," she told him seriously, then added with a mischievous grin, "Besides, I have the distinct feeling I need you where I can keep a very close eye on you!"

"Don't you trust me, Miss Kincade?" Steele laughed, his brown eyes bright with humor.

"Not in the least, Mr. Steele. Not in the least," she returned, the light in her blue eyes alive and happy, her anger surprisingly forgotten.

The afternoon hurried by in a rush of errands, and Temerity found herself enjoying Steele's company in spite of her earlier misgivings. He had behaved with perfect decorum; and once they had purchased his new clothing, he had even looked the part of the gentleman his manners suggested. Of course, she was aware that Steele had not really changed and shouldn't be trusted; but as long as his outward demeanor was tolerable, she would be satisfied. On her guard, but satisfied.

Actually, Temerity had to admit she had liked having Steele with her as she carried out the *Intrepid*'s affairs. Though he had taken no active part in her dealings with the St. Charles merchants, waiting patiently in the background as she conducted the riverboat's business, something about knowing he was nearby had given her fragile confidence a mysterious boost—such a boost that she'd been able to convince Mr. Shaffer at the brewery to trust her with ten barrels of beer on consignment, when she would have considered her efforts a success with only one or two!

"We'll have to hurry back to the *Intrepid* and inform the men to expect the shipment later this evening," Temerity chortled excitedly as she and Steele walked along Main Street. Totally elated with her success, she had forgotten her vow to remain aloof and squeezed Steele's hard arm affectionately.

However, Steele remembered his own decision to behave himself and pretended not to notice the warm, cushioned pressure of her breast burning through his sleeve. "I—" he started, his usually mellow voice a surprising croak. He cleared his throat and self-consciously wiped his thumb and forefinger over his mustache twice, then began again. "I've already sent word to them," he managed to announce finally, his voice still not as steady as he would have preferred.

"You did? When?" Temerity asked, dropping her hold on his arm and looking up into Steele's golden-brown eyes. She was shocked to see the discomfort that was evident on the big man's rugged face and couldn't believe it. "You don't need to look so apprehensive, Mr. Steele," she quickly assured him. "It's all right. I'm not angry."

"I'm glad," Steele returned, unable to hide the amused twinkle in his eyes with the realization that the naive girl actually thought his discomfort had been caused by a fear of losing his job. At least he knew his plan to play the part of the dutiful employee was convincing. So why didn't that knowledge make him feel good? He had been successful in gaining her trust again. He was one step closer to her bed. Hadn't that been the reason he'd come on this crazy trip in the first place? Hadn't that been what he'd wanted? Of course, it had.

So why didn't he feel successful? By letting Temerity Kincade believe he could be browbeaten, he had secured his place on the *Intrepid* for a while longer, and that was what was important right now. The fact that he felt like a liar and cheat was of little consequence in light of the loss he would realize if Temerity Kincade went on to Ft. Benton without him—a loss he was growing more and more determined not to suffer. If he could only blot out the memory of her full breast on his arm . . .

"Then, let's go on back to the *Intrepid* and make sure everything's ready for Mr. Shaffer's beer," she said with an encouraging smile, taking his arm again, unaware of the grimace that played briefly over Steele's features.

"I thought we might have supper at the Fawcett House before we return to the dock," Steele suggested, inadvertently bringing his free hand up to cover Temerity's smaller one where it rested on his sleeve. However, he caught himself just in time and diverted his hand's forward motion, flicking at a piece of imaginary lint on the dark cloth that covered his arm instead of touching her, then allowing his hand to drop at his side once more. "To celebrate your success," he added quickly, and looked away.

Temerity had been aware of Steele's large hand hesitating over hers before leaving to brush at his sleeve, and she had felt an odd sense of disappointment at his actions. What was wrong with her? She'd finally gotten Steele to behave with the proper respect and here she was wanting something else. Chiding herself for her inconsistency, she declined his invitation. "We really should be getting back to the *Intrepid*. I'm afraid we'll have to settle for having our celebration there."

"That won't be the same. After all, this deserves

something special. Not many women would have been able to talk old Shaffer into trusting them with ten barrels of his beer. But you did."

"I did, didn't I?" Temerity returned, as pleased that she had impressed Steele as with the sale itself. "Did you see his face when I walked in and presented my suggestion?" she giggled.

"I wouldn't be surprised to learn that you were the first woman to set foot in his brewery to do business. You really do deserve a special celebration. However, if you think we should go back to the *Intrepid* right away, I understand."

"We really should go back," she drawled, unable to hide the fact that she found the thought disappointing. She told herself the reason she was tempted by Steele's offer had nothing to do with wanting a chance to spend a little more time alone with the man. She simply felt like celebrating. Not only had the barrels of beer been her first acquisition of cargo by herself, but the fact that the *Intrepid* had left St. Louis at all was cause for celebration. And the fact that the first day of the up-river journey had been so successful. Still . . .

"We'd better not, Mr. Steele," she refused with determination, the regret obvious in her blue-gray eyes as she glanced up into his waiting face.

"You still don't trust me, do you?" His question and expression were serious, but his eyes were teasing, challenging. "Haven't I shown you I can be a gentleman up there with the best of them?"

"It's not that. It's just . . ."

"What?"

"It's just that . . ." she began again, but couldn't go on. "Actually, Mr. Steele," she started a third time, only now there was a mischievous lilt in her voice, "you're right. I do deserve a celebration. And I can't think of a single reason why it shouldn't be with you.

After all, it was because of your contacts that today was possible."

"My contacts?" Steele coughed nervously. "What do you mean? I didn't sell your idea to Mr. Shaffer. You did it alone," he reminded her.

"The beer, yes, but I wouldn't have been in St. Charles to sell to Mr. Shaffer or anyone else if you hadn't found my crew for me. You knew all the right people to hire. So let's do go to dinner at the Fawcett House. We both deserve it!"

With a sigh of relief, Steele looked down at the vibrant young woman, who was now accepting his suggestion with gay enthusiasm. *There just might be something to this subtlety after all!* Pleased with the outcome of the afternoon, he was barely able to hide the smug satisfaction that filled his thoughts, recognizing the fact that if he'd continued to try to force his will on Temerity Kincade they would be on their way back to the *Intrepid,* rather than looking forward to an intimate dinner for two. "If you insist, Miss Kincade," he answered smoothly.

"I do, Mr. Steele. I most certainly do!"

By the time Temerity and Steele stepped out of the Fawcett House, both comfortably replete, it was dark. But neither the man nor the woman seemed to notice as they strolled along Main Street enjoying an amicable silence that only good food and good company could induce.

"I really did enjoy our celebration, Mr. Steele," Temerity said dreamily, finally breaking the silence. "I'm glad you suggested it," she added, looking into the eyes of the tall man who gazed down at her.

"I am too," Steele replied softly, stopping and turning to face her, his expression filling her with a warm

76

excitement that thrilled, as well as frightened.

Flushing beneath Steele's scorching scrutiny, Temerity was suddenly aware of an unexplained fire raging uncontrolled through her body. The heat was so intense that her limbs became weak, seeming to melt. Feeling as though she was falling, she inadvertently swayed toward the large man, instinctively tightening her grip on his arm and catching herself against the hard wall of his chest with her free hand. "We really must be getting back," she said at last, her voice an uncertain whisper.

"Must we?" Steele closed his fingers over the small hand resting on his shirtfront. "Not yet."

"Mr. Steele, please don't . . ."

"Don't what?"

Temerity studied Steele's face for a long silent moment, her eyes searching his for the answer to something she didn't understand. Yes, don't what? *Don't look at me like that? Don't make me tremble all over when you touch me? Don't make me wonder what it would feel like to be kissed by you? Don't make me wonder what your mustache would feel like if I reached up and touched it? Don't make me wish you'd put your arms around me again?*

Frustrated and embarrassed by the outrageous ideas storming through her brain, and unable to bear the thought that her own eyes were betraying her feelings, Temerity tore her gaze away from Steele's. She glanced curiously at his hand clasped lightly over hers. His grip was so slight that it couldn't even be considered a hold, yet a steel bracelet could not have been more restraining. She told herself that all she had to do to gain her release would be to remove her hand from where it lay, trembling and useless, on his chest. So why didn't she? Why couldn't she? Why did she want to reach up with those same fingers and brush their tips over the thick mustache that fascinated her as much as the rest of the man?

"You don't need to be afraid of me, Temerity. I'm not going to hurt you."

Steele's words freed Temerity from the almost hypnotic state his hand over hers had caused, and her gaze shot upward in alarm, as though she'd been caught in a lie of some sort. "I'm not afraid of you!" She realized her protest was a little too emphatic to be convincing. She even sounded guilty, and she tried again, this time a bit less forcefully. "I'm really not!"

"Then what happened?"

You! That's what happened. You forced your way into my life and made me need you, depend on you! You looked at me with those brown eyes that make me feel as though you can read my thoughts, and your strength and self-confidence make me feel unsure of myself!

When Temerity didn't answer, Steele asked again. "What are you afraid of, Temerity?"

Me! she wanted to shout at him. *I'm afraid I'll place more importance on our relationship than it deserves. I'm afraid that I'll behave like those silly girls on the* Intrepid *and make a fool of myself. I'm afraid you're not what you seem to be. I'm afraid I'll grow too dependent on you and then you'll leave.* "I'm afraid that if we don't get back, they may send a search party out for us." She laughed with forced gaiety, her eyes still focused on his, unable to shift away.

"I sent word we would be late."

"Oh," Temerity murmured, surprised by the sudden breathlessness that attacked her. Her tongue flicked nervously over her dry lips.

Steele watched as the pink tip slid along her innocently provocative mouth, and he ached to taste its sweetness with his own tongue. "I'm going to kiss you,

Miss Kincade."

A shot of excitement and terror ricocheted wildly through Temerity's system, bouncing off the floor of her stomach, painfully, exquisitely. Her eyes locked on his lips, her throat went totally dry, and her tongue felt glued to the roof of her mouth. "You can't."

"I have to," he said in a hypnotic whisper as he lowered his head slowly toward hers.

Her heart hammered violently in her chest as she continued to stare at him. Her blue-gray eyes enormous with awe, she was unable to move away as she knew she should. "You promised that our relationship was to be a business relationship, Mr. Steele," she insisted weakly, unaware that she leaned toward him as she spoke.

"This *is* business, Miss Kincade. Important business," he assured softly, his lips so close to hers that she could feel the heat of his kiss even though their mouths were not touching.

"We shouldn't," Temerity whispered, unconsciously lifting her heels off the ground to raise up on her toes and bring her mouth closer to his.

"Don't you think I know that?" he asked with a groan as he slanted his mouth over hers.

Except for kisses from her father, Temerity had never been kissed by a man, and nothing—not even the romances she and her friends had read while she was at Lindenwood College—could have prepared her for the astonishingly wonderful experience. And she couldn't stop herself from responding.

Forgetting all the *sensible* reasons why she shouldn't become involved with an employee, she gave herself over to Steele's kiss. She only knew she couldn't ignore the pleasant throbbing coiling deep within her belly, the exotic tightening of her breasts, the wild desire to wrap her arms around Steele and press herself hard

79

against him.

The sweet, naive surrender of Temerity's mouth was Steele's undoing, and he was filled with a desire like none he'd ever known. It was more powerful, more explosive than anything he'd ever felt, and he was stunned by his own reaction to the chaste, closed-mouth kiss Temerity offered. He knew that if he deepened the kiss, using his tongue to deflower her mouth as desire called out for him to do, he would have difficulty stopping himself until he had possessed her totally.

Exerting superhuman effort, Steele slid his hands up to grasp Temerity's shoulders. He pulled her away from him, a bit more roughly than he realized.

"You're right. We'd better go back," he said, his tone hoarse and annoyed.

Still dazed by his kiss, Temerity had difficulty understanding what had happened. One minute he was kissing her, and the next he was pushing her away. What had she done? Hadn't she kissed him the right way? Had she disappointed him? Or did he think she was loose because she had responded so easily to his kiss? She should have slapped him when he first told her he was going to kiss her. That's what a *lady* would have done. A real lady wouldn't have let him take such liberties.

Sick with embarrassment and shame at her scandalous behavior, Temerity took an unsteady step backward and searched Steele's hard gaze for an answer to the reason he had broken their embrace so suddenly. But she saw nothing in his contorted, almost angry, expression to alleviate her decision that he had found her wanting. Well, if he didn't like kissing her—for whatever reason—she would certainly spare him the unpleasantness of being forced to repeat the incident. Never again would she allow him—or any other man for that matter—to get close enough to hurt her like this.

"Yes, we must go back," she said, turning and walking away from Steele with as much aplomb as she could manage, hurrying toward the *Intrepid* to the safety of her cabin, where she could release the tears that were threatening to spill down her cheeks at any instant.

Chapter Five

"There's a fire in the hold!" a panicked shout cut cruelly into Temerity's consciousness. "Get more water!" the hoarse voice called out, his alarm frighteningly obvious.

"Oh, my god!" Temerity gasped, leaping up from the bunk where she had indulged herself with half an hour of tears and self-pity. "Please, not a fire," she prayed fervently, immediately forgetting her embarrassment and chagrin at the hands of Mr. Steele. The only thought that filled her mind now was what the dreaded word *fire* meant on a riverboat. A flimsily built Missouri River steamer could ignite like a bonfire, burning to the water in a matter of minutes if a blaze wasn't immediately brought under control. It was one of the steamboat owner's worst fears. And despite its dauntless name, the *Intrepid* was no less vulnerable to the total destruction fire could wreak than any other steamer on the river.

Unconcerned with her tear-streaked face and mussed hair and clothing, Temerity yanked open her cabin door and ran down to the main deck, arriving just as Steele and several deck hands, their skin and clothing blackened with soot, ascended from the hold. "It's all right, everybody," Steele assured the milling passengers and crewmen, who were already making frenzied preparations to leave the steamer. "Nothing serious," he announced, hoping to ease the passengers' minds, even though the workers all knew that any fire on a steamer was always serious.

"What happened?" Temerity asked, hurrying to Steele's side and gripping his arm with one hand. She didn't notice the instinctive wince of his muscles when she touched the torn shirt he wore.

"It was an accident. Looks like someone got careless with a cigarette," he told her. "No real damage was done. It ruined a couple of bolts of cloth," he consoled casually, not wanting Temerity to know what he was really thinking.

Temerity glared at the gathered roustabouts and engine workers, her expression angry. "Who was smoking in the hold? Don't you realize what could've happened if the flames hadn't been discovered when they were?"

"We know, ma'am, and there ain't no rooster worth his salt woulda done nothin' that dumb," a large, bearlike man offered bashfully.

"It couldn't 'a been one o' us, Miss Kincade. We know what a fire can do t' a steamer," another defended sincerely. "None o' us would o' done nothin' like that."

"Then who?" Temerity asked, looking back to Steele for a solution to the puzzle.

"Yes, who?" Charles Rawson, who seemed to appear out of nowhere, asked. "Perhaps Mr. Steele can give us the answer to that question since he was in the hold only moments before the fire broke out," he suggested, his expression triumphant. "He could have seen something."

"What are you insinuating, Rawson?" Steele asked. His eyes narrowed cruelly as he took a step toward the other man.

"Were you the last one in the hold, Mr. Steele?" Temerity gasped, her eyes round with shock to think that he might have been responsible for accidentally starting the fire that could have destroyed the *Intrepid*—and her father's business.

"I was merely suggesting that Mr. Steele might've spotted our culprit before coming back onto the main deck," Rawson explained quickly, pleased with the way Temerity Kincade was searching Steele's face as if she already knew who was responsible for the fire.

"Mr. Steele?" Temerity asked hesitantly, hating the answer she sensed she would receive but knowing she had to ask. "Was there anyone in the hold besides you?"

Steele cast a hard glare toward Temerity. "No, but I didn't start the fire, as Mr. Rawson is doing his damndest to make you believe!"

"Don't be foolish, Mr. Steele. Mr. Rawson isn't accusing you. No one is. We're just trying to get to the bottom of this accident so the guilty party can be made to understand the seriousness of what has happened."

"Oh, I'm certain that whoever's responsible is very aware of what he did and what could have happened if the fire hadn't been discovered when it was," Steele ground out through clenched teeth, leveling his accusing glare on Rawson, his tone an obvious threat. Rawson chose not to retaliate.

"Now if you'll excuse me, *Miss Kincade,*" Steele said, turning back to Temerity and glancing down at the arm she still gripped. "I'd like to get a little salve on this hand."

"Oh, Mr. Steele! You've been injured! Why didn't you tell me?" she exclaimed, anxiously lifting his burned palm and wrist to judge the extent of the wound.

85

"It's nothing," Steele said, looking at his injury for the first time and suddenly becoming aware of the throbbing pain that was burning its way along his entire arm. "I just need to put a little medicine on it and it'll be fine," he promised, suddenly becoming light-headed and nauseated from the pain. *Damn. I can't faint,* he thought, fighting the overwhelming dizziness that was consuming him.

"You shoulda seen 'im, Miss Kincade," one of the soot-blackened roosters offered proudly. "When he saw that burnin' bolt o' cloth, he grabbed it away from the other cargo before it could catch and then smothered it with his jacket."

"Mr. Steele saved yer boat, Miss Kincade," another firefighter offered.

"Take him and anyone else who's burned to my cabin," Temerity ordered two burly crewmen. "I have medical supplies up there. And, Jimmy," she said to the red-haired cabin boy, "run into town and find a doctor."

"I don't need a doctor," Steele protested back over his shoulder as he was guided up the stairs to the boiler deck where the cabins were. "Just some salve and bandages will be plenty," he grumbled, finally giving in and going along peacefully, unaware of the look of total loathing Charles Rawson shot at his retreating form.

You may've won this round, Steele. But the next time you have a chance to play the hero for Miss Kincade, you won't be so fortunate. You're going to regret that little incident on the levee this afternoon, my friend, Rawson thought wrathfully, hate contorting his handsome features.

"You men check out the hold to be sure nothing else was damaged," Temerity told two workers. "And for heaven's sake, don't smoke while you're down there."

She laughed, relieving the tension among the workers, telling the men that she would not seek out someone to blame for the accident, but that she certainly didn't intend to re-experience the near tragedy.

"Yes, ma'am!" they responded eagerly.

"Is there anything I can do to help, my dear?" Rawson asked, carefully hiding his resentment of Steele as he approached Temerity and put his arm around her shoulders.

"Oh, Mr. Rawson, how sweet of you to offer!" Temerity said with an anxious smile, still unable to disguise the worry in her expression, despite her gallant effort. "I don't think there's anything, but I do appreciate your asking. Now, if you'll excuse me, I'd better see to the men's injuries." She started for the stairs.

"If there is anything," Rawson called after her, "I hope you won't hesitate to let me know."

"No, I won't, Mr. Rawson," Temerity returned absently, her concentration already on one particular injured man waiting in her cabin. "Thank you," she mumbled offhandedly as she hurried up the stairs, not even bothering to look back at the man who still watched her.

It would be a sin to waste such beauty and intelligence on a man like Mr. Steele, my dear, Rawson thought as he took a cigarette from a gold case and inserted it between his sneering lips. With obvious appreciation, he watched Temerity's gently swaying hips disappear up the stairs. *You should belong to a man of taste, a man of wealth and importance, a man who can give you fine clothing and jewels and furs. And so you shall. So you shall!*

Totally unaware of Mr. Rawson's avid interest in her or his plans for her future, Temerity rushed into her cabin to find only Steele present.

"Was no one else hurt?"

Steele was sitting on her bunk holding his injured hand against his chest. The pain he was suffering was obvious on his perspiring face, but it was just as obvious that he had no intention of admitting to it. "Just me, and I don't know what all the fuss is about," he growled, his attempt to slough off the seriousness of his wound strangely endearing him to Temerity. It was so typically masculine. "It's just a little burn."

Ignoring Steele's surliness, Temerity smiled patiently as she sat on the bunk beside him and took his hand in hers. "Let me see," she coddled gently, flattening his hand, palm upward, in her lap.

Temerity choked back a gasp of horror when she saw the extent of Steele's burn. Blisters were already forming on the burn-reddened hand and wrist, some of them oozing a pinkish, almost clear, fluid. "Well," Temerity breathed, using every modicum of control she could muster to keep the alarm from her voice, "I'm certain this looks much worse than it is. Once it's cleaned up, you'll feel better in no time," she promised, carefully placing his hand back in his lap and rising to retrieve her box of remedies.

"What are you going to do?" Steele asked suspiciously, craning his neck to see.

He reminded Temerity of a small child who isn't certain his mother's cure isn't going to be worse than the pain he's already enduring, and she smiled in spite of the anxiousness rattling through her body. "I'm going to wrap your hand in wet linens until the doctor gets here," she answered casually as she efficiently began to carry out her practiced nursing skills. Burns were not uncommon on a steamer, and Temerity had treated many over the years.

Into a small bowl from the cupboard beneath the washstand, Temerity poured a generous portion of liquid from each of two pharmacy bottles she had retrieved from her medicine kit.

"What's in those bottles?"

"Carbolic acid and laudanum, Mr. Steele," she indulged pleasantly, adding a pitcher of water to the mixture in the bowl before dropping several small linen squares into the liquid. "The carbolic will help clean the burn, and the laudanum will ease some of your pain," she explained, turning back to Steele.

Setting the bowl of cool water on the floor beside the bunk where Steele sat, Temerity took his injured hand in hers once again and draped a folded towel over his lap as she knelt before him. "This won't hurt too much," she soothed, concentrating intently on her work as she gently covered the burned hand with the first cool cloth. "There, doesn't that feel better?" she crooned softly, continuing to cradle his hand protectively in hers until the cool, laudanum-laced water could begin to perform its magic.

Steele stared mesmerized at her head bent over his linen-wrapped hand being held and cared for so tenderly, and an awkward lump of emotion rose in his throat. "Little mother," he unconsciously whispered his thoughts aloud.

"What?" Temerity asked, raising her eyes to find herself trapped helplessly in the golden warmth of his gaze.

"Much better," he said unsteadily, drinking in the beauty of the disarranged wreath of dark hair that made him want to bury his fingers in its thickness.

To gain control of his thoughts, Steele sucked in a deep breath. Unfortunately, the breath meant to control had the reverse effect, taking him even further under her spell as he greedily inhaled the intoxicating lemon scent of the woman before him.

His uninjured hand rose of its own volition to caress

her upturned face, to whisper the backs of his fingertips along the smooth skin of her cheek, gently brushing a lock of the unruly coffee-colored tresses into place. He couldn't have stopped himself if he'd wanted to. His fingers threaded heedlessly into the thick hair at her temple as his gaze traveled over the sweet, flushed face, settling at last on her full, slightly parted lips.

"You're a good nurse," he complimented, for want of something better to say.

"It's nothing," she sighed, unable to tear her gaze away from Steele's face.

"What have you done to me?" he suddenly groaned helplessly, his fist closing in her hair and tugging lightly as he spoke. "That one kiss wasn't enough," he whispered, the light in his eyes a plea for understanding, for mercy. "It will never be enough."

As if there were a magnet drawing them together, Steele leaned forward and Temerity rose up on her knees to meet him, all thoughts of never allowing him to kiss her again shoved to the farthest recesses of her mind, all worry about the burned hand she still held gone.

The touch of his mouth, warm and tender on hers, enveloped Temerity in a wild storm of thrilling sensation, and unknowingly she slipped her free arm around Steele's neck and leaned closer into him, instinctively begging him to deepen the kiss.

Eagerly accepting her invitation, Steele shaped his mouth to hers, slipping his tongue along the pliable furrow that separated her lips, petitioning in a most determined and enticing way for entrance into the blissful kingdom where no man had ever tread.

And Temerity could not deny him, had no thought of trying. Her entire body was responding to the deliberate ministrations of his tongue on her lips, and she became helpless putty in his hands. Her mouth relaxed and opened of its own accord, beckoning him to conquer the untouched domain, make it his own.

Without hesitation, Steele complied, his tongue thrusting between her parted lips, filling her mouth with its hotness as he eagerly mapped the heavenly realm that welcomed him.

Temerity stiffened with surprise—thrilling surprise—and she moved closer. Her head was swimming and she was achingly aware of a coiling desire springing in the heart of her womanhood. Her breasts throbbed with a need she didn't understand—didn't try to understand. Totally motivated by instinct now, she moaned softly and pressed herself against Steele's hard chest in an instinctive effort to alleviate the exquisite discomfort swelling in her.

Steele groaned and shifted his weight slightly, abruptly bringing Temerity to her senses. "I've hurt you!" she gasped, remembering the injured hand trapped between their bodies. Pushing herself away, she flustered anxiously, "I'm sorry! Is your hand all right?"

"My hand doesn't hurt, Temerity," Steele assured quickly, his voice a rasping croak, the dimpled smile on his face crooked. With a sense of urgency, his hand burrowed through her hair to cup the back of her head and haul her against him to resume their kiss.

"I can see it in your face," she insisted against his lips, refusing to let her desire to gorge herself on his delicious kisses make her forget his injury again. "You're in pain."

"I'm in pain all right, but it's not my hand, love," Steele explained sheepishly, unbearably aware of the heat of her small hand in his lap. Sometime during the unexpected passionate kisses, Steele had opened his long legs and Temerity had become nestled between them, her soft curves melding gloriously with his hard corded body from breast to hip as she knelt before him. Hard and throbbing, this ache made his burn seem minor in comparison.

"Then wh—?" Temerity started to argue, the question dying in her throat, her mouth remaining open in stunned surprise. Suddenly conscious of the rigid pressure burning into the back of her hand, her eyes opened wide, her expression alternating between horror and embarrassment.

"Is this the kind o' medical treatment the whole crew can expect?" Uriah Gunther's fierce voice accused from the doorway of the cabin.

"Uriah!" Temerity gasped, jerking herself away from Steele and wishing she could dive under the bunk and hide. Why hadn't she closed the door? *Because you didn't want anyone to get the wrong idea about you in here alone with Mr. Steele,* she chided herself mercilessly. *At least if the door had been closed they would have only wondered—but now there's certainly nothing to wonder about, is there?* she groaned inwardly.

Uriah pretended not to notice his employer's extreme discomfort and went on talking. "I always say the old cures like 'kiss it and make it better' are the best, but the doctor you sent for is here," he announced just as the middle-aged physician, black bag in hand, bustled into the room.

The expression on her face wild and trapped, Temerity exploded up from the floor, bumping the bowl of medicated water and splashing its contents over the floor as she rose. Her face glowed bright crimson as she opened her mouth to explain that she had just been nursing Steele's hand until the doctor could get there. But glancing from the doctor to Steele to Uriah, she knew anything she said would only make matters worse.

She clamped her lips together tightly and turned her back on the three grinning men. Pretending to be concerned with tidying the washstand and rearranging the articles in her medication box, she made an overt show of activity. But no one was fooled, and she knew it. The heat of her mortification intensified, inflaming her whole body. If only she could run from the room and never have to see Steele or Uriah again.

"Let's take a look at that hand," the doctor said to Steele, seemingly oblivious to the tension that crackled through the small cabin. "Hmm," he mumbled as he removed the wet cloth Temerity had placed on it. "I don't think it's too serious. It oughta heal up real nice in the next week or two," he promised, spreading a salve made of pure hog's lard on the wound. "Don't smell too good, does it?" The doctor laughed when he noticed the expression of disgust wrinkling Steele's face.

"Not too good," Steele agreed, venturing a glance at Temerity's back, feeling guilty for the shame and embarrassment she was obviously experiencing.

Efficiently wrapping Steele's fist in bandages, the doctor began to speak to Temerity, making it impossible for her to continue to ignore the presence of the men in the cabin. "Keep it clean and wrapped up for the next few days, and it should be fine. For pain and infection, I want you to make a liniment to put on it. Add a quarter of a bottle of carbolic acid to a mixture of laudanum, linseed oil, and lime water in equal parts. It should do the trick. Do you have enough supplies on hand, or do I need to have the pharmacy opened tonight?"

"Yes, Doctor," Temerity murmured, concentrating her attention on the man's hands as they worked efficiently on Steele's wound. "I have everything you've prescribed."

Speaking to Steele again, an impish grin suddenly

broke across the physician's serious expression. "Course, all the medicine in the world ain't gonna be as good as the lovin' care of a good woman, is it, young feller?"

Temerity inhaled sharply, the gasping squawk of her shock filling the room. He had known what he'd interrupted all along! She wanted to dissolve into the deck.

"No, Doc, it sure isn't," Steele agreed, sneaking a glance at Temerity out of the corner of his eye.

Open-mouthed and furious and looking as if she would throw something at him if another mention was made of the compromising situation the doctor and Uriah had caught them in, she sought refuge beside the washstand again.

Steele wisely changed the subject. "Thanks for coming on such short notice. What do I owe you?"

"A dollar oughta cover it," the doctor said as he snapped his bag shut and stood up.

Steele began to fumble in his pocket with his uninjured right hand, but Temerity stopped him. "Mr. Steele, this is not your responsibility. Of course, I will pay for your visit, Doctor." She quickly dug in her purse and came out with a dollar, anxious to be rid of all three men so she could have her cabin to herself once more. She held the greenback bill out to the man.

The doctor looked hesitantly at Steele, who nodded his agreement, and then took the money. Repeating his instructions one last time as Temerity held the cabin door for him, he finally took his leave.

Standing in the open doorway, she turned to Uriah and Steele, her eyebrows raised expectantly, as if saying, *Aren't you leaving too?* However, neither man seemed to be in any hurry to depart. "Well?" she finally said, impatiently placing one balled fist on her hip while the other hand continued to hold the door.

94

"Close the door, Temerity," Steele ordered, his tone ominously serious, all the amusement gone from his expression. "We need to talk."

An alarm clanged in Temerity's head. She should have known Steele hadn't really changed. He was still the same overbearing male he'd been all along; and she'd played right into his hands by letting him charm his way past her defenses, by allowing him the liberty of kissing her. Now, because he had forced her to expose her weakness, he thought he could take over. Well, the arrogant Mr. Steele had a surprise coming to him if he thought he was going to start telling Temerity Kincade what to do!

"You're forgetting who gives the orders on the *Intrepid,* Mr. Steele," Temerity returned peevishly, not even noticing the amused expression that twinkled mischievously in Uriah Gunther's blue eyes as he watched the two opponents draw up their battlelines.

"I haven't forgotten a damn thing, *Miss Kincade!*" Steele ground out through clenched teeth as he rose to his feet, his uninjured hand tightening into a fist. "But if I do, I'm sure you'll remind me, won't you?" He narrowed his hazel brown eyes and glared accusingly at Temerity. "Now will you close that goddamn door before I *forget* I gave my word to help take this damn steamboat upriver?"

Standing stubbornly beside the open door, Temerity glared right back at Steele, her stance making it obvious that she had no intention of backing down. "I don't appreciate that kind of language, Mr. Steele, and will tolerate none of my *employees* addressing me in such a tone!"

Damn obstinate female. It'd serve her right if I just walked the hell out of here and let her lose her boat! His own anger and determination now as impossible to hide as Temerity's, Steele stomped across the space that separated them and scowled down at her, his face only inches from hers. Deliberately intending to intimidate her with his towering height, he gave her an ultimatum. "Well, which is it to be? Do I stay and help you? Or do I go back to St. Louis and let them burn your boat to the water before you're halfway across the state of Missouri?"

"Go ahead and leave!" Temerity shouted, matching his scowl with one of her own. She refused to be bullied by any man. No matter how handsome he was and no matter how much she'd enjoyed his kisses, Steele was no different! "I don't nee— *What* did you say?" she interrupted herself, Steele's words suddenly registering with frightening clarity. "Let who burn the *Intrepid* to the water? What are you talking about? The fire was an accident. You said so yourself! Who would want to destroy my father's steamer?"

If he had planned to do battle with Temerity, Steele had made a tactical error of the utmost gravity. And he knew it the instant the sweet lemony scent of her hair and skin assailed his nostrils in a sneak attack. This close to her, he was powerless to resist the unique combination of fire and vulnerability that had attracted him to Temerity Kincade from the first—before he'd known she was Tim Kincade's daughter, before keeping the *Intrepid* afloat had even become an issue. Who was he trying to kid? He wasn't going anywhere. He wasn't strong enough to ignore his own compelling need to take care of the little spitfire no matter how often she insisted she could take care of herself. Steele drew in a deep breath of resignation. He wasn't going to St. Louis or anywhere else. He was on the *Intrepid* for the duration, and he knew it.

His own anger dissipated, Steele's voice was calm when he spoke again. "Close the door, Temerity," he said softly, his tone no longer commanding but nonetheless leaving no room for refusal as he pried open her tight grip on the door and shoved it closed. He led her to the one chair in her cabin and sat her down before resuming his seat on her bunk. "We've got to talk, Temerity. Are you ready to listen to what I have to say?"

Having witnessed the scene that had just taken place, Uriah wasn't sure the two remembered he was in the cabin with them. Rather than interfere with what looked as if it should be a private conversation, the older man turned to leave. "Stay here, Uriah," Steele instructed, never taking his eyes off Temerity, as if she might bolt at any minute. "This involves you too."

"What's going on?" the river pilot growled. "I don't wanna get caught in the middle o' no lover's spat!" he warned, eyeing Steele warily.

Temerity's accusing gaze shot upward to zero in on Steele too, her lips moving even before she could form the words she had for him.

Before she could speak, before Uriah could make good his escape, Steele shouted at them, the throbbing pain in his hand compounding his frustration and pitching his patience over the edge of his limits. "Will you two please stop all your yammering! Somebody tried to destroy the *Intrepid* tonight, and you two can't get your minds off petty things like who's the boss and lovers' quarrels! Do you understand what I'm saying?" he yelled at the two who stared open-mouthed at him. "That fire was no accident! It was deliberate!"

Chapter Six

Certain that corn *cobs* instead of corn *husks* had been used to stuff her mattress, Temerity shifted restlessly in her bunk. She flipped over onto her back and stared toward the dark cabin ceiling. *I'm going to buy myself a feather mattress the first chance I get,* she vowed silently, trying to drive her thoughts away from Steele's frightening announcement.

But it was no use. She couldn't stop thinking about what he'd told her. Someone had purposely set the fire in the hold. But who would want to destroy the *Intrepid?* And why? What would they have to gain?

She crossed her arms over her chest and squinted her eyes into narrow slits, as though she would be able to see the answer she was seeking in the black surroundings of her cabin if she concentrated hard enough.

At first she had laughed at Steele's suggestion. The entire thing was completely preposterous. For what reason would anyone want to destroy her father's riverboat and its cargo? Steal it, yes, she could understand that. But to burn it? It didn't make any sense.

But when Steele had told her about finding a narrow burn trail, no wider than a candlewick, leading from the main deck down to the bolt of cloth that had been smoldering in the hold, she'd had no choice but to consider the possibility that the fire had not been an accident.

Of course, her suspicions had immediately focused on the Cameron Line. After all, they had certainly made no secret of the fact that they didn't want the *Intrepid* to make the trip up the Missouri River this summer.

But, she remembered with an irritated frown, as Steele had so logically pointed out, why would they destroy what was in effect their own property? No, it couldn't be Cameron. Then who? No one else had anything to gain if she failed.

If the fire was premeditated—which she wasn't ready to admit yet—it had to have been set by someone who had something to gain if the *Intrepid* didn't make it to Fort Benton but nothing to lose if it burned in the water.

"Unless . . . !" she whispered, springing to a sitting position and throwing her feet over the side of the bed. "Unless they didn't intend to destroy the *Intrepid* at all!" she said, her voice breathy with accusing excitement.

Shoving her bare feet into her shoes, Temerity snatched up a shawl and slung it carelessly around her shoulders. Taking no time to grab a lantern and light it, she jerked open the door to her cabin and stepped outside.

All the first-class passengers seemed to be in their cabins on the boiler deck, while the crew and those who were obliged to travel second-class were all bedded down wherever they could find a space on the main deck. So no one saw Temerity, clad only in a white nightgown and shawl, as she disappeared around the corner.

However, her scandalous dress—or lack of dress—and the impropriety of her late-night actions were the least of Temerity's worries as she lifted her hand to knock on the door of Uriah's cabin on the opposite side of the sternwheeler. Fortunately though, just as her knuckles would have made contact with the pine door, she remembered the sleeping passengers in the nearby cabins. She still gave no thought to what they would think if they heard her; but she didn't want to raise an alarm. So she pulled her hand back and reached for the door handle instead.

"Mr. Steele," she whispered as she stepped into the darkened cabin. "Are you awake?" She listened for a moment to the soft sounds of the sleeping man's breathing, and a wave of uncertainty ruffled through her. It had been decided that because of Steele's injury he would sleep in Uriah's cabin while the master pilot kept watch over the cargo in the hold for the remainder of the night. "Mr. Steele?"

When she still received no answer from the sleeping man in the bed, she quietly closed the door behind her and tiptoed toward him. Because all the tiny cabins were identical, she knew exactly where in the room his bunk was, even though this cabin was darker than hers since the moon's light hadn't reached this side of the riverboat yet.

"Mr. Steele, wake up. I think I know what happened!" she announced, her urgent whisper barely disguising her anger-tinged excitement as she reached out, intending to gently shake Steele awake.

The realization that her hand was touching bare flesh was sudden and violent. And with all the energy of a tornado, it attacked her with enervating force, paralyzing her.

Steele was not wearing a shirt!

A charge of electricity spasmed up Temerity's arm,

causing her heart to jerk painfully in her chest. Every nerve and muscle in her body tensed. Her breath became shallow and rapid, her mouth dry.

But instead of yanking her hand back, as her brain screamed at her to do, Temerity's grip tightened involuntarily, her fingers curling harder into the sleep-warmed masculine sinew.

Steele drew in a deep breath, then released it in a long contented sigh, setting off a whole new flutter of fear in her. *Oh, Lord! He's waking up!* She looked around the darkened room frantically. She had to get out of the cabin before Steele realized she was there.

Then Temerity remembered the dose of laudanum she'd given him for pain before he'd gone to sleep. *No wonder he didn't waken when I called to him,* she thought, and laughed inwardly, relief seeping into her frozen muscles and returning them to her control.

Her eyes, more accustomed to the darkness now, made a cursory sweep over Steele's shadowed features. His breathing was slow and even again and he was sleeping soundly once more. She was safe. She would be back in her own cabin in a minute and he would never know she'd been there.

Gingerly relaxing her grip and drawing her hand away from his shoulder, Temerity started to back away. It was in that moment the moon chose to illuminate the small cabin. Before Temerity's startled eyes, the sleeping man in the bunk became more than a shadow. Her gaze flew to his face to see if the moonlight had awakened him. But no, he still slept, unaware that he was not alone.

She really had to leave, she told herself as her eyes roved over his face and shoulders to his . . . It was then she realized the sheet was draped only over his lower half, and that his entire chest, broad and laddered with muscle, was exposed. The dark shadow of the chest hair that she had seen a glimpse of at the collar of his shirt teased at her senses. Her fingers flexed and unflexed with the desire to know what that dark, springy hair would feel like against her palms.

Horrified by the tempting thoughts racing through her mind, Temerity shook her head resolutely and turned to leave. Still . . .

She looked back over her shoulder. Steele hadn't moved. His breathing was deep and regular. What could one little touch hurt? No one would ever know.

Promising herself she would just brush her fingertips quickly over the hair to satisfy her curiosity and then return to her own cabin, Temerity turned toward the bed.

She stood back as far as possible and stretched for a tentative touch, as though testing an iron. The fascinating chest hair tickled the tips of her fingers. And it was not at all an unpleasant feeling.

Temerity jerked her hand back and shot a guilty glance at Steele's face. He remained sound asleep and she breathed a relieved sigh. She was still safe.

Emboldened by the knowledge that he was drugged, Temerity took a step closer and extended her open hand over Steele's gently rising chest. She drew a deep, steadying breath, then carefully lowered her hand to graze her palm and fingers over the enticing bed of hair.

"What the hell are you doing?" Steele charged suddenly, grabbing Temerity's wrist.

She tried to pull her hand back, determined to flee the cabin that had suddenly become the scene of a nightmare.

But before she could respond, she was yanked up off the floor and flipped over onto her back in the bunk beside Steele. "Who are you? What are you doing in here?" he said, rolling on top of his prisoner and pinning her to the mattress.

"It's me, Mr. Steele," Temerity whimpered, her fear making it impossible to think, his weight making it difficult to breathe.

"Who are you?" he repeated, his tone slurred and threatening. He cupped her chin in one hand and turned her face toward his. "Are they so desperate they're sending a woman to do their dirty work?" His grip on her face tightened painfully. "You'd better talk if you want to keep on breathing!"

Her eyes wide with terror, Temerity looked into Steele's angry face. Narrowed threateningly, his eyes were glazed, and though their focus seemed to be on her, it wasn't—the way a blind person directs his gaze toward a speaker but obviously does not really see the other person.

He's still asleep! she realized with horror. *He thinks I'm someone else! An enemy!*

"Answer me! Who are you?" he blasted. Pushing her head back, he arched her neck painfully, his hold pressing against her windpipe.

"It's Temerity, Mr. Steele!" she gasped, her own tears adding to the strangling lump in her throat that threatened to destroy her. "P-Please, s-stop, Mr. Steele! It's Temerity!"

His drugged eyes searched her face, almost as if they really saw *her,* not an imagined enemy. The pressure on her throat eased and her neck was allowed to return to a more natural position, though his fingers stayed clasped loosely under her jaw. His brows drew together, his confusion obvious. "Temerity?"

"W-We're on my father's sternwheeler, the *Intrepid.* I came to t-talk to you about the fire," she said hurriedly, taking advantage of her ability to breathe again.

"Ah . . . Temerity," he said, his cheeks dimpling with recognition and sending relief flooding through her. Thank God, he was awake and knew who she was. He wasn't going to kill her.

Then what she had perceived to be a smile curled into a sneer, hard and cold. "You're right there, little lady. You've definitely got temerity, and temerity's been known to win battles. But not always the war."

Battles? War? What was he talking about? Temerity examined the smirking face above hers and then she knew the answers to her questions.

Her erratically beating heart somersaulted with alarm. Panic pounded in her ears. He wasn't awake at all! He was still asleep. He didn't recognize her. In his mind he was somewhere else and with someone else. Someone who was his enemy.

"Wake up, Mr. Steele. It's me, Temerity!" she said, intending her order to be stern, authoritative, but only managing a small, childlike plea.

But Steele didn't hear her. He was too lost in the unreal world of his laudanum-induced dream.

"And temerity deserves its own reward, doesn't it?" His smile was knowing, as though he shared a secret with her.

Steele's hand stole around Temerity's neck to burrow deep in the dark silk of the hair at the back of her head.

"N-n-n—" she started as his mouth descended without warning to capture hers, silencing her protest before it could completely form.

Though her mind cried out its remonstrations, Temerity's mouth opened instinctively to invite Steele to deepen the kiss—which he did without hesitation. Knowing she had to escape, she managed to work her hands free of his compressing weight. But instead of trying to ward him off, as she'd expected them to do, her hands, seeming to act on their own, wended their way around his rib cage to his back. The skin of his

105

back was soft, baby's-bottom soft, stretched over hard corded muscles that called out to her to investigate further. And all reason was washed from her mind.

Shivers of anticipation and primitive need trembled through her. Every place her flesh touched his seemed to have a golden wire connected to it that tugged on that secret, private part of her in the most deliciously disturbing way. From the tips of her fingers on his back to the welling desire in her lower body. From the warm interior of her mouth, which was being courted by his tongue, to that same pulsing pain deep in her belly.

This is insanity, she told herself, even as her hands fanned open to knead the hard muscles of Steele's back. She knew she should try again to awaken him, should move her head and force him to stop kissing her, and most of all that she should not be returning his kiss, her own tongue urgently caressing his now, her hands clutching him harder against her.

But Temerity knew just as certainly that she would not, could not, stop what was happening, could not control the gentle rocking of her hips as they began to move against his.

Her body was crying out to be relieved of its agony, to know firsthand the things instinct had already taught it; and to deny herself the healing balm necessary to stop this torture would mean her own destruction.

Steele's kiss became gentle, almost worshipful, and Temerity melted into it, reveling in the feel of his body warm and hard on her. When their lips parted, he trailed a line of kisses over her jaw to her ear. He sucked a plump lobe into his mouth as his hand slid down her throat to the top button on her flannel gown. His mouth following in the wake of his hand, he kissed her throat, now willingly arched to give him full advantage, as he quickly undid the row of buttons.

When he brushed aside her gown and touched her breast with his warm callused fingertips, shock and guilt jolted Temerity out of her sensual fog. An infinitesimal fragment of reason returned. She couldn't let this go on. It had to stop. She had to resist him, as well as her own wanton desire.

"Please don't," she whispered, wrapping her fingers around his wrist and making a feeble attempt to move his hand away. Then his hand tightened around the firm mound and his mouth closed over its puckered peak, sending those demanding golden wires radiating through her body to the very center of her soul. And that last tiny bit of lucidity, that modicum of resistance, dissipated into the unreal cocoon of the dark cabin.

Instead of forcing Steele back into the world of wakefulness, as she should have done, she'd been drawn into his dream. She was no longer herself, no longer Temerity, no longer Tim Kincade's daughter, no longer the owner and operator of the *Intrepid*. Now she was only a woman, a woman in a dream, a woman who would be whoever and whatever this man believed her to be.

She no longer resisted, physically or mentally, as Steele's hand roved over her body to raise her gown above her hips. She no longer struggled against her own desire as she held his head tight to her breast. And she no longer feared what would happen in the morning. Tomorrow didn't matter. Only now was important. Only this dream.

His mouth still at her breast, Steele palmed the curve of her femininity and slid his fingers deep into the silky pleats of her sex, made moist and ready by her own need. "Mmm, nice," he murmured against her nipple as he began to caress and explore the opening petals of her body, tracing each channel from base to tip with meticulous care. More and more, his caresses concentrated on the swollen center of her desire, and Temerity felt the thunder begin to gather in her body.

It seemed as if she were rising off the bed, as though she were weightless, held only to the earth by the glorious warmth of the man holding her, caressing her, suckling her.

Then the thunder came, rolling and rumbling through her entire body in an explosive shudder, splintering her emotions into a million tiny pieces.

As she tumbled her way back from the magnificent storm, trembling and shaken, Steele tossed the sheet off his body and rolled between Temerity's legs, entering her with a sure thrust.

Temerity's eyes opened wide with shock, then fluttered closed again as the tearing pain that had seared through her dissipated as quickly as it had appeared. The penetration had been so quick and unexpected, her body so completely and expertly prepared, that the pain was gone almost before she realized it hadn't been her imagination.

With her welcoming body closing snugly around his manhood, Steele moved in and out, slowly at first, then as his urgency grew so did the rapidity of his thrusts until he was pounding into her with uncontrolled frenzy.

Temerity's legs wound around Steele's hips and her hands burrowed into the hair at his temples, catching fistfuls of it in her fingers and pulling herself up to meet his mouth with hers.

Then it was happening again, that building of the thunder in her groin, that glorious explosion into splendor, followed by the exquisite floating, weightless drift back to earth. Only this time she was not alone. This time Steele was with her as his straining muscles shuddered to fulfillment.

When Temerity would have held Steele to her a

moment longer, glorying in the wondrous experience they had shared, Steele rolled away from her, collapsing on his back, his uninjured forearm thrown up over his forehead.

Confused, she held herself up on one elbow and examined his mustached face. "Mr. Steele?" she couldn't help saying, not knowing if she'd done something wrong or if that was the way a man was supposed to act. All she knew was that she was suddenly left feeling disappointed, empty inside—and used. "Mr. Steele?" She touched his shoulder lightly.

Steele jerked, as though he'd been hit, then mumbled several unintelligible words and began to snore. He was sound asleep! As though she were not even there. As if she'd never been there!

The ugly, snorting sounds of Steele's snoring cut into her consciousness, each one hacking at her heart with deadly purpose. With trembling fingers, she redid the buttons on her gown and climbed over the sleeping man and out of the bunk that had been the scene of her disgrace.

Ashamed and embarrassed, she snatched up her shoes and shawl and hurried to the door, like a burglar sneaking off into the night after committing a robbery.

What seemed like an eternity later, but was actually only minutes, Temerity was safe in her cabin again. Sick with humiliation and self-disgust, she threw herself across the lumpy bunk and cried for the second time that day—and all because of Steele. He'd taken advantage of her and she hated him!

But her hatred for Steele was only a fraction of what she felt for herself. How could she have been so foolish, so totally lacking in self-control? How could she have so lightly given her innocence to a man who was a total stranger?

Revulsion roiled through her. She'd ruined everything! Not only had she thrown away her virginity, the gift she'd meant for the man she would love and marry, the man who would cherish her and the knowledge that he was the only man she'd ever been with.

But she'd also destroyed any chance of maintaining a professional relationship with Steele. After what had happened in his cabin, she would never be able to look him in the eye again, much less work with him. She would have to fire him and make the upriver trip without him. And despite the facade of confidence she did her best to affect in public, she wasn't sure she could do it alone. If she couldn't succeed without Steele, her actions tonight had destroyed her father's business just as surely as if the arsonist had burned the *Intrepid* to the water.

Temerity had no idea how long she lay there mentally flogging herself. But by the time dawn was not more than an hour away, she had managed to come to terms with what had happened and her decision was made.

Her virginity may have been destroyed, but the *Intrepid* wasn't. It was still afloat and she would do everything in her power to see that it stayed that way. Her shame and lost virginity be damned, she would make the trip to Fort Benton and back to St. Louis. And she wouldn't fire Steele after all.

However, she would act as if nothing had happened between them. She would have as little to do with him as possible. She would have Uriah deal with him, speaking to him directly only when *absolutely* necessary. And never, *never* again would she find herself in a position of being alone with him.

With her resolution and priorities once more in order, Temerity rose and went about her morning toilette with determination and new resolve. Only when she discovered the dark stain on the back of her white gown did she experience second thoughts. But they were only momentary. *What's done is done. I won't dwell on past mistakes. I'll only look forward, not back!*

Forcing herself to think about the day ahead of her rather than the night before, she rinsed away the telltale evidence of her loss and hung her gown up to dry on the clothesline she'd strung across her cabin.

Even though it was still dark when she stepped out of her cabin a short while later, Temerity felt invigorated and new. There was no obstacle or setback so great that she couldn't overcome it as long as she kept her thoughts on her goals.

Stepping around the second-class passengers and deckhands who'd slept wherever they could find a spot on the main deck, Temerity hurried to find Uriah Gunther. As she put her foot on the first step leading down into the hold, an unexpected feeling of apprehension shivered up her arm and she hesitated. She felt as though she was being watched.

"Don't be so silly," she scolded aloud, holding her lantern higher and hurrying into the darkened hold. "Uriah?" she called out before reaching the bottom step. "How did things go last night?"

There was no answer.

"Uriah?" she repeated, stopping and squinting her eyes to examine the pitch-black of the hold outside the dim circle of her lantern light. "Where are you?"

Then she thought she heard a moan behind her. "Uriah?" she called again in a shaky whisper. "Is that you?"

The moan came again, a little louder this time, helping Temerity to pinpoint the area of its origin.

Without thinking of her own safety, she ran toward the sound. "Uriah!" she gasped as she rounded a group of large wooden crates and found the crumpled heap of

111

bound and gagged master pilot. "Who did this to you?" she asked, fumbling with the bandana over Uriah's mouth. "Hey, up there!" she shouted toward the stairs. "You roosters get me some help down here!" Turning back to Uriah, she asked, "What happened, Uriah?"

"I don't know, Miss Temerity. Everythin' was goin' fine. All the folks was bedded down and everythin' was quiet. Than all of a sudden he was here, holdin' a knife to my throat!"

"Oh, my god! Who was it, Uriah? Did you see who did this to you?" She worked frantically at the ropes on the old man's wrists.

"I don't know, missy. He grabbed me from behind. I didn't see his face."

"Someone get me some help down here!" she shouted up to the main deck again. "Did he hurt you?" she asked Uriah, her voice shaking with concern. She didn't dare think about what she would do if the pilot was seriously injured.

"I'm fine," the older man lied bravely. "I don't know where he come from, Miss Temerity. He musta' been down here waitin' for me. One second I was alone and the next he had his arm around my neck and was whisperin' in my ear."

"Whispering in your ear? What did he say?"

"He said this was just a warnin'. He said that if you didn't turn the *Intrepid* 'round and head back to St. Louis, there was gonna be more accidents."

"His voice, Uriah! Did you recognize his voice?"

"I told ya, Miss Temerity, he was whisperin'. A evil, crazy-soundin' whisper. Didn't sound like no one I ever heard before."

"Did he say anything else?"

"Nope, jest the warnin' and then he clobbered me on the back o' the head. He was gone when I come to, and I was tied up like you found me."

112

"Think, Uriah. Was there anything else that could give us a clue to who he was? His size? Was he a big man? Small? Your height? Mine? Think, Uriah. There's got to be something!"

Uriah thought for a moment. He rubbed the back of his head, wincing when he touched the spot where he'd been hit. "I'm sorry, missy, but there's nothin' else. It all happened so quick. I'm pretty sure he was at least as tall as me, maybe taller. But I jest can't be sure. I'm sorry I let ya down."

Temerity was suddenly ashamed. Here she was interrogating the poor man before she even saw to his injuries. "You didn't let me down, Uriah," she apologized. "It looks like no one's going to come. Can you walk?" She slipped her arm around the older man's back and urged him to stand.

Uriah, leaning heavily on the slender girl's shoulders, managed to haul himself to his feet. "What are you gonna do, missy? Looks like someone don't want you to go upriver real bad. Are you gonna do like he said and turn back?"

"Not on your life, Uriah!" Temerity answered angrily as she strained under the heavier weight. "They're not going to force me off the river no matter what they do!"

"Are you sure that's what you wanna do?"

"I certainly am! They'll have to kill me to stop me. No one's going to scare me into losing my father's business to the Cameron Line, Uriah!"

"Somehow I thought you'd say that, missy," Uriah said gruffly, the smile on his face an odd mix of pride and worry.

"After what's happened, I'll understand if you don't want to continue with me, Uriah," she said hesitantly, hating the thought of losing the old river pilot but knowing she had no choice but to give him the option of getting out of their bargain.

"Hell, missy, there ain't no way you're gonna git rid o' me now. I wouldn't never be able to look at this ugly face o' mine in the mirror if I was to give up now. 'Sides, there's nothin' a old river rat like me likes better'n a good fight!"

"Well, it looks as though you're going to enjoy this trip then, because we're up to our chins in a real good fight, Uriah," Temerity said, breathing a sigh of relief. The worried frown on her face deepened, then broke into a determined smile. "But nothing *two* 'river rats' like you and I can't handle!"

"And Steele," Uriah added, aware of the way Temerity stiffened at the mention of the younger man's name.

"And Steele," she agreed harshly, hating the fact that she needed him more now than ever. "No, I can't forget Mr. Steele. Now let's get you upstairs to my cabin so I can look at that head of yours."

"Damn, Miss Temerity, this little old goose egg ain't nothin'!" Uriah protested. With that brave denial, he pitched forward in a dead faint just as two roustabouts came down the stairs in time to catch the crusty old man and carry him up to the boiler deck.

Chapter Seven

Steele rolled over onto his back with a tortured groan. His mouth was dry; his throat was parched; and his tongue felt thick and swollen. "What the hell happened?" he croaked through cracked lips, making a vain effort to open his eyes. But it was no use. His eyelids felt as though they were glued shut. "Damn," he muttered, lifting one of his hands, thinking to rub his eyes open. But his hand felt as leaden as his eyelids did and he was forced to let it drop to his side again.

This had to be, without a doubt, the worst hangover he'd ever had; and he swore on his grandfather's grave never to touch another drop of whiskey as long as he lived. Funny, he couldn't even remember having anything to drink the night before, much less enough to produce this rough a hangover. *Must have been some powerful stuff.*

His brows drew together into a frown of concentration as he tried to remember where he'd gotten so drunk—where he was now, for that matter. He raised his eyebrows, stretching the lids so they opened in the barest slits. But the torture was too unbearable, the sunshine beaming into the room too blinding. With an exaggerated wince, he squeezed them shut again.

Turning his head away from the glaring light, he rested a moment, then knowing there was no escape from it, tried to open his eyes again. This time only one stinging eye opened, but it was a bit wider than before—at least enough to determine he was in a bed and not in an alley behind some St. Louis tavern as he'd feared. That decided, he managed to open his second eye.

Suddenly, a rumbling sound roared through his head, louder and louder, competing cruelly with the relentless pounding already berating his temples. Before he could wonder about the source of the mysterious rumble, his bed began to vibrate. A loud whistle sounded, a bell clanged three jarring, brain-destroying times, and the room around him began to move, literally.

He slammed the palms of his hands over his ears in a reflexive defense of his sanity.

Familiar agony shot its way up his left arm. "Aagh!" he yowled, the pain in his hand bringing him fully awake and forcing him to remember the night before with clarity: the fire in the hold, his burned hand, Temerity's gentle nursing of his injury, *and* the laudanum toddy she'd given him so he could sleep. *At least it was good for that,* he thought groggily.

With the slow, cautious movements of a very old man, Steele levered himself to a sitting position and swung his feet to the pine-planked floor. "Unfortunately, the cure's worse than the cause," he groaned aloud, holding his head with his uninjured hand and rocking back and forth, his throbbing left hand limp at his side. "Someone remind me to bite a bullet or something next time," he said to the floor of the cabin as he forced himself to stand up and stagger toward the washstand in the corner. "I couldn't have been this hung over if I'd drunk a gallon of the worst rotgut."

Fifteen minutes later, through sheer determination, Steele managed to drag himself up to the coffeepot in the main cabin, where the cook, Gus, and the cabin boy, Jimmy, were clearing away the remains of breakfast.

"Mornin', Mr. Steele," Gus called out cheerfully. "Breakfast things are all put up, but it wouldn't be no trouble to rustle you up a coupla eggs and some biscuits."

"Thanks, Gus," Steele ground out through a strained grin. *Damn, even my face hurts!* "I'm not all that hungry. Just a cup of coffee to get me going."

"I'll get it for you!" Jimmy announced, snatching up a cup and sloshing coffee in it before Steele could answer.

"Thanks, Jimmy," Steele said, lowering himself to a bench at a table and propping his chin in his hand. "I guess everything went all right last night," he tossed out off-handedly, certain it must have, because the *Intrepid* was under way right on schedule.

Gus and Jimmy exchanged uneasy glances as the boy set the coffee in front of Steele. "Bottom of the pot, hope it's not too strong," Jimmy said, his changing voice going from low to high and back to low again in the short sentence.

Steele eyed the muddy-looking brew and shook his head. "Maybe after a few cups of this I'll feel like a human being again."

Gus laughed and, with unnecessary enthusiasm, went back to wiping off tables and setting up for lunch.

"Did you say everything went okay last night?" Steele said again, lifting the mug to his lips and blowing on its contents before sucking in a rejuvenating gulp. "There wasn't anymore trouble, was there?"

Gus cleared his throat. "I don't guess you done talked to Miss Kincade this mornin'—you sure you

117

don't want no breakfast? A coupla biscuits and a slice of ham, maybe?"

An uneasy feeling began to tighten in Steele's gut. He studied the nervous cook and shook his head. "No tha—why should I have talked to Miss Kincade this morning?"

Jimmy's freckled face reddened and he headed for the door.

"Hold on there, kid. What the hell's going on? Why are you two tiptoeing around giving me a straight answer? What's Miss Kincade going to tell me?"

"Well . . . uh . . . I guess you're gonna find out sooner or later," Gus mumbled.

Steele knew his head would surely split open if he yelled his frustration as he was tempted to do; so, using herculean effort, he kept his voice calm and even. "Find out what?"

"Well, durin' the night, someone bopped Uriah on the head and left him bound and gagged in the hold," Jimmy announced in his squeaking adolescent male voice.

"What?" Steele yelled despite his common sense—and the stab of pain that tore from temple to temple, causing his vision to blur. "Why didn't someone come get me?" he said, using every effort to accent his words slowly, as he concentrated on recovering from his dizziness and not losing his temper again.

"Miss Kincade said to let you sleep," Jimmy offered weakly.

Steele took a deep breath and waited for the pain in his head to ebb slightly. Gradually becoming aware of the slow, steady cannonading of the riverboat's single cylinder, high-pressure engine as it exhausted steam, some of the tension in his shoulders eased. Everything sounded normal, felt normal. "Obviously, he wasn't hurt seriously," he said.

118

"Oh, Uriah's fine," Gus told him. "A coupla days of rest and he'll be up and around as good as new."

An unbelievable premonition exploded in Steele's pain-racked brain. "Did you say, *days* of rest?" he shouted, standing up suddenly and bumping the table with his legs, oblivious to the brown stain of coffee as it spread over the tablecloth. "Where's Uriah now?" he asked, rubbing his bruised leg as he limped toward the doorway. "He is in the wheelhouse, isn't he?" No one answered, and his horrible sense of foreboding increased. "*Isn't he?*"

Gus and Jimmy shot trapped looks at each other. They hadn't figured out exactly what there was between Miss Kincade and her first mate, but they sensed Steele had more at stake here than just a job, and more say than the average first mate. "Not exactly," Gus finally said.

The trapped looks and Gus's evasive answer were enough to tell Steele what he didn't want to hear, but he asked anyway. "What *exactly* does 'not exactly' mean, Gus?"

"Well . . . he's uh, resting in Miss Kincade's bunk and she's—"

"God damn!" Steele spit out, not needing to hear more. He whirled out of the dining salon and, taking the steps two at a time, raced up to the hurricane deck, where the wheelhouse was located. "Fool female. She hasn't got the sense God gave a gnat!" he mumbled. "Any other woman would have waited an extra day in St. Charles! But not this one! Noooo! Not this crazy, stubborn, mule-headed, bossy, headstrong, unreasonable . . ."

Before Steele ran out of words to describe Temerity, he found himself on the short staircase leading up to the iron-plated wheelhouse that sat atop the *Intrepid*. Putting his hand on the door latch to enter the little building, he stopped short and stared at the young woman who, her back to him, was at the wheel.

She wore a starched white blouse tucked into a tailored blue linen skirt gathered at her small waist. Her dark hair, obviously smoothed into a knot at the back of her head that morning, curled in stray wisps at the nape of her neck and over her ears. Though he couldn't see her face yet, he knew it would be framed with more of those same willful curls that stubbornly refused to conform to the severe hairstyle she tried to force on them every day.

The breath caught in Steele's throat as fragments of a dream he'd had the night before assaulted his memory. He could almost smell the clean, lemony fragrance of the dark cloud of hair. His hands tingled with the remembered feel of silky strands curling around his fingers in the dream.

Forcing his thoughts back to the present with a violent shake of his head, Steele yanked open the door to the wheelhouse. "What do you think you're doing?"

Temerity had been so lost in her own thoughts, she hadn't heard anyone approach; and she couldn't help the gasp of startled surprise that escaped from her throat as she spun her head around to see Steele.

Oh, lord, how had she ever thought she'd be able to look at him again, much less work with him after last night? Even if it was the only way she had to save the *Intrepid,* it was too much to ask of herself. She knew now that every time she saw him, heard his voice, she would remember and be ashamed.

Even now, with bloodshot eyes and a day's growth of beard, his mere presence brought back the feel of his mouth on hers and the thrill of his hands caressing her body. She could feel her nipples tightening and straining against the softness of her chemise. Horrified by her lack of control over her body's reaction to seeing

120

Steele, Temerity felt heat rise from the high collar of her blouse, turning her face a bright pink.

"What does it look like I'm doing, Mr. Steele?" she finally said, as coolly as she could manage, turning away from him and concentrating her attention on the river.

"It looks like you're piloting this sternwheeler, but I'm hoping it's just another dream."

"Another dream?" she repeated, her voice just a bit above a whisper.

"That stuff you made me drink gave me crazy dreams all night long."

"Oh?" Her shoulders tensed and her grip on the wheel tightened until her knuckles turned white. Was it possible he thought last night was a fleeting dream? Afraid to trust the relief she was feeling at the crazy idea that Steele didn't remember what had happened, she spoke, her voice husky, guarded. "What kind of dreams, Mr. Steele?"

Steele's mouth watered as the memory of the taste of warm feminine flesh assaulted his taste buds. He wiped the back of his hand across his mustache as though that would remove the memory. "Just dreams," he answered gruffly. "Now quit trying to change the subject! What are you doing at that wheel?"

Temerity turned her head and looked over her shoulder at Steele, studying him, her blue-gray eyes defensive and wary. Did she dare to believe he didn't remember his part in her fall? Her heart pumped erratically with excitement. If everything was a forgotten dream to him, it could be her salvation. Her secret. And perhaps—just perhaps—she could continue to work with him.

Temerity tried to ignore the hurtful thought that an event that had changed her forever meant nothing more to Steele than a dream, maybe not even that much. How few of her own dreams did she remember? Angry for a reason she didn't understand, she counseled herself silently, *Don't jump to conclusions, Temerity. He could be waiting to throw it up to you later. It would be just like him to use that one mistake against you.* Now *that* was something to be mad about!

"To express the obvious, Mr. Steele," she said angrily, returning her focus to the murky brown water before her, "I'm taking this Missouri River packet up the Missouri River!"

"I don't need any of your smart answers this morning, *Miss Kincade!* Now tell me what happened to Uriah and why you didn't come get me!"

"I'm warning you, Mr. Steele. You'd better not take that tone of voice with me. You're forgetting who's the owner of the *Intrepid*."

"I haven't forgotten a damn thing, lady. But evidently you have."

A panicked frown flickered across Temerity's forehead. Did he remember after all?

"You've forgotten that this riverboat wouldn't have left the St. Louis levee if I hadn't found a crew for you; and you've forgotten that I gave my word to do my best to see that you and the *Intrepid* and your passengers make it up the Missouri safely. In spite of you! And that's exactly what I plan to do—no matter who you say the 'owner' is! Now, give the order to slow those engines and turn this thing around and redock it in St. Charles—or I will." He made a grab for the wheel with his uninjured hand and turned it to the left.

"Who do you think you are?" Temerity shrieked, turning the wheel in the opposite direction with all her strength. "By what right do you come onto *my* riverboat and start giving *me* orders?"

"By the right of the man who—"

Temerity's eyes opened wide with horror. Here it was. He was going to do it now. At the top of his lungs. For everyone on the *Intrepid* to hear. Her hands dropped from the wheel to her sides. "Go on," she said, surprised at the strength in her voice as she waited for him to finish his sentence: *the man who took your virginity.* "The man who what?"

The same stricken look in Temerity's blue eyes was mirrored in Steele's golden brown counterparts as the realization of what he'd almost said slapped him in the face. He'd almost given himself away, come close to ruining everything. His hand fell away from the wheel at the same time Temerity released her hold, and the wheel spun out of control.

In the next instant, everything happened at once. Temerity lost her balance and flew across the narrow space that separated her from Steele, slamming up against his chest.

Unable to stop his own backward momentum with the sudden lurching of the riverboat, Steele's hands automatically grasped at Temerity's waist for support as he toppled back to the deck—taking her with him.

"What in tarnation's goin' on up here?" Uriah's gravelly voice roared as he burst through the door to the wheelhouse. "This ride's about as rough as—" Stunned by the sight that greeted him on the rough planks of the deck, Uriah paused.

On his back, with Temerity lying on top of him, her face buried in the vee of his shirt, her hips nestled intimately between his thighs, Steele was struggling to stand up.

"Uriah!" Temerity gasped, hurrying to push away from Steele and rise up to her knees. This was the second time in less than twenty-four hours the crusty old river pilot had found them in each other's arms; and her mortification plunged to fathomless depths. If she could have dived into the river and never come up again, she would have.

If the wheel hadn't been spinning wildly as the riverboat tried to turn its bow downriver to go with the current, Uriah would have laughed at the embarrassed expressions on the two faces, each a shade redder than the other.

"Seems you two could find a better time and place for that sort of thing," he said offhandedly as he stepped around the sprawling, scrambling people on the floor to grab the wheel and begin to battle to regain control of the would-be runaway boat.

"Let me explain! It was an accide—"

"You don't owe me no explanations, missy." He laughed, bringing the boat under control and back on course with a few experienced spins of the wheel.

"You don't understand, Uriah," she protested, standing up and brushing at her skirt nervously. "This isn't what it looks like. We were just—"

"This should be good," Steele said with a knowing wink in Uriah's direction as he struggled to his feet.

Temerity shot Steele a glare, wishing she could slap that infuriating dimpled grin off his face. "It's not what you think, Uriah!" she went on in a defensive rush of words. "We let go of the wheel at the same—the boat lurched—and we—" She looked for support at Steele, who was smiling for the first time that day, the crooked grin under his mustache threatening to break into laughter.

He held out his arms in helpless defeat. "Don't look at me, lady! You're the one who wants to do all the telling here! You're the boss. I'm just supposed to follow orders!"

"Oooh!" Temerity huffed, spinning on her heel and dashing out of the wheelhouse. She could hear the laughter of the first mate and the pilot long after she was out of ear-range.

About three o'clock that afternoon, still suffering the after-effects of the laudanum he'd had the night before, Steele sat down on a bale of hay and leaned his head against a wooden crate. Just a few minutes out of Hamburg, Missouri, where they'd taken on two passengers, Steele knew they were a couple of hours away from Washington, where they would dock for the night. If he could just rest a few minutes, he told himself as he reached into his shirt pocket, he would be good as new.

Studying the business card he had found near the spot where Uriah had been struck down, he frowned unhappily. "THE CAMERON LINE. St Louis to Fort Benton and all points in between," he read thoughtfully. *It's a good thing Temerity didn't find this. She's already convinced Cameron's behind all her troubles.* "And I've got to admit this makes it look like she could be right—or at least like someone's going to a lot of trouble to make it seem that way."

"Riley's Wood Yard is just up ahead and it looks like he's got wood, Mr. Steele!" Harry Bailey, the mud clerk, called out.

Steele replaced the Cameron business card into his pocket and sat up straight. "Why don't we just go on in to Washington and take on some when we dock for the night?" He knew what Harry's reply would be. Though they hadn't used all the wood they'd taken on in St. Louis yet, he knew the riverboat's ravenous appetite would devour every stick of that as well as the new cordwood and would be demanding more before too many days had passed.

The continuous need for fuel to feed the steamboat's

hungry furnace was the riverman's most exasperating and constant concern. Because most of the upper Missouri River Valley had almost no timber, the wise man bought as much wood as he could carry whenever and wherever he found it.

"It'd be a shame to pass up Riley's wood and then get to Washington and find the other steamers have bought up all the good cedar and left nothing but green cottonwood," Bailey explained. "Never can tell when we'll come to a good supply again. Besides, Captain Kincade always bought from old Riley when he could, and Miss Kincade's already given the order to stop here."

Steele rolled to his feet with a groan. "Yeah, well, we wouldn't want to go against Miss Kincade's orders, would we?"

Minutes later, Steele and Harry were on the marshy riverbank with "Ole Man" Riley, a wizened man of indeterminate age. *Somewhere between forty and ninety,* Steele decided. Harry had told him that the old man had been cutting and selling wood at this spot for as long as anyone on the river could remember. And in a time when woodcutters were around only a few seasons before they traveled on, or gave up and went back East, or were killed by Indians, a stop at "Ole Man" Riley's Wood Yard was somewhat of a tradition. For good luck and a weather report, if nothing else.

"Mr. Riley," Harry began, "this here's Mr. Steele, the first mate. He just might be interested in buying some of that wood you got there."

"Hmp. I jest might be inner'sted in sellin' to ya—fer the right price. Whatcha offerin' fer prime cedar, boy?" Riley asked Steele.

"Prime, you say?" Steele answered, sensing that half the reason Riley was a woodcutter was that he enjoyed haggling. "Looks half rotten to me," he said with a

126

straight face. "But since Captain Kincade dealt with you in the past, you might be able to talk me into five dollars in trade goods per cord for the cedar and two dollars for the cottonwood. Couldn't pay a bit more for such sorry-looking stuff though."

Riley shot a knowing glance at Harry Bailey and laughed. He wasn't insulted. It was all part of the game and he recognized a *player* in Steele. "Where'd you pick up this yokel?" he asked, using his hand to cup the side of his mouth in an obvious aside.

Harry shrugged his shoulders and shook his head.

Riley looked back at Steele, his eyes twinkling with excitement. "Tell you what, young feller. 'Cause I feel sorry for you—bein' so dumb and all—and cause I like a feller with a sense o' humor, I'll give you ten cords o' cedar for four seventy-five cash and five cords of cottonwood for a dollar-fifty cash. How's that sound?"

"Cash?" Steele chuckled, raising an eyebrow suspiciously. "You know we trade in goods, not cash. We've got some good ax handles, barrels of clean flour, sugar. I might even be talked into givin' you a pot-bellied stove for the whole fifteen cords. But cash?" Steele shook his head. "I just don't see how we could go that high in cash." Steele made a show of considering an alternative for a minute, then said, "What do you say to four dollars split half and half between cash and goods for the cedar and two twenty-five in goods for the cottonwood?"

Riley wheezed and pulled a pipe out of his jacket pocket and poked it in his mouth. "No tellin' when you'll come to the next wood yard. This late in the season, the others what come before you got it all." He looked from Steele to Harry and back to Steele again, finally shrugging his shoulders in defeat. "Well, what the hell. You seem like a good boy. Tell you what. I'll give you the cedar for four twenty-five cash and the cotton for two dollars in goods. But that's as low as I'll go. Take it or leave it," he said.

"I don't know."

Riley turned to leave.

"We'll take it," Steele laughed, extending his hand to shake Riley's.

From the rail on the boiler deck, Temerity observed the loading of the firewood with growing anxiety. One of those men down there could easily be the Cameron saboteur hired to stop her. Or it could be one of the passengers. For that matter, it could be anyone! Her mind did a rapid recounting of the people on the riverboat, but she still came up empty.

All day she had walked over the decks of the *Intrepid*, talking to everyone she met, young and old, hoping against hope that someone might have noticed something or would say something that would give her a clue to who the culprit was. But she'd found nothing. In fact, after a while, everyone she talked to seemed guilty and sounded as if he were hiding something from her.

"Damn!" Temerity murmured in frustration, hitting the railing with her fists. Someone on the *Intrepid* was her enemy and intended to destroy her, and she was still no closer to finding out who it was than she'd been that morning. All she could do was wait for him to strike again.

In spite of her resolution to put Steele out of her mind and ignore him until she could decide what to do about him, Temerity's eyes sought out her first mate. Viewing the scene on the main deck below, she was forced to admit that the roosters worked exceptionally well for him—much better than they usually did for a crude-talking, whip-toting bully boy ordinarily found on a riverboat. He treated them with respect and as equals; and in turn his men seemed to do their best to live up to what he expected of them. She couldn't help but wonder if they would work as well if he were gone.

Then an annoying thought crossed her mind. Could she, herself, work as well if she didn't have his support?

Of course I could! Shaking her head to rid her mind of that idea, she forced herself to think of something else.

The deal he made with Riley for the cordwood was as good as any man could have made, she admitted to herself. As with all riverboat transactions, she would have preferred to save her cash and handle the entire transaction by trading goods. But this late in the season, when the old man was probably already up to his whiskers in ax handles and flour, she knew they'd been lucky to get him to take any supplies at all. Begrudgingly, she admitted her father probably couldn't have done any better with old Riley—had in the past even done worse on more than one occasion.

And that brought her back to the other problem that had plagued her all morning. What was she going to do about Steele? Seeming to have taken to the river as though he were born to this line of work, he was too good at his job to let go. And hadn't he proven he could be trusted? And hadn't she decided she could bear anything she had to bear in order to ensure a successful journey?

But that was before I had to see him this morning!

Now she wasn't nearly so certain she could continue to work with him—no matter what. The strain of seeing him day in and day out would be too great if he stayed on. For the next three months she would be listening to everything he said, waiting for him to say something to remind her of last night and humiliate her. This trip was too important and would be difficult enough without spending it in a constant state of agitation and fear. And that was exactly what would happen if they both stayed on the *Intrepid*.

There was no other answer. One of them had to leave. *And it surely won't be me!*

As she watched, Steele suddenly ripped off his shirt and tossed it onto the deck. The breath caught in her throat as the muscled flesh of his back, already gleaming with sweat, was exposed to the sunshine— and her vision. Her mouth grew dry and her body temperature seemed to rise. A trickle of perspiration trailed between her breasts in an intimate caress, and she remembered how the smooth flesh of his back had felt under her hands. The warmth of her body seeped deep into her belly, where it radiated downward.

Unaware of her observation, Steele stepped into the relay line with the roosters and hefted some wood with his uninjured hand, then turned to pass it to the next man. As though he suddenly felt her intense gaze burning over his flesh, hotter even than the sun, he stopped and looked up to where she stood gripping the rail.

Drawn to him like a magnet, her blue-gray eyes locked with his; and though she knew she should look away, was in fact making a fool of herself, Temerity was unable to free her gaze.

The slightest hint of a smile twitched Steele's chestnut-colored mustache. Then giving an almost imperceptible nod of his head, he went back to the job at hand—as though the brief, intimate moment had never happened.

Maybe it didn't. Maybe I imagined it, Temerity tried to tell herself. *But it did and that's all the more reason to fire him. I won't be able to function as long as he stays.*

"Aren't you afraid that much wood will make the *Intrepid* sit too low in the water?" a deep voice asked from behind her.

Startled, Temerity gasped aloud and spun around,

130

her mouth grazing the lips and cheeks of Charles Rawson as he bent to hold his mouth near her ear. "Oh!"

"I must say that's a much warmer welcome than I had any reason to expect!" His blue eyes narrowed teasingly. "Dare I hope this is a special greeting reserved for only me?"

"Oh, Mr. Rawson," Temerity apologized, placing her hand on his chest to push him away from her. But there was nowhere to go. She was trapped between the rail and the tall blond merchant. "I'm sorry. I didn't realize you were so close to me when I turned."

"And now I've embarrassed you," Charles said, assuming a sorrowful moue. He took her hand in his and moved back a step. "It is I who should apologize for startling you—and then for teasing you!"

Still shaken by her reaction to Steele's shirtless torso, Temerity couldn't gather her composure quickly enough to respond to Rawson. "If you'll excuse me, Mr. Rawson, I must see to some business," she said, her words halting and breathless.

Watching after her slender fleeing figure, Charles Rawson smiled to himself. "Soon you won't be in such a hurry to leave my company, little bird." *Soon you'll be begging to have my arms around you.*

Charles looked over the rail to the men below, his unguarded hatred honing in on Steele's back. "Just as soon as something is done about my competition."

Chapter Eight

Temerity stopped walking and thought for a moment. "Mr. Steele, you're fired!" she said in her most authoritative voice. Then shaking her head, she resumed her restless pacing around her cabin. "Too blunt."

"Mr. Steele, though I truly appreciate all you've done for me, I'm afraid I must—" She cut herself off and made a face. "Now I'm being too polite!"

She paused, thought a minute, then tried again. "Mr. Steele, I'm sure it must be as obvious to you as it is to me that you and I cannot work together . . ."

She stopped in front of the mirror to idly smooth an errant curl back from her face. "That's it. Not too blunt, not too polite. Surely he's as eager to get out of this situation as I am. He didn't want to come with me in the first place," she told her reflection. "No doubt he's asking himself why he did. In fact, he'll probably be relieved when I tell him I don't need him anymore."

There was an impatient rap on the door. Temerity looked anxiously from left to right to make certain everything in the cabin was in order and appeared businesslike.

She hurried to the door and grabbed the latch. Then

she stopped. Was she doing the right thing? Did she really dare to fire the only other person on the *Intrepid*, besides Uriah, whom she could trust? Was pride something she could afford to indulge herself in right now? Did she have the right to place crew and passengers, as well as her father's business, in jeopardy by firing the very best first mate she could find? Besides, whom would she replace Steele with? Harry Bailey? Temerity shook her head. No, it would be too big a job for Harry. Someday maybe, but not now. Then who?

Damn! What am I going to do?

The knock rattled the door again, this time more insistent. "Temerity? Are you there?"

The sound of Steele's voice released her from her semiparalyzed state. Taking a deep, stabilizing breath, she swung open the door. "Mr. Steele, do come in," she said, forcing as professional a demeanor as she could manage with her insides jumping and churning with doubt.

"You wanted to see me?" he asked, breezing past her and into the room.

Temerity eyed the doorknob in her hand, indecision weighing heavily on her mind. If she closed it, she would be leaving herself open to gossip and speculation. Yet if she left it open, anyone passing by would hear what they were saying. And there was no telling what Steele might say, she conceded with resentment. She stuck her head outside and took a worried look up and down the deck. When she saw that no one was there to have seen Steele come into her cabin, she couldn't stop the relieved sigh she breathed. Straightening her posture to accept her fate, she closed the door and turned to face Steele.

Determined to get the entire affair—now why had she used that word?—over as soon as possible, and not

134

wanting to give herself a chance to back down, she jumped right in. "Mr. Steele, I'm certain you can see that an impossible strain has been put on our business relationship by . . ."

Steele rolled his eyes in disgust. He was exhausted. The headache he had awakened with that morning had never gotten better, and his burned hand was throbbing like hell. And she was going to start her who's-in-charge lecture all over again. "Yeah, well, I guess I got a little carried away. I was just surprised to find you there."

"A little carried away?" Temerity choked, her businesslike demeanor shattering. "You call what happened a *little* carried away?" she hissed through gritted teeth.

"I guess I assumed too much—"

The color on Temerity's face deepened.

"But luckily no real damage was done," he went on, unaware of the fact that his casual attitude was igniting Temerity's anger to fury proportions.

He could at least pretend to be contrite, even if he wasn't. But he was acting as though they were talking about the weather rather than an event that had changed her forever. Maybe even ruined her life!

"No real *damage?*" Temerity's voice was a rasping squawk as she sputtered for air. "You—you—you—Get out of my cabin!" She pointed a shaking hand toward the door. "Get off my riverboat! You're fired!"

"Fired?" Steele yelled back, his own nerves frayed to the very limit by pain and weariness. "You can't fire me."

"Oh, *can't* I? Just you watch me!"

"I can't believe you'd want to fire me over something so inconsequential!"

"Inconsequential? Is that what you think it was?" Hurt and shame curled through Temerity. Tears began

135

to glaze over her eyes and she turned away from Steele to keep him from seeing.

Frustrated, Steele raked his fingers through his dark hair, then ran the edge of his forefinger and thumb down his mustache. "So what's the big deal?" he finally said. "Don't you think you're overreacting?"

Hot rage dried Temerity's tears and she wheeled on Steele again. "I'll tell you what the big deal is, Mr. Steele. You may have ruined me for—"

"Just because I questioned your ability to pilot the *Intrepid,* you think you're ruined? That's the craziest thing I ever heard. No one was hurt and the *Intrepid*'s still afloat. Nothing's been ruined."

"What's that got to do wi—" Suddenly, an idea hit her in the face like a splash of Missouri River water at midwinter. Her expression stunned, her blue-gray eyes opened wide, her voice was an incredulous whisper when she spoke again. "You're talking about what happened in the wheelhouse, aren't you?"

"Of course, I am . . . aren't I?" Suddenly, he wasn't so certain.

Temerity shook her head slightly, then changed to a hesitant nod, which rapidly became more enthusiastic as realization and relief sank into her brain. He was talking about this morning! Not last night. But this morning! He really didn't remember what happened last night!

"Mr. Steele." She spoke hesitantly, her entire tone different. "Perhaps I've been a bit hasty. I suppose I 'got carried away' too." She smiled, hoping to soften his hard expression some. "Do you think it would be possible to forget what happened between us? . . . uh . . . I mean in the wheelhouse."

"I really ought to let you go on and ruin things with your stubborn ways," Steele said, his expression

136

confused by her sudden change. "It's what you're hellbent on doing if you pull any more stunts like this morning."

She bristled. "If you're referring to my taking Uriah's place this morning—"

"You know damn well I am."

"The *Intrepid* was never in any danger with me at the wheel, Mr. Steele. That is, until you burst into the wheelhouse and started giving me orders." Her voice was starting to rise again.

"Hell, this isn't going to work," Steele said with disgust, turning to leave. "I don't know what ever made me think it could. It was a crazy idea all along. As far as I'm concerned, lady, from now on, you're on your own."

Her mind assaulted by the realization that he was actually going to leave this time and not come back, Temerity hurried after him. "Please don't quit, Mr. Steele," she said, her voice suddenly sounding very young and vulnerable, all pretense of being totally self-reliant gone. "I can't do it alone," she admitted for the first time, the words out of her mouth before she realized what she'd said. She knew she was taking a chance, letting him see the real her: a scared young woman who was fighting for survival. But she couldn't stop now. "I need you."

Steele looked down at the slender fingers gripping his arm, and his anger melted into a warm, protective feeling. He knew what it had taken for the strong-willed Temerity Kincade to make that admission—even to herself—and he also knew he was helpless to refuse her.

Still, he had his masculine pride to protect. He couldn't just curl up at her feet after the way she had acted. He wasn't used to taking orders from anyone, much less a know-it-all female; and he had no intention

137

of putting up with any more of her overbearing ways.

"On one condition," he finally said.

"Anything."

Snatches of his erotic dream from the night before floated through his mind. His mouth twitched in a crooked smile. He ran his fingers over his mustache and studied Temerity. Regretfully aware that her "anything" had nothing whatsoever to do with his own idea of "anything," Steele bit back his automatic response.

"There won't be any more of this 'I'm the owner' stuff. You can go on and make all the decisions as far as cargo and passengers and money. But when it comes to decisions that could affect the safety of the *Intrepid* and its passengers, either Uriah or I will make them. But not you. Is that understood?"

"But I'm the one who—"

"Understood?" he said again, his eyebrows raised expectantly.

"But—"

"No buts, Temerity. That's the deal. Either you agree, or you and I part company right now. So what's your answer? Are we in this together? Or are you going to try to do it alone?" He held his breath, waiting for her to call his bluff, not sure what he would do if she did.

Temerity hesitated, her innate stubbornness battling her common sense for control. "All right, I agree," she finally said. "However, I must insist—"

"Somehow, I'm not surprised." Steele rolled his tired eyes upward. "All right, Temerity, what do you insist?"

"I insist you call me Miss Kincade. If our relationship is to remain on an impersonal basis—which it must if we are to succeed—having you call me by my first name is entirely too familiar. It sets a bad example for the rest of the crew and undermines my authority with them."

Steele started to protest, then decided against it. *Let her save face and have the last word. After all, in the last few minutes, little Miss I'm-the-boss Temerity has come a long way toward admitting she isn't quite as independent as she'd like everyone to think!*

Steele took her right hand in his and shook it. "You've got a deal, *Miss Kincade.*"

Unprepared for the dream visions of her naked breasts against his chest that suddenly invaded his thoughts as his hand clasped hers, he held her hand longer than he had intended to. His forehead broke out in beads of perspiration and his gaze was drawn to the tempting rise and fall of her blouse front.

At the first contact of his warm, callused flesh on hers, Temerity was seized by a jolting realization. No matter how much she fought and denied it, her relationship with Steele could never be on a purely business basis again—if it ever had been. Not after last night. She would never be able to look at him again without remembering.

Perhaps if they could reestablish that feeling of camaraderie they'd had in St. Charles—before everything had become so complicated—maybe that would at least put their situation on a less tense basis. Maybe they could be friends. "I'm glad you're staying, Mr. Steele," she said, timidly making the first attempt at restoring a semblance of friendship to their relationship.

"I'm glad too," Steele said, his voice raspy as he looked down into her upturned face. From out of nowhere came the memory of her lips under his, and he leaned forward the slightest bit.

Unable to fight her own desire, Temerity lifted up on her toes. "Good night."

What are you doing, man? Steele shouted inwardly.

139

Do you want to ruin everything? She's told you over and over she doesn't want a personal situation between us. You'd better pay attention for once in your life. Or she really will kick you off the boat. Face it, man, until we're safely back in St. Louis, she's got to be off limits to you.

Suddenly, it was so hot and close in the small cabin, made an inferno by her nearness. He knew he had to get out of there before, caution and good sense be damned, he grabbed her and threw her down on the bunk and made love to her as he had in his dream.

Panicked and afraid he was going to forget the decision he had just made, Steele dropped Temerity's hand as if it were hot and looked around frantically for an escape, the way a trapped animal would.

"Good night, Miss Kincade," he muttered breathlessly, fumbling behind him for the door handle. Finding it, he yanked the door open and stumbled out into the cool evening air with all the desperation of a man narrowly escaping death.

"She doesn't know who you are, does she?" a deep voice asked the man who gazed pensively into the dark night as he leaned over the rail on the main deck.

Startled, the tall man spun around to face the unexpected intruder. "What are you doing here? I told you to stay in St. Louis."

"I came on board last night at St. Charles. I thought you might need some help. For a bonus, of course."

"I've paid you all the *bonuses* I'm going to pay you, Yeager. You're fired. You'd better pick up your things and head on back to St. Louis and start looking for another job. I don't need you here."

"I would think just keeping my mouth shut about your real name would be enough to keep me employed for at least the next three or four months, don't you, Mr.—"

"Shut up, you fool," the taller man said, slapping a hand over Yeager's mouth and grabbing him by the lapels. Looking from left to right nervously to be sure they weren't being observed, the man suddenly dropped his hold on Yeager's coat. "Then again, maybe I could think of something for you to do."

"You just name it, and I'll do it," Yeager promised, brushing the wrinkles from his coat. "For a price," he added with a satisfied grin.

"That goes without saying, Yeager," the man said, his lip curled in disgust. "Your type never does anything for any other reason, do they?"

Yeager smirked, not bothering to disguise his resentment of the other man. "Not if we can help it," he said with a laugh. He had him where he wanted him, and it felt good. Very good. Finally, Harold Yeager was going to get what was coming to him: a piece of the action. "I knew you'd take care of me," he gloated.

"You just be sure to remember who *is* taking care of you. Because if you breathe a word to anyone, you'll be sorry you ever set foot out of St. Louis. Do you understand?"

"Yes sir, I understand just fine," Yeager said with a smirk and a mocking salute before strutting away from the man at the rail.

It was midmorning the following day when Temerity first became aware of the commotion coming from the main deck. She tried to ignore it. After all, she had promised Steele that she would leave the safety of the passengers and crew up to him. And she intended to stay true to her word. Under the skillful control of the fully recovered Uriah Gunther, the *Intrepid* had left the

Washington dock right on time at precisely 8 A.M. Mr. Steele seemed to have everything below well at hand. And breakfast in the main salon had gone just as well.

Now she finally had the time to work on her accounting log, which seemed to be a constant job in itself. They'd taken on and delivered goods and passengers at every stop the *Intrepid* had made so far, bought wood at Riley's, purchased several hams in Washington, and paid off one rooster who'd been hurt on the job and had to quit. One day alone called for several entries.

Running her eyes over the tiny, neat figures in the "Cash Out" column of her ledger, Temerity sighed heavily. She knew the fuel bill would be over a thousand dollars for the trip, not much less than the cash she had on hand after the second day out. "It's going to be very tight," she mumbled doubtfully, scrutinizing the numbers again and praying she had made a mistake in her addition and had a more promising balance than it seemed. But she quickly realized the figures were correct. Frustratingly correct! She would have to do something, and soon, if they were going to stretch her cash enough to last all the way to Fort Benton.

She immediately vowed to talk to Mr. Steele about passing up the next wood that couldn't be bought with goods. *We'll just have to cut our own wood whenever we can. That'll save some. The catfish are biting, so I won't have to buy any more meat for a while. Jimmy and Gus and I can take care of that. And when we get further west, I can send the men out to hunt. The male passengers might even enjoy taking part in that type of outing.*

Suddenly, a hysterical scream, followed by moans and cries, cut into Temerity's thoughts. She jolted up from her chair and hurried to the door of her cabin and flung it open.

All up and down the rail that edged the deck, passengers were peering over it, straining to see something below. "What is it?" she gasped, asking no one in particular as she moved to the rail.

"A body, Miss Kincade. Someone said they found a dead man in the hold!" the woman beside Temerity said, her voice tingling with a combination of fear and excitement.

Mr. Steele! was Temerity's first thought as a wild rush of horror exploded in her head. Even though the night had been warm enough for sleeping out on the main deck, as the second-class passengers and crew had done, he had probably slept in the hold to guard against any further mischief. "You must have misunderstood," she accused the woman harshly as she shoved away from the rail and began to run toward the stairs leading down to the next deck.

When Temerity reached the bottom of the stairs, her eyes frantically searching the crowd for Steele, the first face she recognized was that of Charles Rawson. "Oh, Mr. Rawson!" she cried, running toward him. "Is it true? Have they found a body in the hold?"

Charles wrapped his arm around Temerity's shivering shoulders and tried to turn her away from the wide stairs leading down into the hold. "Don't go any further, my dear. It's too ghastly for a lady's eyes."

"Who is it?" Temerity asked, her voice a frightened scream as she tore out of Rawson's grasp and pushed her way to the front of the crowd. "Is it Mr. Ste—?"

Temerity stopped and stared down at the horrible sight at her feet. She let out a weak cry and her hand flew to her mouth. The first person she saw was Steele. Steele, who'd made her a woman. Steele, who drove her crazy with his domineering ways. Steele, who was always there when she needed him. Steele, who made her feel

143

things she'd never believed possible.

"Mr. Steele—are you—they told me—I thought you were—"

"Somebody get her out of here," Steele ordered, looking up from the bloody body he was squatting down beside.

Two men came from behind her and tried to take her away, but she shook them off and took a step closer to Steele, really noticing the dead man for the first time.

Shock and surprise transformed her face. "It's Mr. Yeager from the Cameron Line!" she gasped.

She was vaguely aware of the echo of her words as the identity of the dead man whispered its way rapidly through the crowd.

"What's he doing on the *Intrepid?*" Temerity choked. "What happened to him?"

"His throat's been cut," a deckhand beside Steele volunteered. "Someone musta wanted to shut him up real fast."

"Is that what you think happened, Mr. Steele?" Charles Rawson asked, coming up to stand close behind Temerity. "Do you think this Mr.—did you call him Yeager?—do you think he was killed because he knew something he shouldn't?"

"How should I know why he was killed?" Steele mumbled, going through the pockets of Yeager's cheap suit.

"I thought he might've given you a clue when you talked last night," Rawson said pointedly, aware of the way Temerity Kincade's slender body tensed at his words.

Barely conscious of the expectant hush that Charles Rawson's question brought over the crowd, Temerity was only aware of the way Steele's head snapped up and his shoulders bunched into tight knots.

"What gives you the idea we spoke last night?"

"I was on the next deck at the rail and saw the two of you." He pointed up to the boiler deck.

As though controlled by one brain, the eyes of the people in the crowd moved up to the indicated spot on the deck above; but Temerity continued to stare at Steele.

"You were arguing," Rawson went on. "I remember because I didn't recall seeing the man you were talking to before then and wondered who he was."

"Is that true, Mr. Steele?" Temerity asked, unable to believe Steele had known the man from Cameron had been on the *Intrepid* and hadn't told her. "Did you talk to Harold Yeager last night?"

Steele looked from Temerity's astonished face to Rawson; his gut wrenched with foreboding. His expression furious, he stood up. "We need to talk, Miss Kincade," he said through gritted teeth, signaling with his head for two roustabouts to take care of Yeager's body. He took Temerity's arm and turned her away.

"Why didn't you tell me he was—"

"Privately."

"But—"

"Now, Temerity!" He gave her arm a rough jerk and set her into motion. "We need to talk now!"

"See here, Steele," Rawson interrupted, stepping up to take Temerity's arm. "Miss Kincade doesn't have to go with you if she doesn't want to." He didn't intend to pass up this chance to make his obvious rival for Miss Kincade's attentions look bad. He looked around at the curious crowd to be sure he was heard. "In fact, I'm not certain I want to trust you alone with her. For all we know, you're the person who—"

Steele stopped and released a low, feral growl. "Who what, Rawson?"

Charles took an unconscious step backward, folding slightly under Steele's ferocious stare. "I mean . . . you were the last person to see Yeager alive, weren't you?"

"I don't know what you're trying to pull, Rawson, but it won't work. I had no reason to kill Yeager. So you're barking up the wrong tree. Are you coming, Miss Kincade?"

Temerity had had time to come to her senses and regather her composure. This was definitely "dirty linen" that did not need to be aired before the entire passenger list and crew. She'd already given them more to gossip and wonder about than she should have.

"Yes, Mr. Steele, I'm coming," she said with more control than she felt. What else could happen? First her father's accident, then the fire, then the attack on Uriah, and now this—a murder! Where would it all end?

When you give up, a knowing inner voice whispered to her.

Well, I'm not going to give up! she answered the voice in her head. *They'll have to kill me first!*

And who else?

"Are you sure you'll be all right?" Charles Rawson asked, the concern in his blue eyes very sincere as he searched her face. "Would you like for me to go with you?"

Temerity chanced a glance at Steele out of the corner of her eyes before answering the older man. "I'll be fine, Mr. Rawson, thank you. This is business and I think it will be best if Mr. Steele and I discuss the situation privately. I do appreciate your offer though," she explained over her shoulder as she allowed herself to be propelled toward the steps leading up to the next deck.

No sooner had he slammed the door to Temerity's cabin behind him than Steele began to explain. "I just found out he was on board late last night after I talked to you."

146

"Why didn't you tell me? What was he doing on the *Intrepid?*"

"I intended to tell you about him this morning and find out what you wanted to do, but I just never got the chance. Then . . ."

"When did he come on board? Has he been here all along?" An idea suddenly flared in her mind. "Mr. Steele! Do you think he's the one who set the fire in the hold and hit Uriah?"

"I don't know," Steele groaned, shaking his head from side to side with frustration as he sat down on the bunk. "I guess it could have been him," he said, remembering the Cameron business card he'd found and still had in his pocket. "He said he boarded night before last when we were docked in St. Charles. But I don't believe it was Yeager who started the fire. It just doesn't make any sense for it to be him. It has to have been someone else."

"Why does it have to be someone else? He worked for Cameron, didn't he? And you know how hard they tried to stop us from leaving St. Louis."

"If you're convinced the Cameron Line is behind this, then tell me why they would try to burn your boat when they stand to lose forty thousand dollars. It just doesn't wash."

"Don't you see?" Temerity said, sitting down beside Steele on the bunk without thinking. "They had no intention of burning the *Intrepid!* They just wanted to scare me into turning back. That's what I wanted to tell you the other night when I—"

Her hand flew to her mouth to cover a gasp of horror at what she'd nearly said.

"When you what?"

Temerity searched Steele's face for a sign that he knew what she'd been about to say. Seeing none, she sighed her relief and made a frantic attempt at covering

147

her mistake.

"When I was, uh, interrupted! By the, uh, by the—doctor! The doctor interrupted me. And Uriah!" Damn! She was a terrible liar. She always had been. "Then I forgot to say anything!" she added in a rush of words, studying his expression nervously. But evidently he believed her because he went on talking.

"I suppose it *could* be possible. But why would Yeager be murdered if he was working for the people who're trying to stop you?" He couldn't bring himself to say Cameron. He still didn't believe it was them. But he wouldn't put it past a weasel like Yeager to be working for someone else at the same time he was drawing a salary from Cameron.

"Mmm . . . I haven't figured that out yet," she said thoughtfully. "But I promise you I will!"

"And we still don't know who killed Yeager. Or why?"

"Perhaps he was going to tell you last night when he talked to you and they wanted to keep him quiet—'close his mouth,' like the rooster said."

Steele remembered his conversation with the little blackmailer and shook his head doubtfully. "Okay, I know you think you've got it all figured out, but just listen to this theory. What if Yeager was hired by someone to make it *look* like Cameron was behind all the accidents? Then if that unknown someone saw Yeager talking to me, he might have thought Yeager was selling me the whole story and killed him. Does that make any sense?" Steele added, suddenly not certain of anything.

"But the only person who saw you was Mr. Rawson. Are you thinking he—?"

As much as he would have liked to be rid of Rawson, Steele shook his head. "He's just the only one who *admitted* to seeing us! But we don't know who else might have witnessed my conversation with Yeager. We weren't exactly in a private place. It would have been easy for the murderer or anyone else to have seen us."

"But that brings us back to the same question, doesn't it? Why would anyone but Cameron want to stop me?"

"Maybe an enemy of Cameron's, someone who's carrying a grudge against them, someone who—how the hell do I know why? I just know it's not the Cameron Line who's behind this. And I'd be willing to bet my life on it!"

Astounded by the intensity of Steele's words, Temerity studied him for a long time. "Why, Mr. Steele? Why are you so certain it's not Cameron?"

Now, Steele! Tell her now. Tell her who you are! Steele opened his mouth to speak, then he closed it again and wiped the curve of his thumb and forefinger thoughtfully down his mustache. *How can I? Thanks to Rawson's big mouth, everybody on this boat probably thinks I'm the murderer already. All they'd need to know would be something like this to take me out and hang me.*

"Why are you so certain?"

Steele took a deep, tortured breath and reached out to cup Temerity's cheek in a callused hand. "Temerity . . . things aren't always what they seem. There are things I can—" he began, then stopped. "Can you just believe that I would never let anyone or anything hurt you?" he said softly.

A warm rush of emotion scudded through Temerity. He hadn't answered her question, but it didn't really matter. Unaware of what she was doing, she leaned her cheek into his palm and closed her eyes for a moment.

"I think I've known that from the first day I met you, Mr. Steele. You've always been there when I needed you. But that still doesn't explain why you're defending—"

"You're going to have to trust me this time, Temerity."

"I want to."

"Then do it, please. Just this once, do what I ask you to do without fighting against me," he said, his voice hypnotic as his mouth brushed hers in a kiss so light that she was sure she had imagined it.

"I do. I do trust you, Mr. Steele."

Chapter Nine

Steele searched Temerity's face for an indication that she might already be regretting her hasty decision. But the only thing he saw in her expression was the trust she was offering him. He heaved a sigh of relief. Then his shoulders sagged.

He didn't know which made him feel worse: having her look at him with those innocent, trusting blue eyes, or thinking of the hurt he would see in those same beautiful eyes when she found out the truth about him. Either way, he felt like the lowest of cads.

"Ah, Temerity," he whispered, lifting a remiss curl of hair from her cheek and winding it around his finger. "If only I could—" He stopped and gazed into her eyes, the deep need to find forgiveness in her arms for his deception suddenly overwhelming.

Steele closed his eyes and took a deep breath, then opened them again. "Temerity, I can't help myself," he groaned, burrowing his fingers into the thick hair at her temple and bringing her face up to his. "I really tried, but I can't help myself," he said again, slanting his mouth over hers and muffling any protest she might have offered.

Temerity's eyes widened in surprise at the change in

151

Steele's mood, then fluttered closed as he covered her slightly parted lips with his.

The instant his mouth touched hers, all thought of protest evaporated into the air. All her vows to keep their relationship on an impersonal, purely business level were tossed aside. And Temerity was lost.

Raw hunger and desire driving her now, she wrapped her arms around Steele's rib cage, her hands clawing eagerly up his back to grasp the hardness of his broad shoulders.

Her tongue engaged his in an erotic battle as she fell back on the bunk, bringing Steele to rest with his upper body over hers. Glorying in the remembered delight of his weight on her, Temerity moaned aloud.

In response to her moan, Steele lifted his head, afraid he had hurt her, certain his weight must be too great.

She was no longer able to fool herself and deny the screaming hunger that raged through her loins every time he touched her. The hunger that had begun the first moment she'd met him had now grown to destructive proportions and was too compelling to stop. Temerity raised her head, straining to bring his mouth back down to hers.

Steele held himself above her on one elbow, cradling her head in his bandaged hand as he framed her chin in his other hand. He smiled shakily into her half-opened, passion-drugged eyes. "It's a good thing someone's liable to come bursting through that door any minute, lady," he said gruffly, his voice a hoarse tremble. "Because any other time and place, if you looked at me like that I wouldn't be able to stop. I'd already have your—"

He ceased speaking and glanced down at Temerity's rapidly rising breasts as they strained upward in an innocent invitation that taxed his willpower to the limit. Beads of perspiration glistened on his forehead.

As though controlled by another power, his hand feathered down the column of her neck to the top button of her high-collared bodice.

His gaze held prisoner by the rising and falling breasts beneath the now-wrinkled white shirtwaist, he dragged his tongue nervously along his dry lips. He knew he should leave—now! But he was helpless to stop his fingers and watched in amazement as they undid the top button of her blouse, exposing the sensitive hollow at the base of her throat where her pulse fluttered erratically.

"My god!" he groaned, unable to resist dipping his head to taste the sweet-scented softness of her neck one time before he stopped. "Tell me to leave, Temerity," he pleaded, his words muffled and tortured against her arching throat.

Acting purely on instinct, Temerity drifted deeper into the sensuous haze of desire and pulled him closer to her.

His hand slipped lower to unfasten a second button on her blouse.

"Send me away," he whispered, worshiping each exposed inch of her flesh with his kisses as his lips followed his hand downward, ever closer to the thrusting allure of her breasts.

"Mr. Steele, we mustn't," she finally managed in a husky murmur, squirming restlessly to move the aching tip of a breast nearer to his mouth even as she told him to stop.

"Is that what you want?" he rasped, slipping the next button from its hole and exposing the top of her white lawn chemise. "Do you really want me to leave?" he asked, plunging his tongue deep into the satiny cleavage that peeked out above the lace edging of her undergarment. "Do you?"

Temerity tried to nod yes, but her head rocked from

side to side as she was drawn deeper under the spell caused by the brush of his mustache on her flesh. She tried to speak. She had to stop him. Had to tell him that what they were doing was wrong, that it wasn't what she wanted. But the only sound she could produce was a strangled cry, which he took as a plea for more of the scalding fire that rained over the tops of her breasts.

Skimming his lips over a chemise-concealed mound, Steele opened them and drew the tip into his mouth. He ran his tongue over the beading peak, reveling in the taste of it through the translucent material. His hand caressing and massaging her other breast, he licked and sucked until the delicate material covering her throbbing nipple was slick and wet and clinging to the rosy peak in a gossamer veil.

All reason and practicality reduced to a thread, Steele drew back and examined his handiwork, smiled, then returned to administer his care and adoring kisses to her other breast.

Just as he took the neglected crest into his mouth to polish it to the same glorious perfection as the first, there was the sound of heavy bootsteps on the deck outside her cabin.

The pounding of the approaching feet hammered its way into the small room, bringing with it the crashing realization of what they'd come close to doing. Steele jerked his head up from her breast so quickly there was a sucking, slurping sound as he released the suction on her nipple. But he didn't notice. He was too busy leaping up from Temerity's bunk, where she continued to lie, stunned, for a moment longer before rising to a sitting position.

"Who is it?" she whispered, her voice shaky as she concentrated her gaze on Steele. He was already beside the door, his ear pressed to the wood, his hands slipping nervously into his waistband to right his clothing.

He held his finger to his lips and waited a moment. The footsteps grew louder until it was obvious they were right outside her door.

Frozen with horror, Temerity watched the door handle intently. The only sound in the room was that of her panicked intake of air. The door wasn't locked!

In the next instant, they realized the footsteps weren't going to stop. They didn't even pause outside her door, but hurried on past, fading away as suddenly as they had occurred, as whoever it was made his way to the other end of the deck. They'd been given a reprieve.

Simultaneously, she and Steele exhaled the breath they had been holding while waiting for the ax of exposure to fall on their heads.

"Whew!" Steele sighed, wiping his brow and turning back to Temerity with a relieved grin on his face. "That was close."

Shamed beyond endurance by the horrifying threat of discovery, Temerity looked down at her fingers as they fumbled clumsily with the buttons of her wrinkled blouse. She couldn't look at Steele, couldn't speak.

The sight of Temerity's proud head bent in humiliation, her straight shoulders slumped in defeat, and her shaking fingers fussing futilely with the buttons on her bodice combined in a sobering, heart-shattering kick in Steele's belly. The dimpled kid-who-just-got-away-with-something grin on his face vanished.

You bastard! She trusted you, and look what you did with that trust. She's the first female you've ever met who's exactly what she seems to be and you took advantage of her. Lying to her wasn't bad enough, was it?

155

"Temerity, I—"

"Don't say anything, Mr. Steele," she said in an unsteady whisper, her unfocused gaze remaining on the button her hands continued to twist.

Steele took two long strides to where she still sat on the bunk, and he hunkered down in front of her to bring his anguished face on the same level with hers. "Honey, I didn't me—"

Temerity turned her head to the side to avoid his gaze. "Please, leave."

Seeing that her trembling fingers had yet to put one button through a buttonhole, Steele reached out to help. "Here, let me—"

Temerity shrank back and clutched the material of her blouse tightly to her breasts. "Don't touch me," she hissed, turning her head back toward him and narrowing her red-rimmed eyes at him. "Don't ever touch me again!"

"I just wanted to help you button your blouse," he said, his expression hurt by the very real fear he saw in her eyes, now gray with misery rather than blue with passion. "Don't be afraid of me. I swear I would never hurt you."

"That's what you told me," Temerity said bitterly, her anger rising to the cause and restoring a modicum of her self-dignity—at least enough to see her through the seconds until Steele left her alone. "What else have you lied to me about, Mr. Steele?"

A guilty rush of adrenaline surged through Steele's chest, and his hands dropped to his sides. "I've never lied to you, Temerity," he said with quiet resignation. With a weary sigh, he stood up. He knew the fine line between lying and evading the truth was moot; but it was the only shred of self-respect he could muster at the moment, so he clung to it with tenacity.

Knowing he was responsible for the hurt, betrayed

look in Temerity's eyes, and unable to bear it any longer, Steele wheeled away from her and strode to the door. "I'll arrange for around-the-clock guards"—he paused to clear the lump from his throat—"for the rest of the trip, and then I'll see what I can do abou—" He stopped and threw his head back, staring up at the ceiling for a long moment. Heaving a deep groan, he finally turned to face her again. "Temerity, I never meant for this to happen. Please believe that." When she didn't answer, he exhaled a defeated sigh. "I'll get my things together and clear out when we dock in Portland tonight."

Temerity studied Steele silently, hating the way his miserable expression had the power to tug at her heart. After all the arguments, after all that had happened, how could she still believe him, trust him—want to be with him? How could she ache to be comforted in his arms when she should hate him? And most of all, how could she blame him for what had happened?

With destroying clarity, Temerity admitted to herself that the only person she should really hate, the only person responsible, was Temerity Kincade. No one else. No one but her was to blame.

He'd asked her, begged her, to stop him. But she hadn't. Instead, she had responded like the harlot he'd had every right to mistake her for. With her wanton behavior, she'd actually invited him, urged him to take every liberty he'd taken and then some. Oh, there had been that half-hearted vocal protest she'd made, even as her body had moved against his in direct contradiction to her words.

The sickening realization that she'd deserved worse than she had gotten roiled in her stomach.

When Temerity continued to remain silent, Steele took it to mean that she wanted him to leave. And he didn't blame her. It was a lot better than what he had coming to him. "It's probably for the best," he said Without a backward glance, he opened the door and stepped out onto the walkway.

Temerity stared at the door long after Steele had closed it behind him. She tried to tell herself she was glad the situation between them had finally been resolved. He was leaving; she was staying; and that was that. No matter whose fault it had been, no matter that she felt as though her heart was being ripped from her chest, it was the way things had to be. The only answer.

She'd been a fool to think they could be just friends and work together after the night in St. Charles. Even though he didn't remember, it would always be there between them, lurking in her memory, ready to leap out and attack her senses every time she saw him, ready to dissolve her into a wanton mass of quivering flesh every time he touched her.

Shaking her head to rid her mind of the persistent memory, Temerity sprang up from the bunk as though she'd been hit. With jerky, agitated motions, she peeled off her wrinkled white blouse and tossed it into a pile of dirty clothes in the corner. She told herself that once she was cleaned up and had her hairdo back in order, she would be able to put the entire thought of Mr. Steele from her mind and think rationally again.

But even as she told herself she would forget him, she knew she wouldn't. In fact, she was already wishing she had done something to stop him from leaving.

Thinking that perhaps she should ask Uriah to talk to Steele, she was putting the finishing touches on her restored hairdo when a forceful knock on her cabin door startled her.

It's him! she immediately thought, unable to stop the happy smile that altered her expression. *He's come to tell me he's not going to leave,* she told herself, not bothering to question the wisdom of wanting him to

158

stay. *He's come to say he's staying!*

Giving her reflection in the mirror a nervous check, Temerity smoothed her hands over the front of her fresh blouse. Then wiping her palms, which were suddenly very moist, on her skirt, she crossed to the cabin door with deliberate casualness. "Who is it?"

"Mr. and Mrs. Fisher," a woman's voice answered. "We must speak with you, Miss Kincade."

Taking an instant to erase the disappointment from her face and for the identity of her visitors to sink in, Temerity opened the door, a polite, if disappointed, smile pasted on her face. "Yes, what can I do for you?" she asked in her most pleasant tone.

"Mr. Fisher and I are good, God-fearing people, Miss Kincade," the plump woman announced without preamble. "And we refuse to stay on a riverboat where such scandalous things are going on! Isn't that right, dear?" she said, smiling piously toward her husband, then glaring back at Temerity, oblivious to the fact that her husband hadn't agreed or disagreed with her.

The scene with Steele in her cabin a few minutes before flashed through Temerity's mind. Shame and guilt rose in her throat to form a startled gulp. "I don't understand, Mrs. Fisher."

"First a fire. Then the attack on Mr. Gunther. And now a murder!" Mrs. Fisher explained. "You can't expect us to put up with these dreadful happenings. Who knows what terrible thing will happen next?"

"Oh, that!" Temerity said, nodding her head as she struggled to regain her composure.

Mrs. Fisher went on talking, obviously unaware of the note of relief that had exploded in Temerity's voice. "You cannot expect us to stay on a boat where we could be murdered at any moment just as easily as not." The heavyset woman turned to her husband, giving him his cue to agree, then turned back to Temerity.

159

"Mrs. Fisher, I assure you, the passengers are in no danger. Mr. Steele is doubling the guards, and we don't intend to rest until we've discovered who's behind Mr. Yeager's . . . his accident.". She couldn't bring herself to say murder. "Believe me, there's nothing for you to worry about." She hoped she was convincing the Fishers, because she certainly was having a hard time believing it.

"I'm sorry, Miss Kincade, but Mr. Fisher and I have discussed this at length. And we are going to leave the *Intrepid* when we dock in Portland tonight. We will seek passage on the next riverboat that comes along."

Temerity looked with sympathy at the still-silent Mr. Fisher. Somehow, she had the feeling their discussion had been one-sided. "I'm sorry to hear that, Mrs. Fisher. I do wish you would reconsider. I assure you—"

"So, if you will kindly refund our passage money," Mrs. Fisher went on as though Temerity hadn't spoken, "we'll be on our way."

Mrs. Fisher had said the word that ranked right up there with *fire* and *murder: Refund!*

Panic began to pound painfully in Temerity's chest. Though her funds were short, she could probably manage a refund for the Fishers—if they were the only ones who asked. But if the other passengers started demanding their money back too, she would be ruined. The arsonist might as well have been successful in St. Charles. Either way, the *Intrepid* would never make it to Fort Benton if that happened.

"Please, Mrs. Fisher, won't you reconsider?" Temerity could hear the alarm rising in her voice but could do nothing to control it. All her work would be for nothing if she lost all her passengers and their fares. "It might be days before another riverboat comes along."

"Then we will simply wait. But we will not stay on the *Intrepid* a moment longer than necessary. We demand

160

our money back now!"

"We're doing everything in our power to catch the murderer, Mrs. Fisher. Just give us a little more time before you leave. I'll see to it that your cabin is given extra attention by the guards. And you can push your trunks against the door at night. That will make you feel safer. Please don't leave." Temerity was near tears. "If everyone asks for their passage back, we won't be able to afford the entire trip up the Missouri."

"That's not our problem," Mrs. Fisher said, jabbing her hand out to Temerity, palm up. "Our money, please."

By the time the *Intrepid* docked in Portland that evening, Temerity's mood was as low as her rapidly dwindling cash supply. Twelve passengers in all had demanded the return of their passage money; and though she would have been within her rights to deny them, she hadn't.

Still, it could have been worse. She tried to bolster her battered confidence as she eyed the cash balance column in her ledger. It was less than half what it had been that morning. *More of them could have left and I would have been forced to start selling off my goods to finance the remainder of the journey. At least, the farther we get from St. Louis before I have to do that, the better the price I'll get for everything.*

She refused to let herself dwell on the fact that whatever she got for her goods in the river towns along the way would only be a fraction of what the miners in the gold camps of Montana would be willing to pay for the same supplies. She simply would not think about it. She would just concentrate on making it through this catastrophe, and any more that came along, one at a time—one day at a time.

"Things could be much worse," she consoled herself aloud as she stepped out of her cabin onto the empty deck, which was aglow with the fading sunlight of early evening. "I am going to make it," she swore to the pink and gold sky.

Her wavering resolve strengthened by the magical sunset, she released her grip on the wooden rail and straightened her posture. "No matter how many setbacks I have, and no matter how many people leave, I'm going to take the *Intrepid* to Fort Benton!"

"Miss Kincade, I need to talk to you," a man's voice interrupted her thoughts.

Her new resolve still too frail to sustain another blow right then, Temerity's shoulders sagged slightly. Then, as if a giant hand had yanked her erect by grabbing the collar of her blouse, she took a deep breath and straightened again. "What can I—" Her mouth dropped open, then broke into a wide, relieved grin. "Mr. Bailey!" she exclaimed as she recognized the *Intrepid's mud clerk*—second mate. "You don't know how glad I am to see you. When you said you needed to talk to me, I was sure you were another passenger asking for your money back!"

"No, ma'am, I ain't a passenger."

It was then Temerity noticed the young riverman's solemn expression. But her relief at knowing she was facing friend rather than foe was so great that she paid no heed to the prickle of foreboding that tripped, ever so subtly, over her skin.

"Well, what is it, Mr. Bailey? What do you want to talk to me about?"

"You got to understand, Miss Kincade. This ain't my idea."

An alarm went off in Temerity's head, and the genuine smile she'd given to Harry froze for an instant. Then, it seemed to melt off her face as the slight prickle of foreboding became a full-fledged premonition of disaster.

"Go ahead," she said evenly, unaware of the fingernails cutting into the palms of her tightly clenched fists at her sides.

"Most of the men in the crew want to draw their pay and quit."

Temerity's eyes widened and her bottom lip began to quiver. She shook her head from side to side and her mouth split into a strange grin. There was a kind of bizarre satisfaction in knowing she'd been right. She'd said things could be worse, and she had been right. They had just gotten that way. Only this time there was nothing she could do. She could go to Fort Benton without money, without passengers, even without Mr. Steele. But not without a crew. No matter how much determination and knowledge she had, taking the *Intrepid* upriver with no crew was an insurmountable obstacle no human being, man or woman, could overcome.

"You can't mean what you're saying. Why do you want to destroy me?"

"Not me, Miss Kincade. It's the others. Mostly the roosters. They weren't too pleased when they found out they were workin' for a female. Said it was bad luck. Then, when things started happening, there were some grumblin's 'bout taking off. But because they respected Mr. Steele—"

"Respected Mr. Steele?" she huffed bitterly. "For what? Because he's bigger than they are? Because he's a man? He knows nothing about riverboats, but he earns their respect. While a woman who kn—"

"You're wrong, Miss Kincade. Mr. Steele knows more about riverboats than just about anybody on the *Intrepid*. Except maybe Mr. Gunther."

"Don't be ridiculous. I hired Mr. Steele myself. And

163

I tell you, he knows nothing about riverboats. Nothing!"

Harry shrugged his shoulders in defeat. There was no point in arguing with her. "Well, it don't really matter none, now. He's quittin', and the rest of the crew is goin' right behind him—just as soon as they draw their pay. I'm sorry, Miss Kincade."

"Quitting?" Temerity's expression was stunned. Even though Steele had told her he would leave, she hadn't believed it. She'd been sure that, like the other times when they'd disagreed, he would change his mind. "Who told you Mr. Steele was quitting?"

"He did, ma'am. Right before he left. He said that I should keep an eye on you and help you anyway I could, but that he was headin' back to St. Louis in the morning."

Temerity looked toward the town of Portland, barely aware of the way the last rays of the setting sun reflected off the glass panes in the wooden buildings. "He's already gone?"

"Yes, ma'am."

"How long ago?"

"Just as soon as we unloaded the cargo we were supposed to drop here. What should I tell the crew?" Harry's expression was confused as he watched Temerity squint her eyes and study the river town, as if she were searching the twilight for Steele. She didn't answer. "Miss Kincade?"

"Mmm?"

"What do you want me to tell them?"

"Tell who?" It was obvious her thoughts were elsewhere.

"The men, Miss Kincade. What do I tell the men who want to draw their three days' pay and leave with Mr. Steele?"

Temerity drew a deep, stabilizing breath and turned

to face Harry again. "Tell them? Why, Mr. Bailey, first of all, you can tell them that they signed on the *Intrepid* for the entire journey to Fort Benton. If they want to draw their pay, they'll fulfill their part of the agreement. And secondly, tell them Mr. Steele is not quitting."

"But he said he—"

"You simply misunderstood Mr. Steele's intentions. He'll be back."

"But he had his gear with him," Harry continued to protest. "I know he didn't plan to come back."

"Just take my word for it, Mr. Bailey. The *Intrepid* will leave Portland on time tomorrow morning. And Mr. Steele *will* be on board."

Chapter Ten

Temerity read the sign proclaiming the false-fronted, two-story wooden building simply as HOTEL and sighed. "He's got to be here." Filling her lungs with a steadying breath, she stepped onto the hotel porch, barely noticing the old men lounging in straight-back wooden chairs who watched her pass.

"Sir, do you have a Mr. Steele registered here?" she asked the desk clerk once she was inside, thankful her voice betrayed none of the defeat she was feeling after having failed to find Steele at the first two hotels she had checked. This was the last one.

The bespectacled man behind the registration desk raised his eyes from his newspaper and gave Temerity a lazy, disinterested once-over, as though deciding what type of woman she was before he wasted the energy it would require to give her an answer. Evidently, she had passed his test and was not the sort of female who usually visited men in their hotel rooms, because he gave her a polite smile and set his paper aside. "Who did you say?" he asked, sliding the register to him and pointing a dirty-nailed finger at the top line of the page.

"Steele," Temerity repeated, craning her neck to see the list hidden by the desk clerk's hand.

The man glanced up from the book, giving her a quelling glare, as though she'd committed the worst of indiscretions by trying to peek at the highly confidential list. Then, making a show of covering the page with his other hand, he returned his attention to the register. "Hmm . . . Steele, you say?" He began trailing his finger slowly down the column.

"He would have registered in the last two hours. His name is probably one of the last ones entered," she suggested, thinking to encourage the man to start at the end of the list rather than the first.

Deliberately stopping the progress of his finger down the page, he glanced up over the gold rims of his glasses and narrowed his eyes at her, saying without words that he would do this his way, or not at all—and that he would not be hurried. When her expression showed she was properly contrite, he continued checking the names.

Temerity held her breath—and her tongue.

"Ah ha!" he exclaimed suddenly.

Temerity let out a squeal of excitement, but before she could say anything, the man shook his head.

"Sorry. Mistake. This is Stell, not Steele."

Temerity's spirits slipped another notch.

He resumed his fastidious scrutiny of the list, mumbling as he read, oblivious to the nervous tapping of Temerity's foot on the floor. "Burroughs, Gramm, Drummond, Murphy, Burke . . ."

The nearer his finger got to the bottom of the page, the more discouraged Temerity became. This hotel was going to be the same as the others she'd already tried: "No one registered here by that name."

"Doesn't look like he's registered here," the clerk said, turning the page and beginning his systematic search of a new column of names. "DeBorde, Lancaster, Maxie, Black . . ." He shook his head as he neared the

168

end of the column, still keeping his intent gaze glued to the page. "Nope! 'Fraid not. There's no Mr. Steele here."

Temerity's voice rose. "Let me see," she said, reaching for the book. "He must be here. This is the last hotel."

Retaining his possession on the register with a tight grip and an indignant sniff, the clerk took another look at the book. "Wait a minute. Here's someone named Steele, but it's his fi—"

"Which room is he in?" Temerity interrupted, her voice high with excitement as she cut him off in midsentence and clamped her hand over the hand jealously guarding the page from her eyes.

"You don't understand. Steele is the man's fir—"

Temerity plopped a two-dollar gold piece on the counter and said, "Which room?"

The clerk shrugged his shoulders and snatched up the money. What difference did it make to him if Steele was the hotel guest's first name, and not his last? The impatient woman would find out soon enough, and in the meantime he was two dollars richer. And after all, two dollars was two dollars. "Two-oh-six," he said and turned back to his newspaper.

His attention focused on the cracked ceiling of his hotel room, Steele didn't immediately react to the urgent knock on the door. Determined to ignore the disturbance, he continued to lie on the bed with his hands clasped behind his head. But when the annoying rapping showed no sign of stopping, he finally called out, "Yeah?"

The only answer to his question was an even more insistent pounding on the door.

Giving up, he dragged himself to a sitting position

and swung his long legs off the bed. He propped his elbows on his thighs and, holding his forehead in his palms, rubbed his eyes with the heels of his hands as he burrowed his splayed fingers into his hair. "Who is it?"

"Mr. Steele, please open the door. I must talk to you." Her voice was muffled, nervous, and sounded as though her mouth was right against the door; but he would have recognized that voice anywhere.

A jolt of excitement shook through Steele's strong body. She'd come to him. Then the excitement turned to anger. What was wrong with her? Hadn't this morning in her cabin tempted the fates enough for her? Or was she so enamored by the idea of playing with fire that she'd come to him in a hotel for more of her games? Well, he wasn't going to have any part of it. He already felt guilty enough about what he'd done, and he wasn't going to let her put him in a position of acting like a sex-starved puppy again. He was going to get rid of her—and fast!

He bolted up from the bed and hurried to the door, opening it with a jerk. "What are *you* doing here?"

The breath caught in Temerity's throat at the sight of Steele. His chestnut hair was rumpled, as if he'd just awakened, and his shirt . . . He wasn't wearing a shirt! And there, exactly at eye level, not twelve inches from her astonished face was the muscled expanse of his hair-matted chest that she had fantasized about from the first day she'd met him.

The full force of his masculinity assaulted her senses in a way that made her knees feel weak, as though they had suddenly turned to liquid. She tried to avert her enraptured gaze, but her eyes stayed riveted to the blatant display of maleness in front of her. The memory of the soft, reddish-brown chest hair against her skin made her palms itch to reach out and touch it—as she had that night in Uriah's cabin. It made her long to press her cheek against it—as she had that night in Uriah's cabin. She closed her eyes and took a deep, shaky breath, praying to block out the memory as well as the reality. "May I come in?" she asked, her voice every bit as shaky and uncertain as she felt.

Intending to make it clearly evident that he didn't want her company, Steele braced his elbows on either side of the doorframe and leaned his forehead on his locked hands. His dimpled smile was sarcastic. "I thought we settled everything between us this morning." There was a bitter challenge in his voice.

Temerity's embarrassed gaze sliced up and down the empty hallway. "Please, Mr. Steele, I must talk to you."

"So talk." He still made no move to invite her into his room.

Her face grew hot under his abusive scrutiny, and she wished for nothing more than the luxury of running back to the safety of her cabin on the *Intrepid*. But she couldn't. She had to stay and do what she'd come here for. She had made her decision, and there was no backing out. Not if she was going to save the *Intrepid*. Not if she was going to save her father's business. She'd come this far and she would not retreat now.

"Privately," she said stiffly, painfully aware that merely saying the word intensified the blush on her cheeks.

Steele raised his eyebrows in mock surprise. "Privately?" he repeated, remembering the fear in her eyes when he'd tried to apologize that morning. "Are you sure?" His tone was hard, mocking. He didn't know which made him angrier: his own inability to close the door on her, or her insisting on putting him in this position again.

Straightening up from where he'd been leaning on the door, he made a wide sweep toward the room with a muscled arm. "Far be it from me to leave a lady standing in the hallway. Although I'm surprised you're willing to take a chance coming into my room. I'm sure you remember what can happen when you're alone with a wild animal like me."

Temerity straightened her spine with resolve and took the step that sent her over the threshold into his room. "I'm not afraid of you, Mr. Steele, and I never called you a wild animal."

"But you sure as hell thought it, didn't you?" He closed the door and leaned back on it, crossing his arms on his chest and his legs at the ankles.

"I didn't think that," she said softly, wondering what he would do if she told him it was her own behavior that had frightened her, not his.

Unable to look at him yet, now that they were truly alone, she kept her back to him and surveyed the room. Nothing special or unusual about it: washstand, chair, table . . .

Her gaze zeroed in on the unmade bed, and her heart seemed to stop for an instant, then resumed beating against the walls of her chest with new force. Evidently, he'd been lying down when she'd come. The pillow still showed the depression where his head had been. And the thought of Steele lying on that bed, his head on that pillow, sent new flutters of apprehension—and something she was afraid to put a name to—fleeting through her blood.

But it was too late to turn back now. She was here and she would do it. "What happened this morning was just as much my fault as yours, and I apologize for blaming you."

The sarcastic expression on Steele's face slipped, and his hands dropped to his sides. "You *do?*"

Temerity nodded her head. "Will you accept my apology for the way I acted afterward?"

Steele studied Temerity's ramrod-straight back for a long moment, then shoved away from the door. "All right, Temerity," he said, grasping her shoulders and

172

spinning her around to face him. "what's this all about? You didn't come here to apologize for this morning. You want something. What is it?"

Temerity raised her gaze to Steele's suspicious hazel eyes. They were blazing with angry, golden fire, and she knew he was not going to meet her halfway. She had to go the whole distance alone.

She took a deep breath and spoke. "You're right. I do want something. I want you to come back to the *Intrepid.*"

Steele threw his hands in the air in a gesture of frustration and pivoted away from her, then immediately spun around to face her again. "Haven't you figured it out, Temerity? You and I can't work together! The minute we're within ten feet of each other, sparks start flying. Even if we could get past the who's-in-charge thing, there'd always be a repeat of this morning! And the next time, you might not be lucky enough to be saved by an interruption."

"I have a proposition for you," she said, her voice surprisingly cool, in light of the offer she was about to make.

Steele held up a hand, palm outward, to stop her. "You haven't heard a damn word I've said, have you? Can't you get it through your head, I'm up to my eyeballs with your bargains and propositions? To put it bluntly, *Miss Kincade,* there's only one proposition you could come up with that would make me consider staying on the *Intrepid* for another three months. And I don't think you're ready to offer that."

"I don't suppose you'd consider changing your mind if I promised you a larger percentage of the profits at the end of the trip?" She had to make a last stab, even though she knew what his answer would be before he spoke.

Steele blew out an exasperated sigh and shook his head with disgust. "You don't give up, do you? I already told you the money wasn't the reason I signed on. Nothing's changed."

"That only leaves me with one thing to offer in exchange for your services, doesn't it?" She turned and walked over to the bed and sat down on it.

A warning went off in Steele's head and his mouth dropped open. "What are you saying?"

Temerity glanced down at her hands in her lap. "I'm saying I'm prepared to finish what we started in my cabin this morning—if you'll change your mind about leaving the *Intrepid*."

There! She'd said it. The words had been stiff, delivered in a rush, as if she'd rehearsed them a thousand times, but they were out now. No turning back.

Steele frowned his puzzlement. He couldn't believe his ears. As the total meaning of what she'd said sank into his brain, his eyes opened wide in shock. "You're ready to *what?*"

"I told you I would do anything to save my father's boat, Mr. Steele. And I meant it." She slipped a glove from one of her hands and placed it on the table beside the bed.

His feet still rooted to the spot where he'd been standing when she'd made her preposterous suggestion, Steele's expression remained stunned. His gaze was held prisoner by the innocently seductive motions of her hands as she eased her fingers, one at a time, from the other glove. He wiped the back of his wrist over his mustache. "You'd actually sell your body?" he finally managed to say.

How can I sell you what I've already given you? were the words that flashed through her mind without warning. But she only said, "Do we have a bargain, Mr.

174

Steele?" She placed her second glove on the table and reached up to untie the bonnet strings under her chin. "What I want, in exchange for what you want." She took off the bonnet and placed it on top of the gloves.

Her last words jolted Steele into action. "Stop that!" he ordered, angrily crossing the space that separated them and catching her hands in his as he sat down beside her.

"What's wrong with you?" His voice was low and tortured, his anger with her for turning out to be no different than other women competing with his self-hate for being tempted to take what she was offering.

"That is why you came with me, isn't it, Mr. Steele? Or have you changed your mind since this morning? Don't you want me anymore?"

"That has nothing to do with it!" His attention was suddenly trapped by the sight of his own hands gripping her slender shoulders, and his tone was not nearly as stern and forbidding as he'd intended it to be.

It was then he realized, with shocking clarity, that he'd done what he'd sworn he wouldn't do, had known he *couldn't* do if he were to escape unscathed from his latest encounter with Temerity: he'd gotten too close. Close enough to touch her. Close enough for the warmth of her to already be wending its way up his arms and throughout his body to erode away at his resolve and good sense. And the final, destroying blow to his fragile strength of will: he'd gotten close enough to breathe in the lemony fragrance of her. The scent that had the power to turn his mind to mush and his self-control to jelly.

His eyes narrowed and a muscle twitched in his cheek.

In a last-ditch effort to resist the temptation tugging at him, Steele tore his hands and eyes away from Temerity. But he couldn't quite muster the strength to move off the bed, where they sat only inches apart. "I ought to take you up on your offer—just to teach you a lesson," he grated, his intended threat far from threatening.

She tried to convince herself that the disappointment she was feeling was caused only by the fact that, if she failed with Steele, she had no other recourse but to abandon her journey up the Missouri River. "Are you telling me no?"

"Of course, I'm telling you no!" Steele grabbed her chin in a strong hand and turned her face toward him, his own contorted with frustrated anger. "What kind of a son-of-a-bitch do you take me for anyway? Do you really think I'd force a woman into prostituting herself in exchange for my help?"

Temerity's eyes widened at his choice of words.

"Don't look so surprised, Temerity. I've got to hand it to you though. You had me fooled. I would never have believed you'd be willing to sink that low for anything. Just goes to prove what I've said all along. There's a little bit of whore in all of you—if the price is right!"

Temerity stared at Steele, her blue eyes round with horror as it sank in that what he said was true. She couldn't even slap his face. He was right. What she had suggested was nothing short of prostitution!

Then, almost unnoticed by her, tears began to gather in her eyes, turning them to glimmering puddles of blue as one lone tear spilled over a lower lid to begin a solitary trail down her cheek. Her shoulders sagged and her hands lay limp in her lap.

Steele's face twisted with anguish. His hypnotized gaze was captured by the forlorn tear that dangled for an instant on the ridge of her jaw before falling onto her blouse. "Aw, don't cry," he pleaded, catching her face between his palms and wiping the pads of his thumbs over the tears that were now coming faster than he could wipe them away. "I shouldn't have said that. I didn't mean it. Don't cry."

Temerity shook her head and managed a trembling smile. "You know what really hurts?" she asked with a sad little laugh, covering his hands with her own and removing his from her face. "It isn't what you said. You were right. What really hurts is admitting to myself what a total failure I am."

Steele started to protest, but Temerity went on speaking.

"I was so sure of myself, so sure I knew all the answers. I had no doubt I could take the *Intrepid* all the way to Fort Benton, with or without help. I was going to prove to you and everyone else I was as good as any *man* who ever took a sternwheeler up the Missouri. I was going to show you all how brilliant I was with my 'vast'"—she swept her hand out in a gesture of greatness and gave a bitter little laugh—"knowledge and skills. And all the time—" A new onslaught of crying exploded from her and she buried her face in her hands.

"All the time, the only one I was fooling was me," she sobbed. "I wasn't fooling you or anyone else, was I? Just myself. I thought I knew so much. But I didn't know anything. Nothing. I couldn't do anything right. I couldn't hire a crew. I couldn't keep the passengers from leaving. I couldn't stop the crew from quitting. And I couldn't even make you want me. I'm just one great big failure." Her words were coming in huge gulps now.

Unable to remember why he'd sworn not to touch her, Steele caught her in his arms and hugged her to him, stroking her back and hair as he spoke, his own voice hoarse with unhappiness. "You just hold on there a minute. The Temerity Kincade I know is no failure,

177

and I won't allow you to run down someone I respect so much." He adjusted his embrace and began to rock her. "Hush now, we'll work it out. I'm not going to leave you. Together, we'll make it work."

But Temerity had heard only one thing. "You respect me?" she asked, her voice a muffled sob against his bare chest. "After what I—" Her gaze swerved sideways to the rumpled bed where they still sat.

"Hell, yes, I respect you. More than any woman I've ever known. I respect your fearless determination"—he emitted a defeated snort of laughter—"though it makes you do some pretty crazy things that're liable to turn me into an old man before September. That's one of the reasons I made this trip in the first place. I figured anyone as brave and as determined as you are ought to get a little support when she needed it. And I respect your intelligence, your loyalty to your father, the way you don't quit trying when things get too tough. When most people would throw up their hands in defeat, you just keeping going. And I respect the way you—should I go on?"

Temerity became aware of the warm hand rubbing her back and tilted her head to search Steele's face. It was in that moment she realized how much she'd wanted him, above all others, to think highly of her. "You really respect me?"

Steele grinned and brushed his lips over her forehead. "I really do," he said against her hair as he tightened his hold on her. "You're the smartest, feistiest—"

"Stubbornest, bossiest, contrariest—" Temerity went on for him with a muffled laugh into the soft, masculine hair that covered the hard-muscled chest where she leaned her head.

Steele reared his head back and studied her for a moment, then chuckled and ruffled her hair, which was already more loose of its pins than restrained by them. "Yeah, that too. But I was about to say—"

Temerity lifted her face from his chest and waited with trusting innocence for him to go on. And Steele was seized by a need to take care of the woman in his arms, to protect her. He wanted to sink himself so deep inside her body and soul that she'd never be able to leave him. An intense need shuddered through his strong body, clear to the tips of his toes, leaving him weak and trembling as it wrenched his self-restraint loose from its moorings—until it hung by a thread no stronger than a spider's web.

Her cheeks glistening with tears, she sniffed, "What w-were you go-ing to say?"

Entranced by her disheveled, unsophisticated beauty that she tried so hard to hide from the rest of the world, Steele was powerless to stop himself from saying what he was thinking. "The prettiest . . . the sweetest . . . the most desirable . . . Oh, hell," he ground out in frustration as his mouth came down on hers. His tongue plunged deep into her mouth in a kiss that was immediately urgent and demanding.

Temerity didn't pause to think about the danger of her response to his passionate kiss as she opened her mouth instinctively to draw every bit of his essence into her. Beyond thought, only feeling—wanting—now, she slid her arms around the corded muscles of his chest to climb desperately up his back with her hands and cling to his shoulders.

By the time he freed her mouth, they were both gasping for air, and Steele made a final effort to stop what her reaction and his own feverish body were screaming to him to make happen. Gripping her shoulders roughly, he hauled her away from him. "I'd"—his chest rose and fell laboriously, his breath coming in rapid pants—"better get you back to the

Intrepid before someone wonders where you are."

"No one will wonder," she said hoarsely, her breathing every bit as ragged as his.

Steele's hold tightened on her shoulders.

"I told Uriah and Harry Bailey that I was going to stay in a hotel so I could get a decent night's sleep."

"Then I'd better take you to your hotel," he said, his tone brusque as he fought to regain control of his passions. "Where are you staying?"

"I had planned to stay here," she admitted softly, still breathless as her blue eyes searched rapidly over his face for a sign he didn't want her to leave.

"You mean at this *hotel*," he said, certain he was misunderstanding the intention in her words.

Temerity nodded her head affirmatively. She couldn't help smiling at the little-boy confusion clouding his golden eyes, eyes that could be so fierce, eyes that could be so gentle. Not even aware she was doing it, she lifted her hand and brushed a reddish-brown lock of hair off his forehead with the backs of her fingers. "In this hotel. In this room. In this be—"

The full meaning of her intentions kicked Steele in the gut. "I told you, you don't need to do that," he bit out harshly, fighting the desire to let his eyes drift closed as he felt himself being drawn under the comforting spell of her stroke on his forehead. "I told you I'd help you save the *Intrepid.*"

"This isn't for the *Intrepid*," she said softly, leaning forward to place a light kiss at the corner of his mouth just where his mustache ended. "This is for me."

"Stop that!" he ordered, his eyes popping open. "You don't know what you're saying."

"Yes, I do, Mr. Steele. For the first time, I'm being completely honest about the reason I came here," she said, stroking her thumb over the furrowed creases between his eyebrows. "Don't you want me to stay?"

She caressed his dimpled cheek with her palm and brushed the tips of her fingers back and forth over his mustache.

Steele didn't answer her question. "Are you sure?" he finally rasped, his tongue flicking outward of its own accord to taste the soft flesh of her fingers as they drifted over his upper lip.

Fire exploded along an invisible line from the wet tip of his tongue on the inside of her fingers to a place deep in the pit of her existence; and Temerity was never more sure of anything in her life. He had taken her virginity; and she knew she would never be whole until she had given him herself.

"I'm sure."

"I'm warning you, lady. If you're going to change your mind, you'd better do it quick," he cautioned in a gruff tone.

"I won't change my mind, Mr. Steele. I want to finish what we began this morning in my cabin." *I want to feel whole again. And this time, I want you to remember, too.*

Chapter Eleven

A low growl of surrender issued from deep in Steele's throat, and his lips closed over Temerity's. Crushing her to him, he reclaimed possession of the warm hollows and sleek crevices of her mouth in a kiss that was hard and punishing yet surprisingly gentle, stern yet playful, sealing their fates.

Ravenous tentacles of ecstasy spiraled uncontrolled to the heart of her femininity, to the very heart of her soul. Burning under the scorching hunger of his lips, she returned his kiss with equal greed and fire.

Bathing her face with tender kisses, he eased her back onto the bed. "Sweet, sweet love," he murmured against her temple.

With senses reeling and the blood thrumming in her ears, she clawed at his back in a wild, out-of-control effort to bring him closer as she sucked in ragged gulps of air.

His hands shaking, as much from nervousness as passion, Steele unbuttoned Temerity's bodice. When the buttons were all free, he gave a rough tug on the tail of the blouse and pulled it from the waistband of her skirt.

Rising up from the bed, Steele grasped her hands in

his and drew her up to stand before him. His hand encircling her wrists lightly, he looked down at her, his expression questioning.

Temerity's gaze lifted to meet his, her own glittering with confusion. Then she realized what he was doing. He was giving her a final chance to change her mind.

With a loving smile, she gave an almost imperceptible shake of her head and slipped her arms around his waist to press her cheek against the wiry softness of the curls that covered his chest.

His muscled flesh shuddered under the evidence of her answer to his unspoken question; and he clutched her tightly against him, burying his face in the tangle of dark hair that crowned her head.

Pleased with his reaction to her decision, her nostrils flared with instinctive desire as the heady male scent of him pervaded her senses. Her tongue flicked out to taste the salty/sweet flesh beneath her cheek, and she thrilled anew to the groan of pleasure her action evoked from him.

Steele bent his knees slightly and cupped the soft roundness of her bottom in his hands, lifting and drawing her close against him. "Ah, sweet girl," he sighed, cushioning the hardness of his desire against the welcoming softness of her. "I've wanted this since the first moment I saw you. I even dreamed of it. Tell me this isn't another dream."

Fragments of a confession that should be made flashed through Temerity's passion-intoxicated mind, and she opened her mouth to speak. But she could not make all the words form on her tongue. "—not—a—dream—" she finally managed to whisper, raising her lips to his.

Steele slid his hand up her back and over her shoulders. Clasping his palms on either side of her face, he brushed her mouth lightly with his, then her nose, the tip of her chin, her closed eyes, her forehead.

When his mouth moved from her face, she opened her eyes sluggishly, her dismay evident in them. But his fingers were already burrowing into her thick black hair to remove her hairpins, the last evidence of her attempt to tame its undisciplinable tendencies. Removing the final pin, he combed through the luxurious waves with his fingers, coaxing it to curl freely and loosely around her shoulders.

Drawing back to admire his handiwork, he smiled. "Wild black silk," he murmured, speaking more to himself than to her. He picked up a strand and brought it to his lips. "Just as I imagined it would be. Just like I dreamed." Luxuriating in its fragrance, he buried his face in a handful of the ebony softness.

Temerity's head lolled back as his kisses moved to the sensitive paleness of her neck and downward to the curve of her shoulder, where he nosed her blouse out of the way. Blazing a trail of moist kisses down first one arm, then the other, he removed the blouse, letting it drop to the floor at her feet.

Unable to wait any longer to unwrap the treasure hidden beneath her clothes, Steele unfastened her skirt and petticoat strings so quickly they swished down her body as one, falling in a dark blue puddle at her feet, along with the discarded blouse.

Standing before him in only her chemise and drawers, Temerity felt an instant of doubt and fought the desire to draw away from him and cover herself with her crossed arms. But the longing that raged in her body was far greater than any sense of modesty she was experiencing; and she didn't move—couldn't move. However, she was thankful for the dimly lit room that had grown progressively darker with the approaching night.

Seeming to sense her sudden hesitation, Steele

brought her against his need again and kissed her mouth.

Pleasure radiated throughout her, and she knew she would not turn away from him. Even if the room suddenly became bathed with glaring light, she would stay, would *have* to stay. If she were to retain her hold on sanity, she would not be able to deny herself the splendor of him one last time.

His kisses resumed their courting of her ears and shoulders, neck, and upper chest. Catching the top of her chemise with his teeth, he lowered it over her full breasts as his hands smoothed the straps of the chemise over her shoulders and down her arms.

Her breasts swelled at the heat of his gaze on her, growing heavy under the intensity. He stooped low and whispered his mustache over each of the tight peaks thrusting toward him.

Scooping her up in his arms, Steele lay Temerity on the bed and stood back to quickly divest himself of his clothing. When he was totally naked, his desire proudly erect, she suddenly wished the room wasn't so dark. She moaned softly and held her arms up to him, but he didn't come into them immediately. Instead, he bent to press his mouth to the gently rising mound at the juncture of her legs as he grasped the waist of her drawers and began to peel them over her slender hips and thighs. Then with painstakingly slow movements, he rolled one stocking then the other off her legs, leaving her clad only in the darkness.

As the last stocking slid off her foot, he kissed her arch, tickling the tip of his tongue along the knob of an ankle, along the shapely curve of her calf, stopping to explore the sensitive crease behind her knee. He nibbled his way up the inside of her thigh, almost reaching the gently rocking center of her femininity, then bathing her other leg in the same torturous kisses.

186

"Please," she groaned, her head tossing slowly from side to side as her hands clawed at clumps of the bedspread beneath her.

When the warmth of his breath disturbed the dark nest of curls at the joining of her thighs, her eyes popped opened in surprise and her head strained up off the mattress. She writhed helplessly beneath him, not certain whether she was trying to escape or move herself closer. Then she was being caught up in a vacuum of passion, where one universal thought controlled, one consummate need ruled; and her head collapsed back on the pillow, her eyes fluttering closed in rapturous defeat.

His fingers lifting her to him and separating the satiny folds of her femininity, he captured the heart of her desire with his lips, bringing her to an immediate and unexpected explosion with his erotic tonguing.

Before she could grasp what had happened, he was over her, his hips positioned between her thighs. His mouth caught hers in his, and he plunged his tongue into its sweet warmth at the same time he sank his manhood into the dark, shuddering heat of her body.

Instinctively, she wrapped her legs around his narrow hips to caress the backs of his hair-dusted legs with her calves and heels. Her hand roved over the perspiration-slicked expanse of his back and shoulders, pulling him closer to her with each hungry stroke.

In the back of his mind, the ease with which he'd entered her struck a wrong chord; but it didn't register in his consciousness. In that moment, the roar of his desire was too great, too demanding, for him to hear anything else—discordant or otherwise. Passion thundered in his ears, matching its rhythm with the motions of his body inside hers. Then it was happening. He had reached the glorious zenith he had dreamed of; and he erupted inside her, the sound of his own breathing, his own heartbeat, all he heard.

Freed from her aching desire by her own spasms of deliverance, Temerity tightened her arms and legs around Steele and clung to him for the tumultuous journey back to earth from the heights they had achieved.

He rolled off her, flopping his forearm back over his brow in exhaustion. "I'll say one thing, *Miss Kincade*— You know how to make a man—"

It was then that the one discordant note in their perfect union sounded its strident echo in his conscious mind. *Temerity Kincade had not been a virgin!*

Not questioning why it should make any difference to him, Steele threw his arm down and rolled his head toward her, his brows drawn together in a deep frown.

"I had no idea anything would be so wonderful, Mr. Ste—" She turned on her side and faced him with a shy smile. "I suppose Mr. Steele isn't appropriate anymore, is it? Not after tonight." She smiled and sifted her fingers through his damp chest hairs.

So that's it! Steele bellowed in his mind, cursing himself for not wondering before how she'd found him. *She saw my name on the register. This whole thing was a trap!* The expression on his face, blissful a moment before, became hard. She'd thought she could use the oldest trick in the book to save her father's business *and* get herself a rich husband in the bargain. *And I fell for it all the way. The distraught little virgin, helpless and alone, nowhere to turn but to me. I bet she thinks it's all over now but the fireworks. I can hear it now: "Steele, darling, I'm pregnant. We must marry right away."* He blew out a snort of self-disgust. *And I'm not even the first!*

"What should I call you now?" Temerity asked, leaning forward to skim his chest with a flutter of light kisses, still too lost in the afterglow of their lovemaking to be aware of the sudden indifference in him.

"Most people just call me Steele."

She drew back and studied his face. "But I thought Steele was your last name."

"But now you've found out differently, haven't you?" He grabbed the hand on his chest by the wrist and flattened it against him to still its disturbing motions. "Who was it?"

Startled by the confusing change in his mood, Temerity replied in a small, frightened voice. "I don't understand."

"Oh, lady, you do that so well."

A thread of apprehension wrapped itself in knots around her stomach. "Do what well? What are you talking about?"

"Dammit, Temerity. Did you really think I'd be so caught up in my desire that I wouldn't notice this wasn't the first time for you?"

His words tightened the thread of apprehension in her stomach. She knew she should have told him the truth when he mentioned the dream. Now it was too late. Now he would never believe he had been the first man, the only man to be with her.

Then anger replaced her fear, and Temerity jerked her hand free of his and sat up. She yanked the sheet up over her breasts angrily. What right did he have attacking her as though she had betrayed him? *Not a damn bit!*

"First of all, Mr.—whatever your name is—you didn't ask. Besides, what difference does it make to you?"

Stunned, Steele stared at Temerity's angry profile, fighting the twinge of confusion he suddenly felt. What difference *did* it make to him? Hardly any of the women he'd ever been with had been a virgin. And he'd never minded before. In fact, he'd preferred it. Things

189

were never as complicated that way; and there was certainly no need for a guilty conscience when that was the case. So why was he upset that he hadn't been Temerity Kincade's first lover? *Because she made you look stupid. You believed her act and walked away from your responsibilities in St. Louis because you thought she was different from the others. Special,* he chided himself with a derisive curl of his lip. *And all the time she was every bit as manipulative and conniving as the best of them. Her act was just a little better.*

Bolting up in the bed, he swung his feet to the floor and bent to retrieve his pants. "It doesn't matter to me what you've done in the past, lady. I just don't like liars. And I don't like a whore who pretends to be a virgin."

"Whore?" she screeched, flying across the bed at him, her fingers curved in punishing talons. "You've accused me of being a whore one time too many!" Her nails sank into the vulnerable flesh of his back and raked its length in eight angry trails, several of them immediately beading red with blood.

"You bitch!" he yelped, twisting around and flipping her back on the bed, pressing her into the covers with his body.

Struggling to free herself of his weight, she pommeled his head and shoulders with her balled fists.

His breathing heavy with exertion and pain, Steele caught hold of her wrists and clamped them in one strong fist above her head and glared down into her fire-spitting blue eyes.

Realizing the futility of fighting his greater weight, Temerity narrowed her eyes and ceased her struggles. She clamped her lips together in a thin, stubborn line and waited for her chance to escape.

Their faces were so close they could feel the warmth of each other's breath, but neither of them moved. For several long, frozen minutes, they stared at each other, neither of them shifting their gazes away, neither of them willing to back down.

It was then Temerity first became aware of the rough caress of his chest hair against her nipples, and the familiar tightening in the pit of her belly. Horrified that her desire could be blossoming again, she was first to break their eye contact.

Steele clamped her jaw in his free hand and forced her to face him again. "How many others have there been, Temerity? How many others have you fooled with this sweet little innocent act of yours?"

The desire to scream the truth at him clawed at Temerity's insides, but she wouldn't give him the satisfaction of defending herself. "Bastard!"

"Careful, Temerity, that kind of language shows your true colors," he bit out.

She opened her mouth to scream a hateful retort at him, then closed it, realizing with instinctive clarity that the only way to fight Steele was to refuse to fight. Sheer determination tightened her mouth into a grim, impenetrable line of resolve and slitted her eyes into deadly weapons, capable of boring their way into a man's very soul.

This time, Steele was the one to break away first, instinctively shielding himself from her relentless glare by lowering his lids for an instant. But like the proverbial moth to the flame, his gaze was drawn back to hers.

"The truth hurts, doesn't it?" he tried, thinking to prod a response from her.

Temerity continued to stare, praying with all her strength that he would back down before her body's natural reaction to him could betray her, as it was threatening to do.

Steele tightened his hold on her chin and squeezed her cheeks together, trying to force her mouth open.

"Go on, Temerity, tell me again what a 'lady' you are."

Temerity's heart skipped a beat, and a flicker of weakening jerked through her.

However, Steele didn't recognize the stirring of response in her. He was too blinded by his own frustration and the confused signals his own body was sending his brain. Determined to control her, he closed his mouth on hers, rocking it punishingly over her tightly clamped lips in an effort to make her yield.

But her defenses held their tenuous grasp against his attack, and she did not respond—on the surface anyway. Only she knew how fragile that grasp was as her own betraying body screamed out for her to open her mouth to him.

"Hell!" Steele growled, raising his head to glower down into her staring eyes, painfully aware of his own growing need and unable to believe his kiss had had no effect on her whatsoever.

Rage and hurt and frustration hurled him the last modicum of the way beyond rational thought. He swore she would respond to him. One way or another!

Still holding her hands above her head, Steele lifted himself far enough above her to yank the sheet from between them. His actions now ruled by primitive desire and an anger he was not capable of even trying to understand, he positioned himself between her legs and entered her with a hard thrust.

Temerity's eyes widened in shock at his intrusion and her mouth opened in an uncontrollable gasp.

He'd won! He'd beaten her.

A sneer of satisfaction crossed Steele's face as her body began to move beneath his, slowly at first, then more rapidly, finally rising to meet each new thrust with ever-increasing fervor.

It was then he saw the trickle of tears that leaked from the corners of each of Temerity's tightly closed eyes. A return to sanity washed over him in a flood of self-recrimination. He'd raped her! He'd actually raped her! No matter what she'd done, or was, she didn't deserve that.

The knowledge had the same effect on his desire as a bucket of ice water splashed in the middle of his back would have had. His manhood, large and rigid with desire a moment before and filling the tight sheath of her body to capacity, went limp inside her.

"Oh, my god, Temerity." He dipped his head to kiss a wet temple. "I didn't know what I was doing," he groaned, his words a plea for forgiveness. "I'm so sorry."

"I would appreciate it if you would get off me," she said with as much control as she could muster, when her own desire was aching with unfulfilled need.

But Steele had no way of knowing the effort the words had required of her, and he was stunned by the chill in her tone. He rolled away from her, knowing there was nothing he could say to make right what he'd just done.

Silently, their backs to each other, they dressed, each lost in private recriminations and self-flogging. Then, with her dignity as restored as she could manage under the circumstances, Temerity tied her bonnet strings beneath her chin and snatched up her gloves. "I'll expect you to be on the *Intrepid* in the morning in time to oversee our loading and departure."

"You *what?*" He spun to face her, his mouth agape.

Finding a warped sense of pleasure at catching Steele off guard, Temerity allowed a cool smile to play across her face. She arched her dark eyebrows. "Why are you so surprised, Steele? Whatever you and I think of each other, I paid the price I offered for your services. Now you owe me. And I expect you to pay the price for mine!" Without giving him a chance to respond, she flung open the door and stepped out into the dark hallway.

She held her posture rigidly erect until she was certain she was out of his sight, breaking into a run the instant the door clicked shut behind her. She knew the fragile supports sustaining her self-control were going to crumble and collapse at any moment, and she was determined to be as far away from Steele as possible when that happened.

Minutes later, unmindful of anything but getting back to the safety and solitude of her cabin on the *Intrepid,* Temerity ran out of the hotel into the dark street.

"Well, well, what do we have here?" a deep voice asked as Temerity slammed up against the solid chest of a man. "What's your hurry, pretty lady?" he asked, catching her by the arms. "You look like you seen Macbeth's ghost."

Temerity's stunned gaze rose to take in the ruddy, square-jawed face of the man holding her. Cleanshaven and about five feet ten inches tall, he was slender and in his early twenties. Dressed in a plain brown three-piece suit, the kind a man might wear to church or a funeral, the sandy-haired man had the intelligent look of a scholar. She felt certain she had nothing to be afraid of and breathed a sigh of relief.

Glancing back over her shoulder toward the hotel before looking back at the young man's hawk-nosed face, Temerity used the time to catch her breath. "I'm afraid I wasn't watching where I was going," she finally said with an embarrassed smile. "I stayed in town longer than I intended, and I was anxious to get back to the *Intrepid* before it got any later," she explained, making an effort to step back from the man.

But he didn't release his grip on her arms, and her sense of panic rose again. After all, just because he

194

looked harmless didn't make it so. This time when she looked back at the hotel, a wish to see Steele standing there sped across her thoughts. But the hotel doorway was empty—as she'd known it would be.

"The *Intrepid,* huh?" The young man's grin broadened with recognition. "That's where I'm headin' too!" Releasing his grip on only one of her arms, he turned toward the levee and started walking, leaving her no choice but to go with him.

"You were?" Temerity choked, not certain what to think of her companion now. She shamed herself for having suspicious thoughts about him. After all, he really hadn't done or said anything that should give her reason to be afraid of him. He'd been perfectly polite. And though he hadn't given up his hold on her arm, escorting her safely back to the riverboat was obviously his only intent—not dragging her into an alley to attack her, as her overactive imagination would have her believe. Yet something about the look in his blue eyes told her that beneath the friendly, easygoing demeanor was a man to fear—if anyone were foolish enough to cross him. A shudder of apprehension rippled through her.

"Do you have business aboard the *Intrepid?*" she asked, doing her best to keep her voice casual and to ignore the ridiculous tremors of foreboding that continued to shake her. She was just spooked, she told herself: by the dark, by everything that had happened that day, by finding herself in the company of a stranger—and by the ugly scene in Steele's room.

"My brother and me been visitin' kinfolk hereabouts and decided to take it easy on the trip back home. I booked our passage on the *Intrepid* not thirty minutes ago." He released his hold on her upper arm and, without giving her a chance to bolt, put her hand through the bend of his elbow. "And you?"

Relief washed over Temerity—on two counts. Evidently, the man was exactly what he seemed to be, no more, no less. *And,* she told herself happily, he'd reminded her of the pleasant fact that at most every stop they would be taking on new passengers to replace the ones to whom she'd refunded passages.

"I own the *Intrepid*—or at least my father does. I'm Temerity Kincade, Mister . . . ?" She held out her right hand, her brows arched expectantly.

"James," the man said, taking her hand in his free hand and raising it to his lips. "Frank James, and it's right fine to meet you, Miss Kincade. Right fine, indeed."

Temerity couldn't resist smiling at the young man's overt attempt at gallantry. "How far upriver do you and—did you say your brother?—plan on going?"

"We'll be leavin' your company at Missouri City. We got us a little place at Kearney, about ten miles north of there."

"Oh?"

"Yeah, ever since we come back from fightin' the Yanks in the War, we been stayin' there. Just livin' a quiet life, so to speak."

"I assume you have family in Kearney?"

"Just my ma and stepfather. And, of course, Jesse. That's my kid brother."

As if just saying the name had produced him, a young man dashed up to Frank and Temerity. Though he had the same sandy-haired, blue-eyed coloring as his brother, Jesse's frame was shorter and sturdier. "Where you goin', Frank? I thought you were gonna meet me at the Gilded Cage when you was through bookin' our passage and had the horses on board." The younger man, who looked about nineteen and had almost girlish features, winked at his brother several times in succession.

196

"Jesse, this here's Miss Kincade. Her pa owns the riverboat we're goin' to be travelin' on. Miss Kincade, this ill-mannered young feller here's my brother, Jesse."

Temerity started to extend her hand, then thought better of it—one stranger kissing her hand was enough for tonight. "I'm pleased to meet you, Mr. James. I hope you and your brother will enjoy your trip on the *Intrepid*."

Jesse turned to her and grinned, his eyelids batting in a decidedly feminine manner. "It's a real pleasure, Miss Kincade."

Temerity's breath caught in her throat, but before she could respond with an indignant huff, he winked again—and again—and yet again. It was then she realized he had an eye affliction of some sort and evidently meant nothing by his constant winking. He probably wasn't even aware of it.

"I'll see Miss Kincade safely back to her boat, then I'll meet you at the Gilded Cage," Frank said, seemingly unbothered by his brother's eyes.

"Really, it's not necessary, Mr. James," Temerity protested, seeing this as a chance to escape from the uncomfortably polite Frank and his brother, Jesse. "I can go the rest of the way by myself. I'll be just fine." She tried to remove her hand from his arm.

"Nonsense." Frank covered her hand with his and held it in place. "Streets aren't safe for a lady at night. And I wouldn't be able to look myself in the mirror if I didn't see you back to your riverboat."

Seeing no way out but to allow him to escort her back—and admitting to herself she was probably safer with him than she would have been alone—Temerity gave him a slight smile. "Very well."

"Nice meetin' you, Miss Kincade," Jesse called over his shoulder, before making his way up the street toward the Gilded Cage.

By the time Temerity had rid herself of the overly attentive Frank and was safely back in her cabin, it was all she could do to hold her head up long enough to strip off her clothes and take a quick bath. Convincing herself she would rest just a few minutes, then would get dressed again and go tell Harry Bailey that Mr. Steele would be back in the morning—she hoped—she lay back on her bunk, falling immediately into an exhausted sleep.

Long after Temerity Kincade had left him, Steele sat in the chair in the corner of his dark room, still in the state of half-dress he'd been in when she'd stormed out into the hallway.

He had no desire to sleep, yet no desire to light a lamp. The darkness suited his mood. *How the hell'd she managed to come here planning to snare me into marrying her and then leave me feeling like the guilty party for wronging her?*

Steele stood up and began to pace. *I don't owe her anything. She did what she did of her own free will. I didn't force her. And I wasn't even the first!* he said to himself for the thousandth time, trying to justify his decision to wash his hands of her once and for all.

Besides, it's the smart thing to do. With most of her crew gone, she'll be forced to abandon this whole crazy idea, he assured himself as he continued his nervous tour around the small room.

"But knowing her, she'll try to go anyway. She's so stubborn, she won't rest until she's sunk the *Intrepid* and gotten herself and everyone else on board killed."

But no matter how he rationalized, Steele couldn't stop feeling guilty, couldn't get the picture out of his mind of Temerity being robbed by river pirates, or scalped by Indians, or . . .

"Damn!" he cursed viciously, knowing what a condemned man must feel in that instant when he realizes he's helpless to stop his own hanging.

Snatching his shirt from where it was draped over the dressing screen, Steele shrugged his arms into it, muttering his disgust with himself the entire time.

Minutes later, he stomped up to the dozing desk clerk downstairs, his expression dark and scowling. "I'm checking out," he announced, pounding his key down on the desk.

Recognizing the angry man, the clerk came up out of his chair with a jerk. "I tried to tell her you weren't who she was lookin' for, Mr. Ca—"

"What the hell are you talking about?"

"The girl." Beads of sweat broke out on the little man's forehead. "She was tryin' to find someone whose *last* name was Steele. She wouldn't listen when I tried to tell you were the only Steele here and it was your first name and not your last name. She just heard the name Steele and headed upstairs for your room."

The meaning of the desk clerk's words began to penetrate the rage that still had Steele's brain fogged. "You mean she didn't know my last name was—"

The clerk shook his head. "She was in too big a hurry!"

Steele's face broke into a wide grin of relief and he plunked a gold coin on the counter. "You don't know how good that is to hear, friend."

He turned away from the confused clerk and started to run out of the hotel. Then the full impact of his mistake hit him full force. "Damn!" he blasted. "What the hell have I done?"

Chapter Twelve

Her expression pensive, Temerity stood at the rail on the *Intrepid*'s main deck and watched as the crew off-loaded cargo at Yankton. She couldn't help noticing the difference in the small Dakota territory town and the rapidly growing town of Sioux City only sixty-five miles downriver at the junction of Iowa, Nebraska, and the southeast corner of the Dakota territory.

Both towns had been established about ten years before, and their populations had increased at about the same rate for several years. Then the news had come that the railroad was considering one of the two river towns as its westernmost terminus. And the founding fathers and speculators of Sioux City and Yankton had immediately thrown themselves into a heated race to snare the guaranteed huge profits and commercial dominance the chosen town would be assured when the railroad arrived.

But now the race was over. The railroad and all it meant had arrived in Sioux City this past March, and already the Iowa town had left its rival city behind, its dreams of greatness dashed, and its single claim to fame a pork-packing plant.

Only two months after the first railcars had pulled

into the new Sioux City depot, the population of that town had more than doubled; new homes and businesses had been established by the hundreds; and Sioux City had assumed control of the major portion of the shipping to the eight Indian agencies and seven army posts scattered between there and Fort Benton.

In fact, there'd been so much cargo arriving in Sioux City by rail, some of it only eight days out of New York, that the larger riverboat lines hadn't been equipped to handle it all and had been forced to turn business over to the smaller, independently owned riverboats like the *Intrepid*. Most everyone had profited from the bountiful railroad windfall. Everyone, that is, but the people of Yankton.

"Quite different from Sioux City, isn't it?" Charles Rawson said, coming up to stand beside Temerity.

"Oh, Mr. Rawson, you surprised me!" she said, clapping her hand to her chest and looking up with a friendly smile. "And"—she laughed self-consciously—"you read my mind. I was just thinking what a shame it was that the railroad didn't go into Yankton too. It would be a perfect place to headquarter a line of riverboats. The shoreline's solid here and the river channel is deep. There would always be mooring space here. Sioux City's levee is already beginning to be too crowded with the larger lines to make room for the smaller boats."

"Do I detect a note in your voice that says you're ready to concede that the days are numbered for shipping westbound cargo to St. Louis by rail first, then up the river by packet?"

Temerity smiled at Rawson's mention of their familiar argument. "I'll admit that the railroad has had a greater effect on things than I could have imagined. But don't give up on the riverboat yet, Mr. Rawson. The railroad may force us to move our operations further north, but Sioux City is still almost two thousand miles below the head of navigation. I've no doubt there will be more than enough business to keep the enterprising packet owner busy for quite a few years to come."

"But it's just a matter of time until the railroad crosses the Missouri River. And when that happens, there will be no more need for the riverboats. What will you do then?"

"When, *and if,* that happens, I'll make that decision. In the meantime, I'm thinking of purchasing a second sternwheeler to make certain the *Kincade Line* gets a healthy share of the business as long as it lasts!" She laughed and gave Charles Rawson's hand a conciliatory pat where it rested on the rail.

Rawson's blue eyes glittered with humor as he smiled down at Temerity and placed his other hand over hers. "You are a very stubborn young woman, Miss Kincade."

"That's what I've been told, Mr. Rawson," she said, an expression of sadness flitting across her laughing face as his words reminded her of the man who had never been out of her mind for more than an instant during the past two weeks, since that night in his Portland, Missouri, hotel room. In automatic response to her thoughts, her eyes darted to where her crew was loading several cages of yowling cats, to be delivered to the army posts, where it was said the rats ate the grain faster than the horses could.

Her gaze was immediately captured by Steele's intense glare as he watched her from the levee. Even from here she could see the muscle in his square jaw knot as his eyes narrowed angrily. A thrill of satisfaction curled through her. He must feel something for her or it wouldn't bother him to see her talking to Rawson. And it was obvious it bothered him.

A great deal.

Well, that's just too bad! she said to herself with sadistic delight, turning her attention back to Charles Rawson with her most beguiling smile. "I really must go to my cabin and work on my ledgers, Mr. Rawson," she said with a teasing tilt of her head, which she hoped from a distance looked as if she were saying something wonderfully clever and flirtatious.

Rawson affected a disappointed moue, then smiled. "I suppose it's just as well, I have some business to attend to in Yankton. But at least allow me to escort you to your destination," he said, taking her hand and placing it on his arm.

"Thank you." Temerity fell into step beside the older man, concentrating on keeping her forced smile in place, despite the feel of Steele's scorching glare as it bored into her back.

Alone in her cabin minutes later, Temerity slumped back against the closed door and let a long sigh as the torturous facade of gaiety slid off her face. She was miserable.

True, the problems that had plagued the first few days of the journey seemed to have stopped, and the unexpected boon of cargo they'd received in Sioux City had provided the funds to make it to Fort Benton—if she remained frugal and if nothing unforeseen happened. Equally important, she and Steele had not had any arguments since she'd left him in his hotel room in Portland. But his cold, accusing silence had proven to be worse than a direct confrontation, haunting even her dreams at night.

When he had come back to work, ensuring that she wouldn't lose her crew, she'd been so relieved to see him that she would have been willing to forgive and forget everything that had happened between them. And when he'd said "Good morning" to her, she'd let herself believe there was the tiniest glimmer of uncertainty and contriteness in his expression. However, before she'd been able to respond to his greeting, her attention had been averted by Frank James as he had spoken to her from behind, telling her how much he'd enjoyed their time together the night before.

When she'd seen Frank on his way with a friendly reply and turned back to Steele, he'd been gone. Wanting to finish what had started with his "Good morning," she had searched the deck for him, finding him already shirtless and shouting orders to the crew.

Before she could call to him, he had looked up at her, the expression on his face a mixture of such hatred and hurt that Temerity's words had frozen in her throat.

She would never forget how their gazes had locked for the slightest instant before the muscle in his jaw jerked spastically in his cheek and he had turned his back on her, deliberately showing her the eight scratches that ran the length of his back.

In that chilling moment, she had known not only why he'd taken off his shirt before the day was hot enough to warrant it, but why there could be no forgiveness between them. It was obvious he'd meant to shame her in a way that words never could, and to make certain she knew the bridge between them was too wide ever to try to cross again.

That had been the last time they'd had any real contact.

For two weeks, he'd done his job perfectly, dealing with her through Uriah or Harry Bailey, but never directly. And she'd gone about her duties with efficiency, making it a point to show no more interest in her first mate than any other member of the crew. But he'd always been there, always watching her with those golden hazel eyes of his. And not a minute had passed when she hadn't been painfully aware of him.

Still leaning back on the door, Temerity buried her face in her hands.

A rapid knock on the door made her jolt upright. Looking around frantically in an instinctive response, she took a deep breath, pasted a brave smile back on her face, and opened the door. "Did you forget something, Mr. Raw—" Her mouth dropped open and her eyes widened with shock. "What do you want?"

"Sorry to disappoint you, boss lady," Steele said, his voice teeming with sarcasm as he brushed past her into the cabin. "We've got to talk. But don't worry, I'll be through before your boyfriend comes back."

"My boyfriend? What are you talking about?" She slammed the door behind her with more force than necessary, not realizing until it was too late the position she'd put herself in.

"Your latest conquest just left for town a few minutes ago. I'm surprised he was willing to let you out of his sight that long. Evidently, he doesn't know you as well as I do—yet. A situation I'm sure you'll remedy before long, won't you?"

"Are you suggesting that I—"

"Maybe not yet, but it's obvious what you're leading up to. Everywhere I look, there you and your adoring shadow are, laughing and holding hands. What do you expect to get out of it, Temerity? A wedding ring? Take my word for it, honey, you'll have a better chance of getting Rawson to propose if you wait until he pops the question before you—"

The only sound in the room was a wheezing intake of breath as Temerity flew across the room at him. "How *dare* you come in here and make such a vile suggestion?" Her open hand arched toward his tanned cheek.

Steele caught her wrist in midair and twisted her arm behind her back, jerking her up against his chest and

206

trapping her other arm between them. "Don't ever try that again, Temerity."

"Let me go!"

"We haven't finished talking yet."

"Talking? You call attacking me with your ugly allegations *talking?*" Her voice was beginning to shrill, but she didn't care. "I've heard enough of your *talk,* Mr. Steele. I want you to leave." She struggled against his hold on her.

"Not until I say what I came here to say," he said, tightening his grip on her.

"Then say it and get out."

"Before you come to an *arrangement*"—the way he said the word left no doubt about what type of "arrangement" he meant—"with Rawson, I want to be sure you're not pregnant with my baby."

Temerity opened her mouth to speak, but before she could utter her indignation, he went on.

"And if you are expecting a baby, I want you to know I'm willing to marry you."

"*Willing* to marry me? Why, you pompous ass! What makes you think *I* would be willing to marry *you?* Baby or no baby, I wouldn't marry you if you were the last man on earth!"

"I'm telling you right now, lady. If you're pregnant, you're going to marry me. And until you know if you are or not, I want you to stay away from Rawson. Is that understood?"

Something in his tone of voice tugged unexpectedly at Temerity's emotions, and her own anger seemed to dissipate. Steele was jealous! What else could explain his preposterous behavior? Unless he cared for her, it would make no difference to him whom she spent her time with. An exalting thrill raged through her blood. He cared! Steele cared for her! That was why he was jealous of Charles Rawson. That was why every time she'd stepped out of her cabin in the past two weeks, he'd been there watching her every move. That was why he was using the excuse of a possible baby to talk to her. Even if he hadn't admitted it to himself yet, she knew without a doubt that Steele had to feel something for her!

"Why, Steele?" she asked him, her voice soft, coaxing. "Why would you want to marry me?"

"Because no woman is going to brand a child of mine a bastard, that's why?"

"That's the only reason?"

Steele frowned at the change in her. "No kid should have to grow up without knowing his father," he added, his words sad and coming more slowly now as he stared confused into her understanding blue eyes.

"Is that what happened to you, Steele? Is that why this is so important to you?" The hand trapped between them worked its way up his chest to caress his cheek. "Didn't you know your father?"

Startled by her perceptiveness, Steele drew his head back to examine her. "Who told you that?" he asked suspiciously.

Temerity noticed the self-protective shell that suddenly seemed to surround Steele. "You just did." In a gesture that was universally maternal, her hand rose to brush a lock of chestnut hair back off his forehead. "Would you like to talk about it?"

"Why would I want to talk about something that happened years ago?" he barked defensively, tossing his head to shake off her caressing hand.

"Sometimes talking about things we can't change helps heal the hurt."

"All right, if you're so curious, I'll tell you about it. Not that it bothers me anymore. My parents weren't married."

Temerity inhaled a shocked gulp of air.

"Does that shock you, Miss Kincade?" he said hostilely. "Does it upset your delicate sensibilities to know I'm a bastard?"

She shook her head, her expression compassionate, her heart aching for the hurt she heard in Steele's voice. "Not in the way you think."

Steele went on speaking, as though he hadn't heard her reply to his question. "No one ever told me who my father was—if anyone ever knew. And my mother . . ."

"What about your mother?"

Steele dropped his arms from around her waist and wheeled away from her. "I never knew my mother either. She had run away from home when she was sixteen and was never in touch with her parents in all the time after she left. Then, after four years, she showed up on their doorstep, pregnant and begging them to take her back. Of course, they never considered refusing her. They were that kind of people. But as soon as her baby was born—me—she repaid their love and kindness by packing up and leaving again. Only this time, she left them saddled with a baby to take care of. She told them it was because I would be better off with them. She was right about that, of course. But I'm sure the real reason she left me with my grandparents had nothing to do with her concern for my welfare. A baby would have definitely gotten in her way."

Overwhelmed with sympathy for the little boy who'd never known his parents, Temerity's heart felt tight in her chest, and tears formed in her eyes. She ached to take him in her arms and cradle his head to her breast as his mother should have done all those years ago. She ached with the need to make it up to him for all the hurt that selfish woman had caused her son. "Did you ever meet her?"

"Only once," he answered, the bitterness in his tone cutting into Temerity's senses with vicious force.

"When I was about twenty I was in San Francisco on business for my grandfather. While I was taking in the sights, a prostitute approached me and tried to get me to go back to her crib with her. She was filthy and reeked of alcohol, but there was something about her eyes and the shape of her face that reminded me of the picture in the watch my grandfather had given me when I got out of college . . ."

Temerity's hand flew to her mouth to cover a horrified gasp as what he was going to say next dawned on her. "Oh, my god!"

Steele turned to look at her again, the expression on his face taunting. "Do I need to go on?"

No longer able to deny her need to comfort him—the boy he'd been, the man he was—Temerity flung herself across the space that separated them and wrapped her arms around his waist. "Oh, Steele, I'm so sorry," she wept, nuzzling her face against his shirtfront. "Is that why you thought I—"

Without thinking about what he was doing, Steele enfolded her in his arms and buried his face in the lemony fresh abundance of her hair. He breathed in deeply, the way a man deprived of oxygen would have done when given a lifesaving whiff of air just before death would have taken him.

They stood like that for a long time, just silently clinging to each other, drawing on and relishing their united strength, which had been denied them the past two weeks.

"Steele," Temerity finally said, intent on easing some of his pain. "I'm not pregnant," she told him, surprised at the unexpected wave of sadness that swept over her with her announcement. "So you have nothing to worry about."

"Are you sure?"

Temerity told herself she was imagining the note of

disappointment she heard in his voice. "I'm sure."

"Yeah . . . well . . . I guess that's good news."

"Yes, I suppose it is. And as far as my relationship with Mr. Rawson . . ." She felt the muscles in Steele's back and arms tense at the mention of the other man's name. "There's nothing for you to worry about there either. He's just a kind friend. More like an uncle. We simply enjoy talking to each other. There will never be an 'arrangement' between us."

"You may be able to convince yourself that's the truth, but believe me, he doesn't see you as his niece. And he's interested in a hell of a lot more from you than conversation!"

Temerity ignored his comment, chalking it up to jealousy, the sound of it warming her all over. She was suddenly compelled to clear away every misunderstanding they'd ever had. "There's one more thing I think you should know," she said hesitantly. Keeping her hands clasped around his waist, she leaned back so she could see his puzzled face. "You remember that dream you said you had?"

"What dream?" He tilted his head slightly to the side and looked down his cheek at her, his expression wary.

"The one where I came to you in the middle of the night and we—"

"What about it?"

She shot him a silly little embarrassed grin. "It wasn't a dream. Or if it was, I had the same dream."

"What kind of trick are you up to now?"

"No tricks, Steele. Just the truth."

"I don't believe you. You're up to something. I told you about the dream. Telling me it wasn't a dream doesn't prove anything."

"Nor does denying it make it untrue. Did you tell me which night you had the dream or what I was wearing or what you said to me?" Steele didn't answer her, so

211

she went on. "I was wearing a white nightgown and my hair was loose. It was the night you slept in Uriah's cabin. You were drugged with the laudanum I'd given you for pain, but I remembered that too late. I'd had an idea about why the fire had been set in the hold, and in my excitement I went to tell you about it. When I realized you were asleep, I checked you for fever"—she couldn't quite bring herself to tell him the real reason why she had touched him—"and you suddenly grabbed me and threw me on the bed and—and—" She raised her gaze to his, hers begging him not to force her to say it aloud. "You talked as if I were a spy or something and accused me of being there to get some sort of information from you."

A flicker of something akin to recognition enlarged the pupils in Steele's eyes, but he quickly hid his surprise behind carefully hooded lids. "If you're telling the truth, why didn't you call for help?"

Temerity released a puff of embarrassed laughter and turned away from him, unable to stand the harsh scrutiny of his eyes any longer. "Believe me, I've asked myself what I could have done differently. But the answer's always the same. There was nothing I could do. I tried to reason with you, but you wouldn't listen. And if I'd called for help, everyone would have known I had gone to your room wearing nothing but my nightclothes. They would never have believed that I hadn't gone there in the middle of the night for exactly what happened. I couldn't face the shame of having everyone know. So I remained silent."

"Why didn't you mention it to me sooner?" His tone was still skeptical.

"I was embarrassed and, quite frankly, when I realized you didn't remember, I was relieved. I thought the best thing I could do would be put it out of my mind and go on as though it had never happened."

A memory streaked across Steele's mind. There had been a brown smear of dried blood on his sheet the morning after the fire. At the time, he hadn't given it much thought. He had assumed it had come from his burn injury. But now that he thought about it . . .

He studied his hand, its tightly stretched new skin still pink and shiny, rather than tan and weathered like his other hand. There never had been much bleeding, he remembered. And a vague feeling of uneasiness rocked through him.

The meaning of what she had told him sent an unexpected storm of relief and happiness rippling over him. He'd been the first, after all. There had been no one else!

Damn! he cursed himself, suddenly realizing how easily he was falling into her trap again. He was actually starting to believe her.

His head jerked up, his hazel eyes drilling their accusation into hers. "Why are you telling me this now? What do you expect to gain?"

Hurt beyond understanding by the fact that Steele clearly suspected her of lying for some ulterior motive, Temerity wished she could pull back every word she'd said. She couldn't imagine why she'd told him in the first place. But it was too late for that. She had to go forward now. "Because I don't want you to think I'm a—a—" She couldn't say the word. "Because I want you to know I'm not like your—like your—like—*her*. I'd never leave—" Her breath caught in her throat, cutting off her words. Her panicked gaze darted to his eyes to see if he'd detected the unspoken *you* she'd nearly uttered. "—my baby," she quickly improvised. "And I'd never sell—"

"Sell your body?" he said, pouncing on her intended words with zeal. "But you did, Temerity. That's exactly what you came to my room to do that night, isn't it?"

213

He grabbed her by the shoulders and jerked her close to him, his fingers digging into her flesh. "Tell me: If I hadn't shown up on the *Intrepid* the next morning, who were you going to offer your little business arrangement to next?"

"No one!" she shouted, tears springing to her eyes. "I could never do that. Never!"

"Then how do you explain what happened in my room that night, Temerity?"

"That was different."

A thick brow arched suspiciously. "Oh. And how is that?"

"Because it was you. And we had already . . . you know." She tore her eyes from his accusing glare. "And because . . ."

"Because what?"

Temerity looked from left to right for an escape. "Because I couldn't . . ."

"What Temerity? What couldn't you?"

The words exploded from her mouth in an unrestrained cry. "Because it was the only way I could think of to stop you from leaving me!" She wrapped her arms around her waist and examined his face for some sign of understanding. "I didn't want to lose you!" she confessed, her voice now a low, resigned moan, as the reality of why she'd offered herself to Steele sank into her.

"So, that brings us back to the fact that there was nothing you wouldn't do for the *Intrepid*—including sleeping with me, or anyone else who could help you save your precious riverboat!"

"No!" she screamed, raising her arms suddenly and shaking herself loose from his grip. Desperation had crumbled the restraining dam on her words and she couldn't stop now. "Don't you understand? The *Intrepid* was only part of the reason I came there."

"What was the other part of the reason?" he said, his expression hard.

"You!" she shrieked. "I came because I couldn't bear the thought of never seeing you again. I needed you. Not just for the *Intrepid*. But for me. I wanted you for *me!*"

Temerity's eyes opened wide and she slapped her hands over her mouth as she stared in horror at Steele's stunned expression. "I—mean—I—uh—" she began to stammer, floundering for words that would negate the scandalous confession that still hung between them like a dense river fog.

His face unmoving, showing none of what he was thinking, Steele took a step toward her.

Not knowing what she was afraid of, Temerity turned and made a frantic dash for the door. But before she could lift the latch, Steele was there, spinning her around to face him, gathering her into his arms, his mouth coming down hard on hers, telling her with no further words how much he wanted her.

Chapter Thirteen

"Oh god, Temerity," Steele breathed against her cheek as his hands roved urgently over her back and buttocks, clutching her hard against him. "Do you know how miserable I've been since that night? Can you ever forgive me for the things I said to you?"

Temerity lolled her head to the side to make her neck more accessible to the kisses he was raining over its sensitive flesh and sighed her delight. "Mmm . . . I forgive . . . you . . ." Her fingers slid up under the loose riverman's shirt he wore, delving hungrily into the wiry mat of hair that covered his chest.

Bending his knees, Steele nestled his head against her breasts. "I've missed you!" he murmured, his words muffled as he turned his face into the warm cushion of her.

"I've missed you too, Steele. More than I can say." She clasped his head to her, stroking his hair and face with all the feeling she'd been forced to hold back during the past two weeks. Suddenly, nothing mattered but being with this man, comforting him—loving him.

Loving him?

The knowledge rocked over Temerity with bone-dissolving clarity, and she sagged against him.

Yes! She loved Steele! It was as though every fiber of her being had known from the very beginning, but had only just now managed to penetrate her brain with the truth.

"I've even missed our arguments," she confessed with a breathless laugh.

"Me, too," Steele said, straightening and backing up to sit in the cabin's lone chair. He caught her at the waist and drew her between his hard flanks. He rotated his hips gently against her and looked up the length of her. "Can you feel how much I want you?"

Temerity nodded her head and smiled. "And I want you, Steele. More than I ever believed possible."

"This time there won't be any excuses. I'm not drugged and you're not in a position where you can think it's the way to save the *Intrepid*. Our only reason for making love this time will be because it's what we both want."

Clutching his head to her breasts and burying her face in the rich luxury of his hair, Temerity answered him, her words almost a reverent vow. "Because it's what we both want."

Steele breathed a loud sigh of relief and smiled. Then there was no more conversation, no more hesitation, no more bargaining. Only instinct and mutual need remained.

Four hands moved with a common goal, discarding clothes in a frenzy until Temerity and Steele were standing naked, touching from chest to knee.

When Temerity started to move toward the bed, Steele shook his head and slid his hands down to cup the round firmness of her bottom. "The bunks squeak." Bending his knees slightly, he lifted her up, then lowered her onto his manhood with one sure thrust as he sat back in the chair. "Ah," he groaned as the warm, creamy petals of her body grabbed at and closed around his strength.

"Oh, Steele," she moaned, pressing herself down harder on him, her quivering passion desperate to consume all of him. She wound her arms around his neck, burrowing her fingers into his thick hair as her mouth opened on his.

His tongue sparring erotically with hers, he returned her kiss with equal urgency. Curving his fingers into her waist, he lifted her upward, raising her almost the entire length of his manhood, until only the swollen tip of him was inside her. Then, plunging his tongue deep into her mouth, he brought her hips down hard on his thighs to again fill her body to blessed capacity.

Gasping for air, her nails dug into the straining muscles of his shoulders. Temerity flung her head back, presenting her arched neck to him as over and over again she was lifted almost off him, then impaled on his erection with demanding force. Her thinking was totally enshrouded by passion, all concept of time and place wiped from her mind as she whimpered his name softly.

The core of her body was on fire, burning hotter and hotter with each relentless thrust into her raging center. Then the explosion came, taking Temerity beyond this sphere. Her breathing became labored, almost as though each breath might be her last; and the muscles of her femininity contracted violently against the rigid intruder in her body, squeezing and embracing its solid presence as she rode it to blind ecstasy.

His hips still undulating beneath her, more gently now, Steele lowered her back on his strong legs, then bent over her to catch the rigid peak of a breast in his mouth. He rolled the hard pebble of her nipple between his lips, which were folded in over his teeth. One hand securing her on his lap, the second molding and shaping a breast, he licked and nipped greedily at the

219

other sweet mound. Then, as though he were dying of thirst, he sucked the entire nipple and areola into his mouth.

The fire inside her, the fire that surely had burned itself out, flared again, beginning with a tiny spark, yet raging wildly through her blood to her every pore within seconds.

Continuing to suckle at her breast, Steele's fingers slid down her belly to the place where their bodies were still joined. Delving into the dewy folds of her, he caught the tip of her desire between his thumb and forefinger. Relentlessly, he stroked and teased the sensitive bud, using the lotion of her body to lubricate and fire the rigid nub to excruciating sensitivity.

Then it was happening, and Temerity was soaring on wings again. The ethereal light behind her closed eyelids brightened and expanded to another blinding explosion of every nerve and cell in her body.

His control tested to the limit, Steele kept his hand between their bodies to continue his erotic manipulations as he drew her to sit up again. This time, when he thrust himself upward into the dark, slippery glory of her body, there was no holding back. Harder and harder he plunged into her until there was no stopping.

With one final lunge, he spilled his desire inside her, to mix and dance with her fluids as again she achieved the ultimate dream she'd striven for. Her femininity clenching and jerking, it wrung him dry, before they fell against each other, their trembling bodies slick with perspiration, their hearts pounding violently and irregularly in their chests.

"Steele?"

"Mmm?" He nuzzled the curve of her neck and shoulder, taking playful nips of the sweet flesh with his teeth.

"You never told me your last name."

Steele's mouth froze on her shoulder and his chest expanded, trapping the air in it, then seeming to forget to release it. Though neither of them moved, their joined bodies separated as his manhood slipped from within her warmth. "I haven't? I was sure I had," he said with forced casualness.

She frowned her confusion, then smiled. "No, you didn't, and I should know the whole name of the man who—" She stopped talking and cocked her head at an angle, giving him a suspicious side-glance and an impish grin. "You're not trying to hide your identity from me, are you?" When he didn't answer immediately, she went on speaking, her mood too contented to notice Steele's stunned silence. "I know! I'll bet you're a member of a notorious gang of outlaws and you're on the run! That's it, isn't it?" she teased, giving his neck several enthusiastic kisses.

Steele shook his head and gave a forced smile. "It's nothing quite so interesting, I'm afraid."

"Oh?" Then a horrible thought occurred to Temerity and her happy mood plunged. She really knew nothing about Steele. He could be anyone. Could have done anything! He could even be . . . Her hands flew up to cover her gaping mouth. "Oh, my goodness! You're married, aren't you?" She pushed herself off his lap and stooped to snatch her clothes up off the floor. "How could you? How could *I?*" she muttered through heartbroken tears as she tried to untangle her clothing, her distraught actions only complicating the process.

"Temerity," Steele said, crossing to her and wrapping his arms around her waist from behind and kissing her shoulder. "I'm not married."

But the meaning of Steele's words didn't immediately infiltrate the haze of mortification that had clouded her thinking. "How could you do such a thing to me? To your wi—" Her words were cut off, as realization clapped across her mouth like a huge hand. Her gaze shot over her shoulder to meet his. "You're not?"

Steele shook his head and flashed his dimples. "Never."

"Then why?" she said, her look disbelieving.

"Because I've never met anyone I wanted to spend the rest of my life with, I suppose."

"Not that. I want to know why you haven't told me your last name, why you let me go on thinking it was Steele."

Think fast, old man, or your ass is cooked. "Cook! My name's Cook." He turned away from her and began to dress, his casual motions betraying none of the inner turmoil the lie on his lips had caused to his gut.

"Cook? Steele Cook," she said, trying the name out on her tongue. "Somehow it just doesn't fit you."

"I know it. That's why I just use Steele." He was dressed and sat down to put his boots back on. "I don't usually tell anyone it's Cook. Using just one name keeps things simpler." *Go ahead, man. Dig yourself in deeper.* "Besides, I'm told my father's name was Steele—though I don't know if it was his first or last name." *At least, that much is true.*

"So you were given your mother's last name at birth because—"

"Yeah," he said, the bitterness difficult to hide in his voice. "If you don't mind, I'd like to drop this. Quite frankly, I'm getting more than a little tired of this conversation. I am who I am. And no matter what my name is, it doesn't change what I am." He rose and walked over to the door. "Besides I've got business to take care of below." He cracked the door and turned back to her. "I'll see you later."

"Steele!"

"What?"

"I'm sorry. I didn't mean to pry or bring up bad

222

memories. It's just that I want to know everything about you because . . ."

Her expression was hurt and confused, like a happy puppy who in his enthusiasm at seeing his master had jumped on him with dirty paws—then been punished for it. Steele's heart tumbled over in his chest and guilt wedged itself like a cold fist in his belly. He raced back to her and gathered her into his arms, showering her face with little apologetic kisses. "You've got nothing to be sorry for, honey. It's me. I'm the one who's sorry. It's just that certain subjects make me—"

Temerity placed two fingers over his lips. "I know. And I promise I won't ask you about the past again, until you're ready to tell me more." She raised up on her tiptoes and placed a light kiss on his lips. "Now go on. I'll join you on the main deck in a little while."

Some mess you've gotten yourself into this time, pal, Steele berated himself a minute later as he stepped out of Temerity's cabin, the sweetness of her last kiss still warm on his lips. *I've found the woman I've searched for all my life, and I can't do anything about it because everything between us is based on my stupid deception. If only I'd told her the truth from the very beginning, maybe she would have been able to accept me, in spite of who I am. As it stands now, once she learns the truth, she'll never believe me when I tell her how I feel. She'll feel angry and betrayed. She'll think everything I did was for my own selfish motives and not out of any genuine feeling for her.*

Steele was so lost in his own miserable quandary, he didn't notice the pair of blue eyes narrowed at him from a distance as he left Temerity's cabin and strolled down the stairs to the main deck.

"So, my friend, you and Miss Temerity have decided to put your differences aside," the man at the end of the deck muttered with an angry sneer as he stepped out of the shadows. *Well, you have made a very serious misjudgment if you think your youth and rugged good looks are enough to win a woman like her. "A very serious misjudgment." She may choose to dally with your type out of curiosity, but in the end, a lady such as Temerity Kincade will choose someone like me, an older, more settled man of good breeding who can give her everything she could ever want.*

Watching Steele's back until his head disappeared below the top edge of the stairs, Charles Rawson smiled to himself as an idea occurred to him that would surely end Temerity Kincade's interest in Steele once and for all—before her temporary fascination with the man caused her to commit a mistake that couldn't be undone.

"Uriah," Temerity said idly the next day as she relieved the pilot at the wheel during an easy stretch of river so he could eat his lunch in a more leisurely fashion than usual. "What exactly do you know about Mr—" She caught herself. Somehow she couldn't manage to call him Cook yet. "About Steele's background?"

His mouth full, Uriah stopped chewing and studied her profile, her gaze intent on the muddy water in front of her. "Why do you ask, missy? Are you two still not gettin' along?"

Temerity laughed. "No, it's nothing like that. In fact, we've come to an understanding—of sorts. It's just that I sense he's troubled by his past."

"Did you ask him about it?"

"He doesn't want to talk about it."

"Then I suggest you drop it, missy. A wise woman doesn't go behind her man's back tryin' to find out his secrets."

Stunned by Uriah's choice of words, Temerity jerked her head around to face the grinning man, who was once again chewing a mouthful of food. "Why would you imply that he's *my* man?" she asked indignantly. "And I certainly had no intention of 'going behind his back.' I just thought I might be able to help him if I knew the whole story."

"Well, I reckon any troubles that boy's got he's gonna have to work out for hisself, missy. And one of these days when he's got'em all figgered out, he'll probably tell you everythin' you're wantin' to know about him." Uriah's eyes suddenly sparkled with a teasing glance. "I mean if he *was* your man, of course. In the meantime, all you can do is just give that young feller time, and be there to listen when he's ready to talk."

Uriah went back to his lunch and a copy of the *Press and Dakotian* newspaper he'd picked up in Yankton the day before. "Says here the Senate didn't get the two-thirds vote it needed to impeach Andrew Johnson. If you ask me, it's disgraceful they even tried it. Their trumped-up charges against him were so weak it's a wonder they got as far as they did with them."

Temerity grinned at the old man's not-too-subtle change of subject and nodded. "All right, Uriah, I've been properly put in my place. We won't talk about Steele anymore."

Steele dipped a pan of murky water from the river and set it down on the sandy bank. Opening his shaving kit, he took out a mirror, razor, and razor strop, which he lay on a towel beside the water pan. He'd just never gotten the knack of shaving on the riverboat, even when it was docked, so in spite of the fact that he had his own cabin now—one vacated by the Fishers when

225

they'd "deserted ship" in Portland—he still preferred to take care of that aspect of his grooming with solid ground beneath his feet.

Enjoying the moment of privacy, he stirred his shaving soap to creamy whiteness, then lathered it generously over his suntanned cheeks and chin and neck with his shaving brush.

He was in a good mood and was looking forward to the evening. Since Yankton had been the last of the real towns they would be docking in for quite some time— from here on out they would be spending most nights at small river crossings, woodyards, Indian agencies, army forts, or more often than not just along the bank as they were tonight—all the passengers would be staying on board at night from now on.

To take the passengers' minds off the fact that they had left the last signs of civilization behind—and had now entered Indian country to boot—Temerity had arranged a dance and early evening picnic for that night. He smiled at the thought. If that wasn't just like her. Here they were in the middle of nowhere and she had all the passengers and crew sprucing up for a party with as much excitement as they would have felt if they'd been preparing for the biggest social event in St. Louis. There was just something about Temerity Kincade that created beauty and good feelings wherever she went.

Look at the crew. Three weeks earlier, they'd been talking about leaving, and now they fought with each other to carry out her requests. In more than one situation, they'd seen the difference her quick thinking and hard work had made, and their respect had grown daily. By never failing to notice and compliment the smallest bit of extra effort, she'd actually given them pride in their work—something unheard of in the roustabouts that worked the Missouri River, where the

226

usual way to control a crew was with a whip. In fact, because of their growing loyalty to Temerity, the crew of the *Intrepid* was a relatively sober, clean-talking—at least cleaner than any Steele had ever seen—hardworking bunch of men Steele would have matched against any crew on the river.

She's the kind of woman a man could spend a lifetime with and never grow tired of. She would be everything to the man she married: a partner, a friend, and a lover. "But not yours, Steele," he said aloud. *Not when she finds out how you've deceived her. She won't come near you with a ten-foot pole once that happens!*

It was in that instant that Steele realized he wanted more from Temerity than just her forgiveness and understanding. He wanted her for his wife! He wanted to spend the rest of his life with her, have children with her.

Taking a last angry swipe at his cheek with the razor, as though to remove the forbidden thought he'd just had, he nicked his skin. "Damn!" He tossed the razor down and pressed a handkerchief to the cut that was already streaming blood down his freshly shaved face.

I'm just not going to think about that until the time comes, he told himself, lifting the handkerchief from the cut and peeking in the mirror to see if the bleeding had stopped. Another rivulet of red trickled down his cheek. He put the handkerchief back. *Maybe by the time we get back to St. Louis, I can have her so dependent on me that she'll at least listen when I explain why I did it.*

An idea that would solve everything popped into his head. *If she were pregnant she'd have to marry me, no matter who I am. And sooner or later she'd have to forgive me if we were married!*

Steele chuckled at the idea. How many times had he heard of a man being trapped into marriage by a female who was pregnant. *Turn about's fair play,* he told himself. *But only as a last resort. But one way or another, sweet Temerity, you're going to be mine.*

His bleeding stopped and his hopes fortified with the confidence there was a way to get out of the mess he'd created for himself—and have Temerity—Steele bundled up his gear and raced back to the riverboat, where preparations were already under way for the festivities the enterprising Temerity Kincade had arranged.

To be lit after dark by gaily colored Chinese lanterns strung from the bottom edge of the boiler deck, the main deck had been cleared of a great deal of its cargo, most of which had been stacked on the riverbank, to make room for the dancing.

Everywhere Steele looked, there were people dressed in what appeared to be their Sunday clothes, talking and laughing excitedly. On the bank, Gus, the cook, was overseeing the turning of the several spits required to roast the ducks and jackrabbits the hunters had shot that day. Already the fragrance of the expertly seasoned meat was wafting through the air.

"What do you think?" a soft voice asked beside him, setting Steele's heart thudding in his chest like a schoolboy's.

He grinned and turned toward Temerity, resting his hip against the white wooden rail. The first thing he noticed was that she was wearing her hair down, letting it curl past her shoulders in a black cascade of shiny satin and tied back from her face with a simple pink ribbon. Her dress was the same pink as the tie in her hair, its bodice becomingly low, its skirt stylishly full, nothing like the starched and tailored skirts and blouses she usually wore while performing her duties on the *Intrepid.*

He ached to take her in his arms and kiss her, but he knew her strong sense of right and wrong would be

228

offended by such a public display of affection, so he just gazed down at her with what he was sure was the look of a silly, lovesick puppy. He ran his thumb and forefinger down his mustache from below his nose to his lip. But it was no use. He couldn't wipe the happiness off his face—not that he had any desire to. "Everything's beautiful. In fact, it's the second most beautiful thing I've ever seen in my life."

Temerity's eyes jerked upward, their blueness sparkling playfully. "The *second* most beautiful?" she said, arching her eyebrows in mock indignation. "And what, pray tell, kind sir, could you possibly have ever seen in all your travels that could match, much less surpass, all this splendor?" She spread both her arms to include the main deck and the grassy, treeless riverbank, where brightly dressed people were milling about and conversing gaily.

"Why, you, Miss Kincade!" Steele took her hand and bent in a dramatically gallant bow to kiss it. "You are the most beautiful sight my eyes have ever seen," he said, looking up from her hand as he spoke, then turning her hand over in his and brushing his lips and mustache across the center of her palm before straightening up.

"Steele! What will people think?" Temerity asked, reflexively pulling her hand free and holding it to the exposed creamy flesh above the ruffled edge of her bodice. She was more thrilled by the intimate kiss on the inside of her hand and his compliment than she was worried about who might have seen it occur.

"They'll think I'm the most intelligent man on this riverboat because I'm courting the most beautiful woman here."

Temerity looked up the length of him, searching for some sign he was teasing her. His hair, still damp from his bath, curled casually over his head, as though he'd combed it with his fingers, and the pleasant smell of bay rum rose from his skin and the clean white shirt he had donned for the party. And Temerity was certain she'd never seen anything or anyone as perfect as this man. "And are you?" she said, her voice nearly a whisper.

"What? The most intelligent? Probably." His eyes sparkled with a mischievous gleam, his dimples deepening impishly.

"Courting me." Her chest rose and fell rapidly as she waited for his answer, for though Temerity had been raised on riverboats and around men all her life—except for the years at Lindenwood College for Women—no one had ever courted her.

Steele's expression grew serious and intent, and he took both her unresisting hands in his. "That I am, Miss Kincade. I am most definitely courting you—that is, if it's agreeable with you."

Her heart pounding so hard in her chest that it drowned out all the sounds of the activity around them, she used every shred of strength she could muster not to give in to the impulse to throw her arms around Steele's neck and shout for all the world to hear that it was more than agreeable. What it was, was wonderful! Glorious! The answer to a dream! The man she loved and was determined to marry was courting her!

"I believe that will be quite agreeable, sir," she said, the pleased grin on her lips completely destroying the degree of casual sophistication she was striving for.

Smiling his jubilant relief, he tucked her arm in his and started for the gangway. "Then let's go, my lady!"

Several hours later, after the sun had gone down, when the passengers and crew had eaten their fill of the delicious food, and the fiddle players had played every number they knew at least twice, Temerity flopped down on a bale of hay, all worries gone from her expression. She'd danced every dance—not all with Steele, as she would have liked—and was exhausted. She was sure she had danced with every male passenger, young or old, and with almost every member of the crew, and now all she could think of was resting her feet for a few minutes. It had been a wonderful evening. Even now, when most people had gone to bed for the night, a few couples were still dancing, determined to hold on to the enchanted night for as long as possible.

Using the toe of one slipper behind the heel of the other, she slipped her shoes off and wiggled her toes happily, sighing contentedly. She glanced around, hoping Steele would see her and come join her for a few quiet moments before the party was completely over. He was nowhere in sight. Sitting up straighter, she squinted against the night, thinking he might still be on the dance floor. He, like she, had been in great demand as a dance partner, and every female on board, from giggling teenager to clucking matron, had insisted on having him ask her to dance. But he wasn't among the dancers.

Scolding herself for the silly frisson of concern trickling through her veins, Temerity stood up and raked her gaze over the bank where the cargo was stacked. She studied the outlines of each of the guards protecting the cargo, quickly determining that Steele was not among them.

"What's this?" a familiar voice asked from behind her. "Is it possible the lovely Miss Kincade has run out of dance partners?"

"Hello, Mr. Rawson," Temerity said, taking one last look at the torch-lit bank as she turned to greet the passenger. "I'm afraid my feet gave out before the fiddlers did." She looked down at her bare toes peeking from under the hem of her dress.

"Surely you're not going to deny me the pleasure of one last dance with you," he said, stepping close to her and taking her in his arms before she could stop him.

"Really, Mr. Rawson, I just don't think I can dance another step. Please forgive me." She had her hands on his chest and tried to give him a little push, but Rawson hesitated longer than necessary before dropping his hands from her waist.

"Would you be too tired to dance if it were Steele asking you?" he said, with a knowing gleam in his eyes. "Tell me, where is your beau?"

Thinking Rawson was just teasing her, the way Uriah had more than once that evening, Temerity smiled and stepped back, the man's closeness making her uneasy. "He's not my 'beau,' Mr. Rawson, and I don't know where he is. Probably attending to some necessary work."

"Don't you think it's time you stopped calling me Mr. Rawson, and started calling me Charles?" he said, stepping closer to Temerity and backing her up against the hay bale. One more step and she'd fall back over it.

She looked from left to right nervously. Where were all the people who'd been watching her every move all evening when she needed them? "I think it's best to keep our relationship on a more formal footing . . ."

Without warning, Charles took another step and grabbed Temerity by the tops of her arms and pulled her against him, closing off her shocked squeal with his mouth on hers. But before she could free herself, a girl's voice called to her.

"Oh, Miss Kincade, I'm so glad I found you."

Temerity broke out of Charles Rawson's hold, and glaring at him from the corner of her eye, she answered the girl she knew was Mary Rigby. She was the younger of two sisters who were supposedly going up the Missouri to Fort Randall to visit an uncle. But because of things Temerity had heard about the reasons the two had left the last town they'd lived in, she had her suspicions about the real reasons they were going to Fort Randall. But who was she to judge anyone else? "What is it, Miss Rigby?" she said, sidestepping out from between Rawson's blocking frame and the hay bale.

"It's my sister! I can't find her anywhere! I'm afraid something's happened to her."

"I'm sure she's here somewhere. Where did you see her last?" Temerity put an arm around the smaller girl's shoulders and walked her away from Rawson.

"Well, let me see. It was when . . . Oh, I remember. She had just finished dancing with Mr. Steele, when I heard him tell her he had something down in the hold to show her. Yes, I'm sure that's the last time I saw her . . . when they went down the stairs together."

Chapter Fourteen

"All right, Miss Rigby," Steele said to the small blonde who'd insisted he accompany her into the hold. "Where's this supposed clue to solving Yeager's murder you say you found while rummaging through your trunks for your party clothes?" He didn't bother to hide his annoyance at being called away from the dance. After all, he'd gone over the hold a dozen times in the weeks since the murder. It hardly seemed likely any new evidence would turn up now. Besides, the murderer was no doubt long gone after this much time. Since there had been no further occurrences, Steele was convinced that whoever had killed Yeager was gone. And he had decided the murder was a mere coincidence and had nothing to do with either the Cameron Line or the Kincades.

"Mmm," Rosalie Rigby said, squinting her eyes and circling in place. "I'm all turned around now. Everything looks different at night. Can you hold your lantern a little higher? Oh, there they are!" She hurried to her trunks and pointed to the narrow space between them that had been created when the trunk had been pulled out for her. "It's in there. A handkerchief with dried blood on it."

Steele raised the lantern to see better. "It looks like a handkerchief all right." Placing the lantern on top of the trunk, he stooped to retrieve the handkerchief from the crack. "And I've no doubt this is dried blood on it. Still, there's really no reason to believe it belonged to the murderer. Anyone could have left it down here."

A strong sense of foreboding swept over Steele. Something felt wrong. He looked more closely at the handkerchief. Except for the bloodstains, the handkerchief was snowy clean—entirely too clean to have been on the dirty floor of the hold for several weeks. For further confirmation of his theory, he held the handkerchief to his nose and breathed in. Just as he expected, the smell was not the least bit musty—as it would have been if it had been down here for three weeks.

"Look, it's got initials on it!" the girl said excitedly, lifting a corner that hung off the edge of Steele's hand. "What do they say?"

"Let me see," Steele said, only mildly curious. He'd already decided this had nothing to do with the murder. "S . . ." *Hell! This is my handkerchief!* he realized as his eyes focused on the second initial. "C," he said with resignation.

Without warning, Rosalie Rigby suddenly flew toward him, flinging her arms around his neck and pressing her voluptuous body to his. "I'm so glad you're here. It's so frightening to think the murderer may still be on the boat," she said—just as he heard voices on the stairs.

Illuminated by the lantern on the trunk, the tableau that greeted Temerity's eyes was more horrible than any she could have imagined. The warm feeling of happiness that had kept her glowing all day turned cold and ugly.

"Temerity," Steele stammered, peeling Rosalie's

arms and body from his. "Let me explain."

"You see, Miss Rigby?" Temerity said, her voice higher than usual and artificially cheerful as she turned to the younger Rigby sister with a forced smile. "I told you there was nothing to worry about. Your sister was in good hands all along. Now, if you will excuse me, I believe I'll retire for the evening."

Her posture rigid, her head high and her mouth set in a grim line of determination, Temerity wheeled around and started back up the stairs to the main deck.

"Allow me," Charles Rawson said, jumping to attention and taking her arm in his, but not before he took a moment to shoot Steele a triumphant smirk. Then he turned back to Temerity, his voice oozing with conciliation and sympathy. "This has obviously been a great shock to you, my dear." His expression and tone were the epitome of fatherly concern.

"Thank you, Mr. Rawson," she said, not forgetting the incident on the main deck, but unable to cope with that now. At the moment, she just wanted to get away from Steele before she disgraced herself further by betraying how hurt she'd been by his actions. The only thing she could concentrate on now was getting back on deck before she became ill. And she wasn't certain her own legs would hold her up that long, so she accepted Rawson's arm.

The realization that Steele had been toying with her the entire time cut into her with sharp, jabbing agony. He hadn't meant a word he'd said. He'd led her to believe there was something special between them. But the whole thing had been nothing but a game to him, a cruel, vicious game. How many other women had he seduced with his charms? Probably dozens. How he must be laughing at her little girl naïveté right now. To think she'd actually been stupid enough to picture herself in love with him! Even married to him!

237

I suppose I should be thankful I didn't make an even bigger fool of myself by telling him how I felt! Unfortunately, that one small saving grace did nothing to relieve the ache in Temerity's heart, in her soul.

"... on the magic of the moonlight and your beauty," Charles Rawson said.

Temerity looked at the speaker, her expression confused and embarrassed. She realized she was outside her cabin door and that Rawson had been talking to her for several minutes. "I—I'm sorry, Mr. Rawson. I didn't hear what you were saying."

"I was apologizing for my actions earlier. I was simply overcome by the romance of the evening and your startling beauty. I never should have presumed—"

"Yes, well, your apology is accepted, Mr. Rawson. We all occasionally do things we realize later were mistakes. I'm certain it won't happen again. Now, if you will excuse me, I seem to have developed a terrible headache. Good night." She opened her cabin door and stepped inside, literally slamming the door in Rawson's face.

That is the last time you will close a door on me, my girl. I'll give you a few hours to get over the loss of your deckhand Romeo. Then I will teach you who you belong to. Rawson spun on his heel and made his way down the deck to his cabin on the opposite side of the boat. *At least I know she won't be inviting Steele back in her cabin again.* Rawson opened the door to his own cabin and stepped inside.

"How did we do, honey?" a sultry voice asked from his bunk.

"When do we get paid?" a second, slightly higher voice, joined in from the chair.

Rawson looked from sister to sister and chuckled. "You did very well, ladies. I'm very pleased with the results of our efforts. And believe me, you'll receive your money in due time—" He reached up and yanked off his tie and began to unbutton his shirt. "—in due time. But first I have another urgent matter for you lovely ladies to attend to." He dropped his trousers, exposing his manhood, hanging limp and small between his legs. "For an additional bonus, of course."

"Anything you say, sugar," Rosalie chuckled throatily, falling to her knees and reaching for his flaccid member. "You're the boss."

Temerity sat on the floor of her dark cabin, her back against the door, where she'd been since Charles Rawson had left her. Her elbows propped on her bent knees, she buried her fingers in her hair and rested her forehead on the heels of her hands. She really did have a headache. If she could just gather the strength to get up and go to her medicine box for some powders . . . But it was too much trouble to get up. So she continued to sit there, punishing herself by reliving every stupid thing she'd done from the moment she'd met Steele. How could she have been such a fool?

There was a soft knock on the door. "Temerity, let me in. I've got to talk to you," a deep voice whispered against the door.

"Go away, Steele. You and I have nothing to say to each other." She rose laboriously to her feet and stumbled across the room.

The door rattled, and she realized he was trying the lock. "Dammit, Temerity, let me in!"

"I said go away!"

"If you don't open this door, I'm coming through it," he hissed, his voice a bit louder. "And there won't be anyone on board who won't know I'm in your cabin *or* hear what I've got to say."

Torn between hanging on to the fragment of pride she could perhaps retain if she denied him, and saving what little of her reputation she might manage to salvage by keeping what had happened between them a secret, Temerity went back to the door. "Please, go away, Steele. There's nothing more to say."

"I've got more to say, lady, plenty more. And if you don't open the damned door, I'm going to shout it for everyone on this goddamn boat to hear!"

Hating herself for not being strong enough to tell him she didn't care if he told the whole world, Temerity clicked the bolt out of the lock and turned her back to the door. The last remnant of her dignity brought to its knees, she crossed to the chair and sat down to wait.

Steele entered the cabin and sank back against the door, giving his eyes a chance to accustom themselves to the darkness. "I'm sorry I had to threaten you," he said.

"It's a little late for apologies now, don't you think, Steele?"

Icy fingers of sorrow and regret clutched at Steele's belly. "Yeah, I guess so."

"Go on and say what you came for. Then leave."

"Temerity, what you saw in the hold was obviously staged for your benefit. Someone went to a lot of trouble to have you see me with that girl. We were set up!"

"Set up, Steele?" She snorted bitterly. "Don't make me laugh. You were simply exposed for the rogue you are, and now you're trying to wriggle your way out of it. You needn't have bothered, though. Your job is secure. I've already learned what would happen if I were to fire you. And no matter what you do, I won't let you ruin the *Intrepid*'s chances of success. But I must remember to thank the Rigby sisters for enlightening me to your true character and showing me what a fool I've been."

"While you're thanking them, be sure to include your friend Rawson. I'd be willing to bet he's behind this."

"That's right, try to cast the blame on someone else. That's exactly what I would expect from a womanizing scoundrel like you!"

Steele hunkered down in front of her and grabbed her shoulders. "Temerity, shut up and listen. That girl told me she'd found a clue to Yeager's murder. That's the *only* reason I went down there with her. Don't you know I never would have left with her otherwise?"

"But while you were there, you found your lusts too strong to ignore. I don't blame you, Steele. She's a lovely young woman."

"Temerity, she's trash. Can't you see what kind of woman she is? Do you really think I'd have anything to do with someone like her after being with—"

Temerity lifted her eyebrows and cast him a disbelieving glare but said nothing.

"I began to suspect something wasn't right when I found the 'clue' she led me to. It was a bloody handkerchief stuffed into a crack between her trunks."

Temerity opened her mouth to speak, but Steele went on talking.

"But that handkerchief was no clue to the murderer. It was planted there to point a finger of suspicion at me."

"Now you're being ridiculous. Even if what you say is true, why would a bloody handkerchief point suspicion at you?"

"Because it was mine, dammit!" He yanked the stained handkerchief from his pants pocket and tossed it into her lap, then turned to light a lamp. "Look! It has my monogram on it!"

Temerity examined the neatly embroidered "S.C." on the handkerchief. A horrifying thought popped unbidden into her mind.

What did she really know about Steele? He could easily be the murderer. After all, he'd been seen talking—no *arguing*—with Harold Yeager the night before the body had been found in the hold. And now this handkerchief. It was not too difficult to imagine what might have happened. Steele could have killed Yeager, then used the handkerchief to wipe the blood off his knife or hands afterward. Then to make certain no one found it on his person or with his things, he could have stuffed the handkerchief where he didn't think anyone would see it until the *Intrepid* was unloaded. And, of course, by the time it was found, it would mean nothing to the finder—especially if no one had discovered Steele's true last name! If everyone had continued to believe it was Steele—with the *S* his second initial, rather than the first—no one would ever have connected him with the bloody handkerchief.

Temerity crushed the handkerchief in her fist and raised her stunned gaze to Steele.

Steele had seen the flash of suspicion that had crossed Temerity's face, and hurt twisted his features, to mingle with the anger and frustration already there.

"I know what you're thinking, Temerity, and I guess I can't blame you." He didn't bother to disguise the feeling of betrayal her doubts had caused him. "But it's not true. I had that handkerchief in my pocket the day we left St. Louis. The new ones I bought in St. Charles didn't have my initials on them, so it was the only monogrammed one I had with me—and I had it this afternoon. I used it to stop the bleeding where I cut myself shaving. Someone must have come into my cabin and taken it, then deliberately put it there for Rosalie Rigby to find so she could incriminate me."

"Or it could have been in the hold since the night of Mr. Yeager's death, and you're worried that I'm the only one who knows those are your initials," Temerity said quietly.

Now that she'd spoken the words aloud, the idea sounded outlandish and ridiculous, even to her own ears. Stunned, she suddenly realized with shocking clarity that no matter what logic, circumstantial evidence, or her own wounded ego were trying to make her believe, it couldn't be true. She knew with all her instinct that Steele was not a murderer—and something deep in her core told her he was not a liar either.

"That's what someone went to a lot of trouble to make you think. But smell that handkerchief, Temerity," he ordered, lifting her balled fist still clinging to the handkerchief to her nose. "Does that smell like a piece of material that's spent the last three weeks in the hold?"

The familiar scent of Steele's bay rum and shaving soap filled her nostrils. "No, it doesn't," she admitted. "But why was it down there? Who could have put it there? Why would someone be trying to make you look guilty? Do you think it's the murderer?"

Steele heaved a sigh of relief. She believed him. Or at least she was now willing to listen to him. "It could be the murderer—if he's still on the *Intrepid,* which I really doubt. No, I think it was someone who's jealous of the time you spend with me. Say someone who wants you for himself. Someone like Rawson. After all, our feelings for each other weren't exactly a secret at the dance. And you only danced with him twice, while you and I . . ."

The fact that Steele had kept count of the number of times she danced with other men sent a warm rush of love flooding through her. "You're being silly. Mr. Rawson's not interested in me in that way," she said, for some indefinable reason not wanting Steele to know about the stolen kiss. "Why, he's at least my father's age. He only likes me as a friend and someone

243

to talk to."

Steele clutched her hands to his chest and impaled her gaze with a knowing glare. "Are you sure?"

The memory of Charles Rawson's surprising kiss that evening flickered across her mind, and she averted her gaze away from Steele's penetrating glare for an instant, just the barest instant. But it was long enough to tell Steele the answer to his question.

"I knew it! That bastard! What did he do? So help me, if he—"

"Nothing!" she lied, frightened by the violence she saw in Steele's expression and heard in his voice. "Mr. Rawson did nothing. I think you're judging him all wrong."

"Well, I think I'll have a little talk with the Rigby sisters tomorrow anyway. I'm going to know who hired them to set me up before they leave this riverboat at Fort Randall tomorrow night. And my money's still riding on Rawson."

"And I'm sure it's someone else. What if for some reason Mr. Yeager's murderer thinks we've gotten too close to discovering his identity—even though we aren't aware of it—and he decided to divert our attention?"

"I guess that's possible," Steele conceded. "But you do believe that girl tricked me, don't you? You do know I'd never have anything to do with someone like her. Especially not since you and I—"

"I believe the handkerchief was a trick but . . ." She looked down at the floor, unable to forget the scene in the hold. "You *were* holding her in your arms, Steele."

"I wasn't! She threw her arms around me the same time we heard you on the stairs. It was part of the act. You've got to believe that!"

The right side of Temerity's mouth turned upward in a weak smile. "I suppose I do. But I'm warning you,

Steele—" She held up a finger and pointed it at him. "—if I ever find out you've lied to me, I'll never forgive you for as long as I live."

Steele exhaled a sigh of relief and leaned his forehead against hers. "You won't be sorry you trusted me on this, Temerity. I swear it. And when we get back to St. Louis, there are some things I want to—well, we'll talk about that when all this other stuff is cleared up. But for now, you just remember, you're mine, and I won't ever willingly give you up or hurt you."

Temerity wrapped her arms around his back and kissed his mouth. "I'm sorry I doubted you. It just looked so—"

"Shh, I know," he whispered, kissing her forehead and backing away from her embrace. "Now you go to bed and get some rest. It's been a big day, and tomorrow will be here in a few hours—in fact, it's already here. I'm going to go check on the guards, then I'll sleep too."

"But—"

He kissed the end of her nose and crossed to the door. "No buts. We both need our rest, and if I stay here any longer, we're not going to get any. I'll see you in the morning."

The *Intrepid* had been out for only about thirty minutes the following morning when Temerity, working on the ledgers in her cabin, heard a grating sound that she recognized from years on the river. The *Intrepid* had run aground on a sandbar! "Damn," she mumbled, glancing at her lapel watch and hurrying to determine the seriousness of the situation. She knew they'd been lucky so far. After all, this was the first sandbar that had slowed them down. But any sort of delay could prove disastrous, even those to be expected, like the constantly shifting sandbars that made travel on the shallow Missouri River so unpredictable.

The roar of the engines grew louder, and it became obvious to her that Uriah had yelled down the speaking tube from the pilothouse to the engineer on the main deck and ordered more pressure in the boiler. He was going to try to use the extra power to carry the *Intrepid* across the sandbar.

However, from her position on the bow of the boiler deck, Temerity quickly saw that they were not going to make it. Perhaps if they had been lighter . . . As it was, the *Intrepid* was carrying too much cargo and needed at least three feet of draft. The water over the sandbar was no more than eighteen inches at its deepest, and even less in some places.

Temerity knew steamboat engineers had no way of determining the amount of pressure in their boiler engines, using only instinct and their ears to estimate an engine's limits. So in times like this, they just ordered more fuel into the fireboxes and listened astutely to the vibrating engine, to determine how much more strain the engine could take—before it blew up.

Temerity cocked her own experienced ear to listen to the cannonading sound of the engine as its intensity grew, in relation, she knew, to the mounting pressure inside the boiler. "Oh, lord! He's crazy! He's going to keep trying!" she choked, taking the stairs to the hurricane deck two at a time, praying she could get to Uriah before he blew them up.

As she topped the last stair, the intense roar of the engine suddenly slowed, and Temerity heard the welcome hiss of escaping steam as the safety valves were finally released to relieve the mounting pressure. Feeling ashamed of herself for doubting the experienced pilot, she realized she should have trusted Uriah's senses. With an apologetic glance at the pilothouse, though Uriah didn't see her, she spun around and hurried down to the main deck to be certain the sparring operation was getting underway.

Also called *grasshoppering,* sparring was a process of literally *walking* a riverboat over sandbars with strong wooden poles—spars—lowered at a forty-five-degree angle into the water to be used like huge crutches to move the boat over a sandbar and into deeper water. The process was then repeated over and over until the boat floated free again—and would no doubt be used many times before the journey to Fort Benton and back to St. Louis was complete.

Temerity watched with anxious admiration as the *Intrepid*'s crew worked together to bring the boat across the sandbar with the use of a steam capstan and the sparring poles. The bow had just cleared the shallowest point in the bar, when the boat suddenly stopped its forward momentum. Several men, including Steele, immediately leaped over the rails of the riverboat into the muddy water, grabbing strong guide ropes to lend their muscle power to that of the capstan and spars in the fight against the current and the sandbar.

At first, the boat refused to move forward, but then slowly it surrendered to the combination of straining muscles and the grasshopper poles and glided the rest of the way over the sandbar with ease.

A cheer rose from the spectators and the crew members on deck and in the water, as the sternwheeler freed itself. Then there was a mad scramble of activity as the capstan ropes were rewound, the sturdy spars were put back in place, to be used again in the not-too-distant future, and the men in the water climbed back onto the boat. The sound of the engines increased and

Uriah offered his congratulations on a job well done with two long pulls on his whistle, its shrill sound audible for several miles in every direction.

His tanned cheeks dimpling smugly, Steele joined Temerity at the bow, directing a saucy salute up to Uriah in the pilothouse. Resting his buttocks against the rail, he stretched his long legs out in front of him, crossing them at the ankles as he folded his arms across his chest. "Not bad for a crew of last-minute recruits, huh?" he said to her, the pride evident in his cheerful tone.

"Better than 'not bad.' You worked together perfectly. If I didn't know better, I'd say you'd been together for years rather than weeks. I was afraid we'd have to double-trip." Double tripping was the process of unloading half the cargo and passengers to lighten the boat, then unloading the second half on the other side of the sandbar, then returning for the first half. "We would have lost several hours that way. As it is, we didn't lose more than one."

"This time!" Steele added wisely, bending over to remove a wet boot. Emptying muddy water out of the boot onto the deck, he laughed. "As we get closer to Fort Benton, we probably won't be so lucky."

"Where did you learn about riverboats, Steele? I thought you didn't know much about them, but you seem to know a great deal."

Startled by her question, Steele glanced up at her, then busied himself with wringing the water from his pant legs. "Let's just say, I'm a quick study."

"Steele—"

He straightened and smiled apologetically. "That's another one of those things that had better wait until St. Louis. Be patient with me, Temerity. I'll answer all your questions soon. In the meantime, you'll just have to trust me."

Before she could answer, Uriah's whistle sounded the alarm with three long pulls on his whistle, and further conversation was impossible.

"What the hell?" Steele asked, tugging a wet boot on his foot and wheeling around to determine what the problem was.

"Indians!" a man's voice warned.

"We're being attacked!" another added.

"Oh, Lord, we're going to all be killed!" a woman cried.

Temerity glanced out to see a line of about thirty mounted Sioux Indians, angling into the river from both banks. Though their bows were in readiness, they wore no war paint and were waving a flag indicating they wanted to parley.

"Don't shoot!" Temerity shouted, more frightened by the viciousness she saw in the faces of the men on board as they scurried to bring their rifles and handguns into play, than she was of the Indians. "They want to talk! Stop the boat, Uriah!" she ordered, already waving her agreement to the Indians. "Don't anyone shoot!" she repeated.

There was a moment of silence and hesitation as the crowd behind her seemed to freeze at her command. Then Temerity became aware of the low murmur of curiosity and differing opinions as it hummed through the uneasy passengers of the riverboat.

But no firearms came into view. Evidently, they were going to give Temerity the benefit of the doubt. *For a few minutes, anyway!* she told herself, fully aware that behind her, every man on the deck had fingers perched in readiness on a revolver handle or clenched tightly around a rifle butt. All it would take to start a full battle would be to have one hotheaded "redskin hater" fire a shot, or to have one Indian raise a hand with a bow in it—even if his intent was nothing more than to scratch

249

his nose!

Now I know what they mean when they say "between a rock and a hard place"! she said to herself, stepping onto a bale of hay and waving to the Indians.

"What are you doing?" Steele said, reaching out to stop her.

"Smile and wave, Steele!" she hissed out of the corner of her smiling mouth. "No time to explain. This is one time you have to do the trusting!"

"Leaping Bear!" she called out, her wide, friendly grin showing none of the fear she was feeling as she began to sign her words. "It's good to see you again."

Chapter Fifteen

"Are you sure you know what you're doing?" Steele asked as he helped Temerity into the waiting yawl that had been lowered into the water to transport them to the river bank. "I'd feel better if you stayed on the *Intrepid* and let—"

"Don't you trust me, Steele?" she asked, her eyebrows arched in mock surprise. She'd made no secret of the fact that she was taking great pleasure in tossing his frequently said words back in his face. "I'm crushed."

His uneasiness growing with every second, Steele was not aware of the low, frustrated growl that issued from his throat. "It's not that I don't trust you, Temerity. It's just that these Indians usually have all kinds of tricks up their sleeves and . . . Hell! I shouldn't have let you come."

"*Let* me come? Aren't you getting things a little mixed—" The discordant melody of their old argument sounded loud and ugly in her ears. Now was definitely not the time for anything so petty. She stopped herself in midsentence and studied Steele. He had a right to be nervous. After all, the Indians who stopped the riverboats usually did so to burn and kill the noisy invaders of their river, rarely to invite them to tea. Besides, if she were honest, she had to admit she rather liked the way he was so protective of her. "I'm sorry—I know you're only worrying about me and the people on the *Intrepid*."

"Then go back. Let me and Uriah talk to them!"

"I can't, Steele. How would it look if the daughter of Leaping Bear's old friend, Tim Kincade, refused his invitation? It would be an insult. Then we *would* have something to be afraid of! Besides, it would never do to have him think I was afraid."

"But you're a woman! Women aren't expected to—"

Temerity shot Steele a humoring glare that said she could hardly be unaware of that fact since he insisted on reminding her of it with such frequency. But all she said was, "The Sioux respect bravery wherever it's displayed. And—" Suddenly touched by his concern, she smiled and reached out to wipe away the frown lines between his eyebrows. "—they can sense fear. Now take that scowl off your face and let's go see what my father's old friends want to talk about!"

I'll be damned! She's actually looking forward to this! Why me, Lord? Why couldn't I fall for a helpless little female who gets vapors at the mention of an Indian, much less at the sight of one? One who not only would let the man make all the decisions, but would actually prefer it that way! Steele's mouth spread in a stiff grin that showed clenched white teeth and no pleasure whatsoever.

Temerity laughed aloud at the strained smile on his handsome face. "Come on, Steele, you can do better than that. You look like you've got a bellyache!"

Steele did his best to scowl at her again. But he couldn't dredge up even the weakest glower, much less work up his dwindling anger again. She wasn't one of those other women—and damned if he wasn't glad of

252

it. Damned if he wasn't glad Temerity Kincade was just exactly as she was: impulsive, overconfident, audacious, stubborn . . . and bossy. *Well, four out of five's not too bad.* A rumble of deep laughter exploded from his mouth as it split into a genuine, dimple-flashing grin.

"You're really enjoying this, aren't you?" he accused, the knowing sparkle in his eyes washing away the cloudy concern that had been there.

"I find that if I think of every obstacle as a new adventure and challenge instead of with dread, it makes doing what I have to do a little easier."

"You're pretty smart, aren't you?" Steele said, aware that his own worries had eased greatly. "How'd you get so wise?"

Embarrassed by the unexpected compliment, Temerity coughed self-consciously. "'Wise' may be overstating it. I'd call what I am 'practical.' I'm just practical. Everyday, we have to face obstacles we don't particularly want to face and problems we may not be able to overcome. But worrying and fretting about what *could* happen, before it happens, doesn't change anything. It usually just builds things all out of proportion in our imaginations—and wastes a lot of energy. Besides, in the end, worrying about it never made a problem go away. Sooner or later we still have to face it. And nine times out of ten it's never as bad as we expected it to be." She smiled and shrugged her shoulders in embarrassment. She hadn't meant to get so philosophical. Well, there wasn't time to *worry* about that—or the fact that men weren't supposed to like smart women. Right now, she had more important things to think of.

Temerity was relieved when the grating sound of sand on the bottom of the yawl as it ran up on the bank ended their conversation. "And speaking of adventure . . ." Taking a deep breath, she stood up.

"Leaping Bear!" she said, extending her hand and showing no concern that her boots had gotten wet.

"Who is this grown-up woman?" a tall, bronzed warrior called out in very good English as he stepped forward and took Temerity's offered hand. "Surely she cannot be the child I remember as the daughter of Tim Kincade!"

"It *has* been a long time, hasn't it, Leaping Bear? I have changed, but you have not. I am no longer a small girl, but you are the same. The years have been good to you."

A shadow of sadness passed over the chief's weathered face. "It is about that we wished to speak to your father, Little River Flower. Kincade has always been our friend and we know he will not lie to us as the agents and soldiers and other white men do. He will tell us the truth."

"My father will be sorry when he hears he missed you, but he is very ill right now. So I will speak for him, as will my first mate, Steele. I give you my word that you can trust us both, as you do my father."

Steele came forward and shook Leaping Bear's hand. "I'm very pleased to meet you."

"Steele—it is a strong name," Leaping Bear commented, sizing up the larger man. He looked down at the grip on his hand and smiled. "Your brave is very strong, Little River Flower. He will give you many strong sons."

A flush of embarrassment crept up from her collar to color her face. "I've brought you a gift, she said, anxious to change the subject. She dug in the pack she had over her arm and produced an ornate pair of sterling silver salt and pepper shakers from the *Intrepid*'s dining room. "I understand these make very good shakers in place of gourds," she said, jiggling the shiny metal containers she had filled with beans before leaving the riverboat.

Leaping Bear took the shakers from her and smiled, but his smile was sad. "These are very nice, Little River Flower. Thank you." He removed a copper arm band from his own wrist and gave it to her. "And I have a gift for you. This bracelet will protect you wherever you go in the land of the Lakota."

"Thank you, Leaping Bear," she said, never considering refusing the gift, knowing her refusal would be an insult. "I will wear it with pride. Now what is it you wish to speak to me about?"

"Is it true your riverboat carries our annuities to Fort Randall?"

Sensing trouble she wasn't sure she could handle, Temerity balled her fists tightly and stiffened her posture, her tension easing only slightly as she felt Steele's warm, reassuring presence close behind her.

"We took on some cargo for Fort Randall," she replied hesitantly. "A portion of it could be *your* annuities. But I have no way of knowing if that's the case or not. Why do you ask?"

Leaping Bear nodded his head. "It has been a long, hard winter, and we have not gotten our promised rations. They say go to Fort Randall. We go. There, they dole out small amounts of flour and tobacco, much less than we were promised, and none of the meat or supplies we were promised and need to keep from starving. I ask why we do not receive our whole gift. They tell us we will, but we must go north to the agency to get it. We go there and are told by the agent that we must pay a storage fee for everything we get from the agency. We cannot pay, because we have nothing to trade with since we no longer hunt the buffalo."

"Why, that's robbery! You aren't supposed to pay for those annuities. They're already yours."

"That is what I say to Winniker, the agent. But he

says, 'No pay, no goods.'"

"What can Miss Kincade do?" Steele asked.

Leaping Bear produced a tattered list from under his belt and gave it to Steele. "You will give us our annuities from your boat."

"I'm not authorized to give them to you, Leaping Bear. They're not mine to dispense."

"But you say they are mine, Little River Flower. You say I do not have to pay for them. So, why can we not have them?"

Temerity looked helplessly at Steele. This was almost worse than being attacked. On the one hand, she hated what the government was doing to these innocent people, literally stealing the food out of their mouths for their own profit. But on the other hand, if she handed the supplies over to this tribe, not only would she never carry another government shipment on her packet, but she would be stopped by every tribe on the Missouri River who'd had trouble with the agencies. And if that weren't reason enough, the fact that she would no doubt be arrested for stealing supplies from the United State government, if she gave in to the Indians, should alone decide her answer.

"Look, Leaping Bear," Steele said, responding to the desperate plea for help in Temerity's eyes, even though he, too, was at a loss as to what to do. "You're asking Miss Kincade—Little River Flower—to do something she can't do."

Temerity turned back to the Sioux chief and nodded her head. "I swear to you I would do it if there were any way I could! But I cannot steal—even for the oldest and dearest of friends."

The look on Leaping Bear's face was lost. It was evident he hadn't made an alternate plan in case he was turned down. "My people say we kill the riverboats and take what is ours. But I say no. I tell them my friend

Kincade will know what to do."

"Let me see your list," Temerity said with resignation. Even if it meant going to jail herself, she couldn't let the chief lose face before his people.

Leaping Bear handed it to her and she studied it carefully, stalling for time and praying she would think of *something*.

"Would you and your people be willing to let us give you a gift from our own cargo of enough supplies to last you until we reach the agency?" Steele asked suddenly. "We could give you a barrel of good cornmeal, and a few of the emergency items you're needing—including dried fruit for the children." He reached into his pocket and came forth with a paper sack of dried raisins and apricots, offering them to each of the chiefs. "Then when we arrive at the agency, Miss Kincade and I will speak with the agent for you."

"In fact," Temerity added, grabbing at Steele's plan with enthusiasm, "we'll tell them at Fort Randall what the agency is trying to do to the Indians."

Leaping Bear turned to the other chiefs, who were chewing enthusiastically and noisily on the sweet fruit, and explained Steele's proposition to them in their own language.

After much conversation between them, Leaping Bear said, "It is good. We will go with you to the agency to get our supplies."

He raised his hand high over his head and beckoned someone out of the brush and trees that lined the bank. In a matter of minutes, the clearing was solid with women and solemn-faced Indian children, who stared up at Steele and Temerity with large eyes that were wise beyond their years.

"I have an idea!" Temerity said, her cheerfulness not quite disguising the sheen that had glossed over her blue eyes at the thought of anyone denying these

257

helpless children food that was rightfully theirs. "Would you and some of the chiefs—and the children—like to ride on the *Intrepid?* There wouldn't be room for all of you at once, but you could take turns. By the time we reach the agency tomorrow night, everyone who wants a ride should get a chance."

Minutes later, Temerity and Steele, accompanied by four excited but wary children, shoved off from the bank in the yawl. "You were wonderful back there," Temerity said to Steele. "I don't know what I would have done if you hadn't offered to speak for them at the agency."

"I was just thinking the same thing about you. I don't think there's another woman in the world who would have walked into that group of Indians the way you did."

"I cheated. I've known Leaping Bear since I was a child. I was sure he wouldn't hurt me."

"Still, it was a very brave thing to do."

"Well, I'm awfully glad you were with me. I probably would have been a lot less 'brave' if you hadn't been! Now, tell me, how am I going to explain our guests to our passengers and crew? For some reason, facing a boatload of white bigots with this news is more frightening than facing the Indians in the first place! Do you think I overstepped the bounds of good sense when I invited them to ride with us?"

Steele stopped rowing for a second and grinned, his cheeks dimpling admiringly as he studied her. "I'd say you most certainly did that, Miss Kincade. But then what's new about that? You've never let 'good sense' stop you before!"

"Are you laughing at me?" she said, smiling over the black-haired heads between them. "This is serious.

258

What am I going to tell the people on the *Intrepid*? They aren't going to like it a bit!"

"No, they're not, but you're going to tell them that Leaping Bear's braves have promised us safe conduct through heavily populated Indian territory for the next two days—in exchange for rides on the riverboat. How can they be upset by having them on board when it's a choice between that and being scalped?"

"Leaping Bear would never make such threats!"

"No one on the *Intrepid* knows that!"

Temerity giggled. "No, I don't suppose they do. And now that I think about it, I don't see much necessity in telling them, do you?"

"Not a bit!"

To say the following thirty-six hours were pleasant would be an absolute falsehood; but all in all, the passengers and crew accepted the *Intrepid*'s unconventional guests with much more grace than could usually be expected in a society where the only stories most whites had heard about Indians had been horror stories of rape and torture.

During the day, most passengers, second class as well as first, stayed on the upper decks of the riverboat, the women in the salon, the men patrolling the decks, their eyes carefully alerted to any danger. This reserved the main deck almost exclusively for the Indian chiefs and children who boarded every two or three hours for their turn on the riverboat.

By the time they arrived at the Indian agency the following night, miraculously without incident, Temerity's nerves were stretched to the point of breaking. So when she and Steele, accompanied by Leaping Bear and his entire tribe, presented themselves to the agent, Alfred Winniker, she was more than ready for a confrontation.

"You don't understand these Indians, Miss Kincade," the swarthy, buckskin-clad man said in response to Temerity's impassioned demand that Leaping Bear's people be given what was theirs. "They ain't like you and me. They're like children. If I give them all their annuities at once, they'll use them up or trade them off for whiskey. Then they won't have any food next winter. My way, they only take a little bit each time they come to the agency, and their supplies will last through next winter."

"And you'll make a nice extra profit in the bargain, won't you?" Temerity's voice was hard, her eyes narrowed knowingly on the dishonest agent.

Winniker's gaze shifted nervously under her intimidating glare. "That ain't exactly—" His uneasy glance darted from Temerity to Steele, who shrugged his shoulders and grinned helplessly, then back to Temerity. "It's not like all the agents don't do the same thing."

Temerity realized the truth of his words, and an ache of shame washed through her that she could be a member of a race that could behave so callously against their fellow man. She couldn't do anything about the other agents right now, but she could do something about this one. And she had no intention of wasting another minute of her patience on him.

"I don't have the time or the inclination to argue the ethics or morality of what the other agents are doing. You're the only agent I'm interested in right now, Mr. Winniker. And you're a thieving weasel who should be strung up by your thumbs. However, I'm going to give you a chance to redeem yourself by giving Leaping Bear and his people the items on their list." She shoved the document at the agent.

"Hold on there, miss. You ain't got no cause to be callin' me no names. And you got no right to be givin' me orders! This is my agency and I paid good money for this appointment. Now you and your Indian friends git on out o' here before I lose my temper and decide not to sell to them at all!" Winniker grabbed Temerity by the upper arm, and started to shove her toward the door. He knew before he'd forced her to go one step that he'd made a grave error in judgment!

With a gutteral growl and one long stride, Steele was across the small room and had Winniker's shirtfront wadded in his hand. Lifting the scheming agent off his feet with one hand, the larger man sank a balled fist in the agent's middle, hurling him backward across the room, to land in a crumpled heap on the dirt floor of the cabin.

"No! You hold on, you cheating bastard. These people signed a treaty with our government on good faith, and you're going to honor their agreement! Is that understood?"

Winniker, his watering eyes brimming with hatred, nodded his head.

"And you're going to apologize to Miss Kincade." When Winniker didn't say anything, Steele lurched forward as though to take a step toward him. "Aren't you?"

"I'm sorry, Miss Kincade," the agent mumbled, quailing back from Steele.

"That's what I thought. Now, if you'll sign that list, I'll have my men dispense Leaping Bear's supplies so they can be on their way. I'm sure they feel they've wasted enough time on you and are anxious to get back to their village."

Snatching the pen from Steele's hand, Winniker signed the offered paper begrudgingly. "I'm not goin' to forgit this!" he said with a snarl.

"Good, because we want you to remember it the next time you try to steal food and supplies from the

Indians. And just to be sure you do, I'm going to be checking on you frequently. I'd better not hear you scratched your nose wrong, or I'll be back. And next time I won't be so polite!"

"Did you see the look on his face when you grabbed him? I wish we'd had a photographer there!" Temerity said with a giggle as she and Steele walked arm in arm back to the *Intrepid*. Then her face grew sad. "I wish there were a way men like Winniker could be stopped."

"As long as there are ways to make large amounts of money off other people's misery, there will always be men like that, I'm afraid," Steele said, stopping and turning to face her, his eyes glistening with admiration. "But as long as there are fighters like you who are willing to defend their fellow man, those snakes are going to have a struggle on their hands."

Temerity looked up, losing herself in Steele's tawny-colored eyes. "And as long as people like me have people like you to get us out of trouble when we get in over our heads, the meek might inherit the earth yet—or at least get to keep the share that is rightfully theirs! Thank you, Steele!"

"Yeah, well, it was my pleasure," he mumbled, suddenly embarrassed. He began to walk again. "But now do you suppose we could just get back to a nice easy trip up the Missouri with nothing but a few sandbars, rapids, broken rudders, and tornadoes to slow us down? I think I've had enough excitement for a while!"

"Me too!" Then Temerity remembered the blood-stained handkerchief from the hold. "Did you ever find out from Rosalie Rigby who put her up to tricking you?"

Steele shook his head irritably. "So much happened

the next day, the sandbar, the Indians, that I just forgot. Then when we got to Fort Randall, I remembered, but they'd already gotten off. I thought about going after them, but I didn't want to leave the *Intrepid*—not with the riled-up passengers and all those Indians nearby."

"Oh, well, she probably wouldn't have admitted it anyway."

"Yeah, I guess you're right. But I sure would have liked to have had a chance to try to get the truth out of her—just so I could prove it to you."

"Steele, you don't have to prove anything to me. If I had any doubts before, they're all gone now. I know with all my heart that you could no more be a liar than you are a murderer."

A pang of guilt tore a jagged trail from his brain to his gut. How the hell was he ever going to get himself out of this mess without losing her? "Still, I'd like to show Rawson up for what he—"

"Shh," she ordered, stopping in the path and turning him to face her. "Let's not argue anymore!" Without giving him a chance to respond, she raised up on her toes and gave his lips a light peck.

"Temerity," he groaned, wrapping his arms around her trim waist and lifting her off the ground as his mouth came down hard on hers in a kiss that made all the explanations, all the apologies, he could not say in words yet. "You're the best thing that's ever happened to me," he said. "I don't ever want you to hate me."

The sadness and insecurity in his voice tore at Temerity's heartstrings. "I could never hate you, Steele. You're the best thing that's ever happened to me, too!"

Steele took a deep breath and set her back down, though he retained his tight hold on her, as though he was afraid she'd be lost if he let go. "I hope you always feel that way." He ran his hands over her back and buttocks, not in a sexual way, but as if he had to keep checking to be sure she was there.

Confused by his behavior, Temerity felt the need to comfort and reassure him. "Why don't we continue this conversation in a less public place?" she whispered, cupping his face between her palms and kissing his lips, his nose, his chin, his neck, between words. "Say, in my cabin?"

"I'd better stay on the main deck tonight. I don't think we've seen the last of Winniker yet. His type may back down from a face-to-face confrontation. But they aren't a bit bothered by seeking revenge in other, less-than-honorable ways."

"Surely he wouldn't try anything."

"You're probably right. But still, it won't hurt to be extra careful until we've put some miles between the *Intrepid* and this excuse for an Indian agency." He kissed her nose and loosened his squeezing hold on her, though he left one arm draped possessively around her shoulders as they continued their walk to the riverboat.

Temerity hadn't realized how totally exhausted she was by the strain of the past two days until she collapsed in her bunk forty-five minutes later, asleep before her head was completely nestled on the pillow. And two hours after that, she had no concept of the time when she heard a soft knock at the door.

Rolling over onto her back, her eyes opened sluggishly, then fell shut again as her brain fought to recapture the bliss of deep and dreamless slumber.

But the knock came again, this time more insistent. "Mmm," she grunted, trying to unglue her eyelids, but failing.

More knocking. "Who is it?" she mumbled incoherently. The knock was accompanied by the rattling of her door. "Who is it?" she said again, this time a little louder and more clearly.

"It's Steele," came the whispered reply.

"Steele?" What could he want? She struggled to a sitting position and stared at the locked door, her eyes blinking open and shut slothfully.

He knocked again. "Open the door."

She stumbled from her bed, yawning and rubbing her eyes as she crossed to the door. "What do you want?" She turned the latch and spun around to stagger, eyes closed, back to her bed.

The door burst open, bringing Temerity fully awake with thunderbolt force. But before she could react, a rough hand was clamped over her mouth and a hard arm wound around her waist in a rib-crushing hold, lifting her bare feet off the floor. "Not so tough without her watchdog here to protect her, is she?" a man's rough voice snarled. "Come on, let's get her out of here!"

"Yeah, I can't wait to get a taste of this sweet morsel," the man holding Temerity answered. "It's been a long time since I stuck a white woman." He raised his hand from her ribs to catch an unbound breast roughly in it.

"Is your brain in your pants? We gotta get her out of here first. I told you there'd be plenty of time for that when you get her to the hideout. Now, get movin' before someone comes along!"

Temerity had not seen the men yet but was almost sure she recognized the voice of the man who was not holding her as belonging to Winniker, the Indian agent. Steele had been right. The man was the kind to work better under cover of darkness and behind people's backs. But he would be no match for Steele when he came to save her—and there was no doubt in

Temerity's mind that any minute now Steele would come bursting through the door to save her. Just like every time she'd gotten into trouble since the day she met him, he would come. With that thought, she forced herself to go limp in the man's arms, thinking to save her strength so she'd be able to help Steele when he came.

Then a white handkerchief replaced the hand on her mouth and she opened her mouth to scream, but the scream was never made as Temerity slipped into the black void of unconsciousness. Her last thought was, *Steele! Hurry!*

Chapter Sixteen

A sense of alarm jarred Steele out of his dream-filled slumber. Glancing around frantically, he bolted up from where he dozed on the main deck. Seeing nothing out of the ordinary, he laughed at himself and plowed his fingers through his hair. There was nothing wrong. It had only been a dream. Nothing else.

Like every other night, second-class passengers and roustabouts were sleeping wherever they could find a place among the crates of cargo that covered the deck, and guards were patrolling: four on the main deck, two on the boiler deck where the first-class passengers' cabins were.

Automatically making a mental count of the guards, he spotted two: one walking away from the bow, the other coming toward him from the stern, as they circled the boiler and firebox on opposite sides of the lower deck.

His sense of panic slightly appeased, Steele's eyes raked over the sleeping bodies, coming to rest on the guard who was posted at the entrance down to the hold. His back was propped against a post and he, too, seemed alert. *The fourth should be in the vicinity of the paddle wheel,* he calculated, refusing to give in to the feeling of uneasiness his dream had left with him.

His gaze rose to the second deck, immediately zeroing in on the guard patrolling past Temerity's cabin door. Evidently, the second man was watching the cabins on the other side—just the way he was supposed to.

Steele shook his head in a futile attempt to shake away the nagging edginess that continued to plague him. He stared up at the boiler deck again. The guard who'd been outside Temerity's cabin had disappeared around the end of the deck as he continued his tour along the walkway surrounding the first-class cabins and dining room.

Then it hit Steele in the pit of his stomach, as if someone had planted a hard-soled boot there. Something was wrong! From where he stood, he should be able to see one of the guards at all times! The second boiler deck guard should have appeared within seconds of the time the first guard disappeared around the far corner cabin.

"Maybe they stopped to talk," he said to himself, praying that the persistent apprehension gnawing at his gut was nothing more than a case of an overly active imagination and the tension he'd been under since the night he'd found his handkerchief in the hold.

Mentally berating himself for falling asleep, Steele took the stairs two at a time as he raced to the door of Temerity's cabin, telling himself the entire time how foolishly he was behaving—yet knowing deep in his belly that he was too late!

"Temerity?" he called out as he raised his fist to pound on the door, not bothering to keep his voice low.

Giving way under his first touch, the door swung open with an ominous squeak and the ease of a door that had not been pulled completely closed.

Steele's heart plunged to the pit of his stomach with a

sickening thud. Temerity never left her door unlocked!

His apprehension gave way to full-fledged terror.

"She's gone!" he shouted, racing into the room and tearing the sheets and mosquito netting away from her bed in a crazed effort to find her there after all.

"What is it, Mr. Steele?" a man's concerned voice interrupted.

The sound of scurrying boots and the guard's voice brought Steele's search up short. But the white hot rage and guilt that roared within him would not be contained.

His eyes wild with horror, he flew at the unsuspecting guard. Grabbing him by his shirtfront, he lifted him off his feet and shook him with the strength of a madman. "Where is she?"

"I-I-I d-d-don't k-k-know!" the guard stammered, his teeth clacking loudly under the force of Steele's hold on him.

"You were supposed to be guarding her!" Steele hollered, taking out his own guilt on the defenseless roustabout who'd drawn guard duty that night.

"I-I-I t-t-thought s-s-she was in her c-c-cabin."

"Steele, put him down!" Uriah's gravelly voice interrupted sternly.

Still holding the smaller man up off the floor, Steele drew back a fist. "So help me, I'll kill you if anything's happened to her!"

"Get hold of yourself, man!" Uriah yelled. "You ain't doin' Temerity no good actin' like a crazy man! If this boy's to blame, we ain't gonna find out if you kill him. Now put him down!"

In the instant Steele's mind began its journey back to sanity, he heard the blast of a pistol—only a fraction of a second before he felt the bullet sear through the muscled flesh of his shoulder where it curved into his neck.

269

Steele dropped his hold on the deckhand and grabbed at his own neck, only slightly aware of the blood that spilled through his fingers or that he was falling as his body folded accordion-style to the floor.

"What the hell'd you do that for?" Uriah screamed, dropping to his knees beside Steele.

"You saw him. He was going to kill the kid!" an angry voice defended.

"He wasn't gonna kill nobody!"

"Well, I didn't intend to wait around to find out!"

Temerity jerked awake as a muscle spasm wrenched through her neck and shoulder. Unaware where she was, she attempted to raise her hand to rub out the knotting cramp.

A ripple of confusion skidded through her with the rocking knowledge that she could not feel or move her hands.

It was then she realized she was not in her cabin on the *Intrepid,* and the crick in her shoulder had not been caused by anything so simple as sleeping in a bad position.

Suddenly, everything that had happened came rushing into her memory, bringing with it a violent shudder of the hopelessness she'd made it a rule of life never to give in to.

Now painfully aware of the ropes cutting into her ankles and wrists and the foul-tasting gag on her mouth, she squirmed in an effort to change position. She refused to surrender to the threatening panic already thrumming its way through her veins.

There had to be something she could do. She would just relax and think for a minute. That always helped. Draw back and examine your options. Then act. *First, I'll figure out where I am.*

Fighting the scalding tears welling in her eyes despite her will, she blinked and tried to see something in the darkness. But there was nothing. Nothing at all. Never in her life had she seen a darkness so black, so totally devoid of shadows and shapes and light.

And for the first time in her life, she knew the feeling of being completely alone.

The growing panic in her edged its way a notch closer to the surface.

Stop it! You're never out of options until you're dead, she screamed in her mind, taking a deep breath to bolster her courage.

But the silence! The awful silence. It was deafening. Suffocating! It was as though only she lived, as though everyone, everything in this world of darkness was dead, as if by some bizarre mistake she'd been buried in an underground . . .

Crypt! Tomb! Grave! Coffin!

Her flesh broke out in a cold sweat as the horrible words blared out their macabre meaning in her brain. Sheer hysteria rose chokingly in her throat, and her mouth opened to scream. But the only sounds she could produce were the roaring pound of her own heartbeat and the rapid pant of her own breathing as she struggled frantically to inhale enough of the stale surrounding air to survive.

She heard men's voices and the shuffle of footsteps only moments before a rush of cool air and a glaring light washed blindingly over her. Squeezing her eyes closed in automatic defense, Temerity rolled her face toward the voices.

"You sure she can breathe in here?"

"Sure she can."

"She better be. Them Injuns ain't gonna be too happy if we pay 'em for those ponies with a dead woman—even if she is white!"

271

"Hell, I ain't gonna let her die before I get a whack at her. In fact, what's to stop us from havin' a treat right now?"

Her eyes still watering and only slightly recovered from the shocking glare of the lantern light, Temerity was unprepared for the man as he dropped to the floor beside her and yanked her nightgown up over her legs, exposing the dark, defenseless triangle of her femininity.

"What the hell do you think you're doin'?" hissed the man Temerity could now make out as the Indian agent, Winniker.

"What do you think I'm doin'?" the other man asked, fumbling urgently with the ropes of her ankles. "I'm gonna collect a piece o' my pay right now!"

"We said we'd wait 'til the steamboat leaves in the mornin'! What if someone finds out she's gone and comes after her?"

"What if they do? They ain't gonna come here. They'll go to the agency lookin' for her. They don't even know 'bout me or my place—and for sure they don't know nothin' 'bout this secret storeroom down here. Someone could come right in my shack and they'd never know we was down here. But if you're so worried, maybe you better git on back to the agency to head off anyone who comes lookin' fer us!"

"If you think I'm gonna leave her here alone with you, you're crazy. We agreed on a fifty-fifty split and I ain't lettin' you out of my sight until I get my half of them horses—and the rest!"

"Then let's get started—cause I'm about to burst my britches!" With those words he stood up and dropped his trousers around his ankles. "Spread your legs, honey, and if you're real good I'll take that gag off so's I can see your purty face!"

Though she was still frightened, her breathing had slowed to a more normal pace with the knowledge that

272

she had not been buried alive. After all, she was alive. And as long as she was alive she had choices—limited though they might be. And her choice was certainly not going to be to give in to this man without a fight, no matter how futile it might be.

Her eyes accustomed to the light and able to focus again, Temerity forced herself not to think about the way her lower body was exposed to the feral gazes of the two men. She would only think about gaining her freedom. Drawing on an innate strength born of desperation, she bent her knees as though she meant to comply.

"Look at that," he said, grinning and glancing away from Temerity toward the Indian agent, the expression on his unshaven face smug. "One peek at my hard cock and she's itchin' to go!"

That was all Temerity needed. In that instant, before he could return his concentration to his purpose, her feet shot out and up, her aim sure and damaging.

"Uh!" he grunted, doubling over and grabbing at himself. "Why, you bitch! I oughta—"

The trapdoor to the hidden room was yanked open, exposing a broad-shouldered man in the square of sunlight. "Ought to what?" he asked, leaping and firing his gun as he did.

Paralyzed with shock, then relief, then horror, Temerity watched as in one smooth motion, the gunman felled the would-be rapist with an accurately placed bullet in the heart, then twisted toward Winniker and fired a second shot—every bit as accurate and deadly as the first.

"Oh, my god, Temerity! When I learned you were gone . . ." Yanking the gag from her mouth, he drew her to a sitting position and quickly untied her hands, then enfolded her in his arms, covering her face with kisses as he spoke. "I was afraid I wouldn't be on time!

273

Did they . . . hurt you?"

Temerity shook her head, the shock of what had happened only now starting to set in. She opened her mouth to speak, but managed only a croak at first. Clearing her throat, she tried again. "You were in time," she rasped through parched lips.

His shoulders relaxed and he let an audible sigh of relief. "I shudder to think what would have happened if I'd arrived a moment later!"

The full realization of how close the rapist had come to succeeding hit Temerity with gale wind force. She burst into hysterical tears and buried her face against his chest. "Oh, Mr. Rawson, I was so afraid! Thank God you came!" she sobbed, releasing all the pent-up hysteria she had struggled so valiantly to control during her ordeal. "I felt so helpless," she confessed wrapping her arms around his chest and clinging to him with desperate strength. "They were going to— to—" She shot an uneasy glance toward the dead men's bodies.

"There, there, my dear, it's all over now. I won't let anything happen to you—ever again," he vowed, bringing his mouth down on hers in a passionate kiss.

Somewhere in the back of Temerity's shock-fogged mind, which continued to relive the horror of the last few hours, she told herself she should resist Charles Rawson's kisses. But it was as though she'd used her last shred of resistance when she'd fought the rapist. Though she did not return his kiss, was not even fully aware of what he was doing, she did not resist as he lowered her limp body back onto the floor, continuing to kiss her mouth as he did.

"Oh, my sweet, sweet Temerity . . ." he mumbled against her skin as his lips moved from her mouth to her throat. His hand caressed its way over her rib cage to cup a full breast in his palm. "I've dreamed

274

of this mom—"

"Mr. Rawson!" Temerity gasped, the intimate touch on her breast shaking her out of her indifference with scalding reality. "What are you doing?" she gasped, shoving at his chest with strength she didn't know she still possessed.

Taken off guard by her sudden surge of resistance, Charles rolled away from her. And before he could recover his advantage, she leaped to her feet and stood on shaky legs glaring down at him. "How could you insult me like that? I thought you were my friend!"

An impatient frown crossed Rawson's brow, to be quickly hidden behind an apologetic smile. "I am your friend. Can't you see how much I care for you? I would never want to insult you. But your kiss and your embrace led me to believe . . ."

Temerity examined him cautiously, searching for signs of duplicity in his expression. Seeing none, she had to admit to herself that she hadn't been totally blameless for what had occurred. When she spoke again, it was with a more understanding tone. "Obviously you've mistaken my gratitude for something more than it was. And if my actions misled you in any way, I do apologize. However, I must make it clear that nothing like this can ever happen again! Do you understand? There could never be anything like that between us!"

A frown of what Temerity perceived to be anger flickered across his brow and his blue eyes narrowed purposefully. Then, just as suddenly as it had appeared, the anger was gone, and Rawson's expression was once more remorseful and smiling. He took a step toward her, his hand extended as if to console her. "Once more, I must beg your forgiveness."

They heard the sounds of footsteps above them at the same time and glanced up in unison. Still not fully

275

recovered from her earlier ordeal, Temerity stared at Rawson, her eyes wide with fright.

Charles held his finger to his lips and motioned Temerity back against the dirt wall and drew his gun. Stepping in front of her to protect her with his own body, he waited.

"I'm sure those shots came from this shack!" they heard Uriah say.

"Uriah!" Temerity shouted, running out from behind Charles. "I'm down here!" she announced, not waiting for an answer before scrambling up the ladder, totally unconcerned with the splinters that pricked and embedded themselves in the soles of her bare feet.

Uriah peeked over the edge of the trap door, his grizzled face lighting up with recognition. "She's here!" he shouted jubilantly over his shoulder, offering his hand down to help Temerity the rest of the way out of the storeroom. "You okay, Miss Temerity? Lord, but you had us worried!"

"I'm fine, Uriah," she said, almost believing it, now that she was out of the dark prison where she'd spent the last few hours. "But am I ever glad to see you!" she cried, throwing herself into the old man's bearish embrace. "And if it hadn't been for Mister—"

"Rawson! What're you doing here?" Steele yelled, coming through the doorway to the cabin at the same time Charles Rawson's blond head and broad shoulders appeared in the trap door.

"Steele!" she cried, tearing herself from Uriah's arms to run to him. The only thing she wanted was to feel the security of his arms around her again.

Temerity hurled herself at Steele, wrapping her arms around his chest tightly. She burrowed her face against his shirtfront and reveled in the familiar scent of him, drawing strength from it.

Something was wrong. Steele wasn't returning her

embrace. She dropped her hold on him and stepped backward, a puzzled frown on her face. It was then she realized Steele was different. Instead of its usual tan, his face was a sickly ash color; and he seemed to sway where he stood, his tight grip on the doorframe the only thing holding him erect. "What is it, Steele? Why are you looking at me like that?" she asked. "Aren't you glad to see me?"

His face twisted into an angry gray mask. "I asked what you're doing here, Rawson," he said through teeth clenched tight with pain, as if he hadn't heard Temerity speak. "If you've touched her with so much as one of your slimy hands, so help me, I'll—"

"Steele," she said, touching his arm gently. She wanted to tell him he'd been right about Charles Rawson all along. But she couldn't, knowing how obsessed he was with Rawson's interest in her. "Mr. Rawson saved me from Winniker and his friend! He risked his life for me. If he hadn't come when he did, they would have . . . they would have . . ." She couldn't say it. "I'm very grateful to Mr. Rawson."

"I'll just bet you are," he said with a sneer. "Tell me, Temerity, just how grateful were you?"

No more stunned by Steele's insulting words than she would have been if he'd struck her across the face, Temerity's lower jaw went slack with a wheezing intake of breath.

"Steele, you're talkin' crazy!" Uriah warned. "I wouldn't be a bit surprised to find out you're runnin' a fever!"

"Fever? What's he talking about?" Instinctively, Temerity reached up to feel Steele's forehead, her love and concern for him stronger than her own hurt. His ugly innuendo was pushed from her mind for the moment.

Steele released his grip on the door and batted her

hand away from his face, staggering forward as he did. "I said I want to know what you're doing here, Rawson!"

"Are you sure it's all right for you to be up and around?" Rawson asked Steele with a gloating tone of concern. "I mean, after all, even a flesh wound can get infected."

"Flesh wound! What's he talking about, Steele?" Temerity was fairly screaming now.

"How'd you find her so fast, Rawson?" Steele repeated, ignoring Temerity's question.

"The same way you did, I imagine. I remembered the Indian agent's threat, so went there first. When he wasn't there, one of the loafers who hang around the agency told me Winniker had a friend who had a shack out here. I had no other idea where to search, so I borrowed a horse and took a chance."

"Hmp!" Steele grunted, pivoting away from Temerity and taking an unsteady step toward the borrowed horses.

Temerity started after him, then stopped and whirled to face Uriah and Charles. "Will someone tell me what's going *on?* Why's he acting like that?" The men exchanged uneasy glances.

"We'd better get you back to the riverboat," Uriah said, coming forward and putting his arm around her shoulders. "This whole thing's been rough on you! There'll be time for talkin' later on."

"Stop it! Don't treat me like a child. I won't stand for it. Something else has happened and I want to know what it is—now!"

"There was an accident," Charles began smoothly.

"You got to understand how upset Steele was when he realized you were gone!" Uriah interjected. "He was like a crazy men."

"He was on the verge of killing one of the guards!

278

Someone had to stop him," Charles explained. "I had no choice."

Temerity's eyes widened in surprise. "You tried to kill Steele?"

"No . . . I didn't try to kill him! I only wanted to stop him from killing the poor guard!"

"But you shot him!"

"Temerity"—his tone was patronizing—"you've witnessed my expertise with a revolver, so you above all others should know that if I'd meant to kill Mr. Steele, I would have."

Rawson said a silent "thank you" to the curious passenger who'd brushed up to see what was happening and in the process jostled his arm as he was taking aim. Even though in that moment when he'd seen Steele's attack on the crewman as the perfect way to get rid of his competition for Temerity, he could see now that he'd been wrong.

It was quite obvious that he'd misjudged the seriousness of Temerity's feelings for the man. The simplest fool could see she actually pictured herself in love with him. No, killing Steele definitely wasn't the answer—not if he wanted to win Temerity for himself. She'd never forgive the man who'd killed Steele. No, the best way to get rid of Steele would be by destroying Temerity's trust in him.

"Then who shot him?"

"I did, but it was only a flesh wound in the shoulder. I assure you—"

But Temerity didn't wait to hear more. She was already running to where Steele was drunkenly trying to fit his boot into the stirrup—missing it again.

"Here, let me help," she offered, taking the saddle-horn in her left hand and steadying the elusive stirrup with her right. "We need to get you back to the *Intrepid* so I can examine that wound of yours!" she said with a

279

smile that was meant to be consoling. But her genuine concern for Steele couldn't quite hide the strange feeling of joy she felt. He'd been "crazy" with worry about her.

Until that moment, Temerity hadn't realized the sense of disappointment she'd felt when she'd seen that it was Charles Rawson who'd saved her and not Steele. But it hadn't been Steele's fault! He would have come sooner if he could have. And he had come! Despite a gunshot wound, despite his pain, and despite the loss of blood which had drained him of most of his strength—and possibly his good judgment—he had come for her.

"Put your foot in the stirrup, then I'll help you get on the horse."

"Where's Rawson? Shouldn't you be 'helping' him? After all, *he's* the one who 'saved' you."

Temerity smiled patiently, ignoring the slurred words. She was even able to forgive Steele for the ugly accusation he'd made before. After all, every time he did something like that, it gave her another clue to what was really bothering him, one more clue to why he acted so irrationally at times. He was a man in love! A man in love with *her!*

Temerity's heart surged. "Hold on to the saddlehorn," she coaxed, when together they had managed to place a boot toe in the stirrup. "When I count to three, straighten your knee"—she patted the knee of the leg in the stirrup—"and I'll give you a boost from behind." She positioned her shoulder beneath his rump and started counting. "One, two, three—up!"

Steele's knee unbent at the same time Temerity raised up under him, lifting him off his feet and into the saddle with amazing ease. "Not bad, huh?" she said, her tone surprised as she dusted her hands off against one another. "I'd better ride with you to keep you from falling," she said, removing his foot from the stirrup and replacing it with her own bare one. Before he could react, Temerity had swung into the saddle behind him and wrapped her arms around him to take the reins from him. "Which way's the river?"

"What about Rawson?" Steele mumbled.

"I don't think this saddle could hold all three of us," she said, laughing. "Besides, he has his own horse! Now which way do we go?"

Steele pointed feebly toward the agency and slumped forward onto the horse's neck—unconscious.

"What did you give him, Uriah?" she asked over her shoulder as Uriah and Charles mounted their horses.

"Just a little laudanum for the pain."

Temerity nodded her head in understanding. "From now on, it's nothing but whiskey and a bullet to bite for you, my friend!" she said to Steele's back with a laugh as she nudged her horse onward. "Laudanum is definitely not for you!"

Chapter Seventeen

"I'm telling you, I'm just fine!" Steele bellowed a week later, snatching off the towel Temerity had draped around his neck and tossing it onto the plank floor of his cabin. "And I can certainly shave myself!"

"You're becoming impossible to live with," she said with a patient laugh as she stooped to pick up the discarded towel. Giving it a shake, she sat down on the edge of Steele's bunk and placed it under his chin again. "That must mean you're on the mend."

"Then get out of here and let me get dressed and back to work!"

"The doctor at Fort Sully said maybe tomorrow—if you behave," she said, her humoring tone unfluctuating, no matter how he continued to complain and harangue.

"What the hell does he know? He was drunk! Did you hear how he slurred his words?"

Temerity laughed at the ridiculousness of Steele's observation. "He was no more drunk than I am! And you know it. Now quit acting like a baby and let me shave you. I've got other things to do!"

"Don't tell me you didn't smell the rum on his—" Steele brought himself up short, his mouth opened to

283

utter the next word. Temerity was watching him patiently, not bothering to hide the expression of amusement on her face. He narrowed his eyes at her. "Are you laughing at me?" he accused.

"Of course not," she returned—with a snort of repressed laughter she couldn't quite contain. She shook her head and busied herself with lathering the soap in his shaving mug. "Really, I'm not!"

"Yes, you are!" he said with an incredulous tone, his mouth dropping open in a stunned grin despite his bad mood.

She snorted a second time. Ducking her head and hunching her shoulders up, she covered her mouth with the back of her wrist.

"There! I knew it! You *are* laughing at me!"

"Well . . ." She peeked up from under her brows and snickered helplessly.

A corner of his mouth twisted upward slightly, and one cheek twitched into a dimple. "Well, what?"

"Well, it's just that you're so cute sitting there with your lower lip all poked out, pouting and throwing tantrums like a spoiled little boy. I just can't help it. I'm sorry. I promise I won't laugh anymore." She made a conscious effort to wipe the mischievous grin from her face, but her glistening blue eyes were another matter. The smile would not leave them.

"Spoiled little boy?" he quoted in mock anger. "Tantrums and pouting! How can you say that? I've never thrown a tantrum in my life. And I definitely do not pout!" He compressed his lips together and stretched them across his teeth into a false, I-know-I'm-guilty-and-you-know-I'm-guilty-but-I'm-not-admit-ting-a-thing grin that dug an impudent dimple into each of his cheeks.

"You ought to be ashamed of yourself!" she scolded, taking a swipe at a dimple with the shaving brush.

"You'd better not give me any trouble or I'll shave off your mustache!" She dolloped a glob of shaving soap under his nose. "I've been wondering what you've got hidden under there."

"Pleeeease! Not my mustache!" he wailed in exaggerated horror and yanked the towel up over his face. "Anything but my mustache!"

"All right, you can keep the mustache if you let me shave the rest of your face. And . . . if you promise not to give me anymore trouble about staying in bed one more day."

"All right, I'll be good! But I still think all this fuss over a little nick is unnecessary."

"I'll be the judge of that," she said with motherly authority. "I don't want to take any chances on losing my first mate before the really rough part of the trip begins!"

"Is that the only reason you've been taking such good care of me?" he asked, his voice low and suddenly serious.

No! she wanted to scream at him for asking such a dumb question. *I've taken care of you because I love you. Because I can't bear the thought of what I would do if I lost you.* "What other reason could there be?" she asked with a quick pat on his arm. Smiling, she finished brushing the white lather on his face and took up the razor. Holding it beneath one sideburn, she pursed her lips and moved her mouth to the side, indicating it was what she wanted him to do to tauten the skin of his cheek.

"Well, there's—"

"Hush, now, unless you want me to draw blood!"

"Wouldn't want that," he mumbled out the side of his mouth without moving his lips.

"That's better."

They were silent the next few minutes, the only

sounds in the room the scraping of the straight-edge razor over his coarse three-day beard, and the soft tuneless melody Temerity hummed as she concentrated on her work.

"There ye go, laddie! All doon! An' nary a drop o' yer precious blood gone t' waste," she announced in her best brogue as she wiped the excess soap from his face with a damp cloth.

"Aye!" he returned, smoothing a testing palm over his face. "Soft as a bairn's wee behind!"

Watching each other happily, they burst out laughing at the same time. Then, as if their laughter were controlled by one brain, they stopped, the amusement in their eyes suddenly flaring into passion.

"Temerity," he said huskily, levering himself up on one elbow and reaching out to cup her face in his hand.

Possessing no more chance of resisting than a helpless bit of metal would have against a giant magnet, her upper body bent toward him. Her face only inches from his, she spoke in a weak whisper. "I need to go work on the ledgers."

"Not yet," he whispered, his breath soughing seductively over her face. He kissed her ear, dipping his tongue into its sensitive hollow with deliberate purpose.

"Steele, don't," she gasped, lolling her head into the intimate kiss as her hands stole around his neck. "I really have to go. Someone will miss me."

"Not as much as I've missed you," he cooed, taking his shaving gear from her lap and placing it on the floor. "I've missed the feel of you. The taste of you. Do you have any idea what kind of torture you've put me through this past week?" He moved his hands to the buttons on the front of her blouse. "I've thought of nothing but having you naked in my arms. Every time you've come in here, bustling around with your bandages and trays of food and shaving gear, all I wanted to do was to rip these prim lady-riverboat-owner clothes off you and kiss every single inch of your delectable body from head to toe—and back again."

His soft, seductive words and his hands grazing the fullness of her breasts as they continued to work their way down the buttons sent desire radiating through her. Temerity couldn't help the weak moan she released any more than she could fight the heat that raced along her blood stream to her nerve endings. Her entire body was charged with electricity, its paramount energy illuminating the secret part of her body that only Steele knew how to appease and control.

The buttons of her blouse having given way to his gentle coaxing, he eased the blouse from her skirt waistband and spread it open to expose her rapidly rising chemise-covered breasts. "I've imagined myself inside you in a thousand different ways. Just thinking of your sweet body closing around me, holding me, squeezing me, makes me ache with wanting you."

Though it was an almost impossible effort to remember where she was and what time of the day it was, Temerity tried to claw her way back to reality. "Steele, we can't. Not now."

He slid his arms around her waist and pulled her on top of his bare chest. "You're a hard woman, Temerity Kincade, if you can leave me in this kind of pain." Holding her to him with one arm, he grabbed her wrist and slipped her hand under the sheets to his rigid desire. "How can you leave me like this?"

"Steele . . ." she mewed, wrapping her fingers around the tightly stretched silken flesh beneath her hand and caressing the length of it. "You're not being fair."

"At a time like this, being fair is the farthest thing from my mind." He rocked his hips against her hand and captured the swollen peak of a breast he'd managed to bare while her attention was diverted.

"Oooh," she moaned, succumbing to the familiar tug of her passion.

Within a minute, they both were naked and in the bunk together, their hands anxiously reacquainting themselves with the hills and plains of each other's bodies.

Unable to wait another second for him to glove himself with the heat of her body, Temerity lifted herself over him, dropping her hips downward to impale herself on the strength of his manhood.

"I've missed you, too," she murmured, raising and lowering herself on him, her motions becoming more frantic and rapid with each of his upward thrusts.

"Oh, my god," he moaned, flipping her over onto her back and pounding into her with desperate furor. "Come with me, love. I can't stop!" His voice was a command, a plea, an apology.

But Temerity needed no words to spur her on. Already her own body was peaking to the point of eruption and she, too, was beyond return.

Then it was happening, the blinding light, the rapturous unity, the ultimate goal, and together they both cried out as the zenith of their passion hurled them heedlessly into the heavenly sphere where only they existed.

Drawing the last drop of his passion into her with the greedy, milking motion of her femininity, Temerity tightened her arms and legs around Steele's perspiration-misted shoulders and hips for the glorious tumble back to earth with him.

Rolling over onto his back, Steele blew out a long sigh. "I may live after all."

"I'm glad to hear that," she said, suddenly remembering the inappropriate timing of their lovemaking. Anyone who had seen her come into Steele's cabin to shave him must be wondering by now what was taking her so long. In fact, their assumptions and guesses as to what was happening were probably quite accurate.

Embarrassed by the thought that everyone on the *Intrepid* could know what she was doing, she tore herself from Steele's embrace and stood up abruptly, immediately busying herself with dressing.

"What's the matter?" he asked, puzzled as he watched her brusque and unexpected actions.

"Nothing," she said curtly. "I've been here longer than necessary and people will be wondering." She stooped to pick up and put away his shaving gear. "I have to go back to work."

Confused and hurt, then angered by her obvious change of mood, Steele flopped back against his pillow and folded his arms across his chest. "Look, I'm sorry I was in such a hu—"

"Steele," she interrupted, "I have to know something." She was facing the washstand, unable to meet his perplexed stare. "Did you really believe what you said when you accused me of showing my gratitude to Mr. Rawson with anything other than words?" There, she had said it. It had preyed on her mind for more than a week now, and though she'd tried to block it from her thoughts, her efforts had been useless. She had to know the truth. Now! Before her feelings got any further out of hand.

Stunned by her question, Steele hesitated a moment.

When he didn't answer immediately, she wheeled on him, her face white with shock. "You did, didn't you? You actually thought I—"

"I didn't, Temerity," he protested. "I don't."

But he was too late. His hesitation told her all she needed to know. He really did think she was the kind of woman who would use her body in exchange for things. A prostitute!

The horror of the truth hit Temerity with such force,

289

it was all she could do to keep from gripping her belly and doubling over with pain. But what did she expect? Had she ever given him reason to believe otherwise? Look how easily she'd fallen into his arms just now. Without a care for propriety or her reputation, she'd given in to him and to her own wanton desire—again.

Slamming the washbowl down on the chest, Temerity ran to the door. She had to escape, had to go where she could hide from what she'd done.

Before she could jerk the door open more than an inch, a hard, muscled arm shot past her ear and slammed it shut again.

Temerity straightened her spine as best she could. "Please remove your hand."

"Not until we get this thing out in the open."

"I'd say you did a pretty fair job of that in the kidnapper's shack. Only I was too stupid—or too starry-eyed—to believe you meant those ugly things you said."

"Temerity . . ." He cupped her shoulder with his free hand and tried to wheel her around to face him.

She shrugged free of his grip and jerked on the door handle. But the door remained shut.

"Temerity, look at me."

"I can't! And I don't want to talk to you."

"Then don't. Just listen. I'll talk."

Knowing she stood no chance of opening the door if Steele didn't want her to, Temerity leaned against the door, resting her forehead against her interlocked hands. "Go on and say what you want to say. Then let me out of here."

"First of all, I never thought you were with Rawson—or any other man."

"But you said—"

"Ssh," he whispered, brushing the errant curls of dark hair off the nape of her neck with the backs of his fingers and bending to kiss the sensitive hollow he found there. "I'm doing the talking. You're supposed to be listening."

Shivers of excitement rippled up and down Temerity's spine and she rocked her forehead against her fists helplessly. "I'm listening," she said.

"It was just that I felt so guilty that I had let those bastards get past me, and then when I saw that cocky, grinning Rawson pop out of that cellar behind you, I just went crazy. I didn't mean it."

"Then why did you hesitate to answer my question?"

"I had to think for a minute to remember what you were talking about. You, above all, know what laudanum does to my memory." He trailed a line of kisses up the side of her neck from her shoulder to the unguarded depression behind her earlobe.

"You're not going to seduce me with your kisses this time, Steele." She clasped her hands behind her neck to protect the receptive area from his lips.

"You misjudge my intentions, sweetheart," he cooed. Tickling his tongue along the backs of her fingers, he delved deeply into the dividing line at the base of each digit and tasted her neck. "I'm not trying to seduce you. I'm just trying to get you to listen to the truth."

She hated her weak, betraying body for the rising desire that was already beginning to sizzle through it again. Drawing in her bent arms, she pressed them protectively over her swelling breasts and tightened her thighs together, hoping to ease the passion swelling there, passion that had made her ache for release— again. "Well, go on and tell me what you have to say, and then let me leave," she said hoarsely, determined to ignore his mouth on her hands and neck—and failing totally.

"*This* is the truth, Temerity . . ." He reached up and

291

unclasped her hands from around her neck and kissed her nape. "And this . . ." He slipped his arms around her waist and caressed his way upward to cradle her breasts in his palms "And this . . ." He fondled the taut peak of a breast that strained against the material of her blouse. "And this . . ." His other hand slipped into her skirt waistband to cup her softly rotating femininity and pull her hips back against him. "Can you deny it?"

Her resistance crushed, Temerity sank back against him, her head rolling from side to side against his chest. "No . . ." she moaned, close to falling back into the trap of convincing herself he wanted her because he loved her, when all he really wanted was . . .

"No!" she shouted, straining forward against his intimate hold on her. "This isn't truth. This is lust. You're just like all men. You want to use a woman for your own personal enjoyment."

"I could have sworn the enjoyment *was* mutual," he said, bringing himself against her again and moving his hips and fingers and hands seductively. "But if it wasn't, I'd like a chance to make it up to you."

The breath caught in her throat. "It wa—it i—" She released a low tortured moan. "Please stop. Don't you see? This is all wrong. No matter what I've let you believe, I'm not cut out to be a man's mistress. For me, there has to be more than just—than just—'mutual enjoyment.' There has to be trust and caring and—"

She broke off short of saying the words she longed to hear most from Steele, the words she'd foolishly convinced herself she would hear him say if she were patient enough. But now she finally had to admit to herself that Steele would never say those words to her. She'd been a fool to think he would. Men didn't love and marry loose women, and that was exactly what she was as far as he was concerned: loose and convenient. Nothing more!

Steele ached to tell her what he knew she needed to hear: that he loved her and wanted to make her his, totally and permanently, for as long as they "both shall live." He knew what any relationship other than marriage would do to a properly raised lady like Temerity Kincade. He knew how he'd degraded her by taking her virginity without giving her any sort of commitment. And he knew how demeaning a position he'd put her in by making her his mistress. But he couldn't tell her, not yet, not until he could clear up all the deception standing between them—and not until he was sure he wasn't just fooling himself into believing Temerity Kincade was special and not like other women.

He dropped his hold on her and spun away, furrowing his fingers through his hair as he crossed to the bunk. "Dammit, Temerity, there's more to this than just lust and you know it! Why do you think I went so crazy when I thought I'd lost you? And why do you think I was so jealous when I found you with Rawson?"

"Why don't you tell me?" she said acidly, unable to keep the resentment out of her voice, even though what had happened between them had been as much her own fault as his.

"It's because I *do* care that I can't give you what you want from me. Not yet anyway. It wouldn't be fair to you. There are things you don't know about me, things you won't like or understand."

She turned to face him and sagged back against the door, studying him, trying to absorb the meaning of his words. "Tell me, Steele. Make me understand." Her words were a plea.

"I can't. Not yet. When we get back to St. Louis, I'll tell you everything—if you still want to hear it and don't hate my guts by then."

Temerity studied his face and shook her head. "I

293

couldn't hate you, Steele," she finally said. Tilting her head back against the door in defeat, she directed her unseeing, tear-filled gaze at the ceiling. "I love you."

His mouth dropped open incredulously, and Steele stared at her, unable to believe his ears. It was what he had wanted to hear, what he had fantasized and prayed would happen by the time they got back to St. Louis, so that when she found out the truth about him, she wouldn't want to leave him. If she loved him, he could tell her everything now. He didn't have to wait until St. Louis. If she loved him, she would understand why he had done what he'd done. If she loved him . . .

If! That's the word to consider, a nagging inner voice said, reminding him that every woman who'd ever said she loved him had wanted something—beginning with his mother. Women! They were all willing to do and say whatever it took to get what they wanted. *And maybe Temerity Kincade isn't so different, after all. She wants respectability, and I'm willing to bet she wants it enough to lie to get it.*

He sank onto his bunk and held his forehead in his hands, tortured by the war between joy and suspicion that had raged through his mind—and had been lost. "Do you want to get married, Temerity? Is that it? Okay"—he bolted up from the bunk and snatched a pair of pants off the back of a chair—"we'll get married." Shoving a foot into a trouser leg, he went on. "We can get married when we stop at Fort Rice tonight—or better still, let's go right now and have Uriah marry us! A riverboat captain must have the same powers as a sea captain," he growled angrily.

Crossing to where she stood, her expression stunned by his outburst, he grabbed her upper arms, his own expression a mixture of misery and anger. "But I'm warning you, lady, don't come crying to me when you wake up and find yourself married to someone whose guts you hate! Because once we're married, you're mine and I'll never let you go! So, what's it going to be? Is your need for respectability so great that you're willing to gamble on spending the rest of your life with me no matter what?"

Yes, I want to marry you! Yes, I'll take the gamble, she wanted to shout, her heart exploding with disappointment in her chest. She had wanted Steele's proposal more than anything in her life. But not like this. Not without love. Never without love.

Temerity planted her feet on the floor and hung her head in anguish for what she had to do. "I don't want to marry you, Steele. But thank you *so much* for your gracious offer." She dodged away from him and started to open the door, determined to escape from his cabin before he saw her blue-gray eyes glistening with tears and a hurt she never would have believed a person could experience and go on living.

"Wait a minute!" Grabbing her arm, he turned her to face him again. "Why not? Isn't wangling a proposal out of me what this has been about?"

Temerity's gaze scanned up the length of the shirtless man who glowered over her, her hurt roiling into fury. "Why, you egotistical, overgrown little boy! I wouldn't marry you for anything in the world! Now, if you will excuse me, I have work to do."

Truly stunned by Temerity's words, Steele stared at her aghast. It didn't make any sense. If she wanted to trap him into marriage by saying she loved him, wouldn't she have seized the opportunity no matter how *un*gracious the suggestion had been? Of course, she would—unless she wanted something else. "I don't get it. What do you want from me?"

Temerity's hand froze on the door handle. She opened her mouth to speak, then closed it on a huff. "Nothing, Steele. I want nothing from you but to be left alone." She ripped open the door and raced outside, leaving the half-dressed Steele standing in the middle of the cabin, alone and confused.

For the next two weeks, Temerity went about her daily routine with a zeal and determination that bordered on obsession. She pushed herself to do more each day, certain that if she gave herself no time to think, filling every waking moment with work, she would be able to put Steele and her disastrous love affair with him behind her. The more time that passed, she told herself, the easier it would be to see him without remembering the sinfully wonderful hours she'd spent with him. Perhaps, after enough time, she would even be able to forget him altogether.

But all her hard work and effort had failed to drive the memories and regret from her brain, just as surely as they had failed to eradicate her love for Steele from her heart. In fact, rather than getting better, her anguish and hopelessness grew more intense and painful each day.

Instead of toughening her heart, as she had told herself it would do, his constant presence, even from the distance she was careful to maintain, had had the reverse effect on her. Each sighting, however brief, had ripped another piece of her heart from her chest, until she wasn't certain she could last the remaining two weeks it would take before they reached Fort Benton.

Staring at the churning water as the *Intrepid* steamed past the juncture where the Milk River flowed into the Missouri from the north, Temerity was unprepared for the sudden wave of nausea that rose in her throat. Stunned, she swallowed hard, closed her eyes, and whirled around to lean back on the rail. This was ridiculous; she'd never experienced motion sickness in her life.

"Miss Kincade, are you all right?" Harry Bailey asked, hurrying to where she stood on the boiler deck. "You're awful pale." He didn't mention the shadows that made her blue eyes lack their usual luster or the fact that she looked as though she'd lost weight since the trip began.

"I'm fine, Harry," she answered, drawing in a deep breath through her nostrils and blowing it out through pursed lips. "I didn't eat breakfast and just had a moment of dizziness. It's gone now."

"That's good," he said, wanting to believe his spunky lady boss but not quite able to. "Steele wanted me to tell you we're gonna have to tie up early today."

"What are you talking about? We've still got a good half a day of light left. You tell him we're not stopping!"

"We ain't got much choice, Miss Kincade. We broke another rudder!"

"A rudder! Well, how long will it take to fix it?"

"I'm 'fraid it ain't fixable this time. We're goin' to have to go ashore and find hard wood to build a new one."

"That'll take two days! Wasn't there one we could salvage off the wrecked boat on that sandbar we poled over yesterday? Sure there was!"

"I'm sorry, ma'am. We took everything we could use from that rack, but most of it was only good for firewood. Someone had already beat us to the rudder."

"Well, if we have no choice, we have no choice," Temerity said, her fists clenched with the effort it took her to keep from screaming at the top of her lungs. Two days had just been added to the fourteen she hadn't thought she could bear! How would she do it?

"That ain't all, Miss Kincade!" Harry ventured hesitantly.

Temerity took a deep breath and expelled a harsh

laugh. "You might as well go on and tell me, Harry. Evidently, this isn't my day!"

"Captain Gunther says the water's readin' like it's low up ahead."

"Low water? Is he sure?"

Harry nodded his head. "He says it's much lower here than it usually is this time of the year, and once we get past where the Milk empties into it, it's goin' to get lower, maybe too low to pass without double-trippin' and polin' most of the way to the Musselshell River. It could delay us a couple of weeks—more if anything else goes wrong."

"If anything else goes wrong," she repeated with a defeated shake of her head.

Chapter Eighteen

"Will you do it, Mr. Rawson? Will you drive one of the freight wagons for me?" Temerity asked the older man a few hours after the *Intrepid* had tied up at Trover Point.

Not wanting to appear too eager, Charles Rawson hesitated a moment, pretending to consider his answer. "What about Steele? I would think he'd be the one to go on this trek with you."

Temerity flashed a surprised glance at Rawson, then studied her hands on the guard rail, hoping he hadn't seen the hurt in her eyes at the mention of Steele's name. "I need him to stay here. The men look up to him, and that's very important—especially now. With the river so low and the necessity to do so much poling and grasshoppering, it's imperative he stays—if the *Intrepid* is going to make the total journey to Fort Benton. And it is going to make it to Fort Benton! Even if it has to be poled all the way," she vowed adamantly.

"Then why take the risk of moving your trade goods overland to the gold camps if you're going to Fort Benton anyway?"

"Because there's no telling how long it will take to get there. At the paltry few miles we're covering each day,

299

it may be late July before we do. And we haven't even come to the rapids yet. But if I head southeast into the mountains with part of the goods, I can get them to Virginia City and the rest of the Alder Gulch gold camps at least two weeks before that—maybe even sooner. Besides, by taking supplies directly to the miners myself, I'll make a better profit than if I sell them to freighters in Fort Benton—which I'll do with everything I don't take with me."

"It seems you've thought it all out."

Temerity nodded her head with a sad smile. Yes, she'd thought it out. At first, the idea had come to her only as an idle wish for a way to escape from seeing Steele every day, a way to stop being constantly reminded of the fact that whatever she had imagined existed between them was not meant to be.

However, after a week of grueling, inch-by-inch progress through the low water of the Missouri River, when she'd learned they could expect travel to become even more impossible the farther upstream they went, the idea that had begun as an insignificant daydream had inflated into positive action.

Answering only to her need to escape from the constant and torturous nearness of Steele, she refused to listen to her common sense. She knew the whole idea was an insane venture for the best of men—though she'd heard of more than one who'd done just what she was planning. But she had to do it, had to get away, had to prove she was as good as a man. So she had purchased two freight wagons and eight mules at Trover Point and had begun her search for someone to drive the second wagon.

Because of what had happened in the cellar at the kidnapper's shack, Charles Rawson was definitely *not* her first choice as a driver. However, there was no one else she could ask. Taking Steele would be defeating her purpose, and none of her other employees could be spared from their duties on the *Intrepid*. Of course, there were other passengers she could have asked, but none of the rough-talking men still on board were men she would turn her back on, much less spend a month alone with. At least Rawson was a gentleman—and clean. And most important, he would never force his attentions on her. Instead, he would accept her refusal to his advances—as he had in the cellar. No, Charles Rawson would never take advantage of a woman no matter how much he desired her; so that left him as her only logical choice.

A sudden shiver of doubt rippled over her flesh as she contemplated Charles Rawson's handsome face. Maybe she was misjudging him. What did she really know about him?

"When will we leave?" Rawson said, interrupting her apprehensive thoughts with a cheerful lilt to his voice.

Shrugging her shoulders as if to shake off the uneasiness that had taken hold of her, and scolding herself mentally for her lack of trust, she smiled her gratitude. "In the morning. Before sunup. I'll have the wagons loaded tonight. And if we get an early start, we could possibly make it to the gold fields within two weeks—three at the most."

"I'll be looking forward to it," he told her, reaching for her hand and lifting it to his lips for a kiss.

Snatching her hand from his grasp before his mouth could graze it, Temerity stepped back from Charles. "There will be none of that, Mr. Rawson. I want you to treat me just like another man on this trip. Anything like hand kisses—or anything else—will be out of the question. Do I have your word that our relationship will be that of two men traveling together and nothing more?" She held out her hand in a deliberately masculine offer to shake his.

301

Accepting Temerity's firm handshake, Charles Rawson tossed her a regretful grin and nodded his head. "It will be most difficult to think of a beautiful young woman such as yourself as simply a traveling partner, but you have my word."

"Good, then I will leave you to prepare for our journey," she said, pirouetting away from him. She paused at the top of the stairs leading down to the main deck and called back to him, "Don't forget to dress in warm clothes—it could get cold at night, especially after we get into the mountains. And wear sturdy boots and a hat. If you don't have anything but your nice clothes, I'm sure I can locate something suitable for you." Deliberately forcing to the back of her mind the doubts that continued to harp at her thoughts, she released an excited little giggle. "After all, a lot of what we're taking is just that kind of clothing."

Charles Rawson smiled as she disappeared down the stairs. "I'll be ready," he promised with a cheerful wave. *You can be certain, of that, my dear!* he said to himself, unable to believe his good fortune. Alone with Temerity Kincade in the wilds of the West with no one—absolutely no one—to interfere with his plans for her! His mouth watered at the thought. *I've been ready for years!*

He made himself a vow. He would have her in his bedroll before the first week was out, and would have her acceptance to his proposal of marriage by the end of the second. *Good things come to him who waits,* he told himself as, whistling a gay tune, he strutted toward his cabin to pack. "Now the waiting is at an end, my dear!" he mumbled under his breath. "For you and I have just begun."

"She told you to *what?!*" Steele bellowed at Harry

302

Bailey, unaware of the slight cringe that lifted the second mate's broad shoulders.

"She told me to oversee loading this list of supplies onto those two freight wagons over there. She said she's goin' to take them overland to the gold fields."

"Damn that woman!" Steele cursed, pivoting on his heel and stomping away from Harry.

"What about these supplies?" Harry called after him, waving the list in the air. But Steele evidently hadn't heard him. He had already disappeared up the stairs to the next deck. Harry shrugged his shoulders and signaled for several roosters to go down in the hold with him to start bringing out the supplies Miss Kincade had requested.

With a loud crack, the door to the pilothouse burst open. "What the hell is going on?"

Uriah and Temerity jerked to attention in unison as they took in the man filling the doorway. Steele's golden-tanned face had assumed a deep red color, and a vein along the side of his neck jumped spasmodically. His eyes were narrowed in a threatening squint, and a muscle in his jaw twitched with the obvious effort it took for him to retain what little control of his actions he had left.

Temerity couldn't help grinning her own satisfaction. Steele was angry, and for some reason that made her feel better. "Why, Steele, come in," she said in her most gracious "hostess" voice, taking special delight in the confusion that flitted across his anger-contorted features. "I was just explaining my plans to Uriah. You might as well listen too."

"Your plans just got canceled, lady! You're not going anywhere!" he shouted.

"Oh, but I am! And you can't stop me."

Recognizing the stubborn set to her posture and knowing how useless arguing could be when she had that look in her eyes, Steele managed to rein in his raging temper to a slow boil and spoke in a slightly more reasonable tone. "We had a deal, Temerity. I can't let you go. It's not safe, and that's all that needs to be said on the subject."

"Our 'deal,' Steele, was for the safety of the passengers and the *Intrepid*, not for mine. And our 'deal' was that I would handle funds and cargo any way I saw fit as long as I didn't interfere with the actual running of the *Intrepid*. So, I see fit to take my goods overland into the gold camps."

"Te-mer-i-ty," he said menacingly, dragging each syllable out to the fullest, aware that he was losing the battle to hold in his anger. "I'm warning you . . ."

"No, I'm warning you, Steele," she hissed, her eyes narrowing to boring spears of blue aimed directly at him. "I don't have to take orders from *anyone* on this packet! And I don't intend to. I *am* moving those supplies to the gold fields by wagon, and I'm leaving tomorrow. And"—she snatched up Uriah's revolver from the small desk and pointed it at Steele—"I'll shoot any man who tries to get in my way. Is that understood?"

Before Steele could respond, she turned back to Uriah, plunking the gun down where it had been. "Now, as I was saying. With so much cargo taken off here, it will make the *Intrepid* lighter. I'll meet you in Fort Benton by August fifteenth. If by chance I'm not there, you go on back to St. Louis. I'll catch a later steamer if I have to. I don't want to chance missing the loan deadline. I'd hate to come all this way and then lose the *Intrepid* to Cameron on a default because we weren't in St. Louis by September thirtieth. I'll trust you to get the best price you can in Fort Benton for the remaining cargo—then to pay off the crew and my father's loan when you get back to St. Louis."

Still ignoring Steele, she stopped speaking and tilted her head back slightly and rolled her eyes from left to right, mentally ticking off all the points she'd wanted to cover. "I can't think of anything else. Do you have any questions?"

"Just one," Uriah drawled, taking the worn pipe from his mouth and tapping it on the heel of his shoe.

Temerity arched her eyebrows expectantly.

"Why are you doin' this? I always thought you were one of the smartest little gals I ever seen. But now I'm not a bit sure 'bout—"

Temerity huffed out an irritable hrump and said, "I told you why, Uriah. It makes perfectly good sense. The profits will be better and we'll all make more money—you, me, the entire crew. Besides, I won't be the first person to do this. My father's friend, Captain LaBarge, did the same thing in 1864 and made a hundred thousand dollars."

"And how're you plannin' on takin' all that gold you're gonna earn past the robbers who watch the roads in and out of them gold camps?"

A flicker of uncertainty skidded across Temerity's brow—she hadn't thought about how she would transport her profits if her plan succeeded. "I'll worry about that," she said with forced bravado. "You just worry about getting the *Intrepid* to Fort Benton in time to get me and all that gold back to St. Louis by September thirtieth!"

"Hmp," he snorted, stuffing the pipe back into his pocket, the sound telling her how much he thought of her reasoning.

Tempted to admit she was already regretting her decision, Temerity stared at the crusty old pilot for a long, silent moment; but unable to admit she could be wrong—especially with Steele glaring at her—she wheeled around to leave. "Well, then, if there's nothing else, I'll go prepare for my trip. I want to get an early start."

Taking care to skirt Steele, who was silently seething with frustration, Temerity held her head erect, even managing an obviously insincere smile and a gloating nod as she swept past him.

"Well, what're you gonna do 'bout this?" Uriah fired at Steele the instant Temerity was out of sight. "Her pa'd skin me alive if he knew what she's plannin'!"

"Don't look at me! You heard her. I'm just a hired hand."

"And Santee Claus jest landed his reindeers on the roof of this wheelhouse! What're you goin' to do?"

Steele looked out over the water and heaved a slow sigh. "Hell, Uriah, I don't know! What do you suggest? Short of locking her in her cabin, I'm fresh out of ideas on how to stop her. You saw how she reacts to me telling her how to conduct *her* business."

"Look, I don't know what happened 'tween you two—I don't even want to know—but you mark my words, boy, if anythin' happens to that little gal 'cause of your shenanigans, I'll personally flay you alive. I went along with this whole business 'cause you said it was the only way. But it's time for this foolishness to end. You got to put a end to it 'fore she gets hurt."

"I don't want anything to happen to her any more than you do, Uriah. I've tried to protect her, but she's so goddamn bent on doing things her way that—"

"Lies usually don't protect no one for very long, boy. They got a way o' comin' back to hurt worse than the truth woulda done in the first place. If you want my advice, you'll tell her the truth—tell her who you are and why you done what you done. Then tell her you love her!"

"Love her? You're out of your mind!"

Uriah would have laughed at the guilty expression on Steele's face if the situation hadn't been so serious. But one way or another he had to get through to Steele, because he was the only way Temerity was going to be stopped. "Hell, boy, it's as clear as the nose on your face that you two love each other. But you're just too stubborn—or too dumb—to admit it! And a feller who don't tell his woman how he feels deserves to lose her to anot—"

"She's not my woman!" Steele interjected with a tone of disgust. "Only a crazy man would call a woman as contrary and set on doing things her way as Temerity Kincade his woman. I only came on this trip for one reason and as far as I'm concerned, Miss *I'm-the-Boss* Kincade can take fifty freight wagons of cargo to the gold fields—or all the way to blazes for all I care. I'm sick of worrying about her and trying to second-guess what crazy scheme she'll come up with next. I'm ready to wash my hands of her and this whole damned boat."

"I could o' swore you two . . ." Uriah affected a convincingly surprised expression, then shook his head. "Well, it goes to show I need to stick to observin' the river and forget 'bout watchin' folks. Still . . . I would o' swore . . ."

Taking care the grin on his face didn't show, Uriah turned away from Steele and busied himself with maps and charts he had strewn on his desk. "Probably for the best though, now that I reckon on it. You two wouldn't never be able to get it settled 'bout who was boss—both o' you spoutin' orders all the time instead of takin' time to listen to each other. Rawson's more her type anyway. Him bein' such a fine gentleman and all . . ."

"*Rawson?* What's he got to do with this?"

"Didn't she tell you?" Uriah asked, his thick white brows arched innocently as he turned to face Steele again. "Rawson's drivin' her other wagon for her. In fact, now that I think of it, I'm probably worryin' for nothin'. With a sharpshooter like Rawson along, she won't exactly be out there all alone, will she?"

Steele emitted a low animal growl, which only hinted at the repressed anger trembling inside him, and his face deepened to an oxblood color. "Over my dead body," he snarled, crashing out of the tiny wheelhouse and storming toward the stairs.

"Somehow, I figgered that's what you'd say, young feller."

Temerity pulled her wide-brimmed hat down farther on her head, adjusted her long-sleeved shirt, and pulled on a pair of heavy men's gloves. With a sigh, she hitched up her baggy denim trousers and climbed up on the seat of the freight wagon. Taking up the reins of the team of four mules she'd hitched to one of the two Schuttler wagons she had purchased, she ran a cursory check over her second wagon and team parked beside the first. In spite of her desolate mood, Temerity couldn't help being pleased with her purchases.

Decorated in patriotic colors, with blue wagon boxes, red wheels, and white canvas covers—as was common for the prairie schooners used by freight haulers—each of the sturdy, iron-wheeled wagons was nine feet long and four-and-a-half feet wide. Together they carried four tons of cargo beneath their high-arched canvas covers, and a ripple of excitement wiggled through Temerity as she thought of the profits that would be hers when she got to Virginia City.

That is, if we ever get there! she reminded herself with a frown as her eyes narrowed on the empty driver's seat on the second wagon.

Temerity glanced down at her lapel watch and

heaved an irritated sigh.

Charles Rawson was late, and her mood, already bad after a sleepless night of tossing and turning and reconsidering her decision, was growing worse by the second. "I'll give you one more minute, Rawson," she grumbled to herself, shooting an angry glare back toward the *Intrepid*.

But the instant her gaze landed on the sternwheeler, her anger with Charles Rawson faded into the back of her mind. In that moment, all she could think of was how she loved and would miss the trusty little riverboat. And she couldn't help feeling that the *Intrepid* was experiencing similar feelings about her. Rising up out of the early morning river mist, it reminded her of a lonely, forgotten spirit; and a feeling of sadness, so immense she could not shake it off, wrapped itself around Temerity's heart and squeezed painfully. What if she never saw the *Intrepid* again? What if she had made the wrong decision?

A lonely, unchecked tear trickled down her cheek, followed by another, then another.

"Good morning," a deep voice said, as her traveling partner finally made his appearance and climbed on the other wagon.

"You're late," Temerity reprimanded him, turning her head away and wiping her sleeve over her face to remove the obvious traces of her misery. "It would have been nice if you could have managed to give me some help hitching up the mules."

"Sorry," he mumbled in a hoarse voice, taking his place on the wagon seat and busying himself with arranging the reins between his fingers. "I overslept."

That's just dandy, she fumed silently. *I'm here hitching up eight damned mules, and he's sleeping!*

Not trusting herself to speak another word aloud, Temerity stiffened her posture and clamped her lips together. With the mood she was in, she was more than ready to tell Charles Rawson he could just go back to bed. However, since she didn't want to waste another day seeking a suitable driver, she kept her mouth shut.

Without further conversation, Temerity took one last look at the *Intrepid,* grabbed her whip out of its holder, and cracked it over the backs of her mules.

With a lurch, her team jerked to attention and, moving as one, pulled out ahead of the second team, leaving the other wagon to catch up.

"Captain Gunther, you'd better come see this," Harry Bailey said in a hushed, obviously distraught voice.

"Be with you in a minute, son," Uriah answered, squinting his eyes for the last glimpse of the billowing covers of the red, white, and blue freight wagons as they faded from sight.

"I'm afraid this can't wait, sir," Harry insisted. "Somethin' needs to be done before the passengers start to rouse."

"All right, Harry," Uriah said, turning away from the guard rail of the hurricane deck to face the younger man. "What's so all fired important it can't wait? I'm warnin' you, though, I ain't in no kind of mood to be settlin' any disputes between hot-blooded roosters."

"It's nothin' like that, sir," Harry started, hesitant now that he had Uriah's attention.

"Well, spit it out, boy."

"Last night when the men were takin' cargo out of the hold for Miss Kincade's freight wagons, they noticed a god-awful smell down there—like about ten cages of cats died down there and no one noticed 'til it was too late!"

"Why are you tellin' me about it? Find 'em and get

'em out of there."

"It's not that simple, Captain. When we finished up last night, it was too late to check it out, but first thing this mornin' I sent a couple of boys down to find out what was causin' the stink."

"Well, did they find out what it was?"

"You remember those two sisters named Rigby who got on at St. Charles and were supposed to get off at Fort Randall?"

"Not many men, young or old, could've forgot those two little ladies," Uriah acknowledged with a nod of his head and a grin. "Fact, I thought 'bout payin' them a little visit on the way back through Randall. But what've the Rigby sisters got to do with dead cats."

"They didn't get off at Randall, like we all thought, Captain," Harry said, the ominous sound in his voice wiping the smile from Uriah's leathery-skinned face.

"What do you mean?"

"The boys found their trunks still down in the hold."

Uriah's posture straightened alertly. "Are you sure they belong to them?"

"Oh, the trunks are theirs, all right." Harry swallowed hard, obviously having difficulty keeping down the contents of his stomach. "I opened them— and—and—God, it was awful, Captain! I never seen or smelled anything so terrible in my whole life. It was all I could do to keep from retchin' my guts out right then and there."

"You mean . . . ?"

"Yessir, both of them dead, one in each trunk."

"How? Could you tell how they died? Or were they too far gone?"

"It looked like their throats was slit," Harry said, his words coming between a series of dry heaves. "Just like that Yeager feller in St. Charles!"

"Damn!" Uriah cursed, looking off in the direction

311

Temerity's wagon had disappeared, the worried lines of his face deeper even than his age could account for.

"What are we goin' to do with them? We can't just leave them in the hold. The stink alone . . ."

"Bring 'em up and take 'em ashore. We'll have to bury them—after we go through the trunks to see if we can find the names of any next of kin."

Harry shook his head in revulsion. "I'm not sure I can open those trunks again."

"Then I'll do it, but it's got to be done. We owe it to them to find out if there's anyone we should notify. And we got to look for clues to who the murderer is. I was sure Yeager's killer was long gone, but now I'm not so certain. He might still be here. And everyone's in danger until we find out who he is!"

Throughout the morning, the other wagon kept far enough behind Temerity's to give the dust raised by her rig a chance to settle before riding into it; and no further attempts at conversation were made, which was fine with Temerity. Though the Schuttler wagons she'd bought were built so they could be coupled together and pulled by one combined team and one driver, she had deliberately left them separate for just that reason. Not only did she need this time alone with her thoughts to sort out her life; but she was hopeful that, if she made it a point to have no more personal contact with Rawson than absolutely necessary, he would permanently forget any amorous ideas he had entertained before they left the *Intrepid*.

Spying a line of green grass and cottonwood trees at the bottom of the rocky hill they were descending, Temerity glanced at her lapel watch and smiled her relief. After six hours of traveling over the dry, treeless hills of northeastern Montana, burned brown and ugly by the intense summer sun, she marveled at the accuracy of the instructions she'd gotten from a wise old mule skinner she'd met before leaving the Missouri—and at her own ability to follow his directions. He had said they would come to a creek about ten o'clock where they could stop to let the mules eat and rest for a couple of hours before moving on.

Emboldened by her first flush of success, Temerity tugged off the bandanna she'd tied over her face to protect her nose and mouth from the buffalo gnats that plagued the plains, and she cracked her whip to hurry her mules along. That clear water looked too good to wait another minute.

"We'll stop here to rest the mules and let them eat," she said minutes later when the second wagon pulled up next to hers and the driver jumped down. Temerity was already busy undoing the rig on her mules, expecting the other driver to do the same thing.

"How are your arms and shoulders holding up?" he said, his voice muffled by the protective red bandanna he still wore.

At the sound of his voice, Temerity's head jerked up, and she studied him across the backs of the four mules that stood between them. "My arms and shoulders are ju—"

Her mouth dropped open in a stunned gulp as the man she had believed to be Rawson eased the bandanna downward to expose his smiling features. "My grandmother always told me, 'Close your mouth before you start catching flies.'"

"What are you doing here? Where's Mr. Rawson?" she gasped, her eyes drinking in the welcome sight of the smiling face she had thought she could forget by running away, but now knew she never could.

"Poor old Rawson was suffering from a strange belly ache this morning and couldn't make it out of bed.

Must've been something he ate," Steele said with a pseudo-innocent shrug of his shoulders. "He asked me to apologize for backing out of your arrangement, so here I am."

Yes, here he was, all six feet four inches of him, and it was all she could do to thwart the ecstatic grin that threatened to split across her face, all she could do to stop herself from running into his arms and telling him how glad she was to see him, how much she loved him and how she wanted him on any terms he had to offer. But she didn't and she wouldn't. Her pride wouldn't let her. Not after the way he'd responded to her declaration of love.

"Steele, I don't trust you. I know you did something to him. What did you do? Why are you here?"

Steele's cheeks dimpled impishly, and his mustache twitched in a half-effort to keep from smiling. "Your distrust cuts me to the quick, Miss Kincade. I told you, Rawson got sick. As far as my being here, it's been a couple of years since I was in Virginia City, so I decided to come along for the ride."

Temerity tore her hungry gaze away from Steele and finished freeing the mules. "You're not going to talk me into going back, Steele," she warned, giving the lead mule a slap on the rump and sending the four to the creek to drink. "I still think this trip is a good idea and will bring a good profit. No matter what you say, I know I can do it."

Steele quirked his mouth up in a resigned grin. "Well, if any female can do it, you're the one. And after seeing the way you drove your team of mules and followed the trail today, I wouldn't hesitate to put my money on you—that is if I were a betting man." Sending his mules to the water, he pulled a folded tarp and scythe off the side of the wagon.

"You would?"

"I would," he said, nodding his head as he walked upstream. "I may have called you stubborn and ornery and bossy a few times, lady, but I never thought you were a bit short on the ability to do about anything you set out to do," he called over his shoulder as he spread out the tarp and hefted the scythe to swing at the tall grass growing beside the creek. "Since there won't be much green grass between here and the Judith Mountains, we'd better stock up while we have the chance," he said with an accurate arc of the metal blade in the grass, deliberately changing the subject. "Maybe while I cut grass for our four-legged companions, you could rustle up something to fill the bellies of us two-legged critters."

"I'm perfectly capable of wielding a scythe."

"Okay, then you cut grass, and I'll cook. But one way or another, I want something to eat."

His words suddenly struck her with the ability to see her own unreasonable contrariness for what it was, and her eyes widened in surprise. For the first time in her life, she could see that she had wasted years trying to prove she was capable of doing a man's work, when what she was, the only thing she wanted to be, was a woman. Instead of enjoying the special rewards and pleasures only a woman can know—like being protected and cherished or even cooking in the shade of a tall cottonwood tree rather than getting blisters on her hands as she cut grass in the blazing summer sun— she'd been trying to show everyone what a *man* she could be. Now, perhaps was time to find out how adept she was at being a *woman*.

"I'll cook and you cut," she said, her sheepish grin the only admission she could make right then.

Chapter Nineteen

"Did Mr. Rawson really get sick?" Temerity asked Steele as she helped him bale and load the grass he'd cut before eating the noonday meal she'd prepared.

Squinting his eyes against the sun, Steele looked up from his work and flashed a teasing smile at her. "Why would I lie about something like that?"

"I should have known you wouldn't give me a straight answer," she said with a disgusted grunt as she heaved a freshly tied bale on top of the cargo in the back of her wagon. "But that's all right. You don't fool me. I know what you're up to. And all your clever machinations will do you no good."

"My 'machinations,' huh? I'm afraid you've lost me, Temerity." He shoved a bundle of grass into her arms and began winding twine tightly around its ends. "Why don't you tell me in plain English what you're talking about?"

"All right, I will! I know *you're* the reason Mr. Rawson didn't come with me. *And* I know why you're here instead."

Steele stopped winding the twine and studied her serious expression, his own face twitching with a suppressed grin. "Oh, you do, do you? And just what

317

might that reason be, boss lady?"

"You thought that by getting me alone out here on the trail I would fall back into your arms at the first opportunity. But you are wrong. I meant what I said. I won't be your mistress."

"You have a mighty high opinion of yourself, Miss Kincade, if you think I'd go to so much trouble just for *another* sample of your feminine charms." He turned away from her and bent to gather up a last bundle of cut grass. "Not that I'll turn you down if you get cold all alone in your bedroll during the long, dark night. But believe me, that's *not* the reason I came with you."

He filled her arms with the last of the cut grass and began to wrap string around it.

His words caused an unexpected flutter of disappointment to ripple over her, and her voice trembled slightly when she spoke. "Then why? And don't say it's because you haven't seen Virginia City in a few years. For once, I'd like to have you give me a direct reply to a question."

Steele opened his mouth to speak, another teasing evasion on his lips. Then he closed it, his expression growing pensive as he wiped his thumb and forefinger down his mustache.

"Okay, Temerity, you want the truth, you've got it. I guess it's the least I can do." He took the last tied bundle of grass from her arms and shoved it into the wagon. Turning back to her, he grabbed her hand and led her to a shady spot beneath a cottonwood tree on the bank of what was supposed to be Dovetail Creek— if the map and directions the mule skinner had given Temerity were correct.

"You're right," he confessed, sitting her down in the grass, then stretching out his own lean frame beside her. "I 'arranged' Rawson's indisposition—with Gus's help."

318

"I knew it!" She couldn't help the triumphant grin that split across her face. He had come to be with her! He must care for her!

"But not for the reason you're thinking."

A wave of regret zipped through her, though she tried valiantly to tell herself it didn't matter why he had come. "Then what is your reason?"

"You know I haven't trusted Rawson from the very beginning. To let you go off across the Montana territory with him would be the same thing as leaving a helpless lamb in a pen with a hungry wolf. You wouldn't have had a chance, Temerity. And I would feel responsible if anything happened to you."

Responsible? How dare he feel "responsible" for her? As if she were a child! She was a grown woman, not a child. She jutted her chin defensively. "I don't want you or anyone else feeling responsible for me. And it's you who are the 'wolf,' Steele! Not Mr. Rawson. A gentleman like Mr. Rawson would never take advan—"

"Wouldn't he, Temerity?" Steele asked with a knowing tilt of his head. "Now who's evading the truth?"

"Are you accusing me of lying?"

"Are you telling me Rawson's *never* made any sort of advances toward you?"

"Of course no—" Temerity bit off the lie she'd begun to tell and focused her guilty gaze on the hands in her lap as they shredded a blade of grass. "Well, nothing I couldn't handle."

"Dammit!" Steele yelled, bolting to his feet and pounding his fist in his other hand. "I knew I should have killed that slimy son-of-a-bitch when I had the chance! And you!" he snarled, wheeling to glare down at her. "You were planning to spend a month alone on the trail with that bastard, weren't you? In fact, you

319

were probably looking forward to it! No wonder you were so upset when I interrupted your little tryst—"

"Tryst? How dare you—"

"—with my misplaced sense of responsibility. No wonder you—"

"—make such a vile suggestion. I made it very clear to Mr. Rawson how things would be, and he—"

"—were so anxious to get rid of me. All that crap about—"

"—gave me his word he would respect my wishes and—"

"—not wanting to have an affair. Tell me, Temerity, how long—"

"—keep everything between us on a business basis. Otherwise, I never would—"

"—have you two been carrying on behind my back?"

"—have agreed to go with—" Temerity's eyes bulged and her mouth dropped open in shock. "'Carrying on behind your back'? Why you vicious—" She raised her arm to strike him.

"Hold on there," he said, catching her wrist in his strong grasp and stopping the arc of her hand in midair. "I don't intend to take any more of your abuse."

"*My* abuse? You've stolen my innocence, tarnished my reputation, and accused me of being a prostitute and having an affair with Mr. Rawson. It's more than clear who's the abused party here!" She lifted her other hand and swung at Steele, unaware of the tears streaming down her cheeks.

Catching her second wrist in a tight grip before her palm could make contact with his cheek, Steele's face twisted into a grimace of self-recrimination. When he spoke, it was with the stunned voice of a man who has just awakened from a long sleep. "I never meant to hurt you, Temerity. I only wanted to protect you and take

320

care of you."

"Do you really think I've abused you, Steele?" she asked, the pain in his expression washing away her anger.

"Well, 'abused' is probably too strong a word," he admitted shamefacedly. Loosening his grip on her wrists, he lowered her hands to her lap, but retained his hold on them. "I'll admit you've bruised my ego more than a few times, but you didn't 'abuse' me. I don't know why I said that. I suppose *unmanned* would be a better word for it."

An embarrassed frown creased her forehead. "I never meant to—"

"I know you didn't. It's just that a man likes to *think* he's in charge and can take care of his—I mean *a* woman. So it's kind of rough on a fellow who's used to making all the decisions in his relationships, with men as well as women, when he finds himself working for and taking orders from the woman he lo—I mean *a* woman he can't control. Especially a woman who can do everything as well as any man, and better than most. After a while, it could make a guy doubt his masculinity."

"I'm sorry, Steele. I know my determination to earn enough money to buy back my father's loan makes me overbearing at times, but you have to know I never would have done that to you—or to any man— deliberately. Besides, you're the most masculine man I've ever known. I can't imagine your masculinity ever being threatened—by me or by anyone else."

A cheek dimpled in an embarrassed half-grin on Steele's face. "Me either. Why do you suppose I fought you so hard for control?"

Temerity breathed a soft chuckle. "All my life, I've tried to live up to what I thought my father missed by not having a son—though he never indicated he felt

321

that way. And I've always resented the fact that people automatically assume men are capable and intelligent, just because they're men, but consider women to be stupid and helpless little creatures who have to be pampered and cared for like children, no matter what their abilities. I guess in my desire to prove women are equal to men, I occasionally overdo it, huh?"

"Maybe a little bit," Steele said softly. "But I wouldn't want you to be any different."

"You wouldn't?"

"Actually, I think we make a pretty good team—when we work together instead of against each other." He leaned toward her, his gaze on her partially opened mouth.

Every fiber of her body called out for her to lean into Steele's embrace and meet his kiss. But she couldn't. She couldn't forget the things he'd said about her as though the words had never been spoken. And no matter how much she wanted to lose herself in his arms, no matter how much her body craved to be united with his, he still didn't love her. And until he loved her and was willing to make a commitment to the future, she couldn't allow herself to fall back into the addictive trap his kisses represented.

"The mules should be rested enough by now," she said, averting her face and removing her hands from his. "We'd better be on our way. I want to camp at Cat Creek tonight." It was one of the hardest things she'd ever done in her life, but she did it. She had held on to her pride and not fallen prey to his charms again. So why didn't she feel any better? Why didn't her salvaged pride make her feel content and whole—instead of empty and alone?

"Temerity?"

"Steele, I meant what I said on the *Intrepid*. I won't be your mistress—to be used whenever the mood strikes you, then discarded when you're through with me."

"What makes you think I'm going to discard you?"

"It's what men do when they grow tired of their lovers, and that's not a future I'd wish on anyone, much less myself—to be someone's discarded paramour. Besides, I can't forget the accusations you made about me and Mr. Rawson. I can't forget you actually thought I could . . . thought I could go from your bed to his so easily." She stood up and walked away from him.

"I didn't mean it," Steele called after her. "I believed you when you said you had no intention of being involved with him."

"Then why would you accuse me of such a terrible thing?"

"Haven't you figured it out yet, Temerity?" He was standing right behind her.

Startled, she spun around. She hadn't heard him approach. "Figured it out?"

"I go crazy every time you even look at another man," he admitted, clutching her shoulders intensely. "It's a case of jealousy—pure and simple—in its truest form. Just thinking of another man touching you . . . Half the time, I don't even know what I'm saying when I get that way."

Temerity didn't speak. She couldn't. Her breathing had stopped. Certainly any man who felt such intense jealousy had to be in love. Why didn't he say it?

"Temerity, you're mine. I . . ."

"What, Steele?"

"I—I—" He dropped his hold on her arms and wheeled away from her.

"Steele?" she shouted after him as he strode across the grass toward a dozing mule who'd had his fill of the lush grass on the creek bank. "Why can't you tell me you love me?" she whispered to herself as she, too, approached a mule to hitch up her wagon.

Never in her life had Temerity been so hot. Never had she seen a sunshine so bright, so destructive. All around her, there was blatant evidence that this cruel, summer sun was determined to kill anything that dared to try to live beneath its rays. And except for an occasional creek bottom where grass grew in spite of it, the sun had killed almost everything green on the dry, rocky hills she and Steele had driven their wagons over throughout the long afternoon on the trail.

Even after the sun began its descent, it still burned through the sweltering long-sleeved shirt and denim trousers she had worn to protect her skin.

An unexpected wave of nausea rippled through Temerity and her vision suddenly blurred. Swaying in her seat, she gripped its edge to steady herself and bit back the desire to groan. Determined to ignore the light-headedness she was experiencing, she squinted up at the glaring ball of white-yellow and blew out a grunt of disgust. "You won't win! You're doing your best to stop me, aren't you? Like everything else out here. But this time you're going to fail. I've beaten the Missouri River. I've beaten the male prejudice that said a woman couldn't take a steamer up the river. And today I'll beat you. In another hour you will have done your worst, and I'll still be here. And tomorrow I'll be back, even stronger than today. And I'll beat you again. And the day after that. And the day after that. For however many days it takes."

"Did you say something?" Steele called over the rattle of the wagons, maneuvering his next to hers so its shadow fell over Temerity like a cool breeze.

"I was just telling the damned sun it had met its

match when it met me!" That she'd been talking to the sun didn't seem the least bit odd to her, nor did the fact that she had used a curse word.

"Oh, you were, were you?" he chuckled. Then he looked at her more closely, and he was horrified by what he saw. Her hair hung in limp strings from under the brim of her man's hat. Her face was deathly pale, except for the splotches of red that colored her cheeks feverishly. Her eyes were glazed and her shirt was plastered to her body as though she'd taken a swim in it. "What the hell are you doing? Why didn't you tell me you were like this? You need to stop!"

"No! We can't stop. We're almost there. We're almost to Cat Creek. I can't let the sun beat me!"

"That creek's been there for a thousand years, and it'll still be there if we stop long enough to cool you down before we go on," he reasoned.

But Temerity wasn't listening. "I don't need to stop. I can go on. I'll rest when we get there." She picked up the canteen at her feet and opened it to take a drunken swig of water, unconcerned with the stream that dribbled down her chin and neck.

"Like hell you will!" Steele yelled, jerking up on his reins and halting his mules. The instant his team stopped, he jumped from his wagon and ran to catch up with hers. His long legs quickly covering the few feet that separated the vehicles, he leaped onto the driver's seat beside her and snatched the leather straps out of her hands. "Whoa there, mules!" he yelled with a hard yank on the lines.

"I told you I'm not going to stop until I reach the creek," she said with a distinct slur to her words as she did her best to grab the reins back from Steele. "The sun's not going to beat Temerity Kincade!"

Without warning, the nausea that had plagued her stomach for the past hour suddenly burned its way into

325

her throat. But this time she couldn't swallow away the need to be sick. Retaining the barest grasp on her dignity, she swiveled her body away from Steele just in time and hung her head over the seat rail to pitch the water she had just drunk onto the dry ground.

"When are you going to learn everything isn't a contest to see who's the best, Temerity?" he said when she was through being sick. Coming around to her side, he scooped her into his arms and gently carried her to a spot in the shade of a wagon and lay her down. "But you'd better get it in your head real quick, lady. With Old Man Sun up there, there are no winners—only survivors! And the number one rule for surviving in the sun is to get rid of a few of these clothes!"

Before she could know what he planned, he grabbed the front of her shirt and ripped it open, sending the buttons flying in every direction.

Beneath the heavy shirt, her chemise was soaked with perspiration, rendering it completely useless as a covering for her full breasts. In fact, it made them more alluring where they tried to hide beneath the sheer veil of wet cotton. It was all Steele could do to tear his gaze away when a gust of warm air, cool in comparison to Temerity's probable body heat, hit her breasts and the nipples contracted instinctively.

"Really, I'm fine," she mumbled, already getting a little of her color back.

"Ah, Temerity, when will you ever learn?" he said again with a shake of his head, certain he would love her just as much if she were a little less brave and not quite as unwavering in her convictions. Heaving a sigh of resignation, he poured some water from the canteen into a handkerchief and wiped it over her face, neck, and upper chest. "You're just bound and determined to—"

"And when are you going to learn I'm not like your

mother?" she said sluggishly, her eyes drifting closed. "If you loved me, I would never leave you or betray you like she did."

"What did you say?" Steele gasped, staring at her peacefully sleeping face.

When Temerity didn't answer him, Steele sat back on his heels and studied her. Was it possible? Was that what he'd been doing since he met her? Watching for signs that would indicate she was like his mother? Was his mother the reason he'd accused her more than once of being a prostitute? Was that why no woman had ever been right for him—because he'd seen his mother in all of them?

Steele shook his head and stood up. No, he was more intelligent than that. He knew the world was full of good women, women who could be trusted. *And full of bad ones like your mother,* an inner voice reminded him. "But not Temerity. She's nothing like my mother." *Temerity's strong and moral and giving,* he thought, remembering how she'd been willing to risk everything for Leaping Bear's tribe. *And my mother was weak and immoral and selfish. They're nothing alike. How could I have ever thought they could be?*

Temerity's words and his own personal revelation still absorbing his thoughts, Steele located her pack stored in one of the specially built boxes on the side of a wagon and opened it. Rummaging through it, he produced one of the white blouses she wore on the *Intrepid,* a dry chemise and drawers, and a full lightweight skirt of blue gingham.

Knowing he had to cool her off before she became even more ill, he took a knife from his boot and first cut off the bottom half of each sleeve, then went to work on the collar. When he was through, he had a short-sleeved, scoop-necked blouse that would let some air get to her skin.

Taking the fresh clothing back to where Temerity dozed, he stooped down and caught her shoulders to lift her to a sitting position.

"I'm fine," she mumbled, not fighting as he propped her against a wagon wheel. "I don't need to stop."

"Honey, sit up for a minute," he coaxed, slipping her arms from the shirt and tossing it aside. Steeling himself against the sight of her bared bosom, he took a deep breath and untied the chemise, then yanked the wet garment over her head.

"What are you doing?" she asked, coming awake with a confused frown on her face.

"You need to get out of those hot clothes," he said, handing her the fresh chemise.

Temerity glanced down at the chemise, her gaze landing on her own naked breasts, then jerking upward to meet Steele's sheepish grin. "How dare you!" she sputtered, clutching the fresh chemise up to cover her breasts.

"Don't get yourself in an uproar, Tem," he said, turning away from her. "I wasn't exactly going to ravish you here on the plains. I was just trying to change your clothes. But since you're awake now—and obviously feeling better—you can dress yourself." He tossed the skirt and drawers and blouse in her lap on top of the chemise. "Put these on while I move these mules around and hook the wagons together."

"You don't need to do that." She dropped the chemise over her head and slipped her arms under the straps. "It'll take too much time. I'll drive my wagon the rest of the way. I'm fine now," she argued. "I just felt a little weak for a minute."

"Damn it, Temerity, just shut up and put your clothes on. It's too hot to argue anymore. We're going to travel with these wagons in tandem the rest of the way to Virginia City whether you like it or not. You'll

328

drive in the morning and I'll drive in the afternoon. I don't want to hear another word about it. Now, get dressed and let's get going! We've got another three or four hours of good daylight left, and I don't intend to waste it *discussing* the matter!" Without glancing back at her, he strode over to the second team of mules and began unhitching them.

"I don't have to take orders from you!" She bolted to her feet, clutching the bundle of clean clothes protectively to her chest.

"The hell you don't! It's time you learned to take orders as well as you give them. From now on, I'm in charge and you'll do as I say—or I'll turn you over my knee and give you what your father should have given you years ago!"

Temerity stared after him, momentarily at a loss for words. Then, when she would have made another verbal protest, Steele turned around and glared at her. "Get dressed, Temerity," he demanded, taking a threatening step toward her. "Unless you want me to—"

Temerity needed to hear no more. Turning away from him, she fled behind the second wagon, stabbing her arms into her blouse sleeves as she moved.

The remainder of the day, Temerity sat silently on the seat beside Steele, thankful, in spite of herself, that he'd made her change clothes—though she was still angry with him for his high-handed tactics. At least, the lighter clothing was cool; and fortunately Steele's position on the right-hand side of the bench put her partially in his shadow, shielding the newly exposed skin of her arms and neck and upper shoulders, bared by her "restyled" blouse, from the damaging rays of the afternoon sun.

By the time they stopped for the night beside Cat Creek, Temerity's strength had revived greatly and her mood was improved. In fact, she could even see her earlier actions for what they had been. Childish and foolish.

Anxious to make amends to the man who'd supported her and stood behind her at every turn from the very beginning, she jumped down from the wagon and began unhitching the mules.

"I'll do this. You go on and start the fire for supper," Steele said, his voice weary.

Forgetting there was no need to remind him she was as capable of handling the mules as he was, she opened her mouth to protest.

Steele saw her and shook his head in disgust. "Why me?" he muttered with a roll of his eyes heavenward. "Temerity, not now," he warned through gritted teeth.

To his surprise, she snapped her mouth shut. "You're right. I'll gather some sagebrush for the fire and get it started. I think I spotted a deposit of buffalo chips I can use too. I'll go gather them."

His hands frozen on the harness of the mule beside him, Steele stared after her retreating figure, a disbelieving grin on his face. She had actually backed away from a confrontation! The rest of his work was done with new energy, and by the time he accepted the tin plate of food she offered him an hour and a half later, his mood was downright good!

"Thanks," he said, smiling up at her from his seat on the ground. Appreciatively eyeing the buffalo steak she'd brought from the *Intrepid* packed in bran to keep it fresh, the lima beans, and fried cakes, he inhaled a deep whiff of the tempting odor rising from the plate. "Mmm, it smells good. Where'd you learn to cook like this? I thought you'd spent all your life on a riverboat."

Pleased with his first reaction to the meal, Temerity smiled and picked up a second plate and filled it. "Only my springs and summers," she said, realizing for the first time that Steele knew no more about her than she did about him.

Sitting down across from him, she went on. "My mother was a wonderful cook and could make a feast out of the simplest ingredients. She taught me not only the basics of cooking but how to make do with whatever I have on hand. And then, I did learn a lot from the different cooks on the riverboats—when I wasn't pestering my father to let me 'take the wheel.'"

"This is great. Where'd you learn to cook on the trail?" He stuffed another bite into his mouth and chewed eagerly.

"A couple of times we took our own freight wagons down to the gold fields from Fort Benton. I learned then."

"I guess that's where you learned to handle the mules and a wagon," he said.

"It is. But what about you?" she asked, seizing the opportunity to seek answers to some of her questions about him. "Where did you learn about riverboats and mule teams? You never did tell me what you did before you hired on the *Intrepid*."

Steele straightened up, his eyes narrowing as he gazed past her into the twilight.

"Did I say something wrong?"

"Ssh," he hissed, setting his plate on the ground and picking up the rifle he had positioned on the ground beside him. "Just act natural," he whispered through a forced smile. "I think we're about to have company."

Chapter Twenty

The tiny, invisible hairs on Temerity's arms and the back of her neck stood on end; and she froze in place, a forkful of food halfway to her open mouth. The tin plate poised beneath her chin, her frightened eyes bulged with panic.

"Keep talking," Steele said, inching his stretched-out legs up under him until he could position himself in a squat.

Talk? Act natural? Was he crazy? Her vocal chords were paralyzed. Besides, how could she act natural with who knows what creeping up behind her and the man across from her poised, rifle in one hand, a revolver in the other, like a mountain lion ready to pounce.

"Temerity!" he whispered hoarsely. "I don't need you to go all helpless and female on me now. Snap out of it. Say something."

The urgency in his voice finally penetrated her fear. Steele was depending on her and she couldn't let him down. She had to show him it hadn't been all talk when she'd claimed she wasn't like all those other helpless females.

"I always enjoy a good steak, don't you?" she said in

a falsely cheerful voice that wavered terribly and made her sound like a very old woman. "Whether it's beef or buffalo, I like it."

Drawing strength from the brief nod of approval and smile Steele gave her, she went on. "Of course, it would have been so much better if I'd had milk to add to the gravy, rather than water. But all in all I think it was a good dinner."

"Very good," Steele agreed. "Keep it up."

Not certain if he was complimenting her culinary expertise or the way she was "acting natural," she went on talking, her voice *unnaturally* loud.

"The trick to the fried cakes is not to have the fat too hot when you drop the square in it so you can cook them slowly and they get done throughout, not just on the outside."

"Good girl," he soothed softly, not looking at her as his eyes searched the gathering darkness. "Go on."

"They're easy to make. All you need is a cup and a half of flour and a cup of water. I roll them out to about a fourth of an inch thick, then cut them into two-inch squares. I remember when I was a little girl, I insisted on getting out a ruler to be certain my two-inch squares were actually two inches. No more, no less. How my mother laug—Oh!" she gasped.

Suddenly there was no more need to pretend she wasn't scared senseless. They were surrounded by solemn-faced Indians dressed in breechcloths, moccasins, and braids with feathers in them. Several had rifles, and the rest were armed with bows and arrows. All had knives in sheaths on their hips.

"Oh, my god," Temerity moaned without thinking. "What do they want, Steele?"

Steele put down his weapons, though his right hand rested casually beside the rifle. "Come," he said to them, beckoning with his forefinger in the sign of invitation. "Sit!" He motioned to the ground beside him and pounded it with his closed hand. "We will smoke." He pointed his index finger at them, then to himself, then drew a pipe in the air with his crooked index finger, before waving his open hand away from his mouth in an imitation of smoke curls. "My woman"—he patted his open hand on his chest, then passed it down the side of his head as if smoothing long hair—"will pour a drink for you." He imitated pouring liquid into the palm of his hand, then held it in his mouth.

"I hope you've got plenty of coffee," he said to Temerity out of the corner of his mouth, "'cause I'm going to be in a helluva fix if you can't deliver."

So impressed with Steele's outward calm and knowledge of what to do that her own frantically pounding heart had slowed to a more normal rate, Temerity nodded her head. "I've got lots of coffee. Should I fix it now?"

Steele smiled at the brave he judged to be the leader and raised his eyebrows questioningly. "We drink?" he signed.

The Indians looked from one to the other, and the apparent leader nodded his head to Steele. "We drink," he signed back.

"Fix the coffee," he said to Temerity with a big smile for his guests as he indicated they should share his campfire with him.

Needing no further instructions, Temerity jumped to her feet and hurried to grab a large cast iron kettle from where it hung on the side of the wagon. Filling it with water she'd collected from the creek earlier, she took it back to the fire and hung it from the iron rods wired into a tripod. Vaguely aware of the quiet hum of men's voices as she worked, she hurriedly tossed buffalo chips and more sagebrush onto the fire to build it up again, then returned to the wagon for a sack of coffee.

By the time she came back to the fire, its flames were leaping high, lighting the entire circle so that she could see the sober Indian faces a little better. However, she knew a good Sioux woman kept her head down. And she also knew now was not the time to question the red man's age-old way of treating his women. Digging her scoop into the sack, she brought forth coffee, dark and rich, and dumped it into the already simmering water.

Before she could get the second scoop of coffee for the pot, the leader of the Indian braves grunted and vaulted across the space that separated him from her and grabbed her wrist.

Temerity's eyes widened in absolute terror. She was sure she'd done something wrong, had insulted him in some way. And now he was going to kill her! Her gaze jerked to Steele for help, but she saw that he was as helpless as she. The braves on either side of him held Steele's arms to his side and had knives drawn. "Ste-ee-ele," she wailed, unable to help herself.

"What the hell? Get your hands off her!" Steele shouted, straining against the iron-grip holds on his arms. "I came to this land as a friend, and I invited you to drink and smoke with me as a friend! Yet you—"

"Unh," the brave holding Temerity said, pointing to her wrist. "Where white woman get bracelet?" he asked in English.

Temerity's gaze, bordering on hysterical now, shifted frantically to the copper band on her wrist. Its reddish gold colors glistened and danced in the firelight, and she became aware that an eerie silence had dropped over the gathering. Even the wind and the insects of the night seemed to have silenced their songs to await her answer.

"My friend, Leaping Bear, the great Sioux chief, gave it to me."

336

There was a low rumble of conversation as her answer was translated into the language of the Indians.

"He told me it would protect me wherever I went in the land of the Sioux," she said, her voice quivering in spite of her need to sound confident and brave. It had been so easy to face the Indians when she was on the *Intrepid*—and backed by a hundred white men with weapons. But now . . .

The Indian holding her translated her words, and when he was through, all the men broke out laughing as he held the bracelet-encircled wrist in the air.

Please, God, don't let them be enemies of the Sioux! she prayed fervently.

"Let go of her!" Steele yelled, fighting the restraining holds with all his might. "Take the wagons and mules, but leave her alone!"

"We not hurt woman, white man! She is sister!" the brave announced with a deep chuckle. Holding out his free hand, he showed Temerity the bracelet on his wrist, a bracelet identical to hers. "Leaping Bear is my father."

"Bear Cub?" Temerity asked, squinting her eyes to see if she could recognize any of the boy from her childhood memories in the man holding her.

"Ha, ha!" he laughed triumphantly. "Yes, Little River Flower, Bear Cub! But cub no more. Now Roaring Bear!" he announced, taking pride in displaying the powerful voice that had given him his name.

"Bear Cub! I can't believe it!" she exclaimed, throwing her arms around the barrel-chested brave and hugging him without compunction. "I'm so glad to see you."

"Oh, oh!" the witnesses exclaimed.

Obviously embarrassed by her outpouring of affection, Roaring Bear pulled out of her embrace and set her away from him. "Little River Flower make coffee," he said gruffly, indicating the sack of coffee she still clutched in her hand.

Realizing she'd made a terrible social blunder and had been reprimanded, Temerity looked to Steele for guidance.

Free now, his breathing easy once again, he glanced down at the ground to remind Temerity how a woman—even the adopted daughter of a chief—was expected to act, and said, "Make the coffee, Temerity."

Fully put in her place, Temerity lowered her head and did as she was ordered. She added three more scoops of coffee to the bubbling pot—knowing four was a mystical number to the Sioux and hoping the knowledge would make up for her blunder—then scurried to the wagon for cups. Fortunately, she had a box of twenty-four tin mugs near the top of her tradegoods. If she could just find them.

By the time she had located the cups and unpacked them, the coffee was bubbling and the Indians and Steele were passing the long-stemmed pipe around the circle. The air was sweet with the smell of coffee and burning sagebrush and *kinnickinnick*—Indian tobacco.

When the pipe had made its way around the ring of braves, Temerity stepped inside the fire circle again with her box of cups. For an extra treat, she added a cup of sugar to the bubbling coffee, then began to ladle it into the cups. First serving her Indian brother, who sat on Steele's right in the place of honor, she proceeded to give them all coffee, then hurried back to the wagon to await further need for her services.

"Why are Roaring Bear and his braves in this country?" Temerity heard Steele ask. "We just saw your father, Leaping Bear, a few weeks ago on the Missouri River in Dakota territory."

"We hunt game—antelope, goats, elk, black bears, and grizzly for meat and furs. We go to great

338

mountains in west to hunt. Hunting no good on reservation."

"Hunting's good in the mountains though?" Steele said.

"Good," he repeated, nodding his head. "Why you in this dry land? Why Little River Flower so far from water?"

"She's taking her wagons to Virginia City in the mountains."

Roaring Bear nodded his head in understanding, studying Temerity as she refilled the cups in the outstretched hands of his braves. It was a shame his father had seen fit to adopt his old friend's daughter as his own. She would have made a dutiful and hardworking wife—and affectionate, he remembered, recalling the feel of her breasts as they had pressed against his bare chest in that moment before he'd pushed her away.

The longer he watched her silently going about her duties, the harder it was to think of her as a sister. Giving Steele a sly look out of the corner of an almond-shaped eye, he nodded his head toward Temerity. "Your woman, she pleasing to eyes."

Seeing the lust gleaming in Roaring Bear's eyes, Steele clenched and unclenched his fists at his side. "Yes, she is," he agreed, showing none of the effort it took to hold his building anger at bay. He cursed himself for cutting so much of her blouse away, giving the Indians a glimpse at the start of her breasts each time she bent over to serve coffee. "But now that she is expecting a child, it won't be long before she's fat and waddling around the campfire."

"Some women most beautiful when have baby growing in belly. Tell me, why she not wear ring on finger as other white women who have husband."

Now, that's what I call observant, Steele conceded

339

with a gulp. *Not much is going to get past this fellow!* "Oh, she does!" he improvised hurriedly. "But it's been so hot, her hands have swollen too much to wear it! You know how it is with pregnant women!"

"Hmp," Roaring Bear said, still studying Temerity and giving Steele no indication whether he believed him or not.

Then, suddenly standing, the Indian held out his hand to Steele for a white man handshake. "Our camp not far. We leave you and your woman now, but we go into mountains with you—to see sister and husband have safe journey."

"Yeah, well, that's nice of you. But it's not really necessary. We'd hate to slow you down."

"You not slow us down."

Steele realized he was trapped. "In that case . . . thanks a lot."

When the last Indian brave had disappeared into the night, Temerity turned to Steele and breathed a relieved sigh with a hiccupy little giggle. "Hopefully, that's the last of them. I thought they'd never leave!"

Steele cringed. How was he going to tell her she had to keep up her docile wife act a while longer? He couldn't help the smile that twitched on his mouth at the thought of the proud Temerity Kincade being forced to be obedient and subservient for a few days. *It might even do her some good.* "Unfortunately, your long-lost *brother* doesn't feel the same about you. He's decided since we're headed in the same direction, he's going to give us an escort."

"A what?"

"He said it was to watch over his 'sister.' But I suspect Roaring Bear has ulterior motives. He wasn't exactly watching you like any brother ought to watch his sister."

Remembering the uneasiness she'd felt under Roar-

340

ing Bear's intense scrutiny as his black eyes had followed her around the campfire, Temerity didn't argue with Steele this time. She'd seen that look in more than one man's eyes in her lifetime. "What are we going to do? Maybe we should break camp now and be gone before they wake up in the morning."

"I considered that, but they'd catch up with us and then be angry. Anyway, I suspect we have a guard watching our every move."

Temerity glanced around nervously and took an unconscious step closer to him. "Steele, I'm scared."

As touched by the fact that this was the first time he'd ever heard Temerity admit to being afraid of anything as he was nervous about their unplanned escort, Steele wrapped his arms around her and gathered her into the shelter of his embrace. "You don't need to be frightened. I'm not going to let anything happen to you. Besides, as long as he considers you his sister, he won't try anything. Incest is highly frowned on by the Sioux."

"But I'm not his *blood* sister! I didn't even know the bracelet meant Leaping Bear was claiming me as his daughter."

"That makes no difference. Family is family to them. They won't even talk with their mother-in-laws because it would be incestuous. No, as long as you keep that bracelet on—*and* continue to act like the happy *bride* I told him you were, I don't think Roaring Bear will be anything more than an inconvenience."

Temerity drew back, a reflexive argument on her tongue, but Steele stopped her with a dimpled grin and a finger to her lips. "Remember, Temerity, we may have an audience. It wouldn't do to have your protective big brother think you were unhappy, would it?"

Temerity's eyes sawed from side to side, then narrowed to a threatening glare. "You told him we

341

were married?" she hissed through an artificial grin.

"I'm afraid so." His hands on her waist, he drew her hips against his and flashed her a pseudo-apologetic smile. "And pregnant."

"P—p-pregnant? Why would you tell him that?"

"With only one of me, and fifteen of them ogling you and making no secret of the fact that they wouldn't mind having you for their squaw, it seemed like the best way to protect you. I mean, if I was bitten by a snake or fell over a cliff and was killed and you were suddenly a widow, there'd be nothing to stop one of them from claiming you for his own bride, would there? But there's something not quite as appealing about a woman with another man's baby in her belly. Oh, by the way, the reason you don't wear a wedding ring like other white women do is because the pregnancy and the heat have made your hands swell."

"You seem to have thought of everything," she said, stepping out of his embrace. She couldn't look him in the eyes. Uncertain how to take this turn of events, she began to gather up discarded coffee mugs.

On the other hand, it would be ridiculous to be angry. After all, he'd only done what he'd done to protect her. In fact, now that she thought about it, she was quite impressed with his quick thinking. But on the other hand, she was frightened by the surge of elation that had run through her at the mere thought of even *pretending* to be married to Steele and carrying his baby. If only it were true. But it wasn't, and it wasn't going to be. And the sooner she faced that fact, the easier it would be to give him up when he walked out of her life in St. Louis. To act the part of his bride, even for a short while, would make it that much harder when the time came to abandon the pretense. No, she just couldn't do it.

"I'll do that," Steele said softly, coming up behind

her as she stooped to pick up the box of mugs. "You lay out the bedrolls. You know where everything is. I'll be back in a minute."

Temerity watched Steele's back as he walked toward the creek to wash the cups, obviously not the least concerned with doing what was considered "woman's work." The love she felt for him swelled painfully in her chest, and she wanted to run to him, lose herself in his arms, and tell him again how much she loved him, how much she wished their pretend marriage was real. *If only he . . .*

"But he doesn't, Temerity," she interrupted her thought, wheeling away from the sight of his broad shoulders hunched over the dirty dishes. *He's had every chance in the world to tell me. If he loved me, he would have said so!* "No, he's just interested in one thing!" she muttered as she hauled out blankets and pillows.

After great soul-searching and an attack of common sense, she came to the resolution that she would keep up the pretense of being married to Steele during the day when they were under the watchful eye of her self-appointed Indian protector, but not at night. There, she would draw the line.

When she had laid out a bedroll under each of the wagons, Temerity took a nightgown, towel, washcloth, and soap from her personal things and scampered to the creek to bathe.

"The other side of that brush is far enough," Steele warned in a whisper, reminding her of a fact she'd nearly forgotten. They were probably being watched. Still she had to bathe the dust and grime of the day off her skin or she would never be able to sleep.

Studying the darkness from the shrub shelter she'd chosen beside the creek and seeing very little a man could hide behind, she decided Steele had just been trying to scare her. Unbuttoning her blouse, she jutted her chin in defiance of his warning.

As though they were physically touching her, she immediately felt eyes crawling over her. Clutching the front of her blouse together, she whirled around, certain whoever was watching had to be right behind her. But no one was there, only the rough hills marred by sagebrush.

Well, whoever you are, you're not going to get much of a show! she swore silently, slipping the full nightgown on over her head, but not putting her arms in the sleeves. Shooting a triumphant smile into the darkness behind her, she began to remove her clothes in the privacy of her nightgown tent, until she was naked beneath it. Feeling quite smug with her ingenuity, she quickly washed and dried herself, then slipped her arms in the nightgown sleeves. She quickly brushed her teeth with baking soda, then grabbed up her clothes and scurried back to the wagons.

"That was fast," Steele said, looking up from where he was stooped over the bedroll he had moved next to the other one.

Temerity glanced under the second wagon and back to the one beside Steele. "What are you doing? I told you there would be none of that."

"It's just for show, *wife*. What would Roaring Bear think if his braves reported to him that the happily married couple slept under different wagons?"

Temerity averted her gaze toward the hill from where she'd felt someone watching her. "You're just saying that to frighten me into sleeping with you. I don't even believe there's anyone out there."

"Are you willing to take that chance?" Steele asked in a low, taunting voice.

Temerity peered into the darkness again, then back to Steele, her expression uncertain.

He held up his hand to her and said in a husky voice,

"Come to bed, Temerity. I give you my word I won't do anything you don't want me to do."

Taking a hesitant step toward him, she hazarded one last nervous glimpse at the hill beyond their campsite, then gazed down at the offered hand raised up to her. "Remember, you gave me your word," she cautioned, placing her hand in his and allowing herself to be drawn down to the bedroll beside him.

"Nothing you don't want," he repeated, laying her back on the pillow then drawing a sheet over them.

Oh her back, Temerity stared up at the wagon bottom. Exhausted minutes before, she was now wide awake, every nerve in her body aware of the man lying beside her. Only inches away from her, he, too, was on his back, his hands clasped behind his head. The clean smell of soap assaulting her nostrils, she realized Steele had bathed while she was attending to her own bath. Disguising it under the pretense of a sleepy sigh, she inhaled deeply, drawing in the masculine scent of bay rum and shaving soap.

"You know what I first noticed about you?" he asked suddenly.

"That I was about to be run down by a team of horses and didn't have sense enough to get out of the street?"

She could almost feel him smile in the dark, could close her eyes and see his mustache curving upward, his dimples creasing into his cheeks.

"Knocking you out of the way was more instinct than actually noticing you. No, the first thing I really noticed was the way you smell."

"The way I smell?"

"I had you pinned to the ground. My face was buried in the back of your hair and I got a whiff of lemons. It was the cleanest, most fragrant scent I'd ever smelled. As a matter of fact, I think it was then, at that very moment, before I'd ever seen your face or heard your

345

voice that I began to . . ."

The breath caught in her chest, and her head rolled on the pillow so she could study the dark profile beside her. When he didn't go on, she couldn't stop herself from raising up and laying a gentle hand on his arm. "Began to what?"

"I don't think I ever met a woman who smelled like lemons before," he said, ignoring her question. "Is it some special imported perfume or soap you use?"

Disappointment exploding in her ears, Temerity lay back down and answered in a cool voice. "It's soap. I make it myself. A Mississippi River boat captain we know brings the lemons from New Orleans several times a year. They come from Brazil."

"Temerity?"

"What?"

"I don't really want to talk about lemons."

"You don't?"

"No, I don't."

"Then why did you bring it up?"

"Damned if I know. Maybe because every time I start to tell you how I feel, I get tongue-tied like a teenager and change the subj—Dammit, Temerity! I just want you to know that no matter what happens when we get back to St. Louis, I love you."

Temerity's heart stopped for what she was sure was a full minute. "You love me?"

"From the moment I first smelled those goddamned lemons, I was lost—a condemned man," he said with a defeated laugh. "How's that for crazy? Falling in love with a woman's soap!"

"You really love me?" she said again, only barely daring to breathe again. She had to have fallen asleep and been dreaming. Surely, if he loved her, he would have told her before now. Hadn't she given him every chance? "Why haven't you told me before this?"

346

He picked up her hand and carried it to his mouth to kiss each of her fingertips. "Because I didn't have the right to tell you. I still don't. And I swore I wouldn't, not until we were back in St. Louis and all secrets were out in the open."

"What secrets? What are you talking about? Tell me, Steele. Whatever it is, it won't matter. Not if we love each other."

"There are some things even love can't overcome, Temerity." His voice was sad, defeated.

"You're wrong, Steele. Love can overcome anything. Tell me what it is and we'll work it out together. You said before what a good team we make when we work together. You were right. Together, there's nothing we can't do. Let me help you with whatever it is that's bothering you."

"I can't. Not until we get back to St. Louis."

"Then why break your vow to yourself and tell me you love me now? Why couldn't it wait until St. Louis, too?"

She heard him breathe out a long sigh. "When I jokingly said I could be killed on this trip, it got me to thinking. And I couldn't stand the thought of leaving you believing I didn't love you. Because I do, Temerity. I love you more than I ever thought it possible to love another."

"Then that will be enough for me, Steele. Because I love you too, and right now I can only think of showing you how much."

Before Steele realized what was happening, Temerity lifted the sheet and rolled over onto him, covering his mouth with hers in a kiss she hoped would tell him how much his words meant to her.

Chapter Twenty-One

Burrowing her fingers into the hair at the nape of his neck, Temerity cradled her hips between his thighs and trailed her tongue over his upper lip at the base of his mustache. "Tell me again," she pleaded against his mouth. "Tell me you love me."

Steele lifted his pelvis and rotated it beneath her as he cupped her buttocks and pulled her hard against him, his fingers digging into the soft roundness of her flesh. "Can you have any doubt?"

"I want to hear you say it!" she said, moving her body in a decidedly suggestive response to his blatant invitation.

In the darkness, she felt his mood grow intense. One of his hands moved up her back to clutch her torso against his in an almost desperate squeeze as his other hand continued to mold her to him. "I love you, Temerity Kincade. I love you, I love you, I love you," he whispered, punctuating each word with a kiss on her lips.

"Oh, Steele, I didn't think I would ever hear you say those words," she murmured, her eyes filling with tears.

"Hey, what's this?" Steele asked, the surprise evident in his voice when a tear splashed on his cheek. "Are you crying?"

Embarrassed and not even knowing why she was crying, Temerity buried her face in the curve of his neck and expelled a tearful little laugh. "I'm just so happy."

"Well, you've sure got a funny way of showing it," he said, rolling her to her back. "If it's going to make you cry, I'll stop saying it!"

"You'd better not stop. I've waited too long to hear you tell me you love me. I don't ever want you to stop." She slipped her hands between their bodies and began to work a button out of its hole in his shirt.

"I don't think I could." He raised up so she could reach his lower buttons. "In fact, you'll probably hear it so much in the next couple of months you'll get sick of it," he threatened, shrugging out of the shirt when she was through.

"That'll never happen," she said, reaching up to undo the buttons at the neck of her nightgown. "I'll never get tired of hearing you say you love me."

"In that case . . ." He drew her to as much of a sitting position as the headroom beneath the wagon would allow. "I love you"—he pulled her gown out from beneath her bottom—"I love you"—over her waist and ribs—"I love you"—and over her head, leaving her naked, her pale skin shimmering in the darkness.

"I love your face," he said, catching her cheeks between his palms and accenting his statement by kissing her eyes and nose and chin. Encircling her neck with his hands, he said, "I love your ears," as he drew a plump earlobe between his lips and tugged on it slowly, lazily, as though savoring a rare delicacy.

"I love your neck," he murmured, grazing his hands along her shoulders and trailing his lips over her arching neck in a series of sucking nibbles.

"And your shoulders," he added, taking a gentle bite of her shoulder with his teeth before moving his hands

350

and mouth lower.

"And these. Lord, how I love your breasts!" His fingers on the satiny outer curves, his thumbs cherishing the undersides, he buried his face in the lemon-scented cleavage and crushed them to his lips as though he was afraid they would escape his possession.

Wallowing in the security of her breasts against his face, Steele worshiped them with his tongue and lips, leaving not the tiniest morsel of delicate flesh unanointed by his kisses.

When her breasts had been so thoroughly loved that Temerity's insides were churning deliriously, her groin grinding hungrily, Steele moved his mouth lower still.

Kneeling between her thighs, he scooped her buttocks up off the bedding and bent his head to cherish with his kisses the treasure of her femininity.

As his tongue flicked over the tip of her desire, flames exploded from the heart of her ecstasy and radiated throughout her entire being. Unable to keep from crying her pleasure aloud, she pressed the back of her wrist against her mouth to muffle the sound that would not be thwarted. "Oh, Steele," she groaned, her head thrashing from side to side as his tongue and lips relentlessly propelled her to higher and higher peaks.

With expert and deliberate patience, he carried her to the very edge of the ultimate pleasure with his taunting. When she was certain she could take no more, when she was begging him to release the unbearable constraint in her belly, he drew the swollen evidence of her femininity into his mouth. She became a senseless, moaning lump of desire, no longer human, no longer of this sphere.

The glorious light behind her tightly closed eyes burst into a billion splinters of brilliance, taking her to the sun, to be scattered through the universe.

Not realizing she'd been lifting herself higher to meet

Steele's kisses, her muscles turned to water and her legs, where they'd held her up, collapsed under her. "Hurry," she begged, clutching desperately at his hair and shoulders to draw him up over her. Working her hands between them, she fumbled wildly for the buttons on his pants. When she was unable to negotiate them, she moaned her frustration.

Shoving her hands aside, Steele quickly unfastened the pants and shed the hindering garment, freeing his passion at last. "I do love you," he sighed, submerging himself into the sheath of her body with a relieved cry. "Oh, my god! You feel so good, so good."

"Yes, yes," she moaned. Some of her strength restored, she locked her ankles across his back and fanned her fingers over the expanse of his shoulders. "I've missed you so much, Steele." She moved with the slow, easy rhythm he had established. "How did I ever think I could go on living never again knowing the feel of you inside me?" She spoke in a breathless pant, almost to herself, as the torrid pace of their lovemaking increased with each coming together of their bodies.

"I'll never let you go now, Temerity," he growled, almost angrily, as he slammed into her body harder and harder. The sound of flesh slapping against flesh reverberated off the low roof of their dark hideaway, to mingle in an erotic symphony with their moans and ragged breathing, drowning out all other sounds of the night. "Promise me, no matter what happens, you won't leave me. You're mine."

"For all time," she vowed. "I'll never leave."

"Oh, god! Now, sweetheart. Come be my love," he implored, plunging into her in a final, jerking spasm as he spilled his passion deep inside her.

"Ye—esss, Steee—ele," Temerity wailed in a long, hoarse cry as she reached rapturous fulfillment and her own ecstasy constricted around his manhood, squeezing him, holding him, draining him of all his strength.

"I love you," he sighed, collapsing on her and burying his face in the dark cloud of hair spread on the pillow, his words sounding more like a prayer than a declaration.

Clutching his head to her, she smoothed her fingers over his hair, soothing him, loving him. "And I love you, my sweet, sweet Steele. I'll always love you. Always."

They fell asleep, their bodies still united in their passionate embrace, both vowing to love each other forever, yet neither of them trusting the joyous feeling of happiness they felt at that moment.

Temerity woke up to the sound of a hobbled mule snuffling for breakfast on the other side of the wagon. Smiling softly at the head that rested on her shoulder, the hand that possessively cupped her breast, and the long leg draped over her thigh, she eased herself out from under Steele's sleeping body.

Clutching the sheet to her chest, she glanced around groggily, finally locating her nightgown wadded up on the other side of Steele. She reached over him and grabbed the gown. After shaking it out—to dislodge any possible creatures who might have decided to sleep in it while she wasn't using it—she slipped it over her head and scooted out from under the wagon.

The sky faded from darkest gray at its zenith down to near white on the eastern horizon, and she could hear the sounds of birds as they began their day. Already, she could tell it was going to be another sweltering day, but it didn't matter. As far as she was concerned, this was going to be the most glorious day of her life. This was the first whole day she would spend with Steele, knowing he loved her. She couldn't wait to start it.

Snatching up a towel and washcloth, Temerity hurried to wash up and take care of her personal needs at the bush she had bathed behind the night before. But just as she got back to the wagons, a wave of nausea swept over her, causing her forehead to break out with perspiration and her limbs to go weak.

Glancing up nervously to make certain Steele was still sleeping, she wheeled around and ran back to the creek as fast as her wobbling legs would carry her, her hand clasped over her mouth.

"Oh, lord," she groaned, wrapping her arms across her stomach and sinking to her knees, heaving, gagging. The vomiting lasted only a few minutes, and by the time she had washed her face and brushed her teeth again, it was as though she'd never felt sick. Certain it was just a lingering effect of her reaction to the heat the day before, she straightened herself and started back to the wagons, thankful it was nothing more serious. She would eat a soda cracker or two just to be sure there wouldn't be another recurrence.

"Good morning, Little River Flower," a man's deep voice said behind her, bringing Temerity up short.

Spinning around, she found Roaring Bear approaching her on foot from further up the creek. "Roaring Bear, what are you doing here?"

"I bring meat for morning meal," he announced, holding out a freshly killed rabbit for her to see, unconcerned with the blood that dripped from it.

Temerity's stomach heaved and she couldn't speak. All she could do was clamp her hand over her mouth and run for privacy.

"So, it is true," Roaring Bear said when she stepped back out into the open, her face pale.

"What's true?" she asked, searching for the bloody rabbit, but seeing thankfully that her "brother" had put

354

it out of sight.

"Little River Flower with child."

"What?"

"Husband say baby in belly." He pointed to the area of her stomach. "I not believe last night. But now I believe."

Temerity looked at him with a puzzled expression.

"Morning sick," he explained with a knowing nod of his head.

"Morning sick?" Temerity repeated, unable to deny his assumption without betraying their safety. "Oh, morning sickness! Yes. We're very happy about it." She nodded her head and managed a weak smile. Realizing how her words sounded, she quickly amended them. "Not about the morning sickness, of course. The baby. We're happy about the baby!"

Roaring Bear laughed at her brave attempt to pretend to feel good. "I bring medicine from my camp. *Squaw mint*. It help you feel better. I give meat to your man. He will cook. Have baby in belly, must take care. Make strong brave. Where husband?"

"He's still asleep. We weren't going to cook breakfast. We planned to get an early start and ride until around ten o'clock before we stop to rest and feed the mules and have our first meal."

"No good. Mother need to eat. Make sick go away."

"I'll eat some crackers and have a cup of tea."

"Sister tell Roaring Bear. You are happy with the white man, yes?"

"Oh, very happy, my brother. I love him a great deal!"

"He is good to Little River Flower?"

"Very good. He's wonderful. I could never love another man. He is my life."

Roaring Bear nodded his head, satisfied. "It is good. I wake my brother. Tell him leave soon."

"That's all right, I'd like to wake him up," she suggested shyly, sensing she and Steele were in no more danger from her Indian brother. And she was relieved about that. However, now Roaring Bear had given her another worry to occupy her mind. Could she be pregnant? As much as she liked the idea, she couldn't help hoping she wasn't. It was too soon and Steele had said nothing recently about marriage. She didn't want him to feel he *had* to marry her, which he had said he would do if she was pregnant. She wanted him to ask her because he *wanted* to be married to her, and for no other reason.

Roaring Bear smiled knowingly and nodded his head. "I understand. You not married long time?"

"Not very long at all. And I'd appreciate it if you wouldn't tell him about my morning sickness. He's very protective and I don't want him to worry."

"Little River Flower good wife. Roaring Bear keep secret."

"Thank you, my brother," she said, adding a silent prayer of gratitude. If she was pregnant, Steele wasn't going to know until he proposed—that is, if he wasn't so slow that she began to show before he asked her.

The days developed into a routine of rising before sunup, grabbing a quick snack—even if it was just a piece of buffalo jerky Roaring Bear brought them— and getting on the move before the sun peeked over the horizon.

As Steele had planned, Temerity drove their tandem wagons in the morning and he drove in the afternoon. It was the third day out before she realized he had assigned her the mornings deliberately to protect her from the strong rays of the Montana summer sun. Not only was the morning naturally cooler, but moving

356

southwesterly as they were, the sun stayed at their backs and to the left. As driver, she sat on the right side of the bench, where the brake was—*and* where she was positioned in the shadow of the wagon cover behind her and Steele's large frame beside her. And she loved him all the more for his clever manipulating of her, letting her do her share of the work and protecting her at the same time.

Each day, when they stopped to rest and feed the mules, they frequently shared their meal with Roaring Bear, who usually rode his pony beside the wagons. Then, about two o'clock, they were back on the move for another four-hour stint of traveling across the greenless, broken plains toward the Great Rocky Mountains.

Ordinarily, in the afternoon, about an hour or so on the road, Temerity crawled back into the wagon to nap on top of several new tents she had among her wares. It wasn't all that comfortable. But fortunately, by that time of the day, anything would do for a bed. Even her cornhusk mattress on the *Intrepid* would have seemed soft.

The first day she had argued with Steele when he'd caught her nodding on the seat beside him and suggested she take a nap. She had insisted she didn't need to rest. However, when he'd flashed those dimples of his and said, "Come on, Tem. Just do it for me. Do it because it'll make *me* feel better," she had gone all gooey inside and had crawled in the back, falling asleep so quickly she'd barely been aware of the lumps.

"Since tonight's the last night we'll camp with Roaring Bear and his braves, before they head west and we go south," Temerity said to Steele on the ninth day out, as she crawled up from after her nap, "I'd like to fix supper for all of them. What do you think?"

"It might be nice. But do you think your *big brother*

357

will let you do it? You know how he's been hovering over you like a mother hen ever since he decided I was telling the truth about your being pregnant."

Temerity smiled, buttoning up the high collar of the blouse she'd loosened for her nap, but that Steele insisted she keep closed when in view of the Indians—after the experience with her low-necked blouse the first night out.

What Steele said was true about Roaring Bear. Once he'd believed she was pregnant—a fact Temerity also came to believe more and more with each passing day—her adopted brother had coddled her shamelessly. He had brought her marvelous herbs for her morning sickness to be drunk in tea, which she made the night before and drank cool the first thing every morning; leaves that, rubbed on the skin, discouraged hungry insects; and others that protected her fair skin from sunburn.

He had provided them with small game and dried buffalo strips. But the most interesting, and unexpected, turn of events was the way he'd lectured Steele—several times—on the way a man should treat a pregnant wife. According to Roaring Bear, that was the one time it was not considered unmanly for a husband to help with a woman's work.

As a matter of fact, he had been more than a little angry the first morning he'd seen Temerity holding the reins of the eight-mule team pulling the wagons, and had delivered one of his more memorable lectures to Steele.

"I still can't figure out what made him decide to accept you as his sister so wholeheartedly. It kind of makes me feel guilty for my first suspicions about him."

"Me too. But whatever it was, I'm glad. If he hadn't changed, this past week would have been absolutely miserable. As it is, I've rather enjoyed getting to know him and a few of the Lakota customs." She now automatically used the Indian name of the tribe the whites called the Sioux.

"Yeah, but I'm looking forward to having you all to myself again. There's not that much time left before—" A sad expression of regret furrowed across Steele's forehead. "Before we meet up with the *Intrepid*," he went on quickly. "And I don't want to share a minute of our time together with anyone else."

Touched by Steele's echoing of her identical thoughts, Temerity hooked her hands in his arm and lay her head against his shoulder. "I don't either. Though I think we've managed to compensate fairly well for our lack of privacy, don't you?" she teased, tiptoeing her fingers up his muscular arm, over his chest to his neck, and slipping them into the open vee of his shirt. "In fact . . ."

"I've unleashed a devil," Steele protested playfully. He carefully removed her hand from inside his shirt and, after kissing her fingertips, plopped it back on his arm at the elbow. "Now, behave yourself."

"I can't! I'm in too good a mood. We've come over half the way without any serious mishaps, and the mountains in the distance are so beautiful. Besides, it's so good to be traveling where things are green again— green grass, green trees, green shrubs. The air even smells better here. I thought I'd never breath clean air again."

"Well, I suppose we'd better have your farewell party for Roaring Bear and his pals then—just so you can use up some of your excess energy! But I'm warning you, you'd better not work so hard that he decides he needs to stay around to watch over you a little longer. Do I have your promise?"

359

"I love you, Steele," she exclaimed gleefully, turning his head toward her and kissing him on his surprised mouth.

Though he pretended to be angry at her outgoing show of affection, Steele couldn't hide the look of happiness that brightened his smile every time he heard her say those words. Nor could his happiness make him forget that the bliss he was experiencing was only temporary. At best, it could last only until St. Louis. And he vowed to make the most of the time they had left together.

"I wish for my sister and brother a long and happy life with many babies," Roaring Bear said the following morning as he prepared to mount his pony and ride west. "May our paths cross again. And may *Wakan Tanka* breathe good winds in your direction."

"You have been a good friend, Roaring Bear. Thank you for everything," Steele said.

The two men shook hands, both sentimentally aware of the fact that this would probably be the last time they would ever meet, but knowing there would always be a bond between them because they loved the same woman. "You take good care of my sister," Roaring Bear reminded Steele sternly. "I give her to your hands."

"You can count on it," Steele answered, grinning down at Temerity, the love shining in his hazel eyes.

"You will not forget things I teach."

"I won't forget," Steele promised, wrapping an arm around Temerity's shoulders and giving her an affectionate squeeze.

"And, you my sister, take care of this man called Steele. He is good man."

"I will," Temerity answered through a lump in her

throat. "May *Wakan Tanka* ride with you, my brother."

Roaring Bear looked from side to side, checking to be sure the other braves had ridden on. Seeing none in sight, he grabbed Temerity by the shoulders and pulled her to him for a self-conscious hug, then dropped his hands and spun away from the stunned couple. He was on his horse and almost out of sight before either of them spoke again.

"Well, what do you think of that?" Steele said as they watched Roaring Bear disappear into the west.

"I think we're not the only ones who might have learned something this past week."

When Virginia City came into view as they crested the last hill before the road began to wind down to the camp, Temerity stood up from her seat beside Steele. "Look!" she squealed. "There it is!"

Doing his best to keep control of the mules and the brake, Steele grabbed her arm and jerked her back down to the bench. "Sit down, you little fool!" he shouted with a surprised laugh. "Do you want to get us killed?"

"We've done it, Steele!" she cried, his harsh treatment doing nothing to quell her exuberance. "We've actually done it!" She threw her arms around his broad shoulders and kissed him on the cheek. "Just look at it! Isn't it the most beautiful sight you've ever seen?"

"I suppose if you consider a few log buildings and clapboard shanties and tents surrounded by hills with a few pine trees on them beautiful, it is," he said with a teasing smile in her direction. "Me, personally, I can think of quite a few things I think are prettier. For instance, a bathtub full of hot water, or a real bed with clean white sheets and you in the middle of it, or . . ."

"Oh, you!" she huffed, balling her fist and punching him on his hard-muscled arm. "You know what I mean. I've actually done it. I've beaten the Cameron Line at their own game. With the money I get here, I'll be able to pay off the loan and save my father's riverboat."

A triumphant grin split across her face. "Oh, I can't wait to see the look on old Mr. Cameron's face when I walk into that big gray building of his and plunk all that money down on his desk! He'll bust a gusset."

"I heard old Mr. Cameron died," Steele ventured, his mood suddenly darkened.

"Well, whoever's in charge. I'm going to have the pleasure of personally seeing the shock on his face!"

"Maybe he'll be happy for you, Temerity. He might even have *wanted* you to succeed. After all, the Cameron Line isn't exactly in need of any more sternwheelers."

"Don't you see it yet? They don't care about owning another riverboat. They just care about doing away with all their competition so they can rule the whole river."

"Didn't it ever occur to you that . . . *Mr.* Cameron could have lent the money to your father out of friendship instead of greed, Temerity?"

She studied his profile for a long moment. "I wish I knew what makes you feel compelled to defend Cameron when you've seen . . . Oh, what's the use?" she mumbled, dropping her arms from around his neck and turning her face away. "You and I are never going to see eye to eye on the Cameron Line, so I'd rather not talk about it anymore. I feel too good to have my mood spoiled by an argument no one can win!"

"You're right! I'm sorry. So! What's the first thing you want to do when you get to Virginia City?"

Slanting him a mischievous glance out of the corner of her eye, she smiled and said, "That bath idea of yours sounds very tempting."

"Oh, it does?" he said with a villainous grin. "And what about my other idea? How does that strike the lady's fancy?"

"As a matter of fact, it strikes the lady's fancy quite nicely, thank you," she returned haughtily, doing her best not to giggle and spoil her imitation of an English noblewoman. "If . . ."

"*If?*" he roared threateningly. "You dare to speak to me of ifs?"

Shrinking back from him as convincingly as the heroine in a melodrama, she squealed in a high, dramatic voice, "If . . . your other idea is a meal cooked in a stove—by someone other than me!"

By the time they drove into town an hour later, their argument about the Cameron Line was behind them and Temerity's spirits were high once more, her sides aching from laughing so much.

Looking around the town she knew to be the first incorporated city in the Montana territory and to have been established on the Ruby River only five years before when gold had first been discovered in Alder Gulch, Temerity's mood was whisked to even greater heights. All around her, the streets teemed with activity, causing her excitement to soar. The sounds of wagon harnesses jingling, wheels clattering, miners laughing raucously, women chatting gaily, hammers constructing new buildings of rough-sawed lumber, men shouting orders, animals squealing, all seemed to join with her in a wild chorus to celebrate her success.

"Thank you, Steele!" she shouted over the noise of the streets.

"For what?"

"For helping me get here. I never could have done it

363

without you! I love you!"

"I hope, when we get back to St. Louis, you remember you said that!" he said, undisguised anguish wrinkling his brow.

"Remember what?" she asked with a teasing smile for the man she loved, too taken with the Virginia City sights to notice he wasn't smiling as well.

"You're getting a bit too smart for your drawers, little lady," Steele said, skillfully hiding his worried frown behind the facade of playfulness he'd been able to affect since the subject of the Cameron loan had come up. But how much longer he would be able to put up this front, he didn't know.

Chapter Twenty-Two

"Are you sure the wagons will be all right until tomorrow?" Temerity asked, glancing back over her shoulder at the livery stable as she and Steele crossed Wallace Street and headed for the Ruby Valley Hotel.

"I'd trust Ed and John Lord with my life," he said of the livery stable owners, who had promised to watch over the loaded wagons.

"Still, I'd feel better if we could go on and sell our goods tonight instead of waiting until tomorrow," she said, unconvinced.

"The stuff will be fine, and since most places are closed because it's Sunday, we don't really have a lot of choice—unless you want to stand on the street all night and sell things piece by piece to whoever walks by."

"Of course, I don't want to do that, but . . . maybe we should spend the night at the livery stable as an extra precaution!"

"Temerity, relax. Ed and John won't let anything happen to your wagons. I spent three years with those boys during the war, and I'm telling you, either one of them would lose his life before he'd let a friend down. Now, what do you say we go take care of a couple of those items on our idea list? In fact, if you scrub my back really well, I might even take you to the theater between supper and bed. I saw a poster that said Jack Langrishe's troupe is performing *The Widow's Victim* at the Crown Theater. How's that sound?"

"That sounds wonderful," she said, taking another worried glance back at the livery stable. "Still . . ."

Steele rolled his eyes toward the sky. "For tonight, will you do me a favor? Forget you're Temerity Kincade the riverboat owner, and just be a woman being courted by a lovesick fellow who can't wait to get her alone so he can kiss her!"

Temerity flashed Steele a lovingly exasperated smile and laughed. "As long as you put it like that, I don't see how I can refuse."

"That's them," a gravelly voiced man told his partner as the tall stranger and his dark-haired female companion stepped off the sidewalk to cross Wallace Street. "I'd be willin' to stake a year's diggin's on it."

"Still, we better make sure," the wiry second man said, walking into the street and falling into step several yards behind the handsome couple. "I don't want to make no mistakes. We ain't gittin' paid for no bungled job."

"What's our plan? We gonna steal their wagons?"

The smaller, thinner man shot a disgusted look at his taller, huskier sidekick. "Jest how far do you think we'd get with 'em? 'Sides, even you wouldn't stand a chance 'ginst them Lord boys. 'Member how fast Ed Lord took you down in the boxin' match last Fourth o' July? Hell, boy, you never even knowed what hit you!"

"I been practicin' since then. I'm gonna beat him this year!" the larger man said defensively.

"Either o' them boys're bigger, faster, and smarter 'n you. You ain't got a chance."

"I'm gonna take him, Billy. You jest wait 'n see! This year I'm gonna take Ed Lord."

"Sure, Petey," Billy said, "but for now, we ain't gonna mess with him or his brother."

"Then what're we gonna do?"

"If you jest had half a brain, you'd have it figgered out. We let 'em sell their stuff here 'an wherever they're goin'. We jest foller 'em, like we're doin'. Then when they got their bags full o' gold dust and are on the way to Fort Benton, we jest drop down on 'em and take it away from 'em. Couldn't be no easier!"

"You're real smart, Billy," Petey said admiringly, the worship evident on his big, dumb face. "I wish I was smart like you."

"Don't you worry 'bout it none, Petey. Long as you got me to do the thinkin', you're as smart as you need to be. 'Member, I told Ma I'd take care o' you. An' ain't I always done it?"

"You sure have, Billy. And I always done took care of you, ain't I?"

"Like Ma said, you got the brawn and I got the brains."

"Have you been to the Continental before?" Temerity asked as they made their way down the outside stairway of the hotel.

"No, it's gone up since I was here last. But I've heard it's the most spectacular restaurant west of St. Louis," Steele told her. "How does Wiener schnitzel, noodles, kraut, herring salad, and the finest imported champagne sound for dinner? And for dessert, how about homemade ice cream over a slice of pie a man would ride a hundred miles for a taste of?"

She thought about how hungry she'd been ever since she'd discovered her pregnancy *and* gotten over her morning sickness. "It sounds delicious. But how do you know they'll have that? I thought you said you haven't been to the Continental."

"I haven't, but the Murats own the Continental, and I ate at a combination saloon and barbershop they owned in Denver a few years ago. Katrina's cooking is world famous, and those are her specialties!"

"What's she doing in Virginia City?"

"Katrina and the count—did I mention her husband, Henri, is a count? No? Well, he's supposedly the black sheep of some royal French family. Anyway, he and Katrina go wherever the money is. Rumor has it they've already made and lost several fortunes in their lives."

"Royalty?" Temerity asked, her eyebrows raised with dismay. "Do you think my dress is nice enough? I didn't think I'd have any need for anything fancy."

Steele laughed and glanced down at Temerity's pale blue gingham dress. "You're perfect. In fact, you'll probably be one of the best dressed people in the restaurant or the theater."

Even if his words hadn't been just right, Temerity would have felt better under Steele's admiring gaze, and she squeezed his arm affectionately. "You're just saying that because you're so glad to see me without dust an inch thick covering me from head to foot."

"Yeah, that must be it. It couldn't be because you'd be the most beautiful woman in the world dressed in nothing but rags."

"I'd better get some food in your stomach fast. You're becoming delirious!"

"Deliriously in love!"

"Me too!" she whispered, meeting his warm gaze with sapphire eyes that sparkled brightly with happiness.

*　　　*　　　*

"Oh! What an evening!" Temerity giggled, twirling across their hotel room hours later. "I've never eaten so much or laughed so much or—"

"Or drunk so much," Steele offered, catching his hands around her waist as she spun into his arms.

"Are you suggesting that I'm inebriated?" she asked, arching her back and staring up at his smiling face.

"Who, me?" His cheeks dimpled impishly. "Would a gentleman suggest such a thing?"

"I'll have you know, I am not inebriated! I simply feel good."

"Numb's probably a better word for what you're feeling," he chuckled, grasping her behind the knees and hoisting her into his arms.

"I beg your pardon?"

"I said champagne agrees with you!"

She studied his mustache for a moment, as if analyzing his words, then flopped her head against his chest with a profound, "Oh."

"Oh, is right! Now let's get you to bed so you can sleep this off before morning!"

"Sleep? What about the last item on our list? Aren't we going to make love?" she asked, her face forming a sullen pout.

"I don't think you're in any shape for it tonight."

"What's wrong with my shape?" she giggled, straightening in his arms and jutting her breasts forward. "I thought you liked my shape!"

Steele's mustache twitched up in a smile as he stood her beside the bed. "Now, Temerity, be a good girl and get ready for bed."

She wiped the tip of her tongue along her lips slowly, her expression thoughtful. "If you insist," she cooed with a secret smile as she began untying the waiststrings of her skirt and petticoats, letting them drop together in a puddle of blue at her feet.

"I'll get your gown," Steele offered, not wanting to

take advantage of her in her intoxicated state, but unable to look away from the alluring picture she made as she reached up and unwrapped the crossover bodice of her dress.

"I won't be needing it," she whispered brazenly as she locked his gaze with hers and shrugged out of the bodice. With a nonchalant toss, she pitched it onto a chair, leaving herself clad in only a thin white chemise and lace-trimmed drawers that came to her mid-calves.

"You won't?" he rasped through parched lips.

"Unt-uh," she said with a slow, predatory grin as she fanned her hands over his shirtfront and into his coat to smooth it back and off his shoulders. "And you won't be needing all these clothes either." She let the coat drop and went to work on his shirt.

"Te-mer-ity," he warned in an uncertain voice, but he did nothing to stop her as her fingers, surprisingly nimble considering the amount of champagne she had consumed, quickly dispensed with the buttons on his shirt. The shirt itself was sent fluttering to the floor to join the rest of the discarded clothing.

"You definitely don't need these," she said, giving all her concentration to his trousers.

"You're crazy," he whispered, no longer able to resist this new, sexually assertive Temerity. Recognizing his defeat, he surrendered. He delved his fingers into her thick dark hair, sending pins pinging onto the floor.

His pants unfastened, she dropped to her knees and tugged his boots and socks off his feet one at a time. That accomplished, she looked worshipfully up the length of him and smiled. Reaching up to catch the waistband of his drawers and trousers in her fingers, she peeled both garments down his long frame as one.

"I love you, Steele," she vowed, hesitating only slightly before wrapping her hand around the satiny flesh of his manhood, stretched tight with desire. "I want to love all of you, the way you love me," she whispered, moving her hand up and down the length of him as she inched her head closer.

"Oh, my god," he cried aloud as the warm moisture of her mouth closed over his desire. He dug his fingers into the hair at her temples and held her head to him. "Oh, my god."

Suddenly, Steele caught her under the arms, yanked her up from the floor, and pushed her over onto the bed. "You little witch," he ground out, grasping at her chemise and drawers in a desperate effort to remove the thin undergarments, leaving her wearing nothing but her stockings.

Draping her legs over his shoulders, he plunged deep into her, filling her with the entire length of his swollen desire, exploring and claiming her innermost core.

It was a raw act of possession, like nothing they'd ever experienced together, and Temerity was catapulted into a spasming climax before she was aware it was happening. Crying out her joy, she dug her nails into the hard-muscled flesh of his shoulders and babbled senseless words of love and sex and worship.

Then, before she had fully recovered from the first rapturous rise and fall, he took her soaring again, this time joining her as together their single-minded passion ruptured in a violent flood of fulfillment.

"Mmm," Temerity purred, pulling Steele down to kiss his mouth. "Now, don't tell me that's not nicer than going to sleep!" She smoothed his hair off his sweat-soaked brow.

"I've got to agree with you," he said, his breath coming in rough pants. "That was a helluva way to end a perfect day."

"*End* it?" she exclaimed, deliberately tightening her femininity on his resting desire. "I thought we were just beginning."

"Oh, you did, did you? You're a little hussy, you know," he laughed. "But I wouldn't want it said I couldn't keep my woman satisfied." Giving her a quick kiss on the lips, he withdrew from her and kissed his way down her body to kneel on the floor beside the bed. Her legs still draped over his shoulders, he dipped his head to lave and pleasure her with his tongue before again entering her and achieving his own glorious release.

"If this keeps up, we won't have anything left to sell in Helena when we get there!" Temerity said in an excited, hushed voice as they approached the fourth business establishment they'd been to that morning.

Holding the door open for her, but staying outside so he could keep an alert eye on the wagons, Steele glanced around the mercantile store. Finding it surprisingly well stocked, he whispered. "You're going to have to work for this sale." He indicated a stern-faced woman behind the counter. "That dragon lady over there's not going to be as taken with you as the owners of those two saloons and the feed store were. Want me to use some of my masculine charm on her?"

Rising to the deliberate challenge, Temerity blew out a derisive snort. "Hmp! You flatter yourself, sir. It's obvious to me that the woman behind that counter is of rare intelligence. Why, she'd spot you for the rogue you are the minute you flashed one dimple in her direction! You'd be outside with broom marks on your backside in a matter of seconds. I'll talk to her! One intelligent businesswoman to another!"

Steele shrugged his shoulders and grinned impishly, deliberately dimpling his cheeks. "Okay, boss lady!" He laughed, crooking his index finger and flicking a knuckle off the tip of her nose. "But don't say I didn't offer!"

Five minutes later, Temerity was back out on the sidewalk, her face screwed into a disgruntled frown. "Of all the stupid people I've ever met in my life, that old prune takes the cake!" she said to Steele as she swung up onto the wagon seat. She directed a final glare over her shoulder at the awning-protected store front and said, "We'll go somewhere else."

"Does this mean she's not going to buy anything?" Steele goaded with a wicked twinkle in his greenish-brown eyes.

"Yes," Temerity growled, directing an irritated glare at him. "She's not going to buy anything—even though she's shamefully understocked on many of the items I offered her. And do you know *why?* Do you know why she wouldn't buy my merchandise?"

"Why?"

"She said she makes it a rule never to do business with women! 'They can't do the figures required for large money transactions,'" Temerity mimicked. "Can you imagine anything so ridiculous? What does she think *she* is? Of course, I'm not surprised she didn't include herself in the female population. I wouldn't either!"

"Should I go back and try the dimples on her?" Steele asked out of the corner of his mouth, keeping his amused gaze focused straight ahead.

Temerity opened her mouth to lambaste him for taking the entire situation too lightly. "No!" she shrieked. The shrewish sound of her own voice sliced through her anger, and with lightning clarity she suddenly realized how ridiculously she was behaving.

Unexpected laughter bubbled in her throat, and she clamped her mouth shut in a futile attempt to contain

373

her giggles. But it was no use. The laughter spewed through her compressed lips in a snorting snicker. It really was funny.

"No, I don't want you to try the dimples," she muttered with a conceding grin. "I'd take it all back to St. Louis before I'd sell to her now!"

"Okay, but I'll keep 'em handy in case you change your mind!"

Before the day was out, Temerity and Steele had sold one wagon load of goods and close to two-thirds of the merchandise in the second wagon. "It's amazing how the merchants are willing to buy such large quantities of things," she said to Steele, as together with Ed Lord and his wife, Nettie, they made their way up the stairs to their hotel room under the approximate two-hundred-pound weight of filled leather and canvas pouches.

"When you tell them that they're getting it cheaper by cutting out the freight handlers in the middle, they just can't turn down a bargain," Steele pointed out, opening the door at the top of the stairs. Using his back to prop it open, he held it for the other three, then followed down the hall close behind them.

"You sure had a good day, Captain C—." Ed flashed a nervous smile at Steele and blushed. "Captain," he said.

"Yes, we did!" Temerity chuckled gleefully, sounding more like a little girl than the sophisticated businesswoman she proclaimed herself to be. "Now all we have to do is get this gold back to Fort Benton and the *Intrepid*," she said, a worried frown marring her happiness. "Somehow, I just never thought seventy-five thousand dollars in gold would be so heavy."

"The captain's got it all figured out, Miss Temerity," Ed said admiringly. "Anybody plannin' to steal your gold's got a surprise comin'."

374

"I know, but tell it to me again. Maybe it'll make me feel better."

"My brother's already hidden it at the bottom of four barrels of horseshoe nails to put on the Wells Fargo stagecoach tonight. After dark, we're going to slip you and the 'nails' out to the edge of town and put you on that stage. You'll be in Helena by tomorrow."

"Anybody watching won't expect us to leave tonight, right? Not with another half-full wagon of merchandise to sell."

"And not with me drinking and talking all over town about how we're leaving in the morning," Steele inserted.

"Then, in the morning, you and the captain will load up your wagons and leave town. Only it'll be me and Nettie dressed in your clothes and carryin' these bags of horseshoe nails."

"No one will know until it's too late that we sold you the wagons and mules and remaining freight and that you're going to sell it in Helena," Temerity said. "It sounds good, but I still can't help worrying."

"Why? It's a foolproof plan," Steele said.

"What if Ed and Nettie are hurt?"

"There's not a lot of chance of that," Nettie said. "Ed's brother, John, and my cousin, Fred, are followin' us on horseback, just like the captain's goin' to be followin' the stagecoach. Any sign of robbers and they'll be there in a minute."

"Besides, you oughta see my Nettie handle a rifle." Ed beamed his pride down at the freckled redhead. "Ain't no one gonna take anythin' from her she don't want to give—even if it's just a bag of nails!"

"Still . . ."

"It's part of the bargain, Temerity; we sell the stuff to them at cost in exchange for their help."

"That's right," Nettie said cheerfully. "The three of

us are going to make enough money on this to make any risk worth it."

"Nettie's already talkin' about the ladies' dress shop she wants to open with her share."

Temerity smiled at the vivacious red-headed young woman she'd met just that afternoon, yet knew she could trust. "Then I guess it's all settled," she said.

"All over but the shoutin', as they say," Ed laughed. "Now, Captain, suppose you and me go have us those drinks and let folks in Virginia City know you'll be leavin' in the mornin'. Nettie, you two switch clothes. We'll be back in about an hour."

"You heard what he said, Petey. They're leavin' in the mornin' for Helena. All we gotta do is watch to make sure they go, then ride on ahead and wait for them. It'll be like shootin' flies on a pile of manure."

"I still don't see why you don't want to just go on up to their hotel room while he's gone and get the gold now."

Billy rolled his eyes and snorted, "Hell, boy! First of all, that much gold must weigh a ton. How you plannin' on luggin' it through town without no one seein' you? Second, she ain't there alone. While her man's gone, she's got Nettie Lord up there with a rifle. You can't move fast enough to get out of that little wildcat's way."

"I guess your way's the best."

"Damn right it is. One of these days you're gonna learn. My way's always best!"

About an hour later, as Billy and Petey watched from a darkened store porch across the street, Steele and Ed Lord came out of a saloon down the street and sauntered casually along the sidewalk to the outside stairs of the hotel. Taking the stairs as casually as they had walked along the sidewalk, the two men disappeared into the hotel.

A few minutes after that, they saw a man and a woman, obviously Ed and Nettie Lord, appear in the doorway at the top of the stairs, hurry down them, and disappear around the livery stable into the small house behind it.

"I'm going to be a nervous wreck before this is all over," Temerity grumbled as she lit a lamp in the front room to make it look as if someone were at home at the Lords' house.

"Come on, let's go," Steele hissed tersely, standing beside the back door of the three-room house.

"I'm coming," she called, hiking her carpet bag up under the long cape she wore.

Making a dash across the open yard between the house and a stand of trees, neither of them spoke. Just as they'd planned, John Lord was waiting on the other side of the trees in a wagon with a riderless horse hitched behind it.

Her heart racing with excitement and fear, Temerity bounded into the wagon and lay down in the back with the gold-filled barrels of nails while Steele untied the horse and mounted him. "I'll miss you," she whispered from the wagon bed.

"I'll be right behind you." He bent low on his horse and she raised her head up from the wagon to meet his kiss. "I love you, sugar. I'll see you in the morning!"

In the morning, in the gray half light of dawn, Billy and Petey jumped to attention from the porch benches they had spent the night on across the street from the hotel. "Looks like they're leavin' right on time, Petey boy," Billy crowed. "Here comes one of them Lord fellers bringin' one o' their wagons around from the livery stable. I guess they sold the other one."

"There they are," Petey announced in a hoarse whisper as he pointed to the man and the woman standing at the top of the stairs.

Knocking Petey's pointing finger down, Billy said, "All we gotta do now is make sure they get on the Virginia City-to-Helena Stage Road, and then we'll just ride on ahead and pick a nice private spot. . . . Quick, get back!" he barked, pressing himself back into the shadows.

"What is it?"

"Nothin'. I just thought I saw the feller look over in this direction. I'm probably mistaken. Go on and get our horses ready and I'll meet you in the back as soon as they head out."

"Okay, Billy. You can count on me!"

"You're a good boy, Petey," Billy said, patting the larger man's cheek with an affectionate pat. "Now get movin'."

Nettie squinted toward the eastern horizon and smiled. "Looks like we're gonna get us some company, Ed," the saucy redhead announced, lifting her rifle from where it was propped beside her knee and laying it across her lap.

"You don't suppose it'd be Billy and Petey Sales, do you?" Ed asked, his voice rife with amusement.

"Wouldn't be a bit surprised. Probably just out to give us a friendly sendoff to Helena."

"Howdy, Billy, Petey," Ed called out in a loud voice. "What you two boys doin' out so early in the mornin'?"

The two would-be road agents looked at each other, their expressions confused. As though their motions had been choreographed, they glanced back at the

378

people on the wagon and, necks straining forward, squinted for a better view.

"Is that you, Ed Lord?" Billy called out, his voice beginning to shake with rage as realization sank in. "What're you and the missus doin' drivin' that wagon?"

"Bought two of 'em," Ed replied proudly. "Ain't it fine? It's a Schuttler."

Nettie eased her hand over the butt of her rifle and inserted her finger in the trigger hole—just in case. "We're takin' it to Helena to sell the rest of this stuff up there. Don't s'pose you boys need a tent or somethin' else we could fix you up with?"

"What happened to the folks who sold you the wagon?" Billy asked, not bothering to acknowledge Nettie's question.

"Oh, they ought to be gettin' into Helena 'bout now. They decided to take last night's stage instead of waitin' until this mornin'." Ed hit his knee and shook his head. "Fancy making it all the way to Helena in twelve hours. We'll be lucky if we make it in five days. Course most of them stage drivers drive like madmen. And they hardly stop long enough to take a pee . . ." He grimaced under Nettie's disapproving glare and apologized. "Sorry, hon. Anyway, the stage don't stop any longer than it takes to change horses at the switch stations along the way. But for folks in a hurry, I s'pose it's the only way to go. Me, I'd ruther take it slow and easy. Well, boys, it's been good talkin' to you. You take care of yourselves now." Ed flicked the bullwhip over the mules' backs and told them to, "Giddap."

As they drove past the two stunned riders, they saw Petey turn to his brother and heard him ask, "What happened, Billy? Ain't we goin' to get the g—"

"Shut up, you big, dumb ox! We been had! That's what happened!"

Chapter Twenty-Three

The closer the fast-moving Wells Fargo stagecoach drew to Fort Benton, the more withdrawn and sullen Steele became. He continued to spend the long hours staring out the window at the landscape—even the final thirty-mile stretch between Helena and Fort Benton, where there was nothing to look at! No grass, no trees, no water.

Her heart breaking at being shut out of his thoughts, Temerity studied Steele's intense face. The muscles in his jaw flexed and unflexed, as though a terrible burden weighed on his mind; but he had given her no clue to what was bothering him. She glanced down at his balled fist on his hard thigh. As it had been since the beginning of the trip, it was clenched, intermittently pounding angrily on his knee.

He'd been like this almost since the Mullen Road had begun to climb out of the flat, open plains of the Prickly Pear Valley to wind along the north and west sides of the Missouri River on top of pine- and aspen-covered hills and cliffs.

She searched her mind again to see if she could think of anything she'd done that might have caused him to change so drastically. But there was nothing. In fact, when she'd asked him directly if she'd made him angry, he had wrapped his arm around her shoulders and hugged her tightly to him. "No, love, it's nothing you've done. It's me. I guess I just don't like being cooped up in tight spaces very much," he had told her, trying to laugh it off but failing miserably to convince her that it was anything so simple.

At first, when they met in Helena, after the madcap departure from Virginia City, they'd been so happy with the success of their entire journey that he'd talked her into staying over an extra few days. Because they had covered the last part of their trip by stagecoach, they were ahead of the schedule she had originally projected, so she had given in to his suggestion willingly.

And they'd had a wonderful time, eating in Helena's finest restaurants, seeing several plays at the Helena Theater, taking buggy rides in the surrounding Prickly Pear Valley—and making love in their room at the International Hotel. As a matter of fact, Temerity was certain she had saved up more wonderful memories in those special love- and laughter-filled days than most people could experience in a lifetime.

But when they had boarded the stagecoach for Fort Benton, all the laughter had ended, as if a black cloud had descended on them. Had the love ended too? she wondered again and again. Had Steele stopped loving her? Had she just been a plaything to while away the boring hours on the trail? And now that the trip was at an end, was he having second thoughts about telling her he loved her? Or was "I love you" just something he automatically said to all the women he knew?

Temerity glanced down at her hands resting in her lap and moved them over her flat belly in an instinctively protective gesture. What would she do if he didn't love her, if he didn't ask her to marry him before he learned of her condition? Shaking her head resolutely, she looked out the window. She wouldn't think about that. Not yet anyway.

Maybe it was as he had said, just a mood brought on by being confined in the stagecoach. She prayed that was it. She would know soon enough though. They were pulling into Fort Benton.

In spite of Steele's morose mood, a ripple of excitement gurgled through her. After all, this had been her goal all along. Fort Benton! The head of navigation of the Missouri River. Of course, she had planned to steam in on the *Intrepid*, not bump and clatter in on a stagecoach. But no matter how she had gotten here, she had done it, and no one—not even Steele—was going to spoil it for her.

She strained to see the levee to determine if she could recognize the *Intrepid* from that distance. This late in the season, she could count the sternwheelers docked at the Fort Benton levee on one hand and . . . A sinking wave of panic shook through her. The *Intrepid* wasn't among them! Shading her eyes with her hand, she looked again to be sure.

"They're not there, Steele!" she cried, her voice shaking with dread.

"They'll be here," he said, leaning across her to peer out her window at the river. "We're still a few days early. In Helena, I read in the *Montana Post* that the water's low all the way to Cow Island and getting lower by the day," he said, his tone consoling. "Don't worry. Uriah will get the *Intrepid* here on time."

"You're right," she agreed, relaxing back in the seat of the coach they had been fortunate to have to themselves most of the way from Helena. "Uriah won't let us down."

"Temerity," Steele said, the sad note of urgency in his voice curling around her heart and squeezing it tightly, making her forget the *Intrepid* for a moment.

She turned in her seat to face him. "What?"

He opened his mouth to speak, then closed it again.

Frustration and anger flared in her eyes, immediately to be overcome with the need to understand what was troubling him. "What is it Steele? Tell me. Let me help. Please don't shut me out! Not now! I love you!"

"Enough to forget about going back to St. Louis? Do you love me enough to just turn your back on the *Intrepid* and go with me to California to start a whole new life together?"

Her eyes opened wide. "What are you saying?"

"If I asked you to come with me to California right this minute, would you do it?" His words came out in a strained monotone. "Would you?" His expression was a dare.

Not able to believe he was serious, yet knowing she was being given a test—a test she would fail—she answered him. "You know I couldn't, Steele."

"Yeah, I know," he said with finality, gazing deep into her blue eyes with regret. "It was a silly idea to think that what we had could go on forever, wasn't it?"

"No! It's not silly. What we had—what we *have*—will go on for as long as we love each other."

"I'll remind you of that when we get back to St. Louis, Temerity," he said, his voice wooden, his smile stiff.

"What's going to happen in St. Louis? Why can't you tell me now?"

Because I'm a coward. Because I want to put off having you hate me as long as possible! he thought, but all he said was, "I can't."

Uriah's sage advice zipped through her mind. *He'll tell you what's troublin' him when he's ready. You just be there to listen when he's ready.*

"That's all right, Steele. I love you and I'll be here

when you're ready to talk to me." She turned and looked back out the window at the town of Fort Benton, nestled in the cottonwooded river bottom land of the Missouri River.

When the stage pulled up in front of the Wells Fargo office, Steele was the first passenger out, offering his hand up to Temerity to help her. "I'll take care of the 'nails' and then go over to the newspaper office to see if they've heard anything by wire about the *Intrepid,*" he said, "while you go and get our rooms at the hotel. I read about a new one that opened here in May. The Thwing Hotel. It's supposed to have all the modern conveniences."

"Did you say 'rooms'?" she asked in a stunned whisper.

"I didn't think you'd want our fellow workers on the *Intrepid* to come looking for us and find us sharing a room. Was I wrong?"

"Oh. No, you weren't wrong. It's just that I thought . . . I mean after . . . No, you weren't wrong. I'm sure it will be for the best."

So, it had begun. Already he was severing their relationship! And there was nothing she could do to stop it from happening. He wouldn't even tell her why.

Certain she could hear the sound of her heart breaking, she turned and walked away from Steele without speaking further. He wanted a break; she would give it to him. It would be clean and neat. No crying, no begging, no using her pregnancy to keep him. She would just walk away.

"Temerity!" Steele shouted after her.

She stopped in the street, not daring to turn back to face him for fear he would see the hope that had sprung to her eyes at the mere sound of her name on his lips.

Catching up to her in a few long strides, he clamped his hands on her shoulders and spun her around. "Oh,

385

god, Temerity, I'm sorry. Please forgive me. I never want to hurt you!" He clutched her hard against his chest, a sense of desperation in his tone.

"What happened, Steele? Why have you changed? Have you stopped loving me? Is that it?"

"Stopped loving you? How can you think that? I love you more than anything in the world!"

"Then what is it, Steele? I have to know. No matter how terrible it is, I must know!"

"I'm sorry you had to put up with my black mood all the way from Helena, Temerity. But you won't have to anymore. I've come to a decision."

"A decision?" Alarm knotted in her chest. Was he going to end their relationship here and now? "What decision?" she asked, steeling herself for his final blow. The death blow. For surely she would die when he told her he was through with her.

He bent his knees, bringing his face on a level with hers. Searching her panic-stricken expression, he spoke huskily. "I've decided I'm going to take each day as it comes and not worry about later. I'm going to love you for as long as you'll let me!"

"You m-m-mean you're n-n-ot . . . ?" she stammered.

"I mean I'm going to take the advice a very smart lady gave me not long ago," he said with a dimpled grin.

"You are?" she whispered, reaching up to touch each dimple with her thumbs. It seemed years since he'd smiled at her, rather than hours. "What advice is that?"

"I'm not going to waste time and energy worrying about things I can't change or things I think *might* happen. Instead, I'm going to concentrate on what I've got now. And on what I *can* do something about. Like my mood, for starters, and like that hurt little girl look on your face."

"Sounds like good advice," Temerity said hesitantly, not certain she could let herself trust the relief rushing over her.

"Believe me, it is," he said with a grin that almost, but not quite, erased the last signs of worry from his face. "Now," he said, stopping to clear his throat before going on, "You go on over to the hotel and get us registered. I'll be there as soon as I can."

Temerity peeked up at him, her expression questioning. She knew he was right about the separate rooms for the sake of appearances; but she wasn't totally convinced that whatever crisis they'd just weathered was truly gone. And she didn't want to spend tonight alone.

As though her thoughts mirrored his own, Steele grinned and said with a mischievous wink, "Make sure the rooms have a connecting door."

Temerity's relief burst forth in a head-shaking laugh. "You know you're a devil, don't you! What am I ever going to do with you?"

Steele's expression grew serious. "Just keep loving me, Temerity. Just love me," he said, drawing her into his urgent embrace, despite the outraged expressions of two matronly passersby.

"I will, I do, Steele. I'll love you always," she vowed, wrapping her arms around his narrow waist and clinging to him, unconcerned with anyone but Steele.

"Then we don't even have a problem, do we?" he said, his tone sad. He gave her a hasty kiss on the lips and put her from him, holding her at arm's length. "Now go on to the hotel before we cause a public scandal!"

"For some reason, that's not nearly as important to me as it once was," Temerity said, telling him without exact words that she'd changed—and that he'd been

387

the cause of that change.

"Not a problem in the world," he muttered to himself an hour later as he entered the door of a shabby two-story frame building on the riverfront. Glancing around the smoky gambling hall, he spied a table in the corner and headed for it.

The place was filthy, the smell of sweating bodies and cheap whiskey nauseating. But he made no move to leave. The place suited a lying bastard like him, he decided, his gaze roving over the drunken customers and flirting women who stood at the bar running along the length of the wall. He noticed a rickety staircase leading up to a balcony, where he could see a number of doors, obviously to small rooms used by prostitutes for entertaining.

"Hell," he objected aloud. *What am I doing here, when Temerity's waiting for me?* he asked himself, bolting out of the wooden chair and starting for the door he'd just entered. *What kind of fool am I anyway?*

"Steele?" a husky feminine voice said behind him as a small hand caught his arm. "Is that you?"

Steele spun around, shaking the woman's hand from his sleeve as he did. "I'm not interes—" he began, losing his voice halfway through his words.

"Hello, son."

All the color drained from his tanned face, and his eyes narrowed cruelly on the small, slightly plump whore with hennaed hair. His lips stretched tightly across his teeth, baring them in an ugly snarl. "Well, well, well. As I live and breathe," he said, speaking as though he was trying to rid his mouth of a terrible taste. "If is isn't sweet little Sally. How in the hell have you been, Ma?" he asked the rouged, red-stain-bedecked prostitute. "Last I heard, you were in California—

Nevada City, was it? What brings you to Montana? Did they run you out of California?"

"I know you have reason to hate me, Steele, but I am your mother and I lo—"

"*Mother?* Don't make me laugh. You're not my mother. You don't even know the meaning of the word! To me, you're nothing more than a dirty, used-up old whore." The corner of his mustached lip twitched upward in disgust. He reached into his pocket and came out with several silver dollars. "Here, *Mother,* go find yourself a nice mudhole to wallow in," he said, pitching the coins at her. Neither mother nor son was aware of the pinging clank of the coins as they hit the wood floor.

Steele and his mother stared at each other a long time, each lost in private agony. Tears filled the woman's bloodshot eyes, brimming over the puffy, kohl-smeared lids to leave dirty, gray tracks down her heavily rouged cheeks, before spilling on the perspiration-stained red satin of her dress.

A wave of pity rocked through Steele, a blast of shame for the cruel things he'd said following directly on its heels.

Scolding himself for his momentary weakness, he wheeled away from her, saying, "I wish I could say it's been a pleasure seeing you again." He started to walk away.

"Not a day has gone by that I haven't hated myself for what I did," she said to his retreating back. "But I was young and foolish, and by the time I realized the seriousness of the mistakes I'd made, it was too late. By then, I wasn't fit to be anyone's mother. Once I made the wrong decision, I had nowhere to go but to this life."

"You could have come home," he said, stopping in his tracks, though he didn't turn to face her. His old wound had been reopened and was too fresh.

"Listen to yourself, Steele. You know I couldn't go home. Besides, you were better off without me. Your grandparents gave you everything you needed."

"Try to explain that to a kid who sat in his grandparents' bay window day after day, watching for his mother to come for him, wondering why she didn't love him! I sat there until I was eight years old, *Mother!* In that same windowseat, watching the same street, waiting. Waiting for my mother, who never came. Waiting for you! Waiting for you to love me," he accused, spinning to face her again.

Sally smiled with trembling lips. "I always loved you, Steele," she said softly. "I always did."

"Well, your way of showing love is a lot different from mine. But don't worry about it. I got over it. Now, I don't want anything from you, except to never see you again."

"All right, Steele. I know I can never make up for what I did. But at least I can do that for you. You won't see me again." She turned away from her son and walked over to the flimsy staircase. "See that I'm not disturbed," she said to the bartender. "I'm going to my room for a rest. Give my son anything he wants—on the house. Good-bye, Steele," she said over her shoulder, turning for one last glimpse of the tall, young man she had so foolishly thrown away in her own youth.

When Steele walked into his room at the Thwing Hotel ten minutes later, Temerity was already in the bathtub, sudsing away the grime of the dusty trip from Helena. "I'll be out in a minute," she called from behind the screen. "Did you find out anything at the newspaper?"

"Huh?" he asked, his voice sounding as if his thoughts were miles away.

Temerity could hear him pacing the small square of the room, and fresh alarm flared in her heart.

"Oh, yeah, the newspaper," he mumbled with forced enthusiasm. "They said the *Intrepid* arrived on the fourth."

"The fourth? Then where are they? Why aren't they here now?" She stood in the tub and poured a pitcher of clean water over her body to rinse away the remaining suds. "Has something happened?"

"What?" he asked—still pacing. "Oh, no! At least not to the *Intrepid* anyway. The *Amelia Poe* wrecked downstream in white water and Uriah took the *Intrepid* back down to help bring passengers, machinery, and salvageable cargo on to Fort Benton after he discharged ours."

"Did they tell you when he's supposed to be back?" she asked, stepping out of the tub and grabbing a large white bath sheet from the chair.

"The man at the *Tri-Weekly* said he should be here by day after tomorrow if they don't have . . ." His voice seemed to trail off. "Shit!" he ground out unexpectedly. The pacing stopped.

"Steele, what is it?" Temerity cried, running around the screen, holding the towel in front of her dripping figure. The sight of Steele, his head against the window, his balled fists silently pounding the sill, sent paralyzing fear thundering to her brain. "Tell me. What *happened?*" she yelled, her voice high with alarm.

Steele turned and looked at her, his face a tortured mask of agony. "My mother," he said, walking to the bed and slumping down on it, his head bent. "She's in Fort Benton."

"Here?" she asked, rushing to Steele and wrapping her arms around him, cradling his head against her breasts. "How do you know? Did you see her? Where is she?"

391

"Yeah, I saw her," he answered bitterly, nodding his head. "She works in a filthy saloon and whorehouse on the riverfront. I think she runs it. She might even own it for all I know."

"Did you talk to her? What did she say?"

"She said she was sorry and that she had always loved me. She wanted my forgiveness. Can you imagine her having the audacity to lie to me like that when she knows I know the truth? But that's not the clinker. The real clinker is that I stood there and listened to her lying through her teeth about how sorry she was for what she had done, and *I* felt sorry for her. She left *me,* and I actually felt sorry for *her!* Can you believe that?"

"Yes, I believe it. You're a gentle and forgiving man—even though you go to great pains to hide it from everyone. Today, for the first time, you saw your mother through a gentle, forgiving man's eyes. Not a lonely little boy's eyes, not even a disillusioned teenager's eyes, but a man's.

"Today, you were able to see her for what she is—nothing more, nothing less. She's just a human being trying to get by. She's made some wrong choices, but she's paying for them. So are you—and I know it hurts. But neither of you can go back and undo what's already done. All you can do is let it continue to eat away at you, or decide to put the past where it belongs and go forward from here.

"It's painful to give up an old hatred, something that's been with you for most of your life, something you can bring out and rehash when you're in the mood to feel sorry for yourself, or when you need an excuse for your own behavior. The only thing harder to give up is an old love. And today you realized you can't do that, Steele. You love her. No matter who she is and what she's done, you love her. And you'll never be able

392

to find peace with yourself until you tell her that."

Temerity suddenly became embarrassed by her long preachy speech and stopped. "Go back to her, Steele. Go tell her you love her."

Steele raised his head, his face furrowed with unhappiness. "She probably won't want to see me again. I told her the only thing I wanted from her was to never see her again; and she told me that was the one thing she could give to me and left."

Sensing the meaning hidden in his mother's words, Temerity jumped off the bed and tossed down the towel. Grabbing for her clothes she said urgently, "Go to her, Steele. Now, before it's too late. I'll get dressed and be there as fast as I can!"

"You don't think she'd—" His eyes were round with fright, as Temerity's morbid conclusion filtered through his pain.

"I hope not, but hurry, Steele. I'll be right there," she promised, shoving him toward the door. "What's the name of the place?"

"I didn't notice. It's a two-story clapboard on the riverfront right across from where the *Donna M* is tied up," he said, springing into action.

"I'll find it!" she called as she pushed him out the door. *Please, Lord, don't let him be too late.*

Sally Devereaux sat behind the gilded desk in her office. She examined the chips in the tarnished gilt and chuckled. She'd always meant to have the desk redone when she got a little extra money in her mattress, but she'd just never quite gotten around to it.

Sally held a dirty, whiskey-filled glass to her lips and took a swig.

"What the hell good would it have done?" she asked. "Do you think a pretty shiny desk is going to make an

393

'old used-up whore' pretty and shiny and new again?"

She belted down another swallow, then setting the glass aside, she reached for a brown medicine bottle and opened it. Laudanum would be so much neater than the pistol she had laid beside the bottle. Still, there was something so final about a gun, and so slow about the laudanum. With the laudanum, she would just sort of slip out of Fort Benton, where with the gun she could *leave with a bang*.

Sally chuckled at the thought and poured another healthy shot of whiskey in her glass and tossed it down her throat in one gulp. Picking up her quill, she dipped it into the ink reservoir and held its tip to her stationery.

"My dearest son," she began. "I am truly sorry for the misery and shame I have caused you and pray that one day you will find it in your heart to forgive me for all the wrong I've done. Though I shall never forgive myself.

"I own this building and all the furnishings in it. It is yours to do with as you wish, but if you have no use for it, I would like for the bartender, Harry, to have it—as well as the gold in my mattress. He has been a long and loyal friend to me and should receive something for his loyalty. God knows being my friend couldn't have been easy.

"Again, I beg your forgiveness. I love you. Mother. Mrs. Sally C. Devereaux, August 11, 1868, Fort Benton, Montana Territory."

"Well, that about does it," she concluded, glancing over the letter one last time and making a few minor corrections. "Time to check out, Sally, old girl. You've definitely outstayed your welcome."

She spun in the chair and began to neaten her hair, taking more pains with it than she had in years. When her hennaed hairdo finally met with her approval, she began to work on her face. That took a bit more effort than the hair, but when she was through, her makeup all wiped away, she was sadly pleased. For the first time in years, she could see a touch of the beauty she'd had when she was young, could see the foolish young girl who'd paid such a high price for her moment on the carousel.

"Damn you!" she shouted at her reflection, lifting a heavy silver hairbrush and hurling it at the smug young face she saw. "You thought you knew it all, didn't you? You thought you were all that mattered! And now the only thing you can do for your son is disappear. Aren't you proud of yourself?" She picked up the brush again and threw it at the wide triangular shard of glass that had not fallen from the mirror frame.

Walking back to the desk, she lifted the brown bottle slowly and twisted off the cap. It was time. Without hesitation, she emptied the contents of the pharmacy bottle into the whiskey glass, then topped it off with more whiskey.

"Mother!" a man's voice shouted outside the door. "Are you in there, Mother?"

Sally held the glass to her lips and took a testing sip.

"Mother! Open the door!"

Mother? she thought, her face frowning toward the door. *Who would come to a dump like this looking for his mother? Must be some drunken miner. Nobody's mother is here!*

"Mother! Let me in!"

"Go away," she slurred, taking another sip of the laudanum-laced drink. "I need to be alone."

Without further hesitation, Steele lifted a large, heavy-booted foot and kicked the locked door at the latch. The lock gave no resistance and the door slammed open, banging hard against the wall.

"What do you want?" Sally asked her son, lifting the drink to her mouth. "I'm giving you your wish. You never have to see me again." She took a mouthful of the drink.

"Oh, no you don't, goddammit!" he shouted, hurling himself across the room and knocking the glass from his mother's hand, sending it flying into the faded wallpaper on the wall. "I've suffered enough guilt because of you. You're not going to put this on me. It wasn't my fault you lived your life the way you did, and it's not going to be my fault the way you die! You got that, Sally Devereaux?"

Sally stared drunkenly at the growing brown stain of wetness as it dribbled its way down the wall. "I thought it was what you wanted. It was the one thing I could give you."

"Do you think I wanted you dead, Mama? I never wanted you dead. I just wanted to love you and have you love me. I just wanted you to . . . oh, hell!" He wrapped his arms around his mother and buried his face in her hennaed hair and cried for the first time since he was a small boy. "I just wanted us to love each other."

Temerity appeared in the doorway to find Steele and Sally embracing, both of them crying, and her own heart swelled with joy. Maybe now, Steele would at last be free to love, allow himself to truly love her—and their baby.

Chapter Twenty-Four

"Here they come!" Temerity squealed, her excitement outweighed only slightly by her relief. According to the editor of Fort Benton's *Tri-Weekly* newspaper, who kept the area informed of all the steamers in port, each arrival and departure, how many passengers and tons of cargo they carried, whom the cargo was for, how long it took them to get to Fort Benton, and how the water conditions were, Uriah should have been back on the twelfth. Here it was four o'clock on the fourteenth of August, and Temerity had been near tears with anxiety. But now her worries were ended.

"Steele! They're here!" she shouted, bursting through the connecting door between their rooms at the Thwing Hotel. They just came into view! Hurry! Let's go on down to the levee and wait for them."

Shirtless and relaxed in an overstuffed chair, his long legs crossed at the ankles and propped on the bed—the bed he had yet to use for anything except a footrest—Steele looked up from his newspaper and grinned. "I told you not to fret, didn't I? I knew they'd be here in time. Uriah wouldn't let us down."

"Admit it!" she said over her shoulder as she whirled back into her room and picked up her bonnet. "You were getting nervous too!"

"Not me! I've learned my lesson. I don't waste energy worrying anymore," he teased, standing up and stretching his long arms above his head with a lazy groan. "Besides, I've enjoyed having a couple of extra days to just rest and do nothing." He leaned his large frame against the doorframe and watched her, never tiring of the sight of her.

Temerity turned to him and cocked her head to the side, her features forming an indignant pout. "I resent having time spent with me referred to as 'doing nothing'!" she reproved him with a prissy huff. "In fact, you'd better watch yourself, sir," she warned saucily, "or you'll learn the *real* meaning of 'doing nothing'!"

His brows arched in amused surprise. "Oh, I will, will I?" he said, crossing the room and swooping her up into his arms. "And just who's going to teach me?"

"Steele! Put me down!" she shrieked, kicking her feet and pounding her fists against his bare chest.

"Not till you kiss me!"

"You're incorrigible!"

"Is that one of your big words for wonderful, desirable, and lovable?"

She blew out a snort of pretended indignation. "I'm sure that's what a conceited oaf like you would believe! Now put me down!"

He puckered his lips. "Not until I get my kiss!"

"Oh, all right," she conceded, giving him a chaste peck on his dimpled cheek. "There. Now put me down."

"You call that a kiss?" he snarled, slanting his mouth over hers without giving her a chance to answer.

Her half-hearted resistance melting like ice in mid-July, Temerity's lips opened beneath his and her arms twined around his neck.

"Now, that's a kiss," he said hoarsely, lifting his head minutes later to gaze into her passion-glazed blue eyes.

398

"Do you think you can remember that?"

"I'll try," she promised in a throaty whisper, visibly shaken by the intensity their playful banter had assumed. "But maybe—" Her eyes focused on his mouth and she slowly dragged her tongue along her own lips. "—I'd better—" She held her lips a fraction of an inch from his, ruffling the hairs of his mustache with her breath. "—get a little more practice—" Her tongue flicked out to tease his upper lip, then darted back into her mouth. "—so I won't forget."

"I thought you were in a hurry to leave."

"Was I?" she whispered, trailing her kisses over his chin to nuzzle her face into the hollow at the base of his throat. "Why would I want to do that when this might be our last chance for a long time to 'do nothing'?"

"Now that's what I call intelligent thinking!" he said, lowering her to the bed, his cheerful tone belying the terrible ache the words "last chance" brought to his heart.

Forty-five minutes later, their attire reasonably well in order and their hair quickly arranged, Steele and Temerity hurried down to the levee to meet the *Intrepid*, which had just unloaded the final passengers and the last of the salvaged cargo and machinery from the *Amelia Poe*.

"Uriah!" Temerity shouted, releasing Steele's arm and breaking into a run at the welcome sight of the white-haired pilot. "We were beginning to worry about you!"

"Well, missy," the oldtimer chuckled, catching her in a bear hug and lifting her feet off the ground. "You shoulda known, come hell or *low* water, I'd be here by the fifteenth like I promised."

"I knew you'd do your best, but when you weren't here two days ago as the *Tri-Weekly* editor led us to

399

expect, and when we kept reading reports about low water and broken boilers, not to mention the two hundred Indians camped at the wreck waiting to go in and take whatever's left . . . well, I just couldn't help being afraid for you. But it seems you've fared well and all of my concern was for naught!"

"You're right on both counts, missy. We fared real well. When we got here and discharged all your cargo to the freight companies waitin' for it and collected the gold and greenbacks you had comin', I put it in the bank like you told me. Then, knowin' you weren't expectin' to leave Benton before the fifteenth, when one of the fellers who bought the *Amelia Poe* wreck offered to pay us five thousand dollars to run down there and pick up a load, I figured it was a pretty good idea. Though five thousand ain't all that much compared to the hundred and sixty thousand I collected for your stuff when I got here, every little bit helps, don't it?"

"It certainly does! But what about the Indians? Did they give you any trouble? Do you think they'll still be there when we go past the wreck on the way back to St. Louis?"

"Wouldn't surprise me none. But I don't look for them to be no trouble. Now, tell me about your trip overland. Was it a success?" He looked from her to Steele and chuckled. "By the looks on your two faces, I'd say it was!"

Temerity blushed and Steele beamed, both of them aware that Uriah wasn't giving the business facets of their trip credit for the pleased expressions on their faces.

"You both ought to be horsewhipped," Temerity scolded good-naturedly. "I wouldn't be a bit surprised to find out that you *and* Gus had something to do with poor Mr. Rawson's sudden illness."

Uriah's blue eyes sparkled innocently, and he

clapped an open hand over his heart. "You wound me, missy!"

"I hope he wasn't incapacitated very long," she said, not believing the old captain's innocent pose for one minute, but knowing she would never get him to confess to any part in the mischief.

"Matter of fact, he was fine when he stormed off down the gangplank at Fort Hawley that evenin' when we docked."

Temerity grimaced. "Was he terribly upset?"

"I'd say his nose was a bit more than out of joint."

"Is he still angry?"

"Can't say as I know. He sent word next mornin' that he would be stayin' at Fort Hawley to handle some unexpected business. That's the last we heard from him."

"Well, that *is* good news," Steele inserted with a happy grin. "Let's hope that's the last we see of Mr. Charles Rawson."

Temerity directed a patiently vexed glance at Steele out of the corner of her eye and decided to change the subject. She didn't want another argument about Rawson's motives to ruin this day. "We have a lot of passengers who are hoping to leave on the *Intrepid* tomorrow morning. Are we going to be ready?"

"Just a few minor repairs to take care of and we're all set. Any other steamer plannin' on leavin' before tomorrow?" Uriah asked.

"The only boat that has posted a departure date is the *Mary Ben*. But that's not for a week yet. She's not even expected to arrive in port for three more days."

"So," Steele announced, "we've got no competition and about a hundred and twenty-two miners with their pockets full of gold and in a hurry to get back downstream to spend it."

"Then, let's start booking passages!" Temerity said with glee.

"A hundred in coin, six ounces in dust, or a hundred and fifty in greenbacks still the going rate?" Uriah asked.

"For now at least," she said. "In another two weeks, any steamers that are still here will probably get double that. In fact . . ."

"Hold it right there." Steele laughed, wrapping his arms around her shoulders. "I can already see the wheels spinning in that head of yours. Aren't you satisfied with all the profit you've already made?"

"Of course, I am. But everything extra we take in means more for everyone in the crew. Not just me. If it weren't so urgent that we get back to St. Louis, staying in Fort Benton an extra two weeks would definitely be worth the risk of getting stranded in low water."

"Water's not but eighteen inches at Dolphin Rapids," Uriah reminded her.

"And the level's falling four inches a day according to the newspaper," Steele offered.

Temerity held up her hands in surrender and grinned at the two men. "I know, I know. I'm not seriously considering staying. It was just a thought."

"Yeah, we both know how your 'just a thoughts' work, lady," Steele said, nodding his head knowingly. "Don't we, Uriah?"

"I'll just say a feller has to be a pretty fast thinker to keep up with her!"

Giving them each the sternest frown she could manage with a permanent smile etched on her face, Temerity said, "Enough of this chattering. We've got work to do. Steele, do you want to go tell your mother we're leaving tomorrow? Or should I? One of us should stay here to help Uriah."

Uriah raised his bushy white eyebrows on two accounts. It was the first time he'd heard Temerity Kincade *ask* Steele what he wanted to do, and he liked the sound of it and what it meant. And— "What's this about a mother?" he asked. "I didn't know you had one. I jest kinda figgered you was hatched!"

Steele punched the older man on a bicep that was as hard as a man's half his age. "Just goes to show *old* doesn't mean you know everything!"

"Old? Who you callin' 'old,' you smart-aleck kid?" He put up his fists like a prizefighter. "Let's hear you say that again."

"I give up!" Steele chuckled and turned to Temerity. "I'll go talk to my mother while you book passengers."

"Give her my love."

"I will," Steele said, not thinking about what he was doing and taking Temerity's cheeks between his palms and kissing her—full on the mouth—in broad daylight—in front of Uriah and everyone else!

They'd been alone so long, for an instant he'd forgotten it was time to go back to a more platonic relationship in public. A shocked look of apology on his face, he jumped back as if he'd been hit. "I didn't me—I forg—It was an acci—"

Then it dawned on him that Temerity wasn't looking at him with horror, nor was she frantically searching the levee to determine who had witnessed his lapse from good manners. Instead, she was laughing.

"Don't look so upset, Steele. I don't think it comes as any surprise to Uriah. It hasn't, has it, Uriah?"

The pilot shook his head and gave her a happy wink.

"And I don't really care what anyone else thinks. Do you?"

Steele's face lit up with delight. "Not a damn bit!" He grabbed her in his arms and kissed her again, this time with definite scandal-making thoroughness.

Uriah was on the main deck when Steele and Temerity came on board with the most beautiful woman he'd ever seen in his fifty-nine years on earth.

Judging the neatly dressed woman to be in her mid- to late forties, he couldn't believe this was the same sad "soiled dove" Temerity had told him about. Small and voluptuously round—Uriah had never liked skinny women—she was clothed in a tasteful gray traveling suit, and had her red hair arranged in a demure chignon at the nape of her neck, topped with a stylish hat that matched her dress. Her pale skin was unadorned by makeup, showed only signs of the natural aging process, and gave no hint as to the type of life she had lived.

Realizing he'd been staring, Uriah leaped to attention and hurried forward to meet her.

"Sally, may I introduce our good friend, Captain Uriah Gunther? Uriah," Temerity said to the awed man, "this is Steele's mother, Sally Devereaux."

"It's a pleasure, Captain Gunther," Sally said, using all the charm she'd had drilled into her as a young girl, though there had been little use for it in nearly thirty years. She held out her hand, pleased that she hadn't forgotten.

"The pleasure's all mine, dear lady," Uriah said, taking her petite hand in his big clumsy paw and bending to kiss it.

His eyes twinkling with pride, Steele patted his mother's hand where it rested on his arm and said, "Let's get you settled in your cabin, Mother. Then if we can get Uriah to quit gawking long enough, we'll get his bucket on the way."

"I will look forward to seeing you again, Captain Gunther," Sally said.

"Yes'm," he mumbled with a blush. "Me too."

As mother and son disappeared up the stairs, Uriah turned to Temerity, a confused look on his face. "She's not exactly what I was expectin'," he said, his eyes shifting up to the boiler deck in time to catch a quick glimpse of Sally before she vanished into the cabin beside his.

More than a little pleased with the effect of her efforts to make Sally's reentry into civilization easier, Temerity gave Uriah a cheeky grin and winked. "I noticed," she teased, giving him a warm hug and no explanation. "Now, suppose we 'get this bucket' moving. I'm anxious to get to St. Louis and see the faces on the people at the Cameron Line when a 'helpless female' walks in there and gives them their money!"

A shadow of concern wrinkled Uriah's forehead. "Yeah, that's really goin' to be somethin' to see."

"So! You still haven't told her!" Uriah upbraided Steele at the first opportunity after the *Intrepid* was under way.

"I couldn't exactly take the chance when we were on the trail," Steele said in his own defense. "You know what a temper she's got. I could just see her doing something stupid like taking off by herself with those wagons and trying to make it to Virginia City alone."

"Not to mention leaving you staked out for the buzzards!" Uriah added. "Which is no worse than you deserve! Why didn't you tell her in Virginia City? Or when you got to Fort Benton? Don't you know, the longer you put it off, the harder it's goin' to be to do?"

"I know," Steele said, hanging his head and shaking it. "But I can't risk having her *ask* me to leave her 'employ'—not until we're back in St. Louis anyway. Too much can go wrong on the downriver trip, and I've got a responsibility to look out for the *Intrepid*."

"Do you really expect me to believe this riverboat has a damned thing to do with why you haven't told her? You're in love and you're sure you're goin' to lose her when she finds out you've been lyin' to her all along."

405

Steele didn't answer, but his guilty expression said it all.

"So you keep thinkin' if you put if off a while longer, you'll come up with a way out of this mess you've gotten yourself into, don't you?"

Steele nodded his head. "But I am going to tell her. Before we get to St. Louis, I promise."

"Just you see to it you do. The sooner the better. I don't want to see that little girl hurt. And judgin' the way she looks at you, the longer you wait, the harder she's goin' to take it!"

Before Steele could respond, there was a soft knock at the door to the pilothouse. Both men turned to see Sally opening the door. "Shall I come back another time, Captain?"

"No, Miss Sally. Come on in," he said, rushing to the petite woman. "I always got time for a lady as pretty as you are."

"Captain Gunther promised to let me steer the *Intrepid.*" Sally said to a surprised Steele. "I told him I didn't want to be in the way, but he said it was all right. It is, isn't it?" she asked Steele, the hesitant frown on her face showing her insecurity.

"Sure, it's all right. Uriah's the captain. I'm just the first mate," he said, giving Uriah a sly grin. "But I do wonder why he never offered to let *me* 'steer the boat'!"

Both Sally and Uriah blushed, neither of them having the nerve to look directly at each other to exchange the warm glances they were feeling. "Maybe you don't smell as pretty as your mama does, you smart-mouth kid. Now go on, before I decide it's time you learned a few manners," Uriah roared with a playful cuff on Steele's chin. "And," he added in a more serious tone, "don't forget what I said. The sooner the better."

"I won't," Steele mumbled, bending to give Sally a kiss on the cheek. "Have a good time, Mother," he said, hurrying from the tiny wheelhouse.

Ambling down the deck, Steele felt certain he understood how a drunk who knows he has to give up booze must feel: *Just one more drink, and I'll stop tomorrow.* But tomorrow never comes, because each day he says the same thing—just like him. *Maybe once we get past the rapids I'll tell her. That way I'll have another week or two to win her back and convince her that I did it to help her.*

Lost in his own misery, Steele didn't notice the two concerned faces that watched him from the pilothouse. "He has a great weight on his mind," Sally said, wishing there was something she could do to help her son solve his dilemma.

"Guilt is a heavy load to carry," Uriah said wisely, moving up behind Sally and placing a hand on her shoulder.

"Oh!" Sally exclaimed. Jerking, she glanced down at the rough hand resting so gently on her sleeve. Her unadorned face flushed. "You startled me."

"I'm sorry," Uriah said, removing his hand and busying himself with rearranging his large frame at the wheel. "I forgot myself."

"No! I'm the one who's sorry," Sally said, shyly laying her hand on his sleeve and looking up at Uriah with pleading eyes. "Please forgive me. It's just that starting a whole new life is very frightening, and I'm a little bit jumpy."

"You don't have to be jumpy 'round me, Miss Sally. Missy told me what a brave thing you're doin', turnin' your back on the past and startin' all over again. That takes more courage than most folks ever have. And I just want you to know, you've got nothin' but my highest respect."

Surprised that Uriah knew about her and still looked at her as if he didn't hold the past against her, and relieved that she didn't have to find the words—and courage—to tell him before their friendship progressed

407

any further, Sally smiled timidly at Uriah. "I'm not brave. I'm scared to death. But not nearly as scared as I would have been if I'd missed my last chance to try to make up to my son for all the heartache I caused him."

"Well, I can tell, you're already making headway. Any fool can tell he's pleased as punch to have found you again."

"I just hope that when this trip is over, I'm not the only woman in his life. I'd hate for him to lose Temerity. She's a wonderful girl. You should have seen how she took over and helped me shop and pack and dress for this trip. And they love each other so much. They just have to work out their problems."

"I take it that fool son of yours told you about the mess he's got hisself into."

Sally nodded. "There ought to be something we can do to help. They've both done so much for me! If only . . ."

"Don't go givin' up on those two yet. If you could have seen how they fought when we first started out, you'd see they're both pretty stubborn about getting what they want. If one thing's happened on this trip, they've both learned to give and take, and I've got a feelin' they're goin' to work this out too."

"Do you really think so?" Sally raised her watery hazel eyes to Uriah.

His insides melting like a young teenager's at the sight of the object of his first crush, Uriah nodded and cleared his throat. "I'm positive. My little missy is as stubborn and contrary as they come. And she's goin' to be hurt somethin' fierce when she finds out the truth. But she ain't dumb. She ain't about to give up what she wants because of a little hurt pride. And you mark my words, that little gal wants your boy as much as he wants her."

"I certainly hope you're right."

"Let's just you and me let them handle their own

troubles; and we'll work on ours."

"Ours?"

"Seems to me you mentioned never steerin' a riverboat before. Now that's a situation I can fix right quick," he said, pulling her in front of him at the wheel. "First of all, put your hands right here." He circled her figure with his arms and put her hands on the wheel, covering them protectively with his own callus-roughened hands.

"Don't let go!" Sally said, her heart racing as she nestled in the warm security of Uriah's arms.

"I won't," he promised, his head near the side of her face so he could see what she saw. "Not ever, if you don't want me to," he said, inhaling a deep breath of her intoxicating lilac scent.

"Oh, my goodness," Sally whispered, certain her knees were going to collapse beneath her.

"Do you like it?"

"I love it. It's the most wonderful feeling I've ever known."

"Can you feel how every ripple in the water is talkin' to you, tellin' you, 'The water's deep enough here for you to pass safely'?"

Hypnotized by the deep voice in her ear, by the feel of his warm tobacco-scented breath on her cheek, and by the glassy water of the river ahead of her, Sally nodded. "I think I can feel it, Uriah! I really think I can."

From that day on, Sally went to the pilothouse every afternoon for her "steering lesson." Some days she took the wheel. On others, when the water was too rough with threatening storms, or the danger was too great that they might get caught on snags or sandbars in low water, she was content to sit in the little building and visit with Uriah. And by the time the *Intrepid* reached St. Charles, Missouri, three weeks later, Sally knew she was totally in love with the crusty old captain, who'd shown her more love and kindness in three weeks than she'd known in thirty years.

However, she also knew she had to put the kind of thoughts she was having out of her head. Uriah may have been kind and attentive to her, but that didn't mean he had any plans for continuing their relationship after the *Intrepid* docked in St. Louis. After all, what decent man would? Temerity and Steele may have deluded themselves into believing a new wardrobe and washing the whore's makeup from her face were enough to change her life. But Sally knew differently. She knew that under the stylishly prim dresses Temerity had picked for her, and behind the proper manners she had readopted, was the same jaded woman Steele had found in Fort Benton. No man would ever want her for a wife, especially not a good and honest man like Uriah Gunther.

The last night out, Uriah found Sally at the rail on the main deck, staring up the levee into St. Charles. They would be in St. Louis by noon tomorrow. "Would the pretty lady like to go for a stroll into town?" he asked as he approached her.

"Oh, Uriah!" she laughed, holding her hand to her chest in surprise. "I didn't hear you."

"I don't wonder. You were mighty far away. A penny for your thoughts," he said, placing his hand over hers on the rail.

"Oh, they weren't even worth a penny. I was just wishing the trip could go on longer. I suppose my son inherits his tendency to put off unpleasantness until the last minute from me."

"Unpleasantness? Going home shouldn't be unpleasant."

"That's the wrong word. Frightening is more what I meant. I haven't seen my mother in twenty-seven years, Uriah, and I'm afraid she won't want me back in her life."

410

"Don't be silly. She's goin' to love you just like—" Uriah stopped speaking and coughed self-consciously. "Just like Steele and Temerity and, uh, all of us do."

"Perhaps I've caused her too much shame and unhappiness for her to be able to forgive me. I wouldn't blame her if she couldn't. I can't forgive myself."

"You hush that nonsense. It's all in the past. You've come here to start a new life and nobody's goin' to throw the mistakes you made in the past up at you."

"Does that include you, Uriah?" she murmured, the words out of her mouth before she could stop them.

"Me?" he said, his white eyebrows arched in surprise. "'Specially not me. I've made too many wrong turns in my own life to toss any stones in anyone else's direction, Sally. As far as I'm concerned, the past don't exist before the day you walked on the *Intrepid* three weeks ago. Not for either of us."

Afraid to trust what her heart was telling her Uriah meant, Sally's gaze dropped to his hand on hers. "Pretending we can forget the past is only a lovely dream, Uriah."

"It doesn't have to be, Sally. Not if we don't want it to." He reached across her and took her by the shoulders, turning her to face him. "Not if you'll marry me and make me the happiest man in the world."

"Marry you?" she echoed, her eyes filling with tears of joy as they lifted to memorize his sweet features.

"I know I'm quite a bit older than you, but dangit, Sally, I love you, and I want to spend the rest of my life lovin' you and takin' care of you."

"I don't know what to say. I never dreamed you would want to marry me."

A wave of panic washed over Uriah's weathered face. "Don't worry if you don't love me yet! I know we ain't known each other very long. But I feel like I been waitin' for you all my life, and I got enough love in this old ticker of mine for the both of us. And I'll be good to

411

you. I swear I will."

"Not *love* you? Why, I love you more than I ever imagined possible, Uriah. I feel like a teenager when you're near me, or even when I just think about you. And I think about you all the time. I even dream about you," she said with a smile as she raised her hand to cup his face. "I love you so much!"

"Then why ain't you sayin' yes, you'll marry me?"

"It's just that no matter how you and I may try to deny it, there's always a chance my past will come back into our lives. There have been too many—people— who knew me in the past to think I would never see any of them again. And I can't bear the thought of that happening. I can't bear to see the disgust in your eyes when what I was comes up and smacks you in the face. I'd rather remember your eyes full of love and never see you again than to let that happen."

"You love me," Uriah said, as though he'd heard nothing else, "and that's all that matters. You're goin' to marry me if I have to drag you to the alter kickin' and screamin'. You understand that, Sally? You ain't gettin' away from me!" He pulled her into his arms and kissed her hard on the mouth.

"Now," he said, breaking the kiss for a second to catch his breath, "are you goin' to say yes or do I have to do some more convincin'?"

"Convince me some more," Sally said, raising up on her tiptoes and kissing him as she wound her arms around his shoulders. "But I'm warning you, Uriah Gunther, if you *do* convince me to marry you, you're stuck with me from now on! I'll never let you go."

"That's a chance I'm willing to take if you are!"

"Then I'm willing to. Yes, I'll marry you, Uriah!"

"For better or worse," he said with a happy grin.

"For better or worse," she repeated reverently.

412

Chapter Twenty-Five

Temerity lay her quill pen on top of her closed ledger book and leaned back in her chair, a beaming smile on her smug face. She'd done it! She'd proven everyone wrong who had doubted her; and best of all, she'd beaten the Cameron Line! Not only had she earned enough to pay back their loan, but she'd actually brought back enough money to give every member of her crew a nice share of the profits when she paid them off tomorrow in St. Louis. And after paying off the money she owed, there would still be enough remaining to take care of her father for a long time and perhaps to buy a second steamer. She'd heard tonight that the *Francis Ray,* which had left Fort Benton a week before the *Intrepid,* was for sale.

Her excitement too great not to share, Temerity jumped up from her desk. After a hasty check in the mirror, she snatched up her bonnet and purse and headed toward the door. "Tonight I feel like celebrating!" she said aloud as she stepped out onto the deck.

Without warning, tentacles of foreboding suddenly tripped up her arms and the back of her neck.

"Who's there?" she asked, twirling to the left and examining the deck, gray in the twilight. No one answered. She spun to the right, certain someone was watching her. "Hello? Who's there?" Again, her eyes assured her she was alone.

Still, she couldn't escape the feeling that somewhere in the dim evening light someone was waiting for her. Watching and waiting. But for what?

"You're being ridiculous," she muttered to herself, slamming the door to her cabin and securing the lock. She slipped the key into her pocket and stomped down the deck—as though her aggressive steps could prove she wasn't afraid. *Just because this is where poor Mr. Yeager came on board, you're imagining his murderer is here!* she tried to convince herself. Just the same, she sneaked another cautious look over her shoulder, as she made her way around the corner to the cabins on the other side. *Whoever he was, like Steele says, he's probably long gone.*

Unfortunately, the grisly fate of the Rigby sisters chose that moment to zip across her mind, and her sense of discomfort increased. She picked up her pace. At first, when Uriah had first told her about them, she'd known the same panic she'd felt when Harold Yeager's body had been discovered. But then Steele had pointed out that it wasn't unusual for prostitutes to have some irate or drunken customer end their lives that way, and she'd decided the two deaths had nothing to do with Yeager's.

But what if they were connected? What if the murderer never left the Intrepid? *What if he's been with us all along, just waiting for another chance to strike?*

By the time she reached the door to Steele's cabin, her imagination was taking irrational stabs at everything that had occurred from the first moment of the trip.

She rapped urgently on Steele's cabin door.

And what if those two guards who disappeared the night I was taken at the Indian agency didn't desert after all? What if someone just wanted it to look like that? What if they were murdered too?

Beads of perspiration sprung out of Temerity's upper lip and her palms began to sweat.

Surely five deaths in such a short period couldn't be unrelated!

"Steele, are you there?" she called, continuing her frantic pounding on the door as she looked back over her shoulder again.

Unable to escape the feeling of being stalked, she tried Steele's door. Surprisingly, it wasn't locked. Anxious to escape from the "eyes" on her, she bounded inside the cabin and slammed the door behind her, sagging back against it—only an instant before the echo of boots on the stairs assaulted her hearing. It hadn't been her imagination! Someone *had* been out there with her!

Wheeling around, she locked the door with shaking fingers, listening until the steps disappeared onto the lower deck. "I'm being silly," she said aloud. "What in heaven's name is wrong with me?" she muttered, finding a lamp in the dark room and lighting it. "There, that's better," she sighed, casually raking her eyes over the empty cabin. "That could have been anyone coming out of their cabin. It didn't have to be someone sinister lurking in the dark!" She deliberately ignored the nagging realization that she hadn't heard a cabin door open or close.

The cabin was cluttered with no more than the ordinary masculine disorder she had expected to find: pants draped over the seat of a chair, a shirt hanging on the back, socks and shoes on the floor, and several outdated newspapers scattered across the desk and floor. Two drawers in the chest were open, articles of

415

clothing hanging out of them, as though he'd rummaged through them in search of something.

Temerity laughed, picking up the socks and folding them. "He probably could have found what he was looking for if he'd just looked on the floor." Setting the folded socks on top of the bureau, she opened the top drawer to rearrange its contents so it could be closed properly.

"Not much point in doing this since we'll be in St. Louis tomorrow." *But I might as well keep busy until he gets back. Besides, maybe it'll keep my imagination from overworking itself anymore than it already has.*

Closing the first drawer, she slid out the second one. It was then her gaze fell on a familiar swatch of lime green trim among the other things. *What's this?* she asked, her heartbeat skipping into a panicked, syncopated beat as she snatched up the pink-flowered piece of green. Her horrified gaze fell on the blood stain in the center of the ribbon.

"What is a ribbon from Rosalie Rigby's dress doing in your drawer, Steele?" she asked with a heart-sinking groan. "It has to be a mistake. This can't mean what it looks like. It can't!" she insisted. "There must be an explanation!" she said, rifling through the other contents in the drawer in search of anything that might answer her question.

When she had just about given up finding an answer, something in the back corner of the drawer stabbed painfully beneath her fingernail. Jerking her hand out, she stuck her injured finger in her mouth and sucked on it as she used her other hand to toss the contents of the drawer on the floor.

Caught at the very back corner, where she'd hurt her finger, she discovered a stiff piece of white paper. Bringing it out, she was surprised to see that it was a business card.

Turning it over cautiously in her hands, her eyes caught on the large black letters that seemed to leap out and slap her in the face. "The Cameron Line," she read.

Tendrils of horror radiated through her. Why would Steele have *souvenirs* of two murders in his drawer? Unless . . .

"No! It's too impossible to even think!" she said aloud. "There's an explan—"

"What are you doing?" Steele asked as he came through the door, tossing his key onto the bunk. "What happened here?" He pointed to the clothing she'd tossed onto the floor.

"What's the meaning of this, Steele?" she asked, holding out the business card to him.

A look of hurt and defeat twisted Steele's face. "Since when have you started searching my personal things, Temerity?" he asked bitterly.

Astounded that he made her feel guilty, she yelled, "I wasn't 'searching your things,' Steele. I was trying to straighten this pigsty while I waited for you."

"And you just happened to come across that card at the bottom and back of my drawer?"

"What was it doing there, Steele? I want to know this minute. And your answer better be good, because quite frankly, I'm not having very nice thoughts about you right now. Where'd you get this card?"

"I found it in the hold near where we found Yeager's body," he said. "I was going to tell you about it."

"When, Steele? Why didn't you tell me when you found it—*if* you found it?"

"I knew how you felt about the Cameron Line and I didn't want to add any more fuel to the fire. Anyway, I didn't think it meant anything. It probably just fell from Yeager's pocket."

"All right, suppose I chose to believe you had no other reason to hide the card from me, what is your

417

explanation for this?" She drew the green ribbon trim from her pocket and dangled it in front of Steele's startled eyes. "How did this piece of Rosalie Rigby's dress trim get into your drawer?"

Steele stared at the trim, his mouth hanging slightly open. He shook his head. "I've never seen that before."

"Why are you lying, Steele? You've seen it before and we both know it! It was on the dress she wore the night I found you together in the hold!"

"I didn't notice what she was wearing that night. But I swear to you that ribbon wasn't here before I went out. I know because I went through my drawers looking for a clean handkerchief."

Temerity opened her mouth to speak, then closed it again, staring down at the ribbon in her hand. Suddenly, she wasn't so certain what to believe. He'd readily admitted to knowing the Cameron business card was there, but he seemed genuinely surprised about the ribbon. Besides, wouldn't a murderer have gotten rid of any incriminating evidence by pitching it in the river? He certainly wouldn't have kept it in his chest of drawers in plain sight for anyone to find! "Then how did it get there?"

"I don't know, unless someone planted it there—like the handkerchief in the hold."

"But why? Who would want to indicate you in the murders?"

"Does that mean you believe me?" he asked softly, the ache in his heart caused by her unspoken accusation still painful. "Or do you still have your doubts about me? Do you think I could have killed those girls? Or Yeager, for that matter?"

"No!" she protested adamantly. "Of course, I don't think you killed them. But for some reason someone wants me to think you did."

Steele heaved a sigh and crossed to her and wrapped

his arms around her.

"But who?" she asked, leaning gratefully into his embrace and rolling her head against his shirtfront. "And why? There are just too many unanswered questions, Steele! I really thought this was all behind us. I should have known the trip downriver was too easy. What does it mean?"

"I suspect we're going to start finding our answers soon now. Whoever did this is getting desperate. Evidently he didn't think we'd make it this far, so he let things ride. But we did, and now he's going to have to act fast if he wants to carry out whatever his plan is before we reach St. Louis."

"What are you going to do?"

"Well, since this is our last night out, I thought you might appreciate an evening on the town. I've made all the arrangements."

"Do you think we should? I mean, wouldn't it be best to stay here in case something else happens?"

"No. In fact, I think we need to get this whole thing out of our minds for a few hours and just concentrate on us. We have things to talk about. You just go put on your prettiest dress, and as soon as I change, I'll come get you."

"All right," she said, crossing to the door and putting her hand on the latch. "Steele," she said, looking down at her hand on the door handle, "were you surprised to find your door locked when you came back?"

"No, why should I be? I always lock it. . . . Say, how'd you get in here?"

"The door wasn't locked, Steele. And before I came in here, I was sure there was someone on the deck watching me from the shadows." She looked up at him, her expression desperate. "I'm frightened, Steele. What if it's someone from Cameron looking for my money? What if they're taking this last chance to stop me from paying them off?"

"I told you, it's not Cameron!" he said irritably.

"Then who is it? Steele, I can't let anything happen to that gold and cash. My father's entire future depends on it!"

"Don't worry. The Pinkerton detectives I hired in Sioux City aren't going to let anything happen to those strongboxes of yours."

She blew out a disbelieving chuckle suddenly. "Do you realize what you're asking me to do? You're asking a woman who didn't trust *anyone* when this trip began to leave her entire future in the hands of six strangers."

"You've come a long way, Miss Kincade," he said. "I'm proud of you."

When they finished eating at the Fawcett House, the scene of their first dinner together, Temerity and Steele strolled toward the hotel he'd found on a side street where they would be assured of their privacy.

"Do you realize how miserable I've been the last three weeks, having to sneak in and out of your cabin like a school kid?"

"Do you think it's been any harder on you than it has on me?"

"Well, tonight there's not going to be any of that. I'm going to make love to you all—"

Out of nowhere, two men leaped on Steele as a third grabbed Temerity and jerked her away from him.

Struggling against her captor with every ounce of strength she could muster, Temerity let a bloodcurdling scream for help. But her efforts were useless. The grip around her arms and chest tightened painfully over her breasts, seeming to press the air from her lungs.

The light from the gas street lamp reflected on a

shiny metal object raised above Steele's head in one of the men's hands. "Steele!" she screamed as the lead pipe came crashing down onto the back of his skull.

Steele's long muscular legs folded beneath him as the two men released him with a rough kick in the back and began to run. "Let's get out of here!" one shouted.

Releasing his viselike hold on her, the man who held Temerity shoved her forward, pitching her onto her face on the cobblestone street.

"Steele, are you all right?" she gasped, dragging herself to her hands and knees and crawling toward the place where Steele's large frame lay sprawled on the pavement.

Her own vision blurring from the fall, she scooted up beside his head and sat back. Cupping the back of his head to lift it into her lap, she was immediately aware of the warm, sticky feel of blood. "Oh, my lord," she whimpered. "Help!" she shouted. "Somebody help me, please!"

Terror pounding cruelly in her ears, she hiked up the hem of her dress and frantically tore strips of white material from the bottom of her petticoat. Her reaction instinctive, she lifted the dead weight of Steele's head and wound the emergency bandages around it. "Oh, please, Steele, wake up!" she begged the unconscious man.

"Mmm," he responded, rolling his head in her lap and opening his eyes slowly. "Wha' hap'nd?" he mumbled sluggishly, reaching up to touch the back of his head. "Wha' hi' me?" He propped his elbows behind himself and tried to lift himself up.

"Don't get up!" she pleaded, relieved he was conscious but afraid he would slip away again. "We were attacked by three men."

Steele patted his pockets. "What'd they steal?" he said, the fact that his wallet was still in his pocket causing a confused frown to wrinkle across his forehead.

"Nothing! They just grabbed us, then hit you with a metal pipe and ran away."

"Damn!" He jerked out of her protective hold and bolted to his feet.

"Steele! Don't! You could pass out again! You're in no condition to be walking around!"

"Hurry! We've got to get back to the *Intrepid*," he growled, holding his hand out to her.

"Let me take you to a doctor," she said, scrambling to her feet and ducking under his arm to offer her support to his crazily weaving body.

"No time. We need to go back to the boat. We may already be too late."

"Too late for what?"

"To protect your money!"

"What are you saying?" she shrieked.

"Someone wanted to make sure we didn't come back to the boat too early tonight! If my guess is right, they're trying to steal your strongboxes right about now."

As if in answer to Steele's suspicion, the cracking of gunfire ricocheted up from the direction of the levee. "No!" Temerity cried, her shocked gaze aimed toward the river. "We have to do something!"

"You go for the police and I'll go to the boat and try to help stop them!" he ordered, drawing a revolver from his holster and spinning the cylinder to check the bullets.

"You can't do that. Look at you. You can barely stand up! You could be killed!"

"Let go of me. I've got to stop them."

"Then I'm going too!" she said, tightening her hold around his back and starting forward.

By the time they reached the top of the levee and

could look down on the *Intrepid,* Steele was steadier on his feet. The occasional sound of gunfire popped from the main deck of the steamer, to be answered with gunfire which originated from behind packing crates that lined the stone levee.

"Do you know how to use this?" Steele asked Temerity, handing her his revolver as he quickly assessed the situation on the bank.

Temerity nodded her head and took the heavy gun. "It's been a while though."

"That's okay," he said, taking a second from his other holster. "You won't need to fire it. Just hold it on them in case."

"Then why . . . ?"

"It looks like the Pinkertons have the robbers at a standoff, so you and I are going to go on and tip the scales. You go around those crates and circle up behind where the shots are being fired from as close as you can without being seen." With his right hand, he indicated the route she should take. "And I'll come up behind them from over there." He drew his plan in the air with his left hand. "When you're in position, give a quick whistle, and I'll whistle back. Then I'll call out and tell them they're surrounded and to drop their guns. They'll know I'm not alone because they'll hear the whistles too."

"But what if they don't?"

"Don't worry about it! That's not important. We just want to divert them long enough to give the Pinkertons a chance to take them."

"All right," she said bravely, aware the pounding in her chest was beating its frightened rhythm in her ears as well. She began to run.

"Temerity," he hissed. "Keep your head down!"

"Oh!" she mouthed, crouching down to continue running.

"I love you," he whispered loudly enough for her to hear.

"I love you too," she called back, then disappeared around the crates, all her concentration centered on doing what Steele had told her to do.

A minute later, crouching behind a crate with a stove in it, Temerity stopped to catch her breath and waited to give Steele time. The battle between the men on the *Intrepid* and the men on the levee continued. From the flash of the guns being fired, she determined there were three guns on the bank and six on the steamer.

Her breathing more normal now, she wet her lips and let a shrill, piercing whistle.

Then a thought occurred to her, as she awaited Steele's answering whistle. If two whistles were good, more would be better. She moved behind another crate several feet away, hearing Steele's whistle just as she got there. Quickly puckering her mouth, she signaled a second time. Steele sent another back, and she realized it was from a different place than the first he'd sent. *Great minds,* she thought with a smile, and moved again.

"What the hell's goin' on?" she heard one of the gunmen on the levee whisper to his comrade.

"How the hell should I know?" a second raspy voice replied.

"Drop your guns, boys," Temerity heard Steele's strong voice shout out. "We've got you surrounded."

"Ah, shit!" she heard a bandit mutter, tossing his gun down on the ground and standing with his hands raised.

"What're you doin', Wes?"

"Ain't no job worth gettin' killed for," the standing man said.

"Listen to your friend, mister," Temerity said in an artificially deep voice. "Or we'll cut you down where

424

you stand." To prove her point, she peeked out from behind the crate and aimed at the hay bale that served as a barrier for the second robber.

She had intended for the bullet to miss the hesitant gunman by several feet. Unfortunately, the weight of the six-shooter, as well as the inaccuracy of her aim, joined forces to send her bullet whizzing into the brim of the wavering man's hat and to hurl it from his head.

The clatter of the robber's gun hitting the stones of the levee echoed through the air as he clambered to his feet and threw his hands into the air. "Don't shoot!" he yelled. "I surrender!"

Bolstered by her good luck, Temerity scurried to a new position and waited for Steele to act.

Stunned by Temerity's crack shooting, Steele's attention jerked to the two yielding men standing eight feet apart. "You boys keep them covered," he shouted to Temerity, and returned his concentration to the two closer to him. But something was wrong. He could see only one man now.

"Come on, pal. Why don't you be smart like your friends are?" he called out.

The bandit wheeled around and fired in Steele's direction.

Steele dropped to the ground and rolled to a new position, coming to a stop with his gun pointed at his adversary's temple. However, the rolling took its toll on his dwindling strength and when he stopped, his vision was blurred.

The gunman saw Steele the same time Steele saw him. But the gunman's vision was not doubled by a blow on the head with a lead pipe.

Blinking his eyes to clear his vision, Steele saw *two* white-toothed, leering grins gleam in his direction as *two* men raised *two* guns and aimed them directly at his one throbbing head. Unable to control his aim, he

425

squeezed his trigger twice and tried to roll behind a new cover. But he couldn't move. All he could do was stare at the blurred outlaw and the gun aimed at his own head. He heard the click as the outlaw clicked the hammer.

"Nooo!" he heard a woman scream over the sound of a second shot exploding through the air. As if watching in slow motion, Steele saw the gunman's arm jerk into the air, squeezing off a shot into the night sky before the gun flew from his hand. Like a huge hand had lifted him by the scruff of the neck, the robber's feet lifted off the ground and he was pitched backward into the stack of hay bales.

"Yeow!" the bandit screamed, clutching his bleeding hand against his chest and doubling over in pain.

"Nice shot, Miss Kincade," said the man Steele recognized as the chief of the Pinkerton detectives he'd hired. But Steele couldn't quite assimilate the meaning of his comment.

"Thanks, Stokes," he groaned, trying to pull himself up to his feet, but managing only to struggle to a sitting position. "I thought I was a goner," he said, rubbing his fingers over his eyes.

"Don't thank me," the lean detective said, rushing forward to help Steele. "The lady's the one with the deadly aim. In fact, that feller moanin' over there's lucky she only wanted to wound him and not kill him!"

Steele, letting Stokes help him to his feet, turned his amazed glance toward Temerity as she rushed to his side.

"You?" he said.

"I couldn't very well let him kill you, could I?" she asked with an embarrassed grin, unconcerned that the frilly yellow dress she had worn was now stained with dirt and his blood and torn beyond repair, or that her hair had fallen in wild disarray from its prim chignon.

426

"I had no idea you could shoot like that," he said, still unable to believe the accuracy with which she'd put a bullet through the man's hand.

Temerity's face split in a proud smile. "Neither did I."

Two more Pinkerton detectives prodded the first two outlaws forward and yanked the third gunman to his feet. "You want us to take these hooligans to the city jail and get 'em locked up?" one asked Stokes.

"Yeah, go on. I'll help Miss Kincade and Steele back to the steamer."

"Hey, wait a minute," Steele shouted, stopping short in his tracks. "Where's the other one?"

"The other what?" Temerity asked, wrapping her arm around Steele's waist to help Stokes support him.

"There were four gunmen. There was one over there too."

"I only saw three of them," Temerity said.

"Are you sure?" Stokes asked Steele.

"I'm sure. He was crouched down there behind that stack of sewing machine crates—just watching. He had a gun drawn, but I didn't see him use it."

"Well, whoever he was, he's gone now," Stokes muttered wisely.

"We need to find him. I have a feeling he's the one who set this all up," Steele said.

"Do you realize how many places a man could hide on this levee? I don't have the manpower to search it. Besides, every minute we're away from your money, the more chance there is of losing it to robbers."

"Yeah, I understand," he mumbled, squinting his eyes and trying to see if he could discern anything moving or out of order. "I guess we lost him."

"Don't worry about him, Steele. As long as you're all right and no one else was hurt, except him, of course"—she shot a glance at the wounded outlaw—

"nothing else matters. Not even the money!"

"You really shot him?"

"I really did! How about that? I guess you'll just have to call me 'Dead Eye Kincade' from now on!"

"Temerity, Temerity, what am I going to do with you?" he asked with a shake of his head. "When are you going to learn to follow orders? I distinctly told you that you didn't need to fire the gun. And what was all that whistling and darting behind boxes like a one-woman army? I didn't tell you to do that."

Temerity slanted an impish glance up at him. "When are you going to learn that giving me orders isn't a very effective means of communicating with me?"

Chapter Twenty-Six

"We've got to talk," Steele said, his brow deeply creased in a worried frown as he and Temerity stepped out of the First National Bank of St. Louis the next afternoon.

Her smile bright with happiness and relief, she stopped on the sidewalk and looked up at him. "Then let's talk," she said playfully. "Though I can't imagine what could be so serious on a day like this! Our profits are safe in the bank, everyone's been paid off, and I have a draft to take to the Cameron Line first thing in the morning. Everything is wonderful!"

Steele burrowed ten fingers into his thick hair and shook his head. "Not here. This isn't the place. Let's go somewhere we can be alone." He took her arm and propelled her along the walk.

"I can't go anywhere now, Steele. And neither can you. I have to go home and see my father. And you need to take your mother to your grandmother's house and get her settled."

Steele nodded his head, twisting his mouth to the side and catching the inside corner of his cheek with his teeth. "You're right," he finally said. "But when are we going to talk? I planned to do this last night, but—well, you know what happened!"

Temerity smiled her sympathy. "How's your head this morning?"

"It's fine." He reached up and touched the back of his head, wincing as his fingers made contact with the still tender knot. "Don't worry about my head, Temerity. I've got more important things on my mind right now. Things that can't wait. They've got to be settled right away."

Certain Steele was leading up to a proposal, Temerity tilted her head and studied him. "Maybe after you get your mother settled you can come to my house for dinner tonight. I'm anxious for Papa to meet you. And we can talk after he goes to bed. Is that soon enough?"

Indecision wavered in his eyes, but he said, "Yeah, I guess that'll be all right. Are you still planning to take the bank draft to Cameron in the morning?"

"Yes, I'll meet you there at nine o'clock sharp."

"I don't know if I'll be able to meet you."

"Oh?" She told herself the ripple of disappointment she felt was silly. "But I thought you were as excited about this as I was. I wouldn't think anything would keep you away."

"I want to be there. Really. It's just that, uh, something may come up! I mean my mother and grandmother may need me. After all, they haven't seen each other in twenty-seven years. I'll know more tonight. I'll tell you then. What time should I come?"

Confused, Temerity frowned. "Would six-thirty be all right?"

"It'll be fine," he said, giving her an offhand kiss on the cheek. "I'll see you then." He turned to walk away.

"Steele!" she called out. "You don't know where my house is."

Steele stopped and turned back to her. "Yeah, I

guess that would help."

"And, Steele," she said, digging in her purse for a calling card with her address on it.

"What?"

"Try to get rid of that scowl before tonight. You look like the world's about to end. I promise it won't be as bad as you think."

"What won't?"

"Why, our 'talk,' of course."

"Of course," he echoed bitterly. "Well, I'll see you later. Are you sure you'll be all right alone?"

She shot him an amused smile. "I believe I can manage. And I won't exactly be alone. I have the driver and carriage you hired."

"Okay, then I'll see you at six-thirty." He helped her to the waiting carriage, but stopped at the door. "Temerity, no matter what happens, I want you to always remember that I love you." His hard arms crushed her against him as his mouth covered hers in a kiss that was so intense, Temerity sagged against him, clinging to him, unable to stand on her own.

"I love you, too, Steele. I always will."

No, you won't. Not after tonight.

Temerity watched as Steele strode away from her carriage, a warm smile on her face. *Tonight my love, I'll tell you about our baby. I'll accept your proposal and then I'll tell you. From this moment on, our lives are going to be perfect!*

"Where to, miss?" the driver called down.

"Three-two . . . Wait a minute, driver. Do you know where the Cameron building is? That big gray one on the waterfront?"

"Sure I do, miss. Is that where you want to go?"

Temerity hesitated. She really had looked forward to going with Steele. But he might not be able to go anyway, and if she was going to end up going alone, she

431

might as well get it over with. "Yes, it is! Take me to the Cameron Line offices first," she said, sitting back in her seat and smoothing her hands over her bodice and skirt, then checking her hair and hat. *Yes*, she decided, *I'll get all the unpleasant reminders of the past out of the way today. Then, I'll have nothing to think about but the future with Steele—and our baby!*

When the driver pulled the carriage up in front of the Cameron Line offices a few minutes later, Temerity looked up at the imposing gray building, her blue-gray eyes sparkling with anticipation. Without waiting for the driver to hop down and open the door for her, she jumped out unassisted and hurried to the front door.

"Allow me," the driver offered, dashing forward and opening the door for her.

"Thank you, driver. I won't be long." She smiled, raised her profile haughtily, and swept through the entrance. Looking around for someone to direct her to whoever was in charge, she spied a small, balding, gray-haired man at a scarred wooden desk in an office off the the side. His half glasses perched on the end of his nose, his shirt sleeves held up with black garters, he was certainly not her idea of a shipping magnate. For that matter, the decor of the interior of the building wasn't anything like what she had expected, she decided with an offended little sniff. *You'd think with all their money they'd fix this place up.*

"Excuse me, sir," she began as she neared the desk.

"No more steamers going upriver this season," the old man responded, not even bothering to look up from the ledgers and stacks of papers that covered his desk.

"I'm not here to book passage on one of your steamers, sir. I would like for you to direct me to the owner of your line, please."

"Can't do that, little lady," he said, continuing to

432

pore over his figures and bills of lading. "Mr. Cameron's out of town. I'm in charge while he's gone."

"Out of town? That's impossible!" Temerity said, her bravado sinking in a flood of disappointment. "When will he be back?"

"Can't say. But if I can help—" The front door opened and the bookkeeper looked up. "Mr. Cameron! What a surprise. We've sure missed you around here. This young lady was just asking about you!"

Thank heavens! It would be too cruel a joke for fate to play to let me come this far and then force me to give the draft to an assistant rather than Cameron himself. Temerity pirouetted around, a self-satisfied smile on her face, and offered her hand. "Mr. Cameron, I'm—"

Her extended hand was forgotten, left dangling in midair. Her mouth gaped open and her eyes widened with surprise. "Steele! What are you doing here? I don't understand."

Steele, who'd been lost in a fog of self-accusing depression, had only looked up from his boots when old Banks, the bookkeeper, had called out to him. He stared at Temerity, his tanned skin paling visibly. "Uh . . . Temerity . . . you weren't supposed to, uh, be here today . . ."

"Neither were you. What *are* you doing—"

The sound of the bookkeeper's friendly greeting rushed into her ears in a roaring echo. *Mr. Cameron, Mr. Cameron, Mr. Cameron.*

"Where's Mr. Cameron?" she asked evenly, knowing even as she stretched to see around Steele's large, blocking frame that she would find no one behind him.

"Temerity . . ." Steele said, crossing to her and catching her shoulders in his strong hands. "Let's go into my office. You've got to let me explain."

"*Explain?*" she screamed, comprehension emerging

433

on her face and turning her tanned skin a deep, reddish purple. Her actions instinctive, she brought her fist up from her side and slugged his chin with all her strength. "You insidious, conniving, deceitful bastard! How dare you?"

A look of surprise, which quickly converted to anger, transforming his face, Steele cupped his chin and grabbed Temerity by her upper arm. "We'll be in my office, Banks."

"I'm not going anywhere with you!" she cried, fighting his hold on her arm. "I never want to see you again!"

"Fine, but you're going to hear me out first." He tightened his grip and, taking long strides that forced her to run or be dragged to keep up with him, began walking. He ushered her into another small office with a cluttered desk, three worn chairs, a tattered rug, and file cabinets in it.

"Now! Are you ready to listen to me?" he asked, slamming the door behind them and shoving her into a chair.

Using the scratched wooden arms of the chair to lever herself up out of the seat, Temerity started to leave. "I don't want to hear anything you have to say!"

"Sit down, Temerity!" he roared, forcing her back into the chair with the heels of his hands at her shoulders.

Temerity crossed her arms across her chest, tightened her mouth into a determined line, and turned her face away from him.

Steele viewed her stubborn profile with a choking lump in his throat. "Temerity," he began, his voice croaking with unusual hoarseness. "I didn't mean for you to find out this way."

"Oh? And exactly how did you plan for me to find out?" she asked, her snide remark delivered to the

434

disorganized credenza along a side wall. "Were you hoping to announce it to the entire crew so you could disgrace me more publicly?"

"You know that's not true. A dozen different times I wanted to tell you, but I never got up the courage."

"Don't talk to me about courage, you lying son of a—"

"That's enough, Temerity. You can't call me anything I haven't already called myself. But if you'll just let me explain—"

"Explain what? How you deliberately made a fool of me? Or how you pretended to be helping me because you cared for me? When all you cared for was protecting your investment! Thank you very much, *Mr. Cameron,* but just knowing the truth explains it all quite well!"

"Temerity, you know that's nonsense. Nobody made a fool of you. I only wanted to help you because I love you. The investment meant nothing to me. *Means* nothing to me. If it'd been up to me, I'd have forgiven the whole thing and signed the *Intrepid* back to you free and clear. But I know your pride would never allow you to accept my offer. So I did the next best thing. The only thing I'm guilty of is trying to help make your trip as big a success as possible."

"And *lying* to me about who you were! *Steele Cook.* No wonder the name never seemed to fit you. Maybe if you'd told me it was *Snake* it would have been more believable!"

"Tell me, Temerity," he said, sitting back on the edge of his desk and crossing his arms over his chest and his extended legs at the ankles, "what would you have done if I'd come to you on that first day and said, 'I'm Steele Cameron, the new owner of the Cameron Line since my grandfather died, and I'd like to court you and help make your upriver venture a big success'?"

435

Temerity snapped her head around to glare at him, her lips twisted into a hateful sneer. "I'd have told you to go to hell!"

"My point, exactly. By not telling you who I was, we were able to be together and fall in love."

"What else have you lied to me about, Steele?" she asked with a bitter snarl, deliberately ignoring his mention of love. She was hurting too much right now to tackle that.

"Temerity, haven't you heard a word I've said? I never lied to you. Except when I told you my name was Cook. And I only did that when you pressed me for an answer. Can't you forgive me for that one lie? I only did it because I love you. Never to hurt you!"

She stared at Steele a long silent time, her fingernails digging deeply into the palms of her unfeeling hands. The only thing that kept her from crying was her stubborn Scottish pride. Thank God for her heritage. "How you must have laughed at me."

"I didn't! I've never laughed at you. I never would. I think you're the smartest, most capable, most beautiful woman I've ever known. I love you."

"I don't know why you insist on continuing this masquerade, Steele. It's really not necessary. I can't do anything about what you've done now. I'm just going to give you my draft for the forty thousand dollars plus the percentage of the profits I owe you; and then I'm going to put you and this entire experience out of my mind."

"It's not a masquerade! Can't you get it through your brain that I love you? I want to spend the rest of my life with you, Temerity. I want to marry you."

Tears sprang into her eyes and she slumped. "If you only knew how long I prayed to hear you say those words, Steele." She hated him all the more for saying them now—when he had destroyed everything they'd

436

had—or at least she'd *thought* they'd had. "There were times when I wanted it to happen so much, I had to fight myself to keep from asking *you*. But it's too late. Your proposal is meaningless to me now."

Reaching into her purse, she drew out the envelope containing the draft and stood up. "Don't bother seeing me out!" she said, slapping the envelope onto his desk. "I can find my way. Again let me thank you, *Mr. Cameron*. Doing business with you has been a real learning experience for me. But from now on, you'd better watch your back. Because in the next year, the *Kincade* Line is going to take over the Missouri River! And we'll force you, and any other line that tries to get in our way, out of business!"

With as much aplomb as she could manage, she turned and walked out of the office, leaving Steele sitting back on the edge of the cluttered desk. "Temerity . . ." he called after her.

"You might use some of that money to fix this place up," she called back over her shoulder. "It's really quite disgraceful!"

How could a day that had begun so perfectly have ended this way? she wondered as she gazed out the window of the carriage with unseeing eyes. *Today was supposed to be the beginning of our future,* she thought, dropping her unfocused gaze to her lap. "Poor little baby," she whispered softly, massaging her hand over her still-flat belly.

"Here we are, miss," the driver called down.

Temerity looked up at the familiar two-story house that had been her home all her life. Other than the stained-glass window that decorated the top half of the front door (an anniversary gift her father had given her mother ten years before) and the gigantic oak tree that

437

dominated the yard and shaded the entire front of the house, there was nothing particularly outstanding about the white frame house. But how she loved it!

There had been times when her parents had discussed moving to a bigger home in a more affluent part of St. Louis, but it had always come back to the fact that no one in the small family could bear the thought of leaving the comfortable home with its friendly rocker- and swing-adorned porch that stretched across the front and wrapped around one side.

"Thank you, driver," Temerity said, stepping out of the carriage and opening her purse.

When he realized what she was doing, the driver held up his hand and shook his head. "That's all right, miss. The gentleman already paid me."

Temerity's mouth tightened into a grim, hard line. "Very well, then," she said, snapping her purse shut. "You may bring my luggage up onto the porch."

Leaving the driver to carry out her orders, she turned and hurried up the brick sidewalk, which she noticed for the first time was beginning to crack and crumble. It was then she realized the partitions between the bricks were sprouting weeds, and the untrimmed hedge that lined the walk was more brown than green.

She began to take better notice of the house. To her crushing disappointment, she realized that the white paint was really no longer white. It was now gray and peeling.

Just like the pieces of my life, she thought morosely, noticing that the once red shutters that framed the windows had faded to a dirty rust color. But the hardest discovery to digest was spotting the large cement flowerpots her mother had kept filled with red geraniums all summer and fall. There were no geraniums in them now. There was only dry, packed dirt, a few dried leaves, and dead brown stems.

Temerity paused at the front door and took a deep breath, forcing the thoughts of dying things—the hedge, the geraniums, her love for Steele—out of her mind. The hedge and the geraniums could be replanted, the house could be repainted—in fact she would attend to that first thing. And Steele . . .

Steele was a mistake! she told herself sternly. *I'm better off without him!*

Stabbing a large key in the front door lock, she turned it, shouting out as she did, "Papa, I'm back! Mrs. Winters! It's Temerity! I'm home!"

"Oh, thank goodness you've come," the squatty, overweight housekeeper cried as she waddled into the entry to greet Temerity, a handkerchief dabbing uselessly at her eyes.

"Mrs. Winters, what is it? You weren't worried about me, were you? I told you I'd be back in September!" Temerity drew the round bulk of woman into her embrace and hugged her. "You don't need to cry. I'm fine and my trip was a big success. Now, where's Papa?" she asked, holding Mrs. Winters away from her and stooping to put her face on the same level. "In his room?"

"Oh, my girl, I'm so sorry. I did my best."

A dagger of alarm cut into Temerity's gut, but she refused to acknowledge it. "What are you talking about, Mrs. Winters? Where's my father?"

Mrs. Winters's teary gaze shifted toward the closed door to Tim Kincade's study. "I guess the excitement was just too much for him. I never saw a man so happy when he received the news the *Intrepid* had docked at the levee. He sent me right out to the market to buy flowers and something special for your celebration dinner. But when I came back a few minutes ago, he— Oh, child, I'm so sorry!" Mrs. Winters was overcome with a fresh attack of hysterical tears.

"Stop that crying," Temerity ordered angrily, refusing to believe what her mind was deciphering from Mrs. Winters's words. "Now tell me what you're talking about!" Mrs. Winters sobbed harder. "Oh, never mind!" Temerity said with an impatient shove away from the older woman. "I'll find out for myself."

Refusing to give in to the ominous shroud of horror that was closing in on her, Temerity began to run. She bolted through the study door with an unladylike shout. "Papa! I'm home! I did it!"

Bringing herself up short in the threshold, she released a sigh of relief. There he was, just like she remembered him, a little thinner perhaps, dozing in his favorite chair.

"When am I going to learn not to let my imagination run away with me?" she laughed aloud. Tiptoeing over to Tim Kincade's chair, she knelt beside him and took his hand in hers. "I'm home, Papa," she whispered, not wanting to waken him, but needing to stay. "You rest now, and we'll talk later," she said softly, pressing her cheek to his hand. "Oh, you're cold! I'll get you a cover," she said, looking around the room for one. Spying a pillow and light sheet on the table beside the chair, she tossed the pillow aside and unfolded the sheet. "Here you go," she said, spreading the sheet over him and tucking it in at his sides.

"Honey, he don't hear you," Mrs. Winters said, approaching Temerity from behind.

"Of course, he doesn't. He's always been a very sound sleeper. And snore! He's got a snore that would wake the dead."

"He's not snoring, child."

"That's because he's sitting up. But you should hear him when he sleeps on his back!" Temerity laughed, her voice rising to a higher pitch with each syllable she spoke. "Mama used to threaten to make him

440

sleep outside."

"It ain't because he's sittin' up, Temerity. Your Papa ain't snorin' because he's—"

"Stop that!" Temerity yelled at the woman, slapping at the consoling hand on her arm. "I don't want to hear any more of that. You already scared me to death with all your hysterics in the entry hall. Don't come in here with your foolish old woman lies! I won't put up with them!"

"Temerity, look at him! Look at your pa! He's—"

Temerity clapped her hands over her ears and hollered, "I'm warning you, I'm going to fire you if you utter one more word!"

Stunned by Temerity's irrational behavior, Mrs. Winters said, "But—"

Temerity pressed two fingers to the woman's lips and said, "Not another word, Mrs. Winters."

The housekeeper nodded her head and silently turned to go.

"Would you send for the doctor, Mrs. Winters?" Temerity asked, smoothing the thick, gray-streaked auburn hair back from her father's forehead.

"Yes, miss," Mrs. Winters sobbed as she hurried from the room. She didn't have to send for the doctor though. She'd already sent Randy, the grocery boy who'd carried her groceries from the market, to fetch Dr. Appleton when she'd come home and discovered Tim Kincade's body.

"I hated to talk to her like that," Temerity said. "But she was becoming hysterical."

Suddenly unable to ignore the facts anymore, Temerity stopped speaking and stared at her father. Bursting into tears, she dropped to the floor, burying her face against her father's useless legs.

"Why, Papa? Why did you leave me? I have so many things I need to tell you. I did it, Papa. I took the

441

Intrepid upriver like I said I would."

"Papa! It's so unfair. My little baby will never know you. He'll never hear your wonderful stories of all your adventures, he'll never see the beauty of the upper river at your side in the pilothouse, and he'll never know the security of sitting on your lap when he's afraid.

"I'm afraid now, Papa. I'm all alone and I don't know what to do. I need you so much. I want to be your little girl again. I want to hear you tell me everything's going to get better. I want to hear you and Mama laughing again, and I want to put my hand in yours the way I did when I was learning to roller-skate. Please don't leave me, Papa. I don't think I can go on without you."

Of course you can, a deep, familiar voice said in her mind. *I didn't raise a quitter, did I?*

Temerity shook her head.

Of course I didn't. You're Tim Kincade's kid and Kincades don't quit. They just keep on fightin', no matter how impossible their fight is.

"But how can I keep fighting? Today I've lost everything. The money and the success mean nothing without you and Steele to share my joy," she answered the inner voice.

Don't give me that crap, lass. Those are a quitter's words. How can you say you've lost everything when you've got that wee one growin' in your belly to share your life with?

"I do, don't I?" she said, raising her head and smiling tremulously.

Anything else good that happens is just frostin' on the cake. When you've got a bairn to love and love you back, your life will be filled with more blessings and joy than any human being has a right to ask for.

"Thank you, Papa," she whispered, pulling herself to her feet and smiling down at him.

"I suppose I'd better go apologize to poor Mrs. Winters," she said, swiping at her tears as she walked toward the door.

Just outside the study door, she heard the pounding of the front door knocker. Almost immediately, Mrs. Winters was there to answer it. "Doctor, I'm so glad you—"

"Please tell Miss Kincade that Charles Rawson is calling," a charming masculine voice said.

"I'm sorry, sir, Miss Kincade can't see nobody today. She's just had a terrible shock. You see, her father just passed on a little while ago."

"That's all right, Mrs. Winters," Temerity said, coming up behind the housekeeper and opening the door wider. "Mr. Rawson, please come in."

"My dear, I'm so sorry to hear your dreadful news. Perhaps I should choose another time for my visit," he said.

Without giving Temerity the opportunity to accept his offer to come another day, Charles pushed past the housekeeper and wrapped his arms around Temerity in a way that was a bit too familiar as far as Mrs. Winters was concerned. "Are you sure, miss?" she said.

"That will be all, Mrs. Winters," Temerity said with a sad smile, turning out of Rawson's embrace and starting for the parlor. "Don't worry, I'm going to be all right," she said to the concerned woman. "I know Papa's with Mama now."

"Oh, my dear, how terrible this must have been to find your father dead when you arrived home," Charles intoned sympathetically, guiding her to a sofa and sitting down beside her, still not releasing his hold on her hand. "But you're not alone. I'll stay as long as you need me. Do you have anyone you'd like me to notify? If not, I hope you'll at least allow me to take care of the arrangements for you."

443

"Thank you, Mr. Rawson," she said, studying her hand in his. It was nice to be able to draw on his strength for just a moment. Almost like having her father back. "I couldn't accept your kind offer. Though I do appreciate it. My father had no family, and I doubt that my mother's family in Philadelphia will be concerned. They never forgave him for marrying my mother and making her happy, when they had already arranged a more 'suitable' marriage for her. They didn't even write to us when Mama died last summer."

"At least allow me to make the arrangements with the mortuary. I insist. You must let me do something."

"Thank you, Mr. Rawson, you're very kind," she said, slumping back on the couch. Suddenly all the stamina and self-control she'd managed to gather was gone. "Oh, Mr. Rawson," she cried, bending forward and burying her face in her hands. "How am I going to go on alone?"

Gathering her into his arms and cradling her head against his chest, Charles Rawson smiled triumphantly over her shoulder. "Don't worry, Temerity. You won't be alone. I'll be here."

Chapter Twenty-Seven

St. Louis, Mid-October

The harsh rap of the front door knocker interrupted Temerity's single-minded concentration. Turning her ear toward the door, she paused, her hand on the wallpaper paste brush stopping in the middle of a downstroke. She listened for signs that Mrs. Winters had heard the knocking and was answering the door. But there were no footsteps in the entry hall. Only the insistent pounding on the door.

"Damn," she muttered, laying the brush over the edge of the wallpaper paste bucket and wiping her hands on the tail of her father's old shirt she wore. "She must be in the back."

Doing her best to tuck stray wisps of black hair up under her bandanna, Temerity hurried out of the small room beside her own bedroom and started down the stairs. "I'm coming," she shouted irritably.

Seeing the outlines of two people, a man and a woman, through the stained glass window in the front door, Temerity's face twisted into an irked glower. *Just what I need, more concerned neighbors coming to check on me.*

She threw an annoyed glare in the direction of the kitchen, a desperate prayer in her thoughts that Mrs. Winters would miraculously appear. But no such luck. Temerity looked down at her paint- and paste-spattered clothing and released a quiet groan. She couldn't go to the door looking like this! Maybe if she was very quite, they would just go away.

As if to say, *We heard you call out, and we're not leaving until you open this door!* the knocker sounded again, louder and more demanding than before.

It serves them right if they see me like this, she decided, stepping forward and jerking the door open, an artificial smile on her face. *If they wanted a perfect hostess, they should've waited for an invitation.*

"Uriah! Sally!" she squealed, her smile immediately genuine as she jumped toward the two at the door and hugged them both at the same time. "It's so good to see you! Come in!"

Sally and Uriah exchanged worried frowns and then smiled back at Temerity. "We would have been here sooner, but we thought you two could work out your problems without our interference," Sally said, sweeping into the entry hall.

The look of determination on Sally Gunther's face said she had no intention of wasting time or words getting to the point. And Temerity winced as she closed the door behind them.

"I don't understand," she said, following Sally into the parlor, where the fashionably dressed woman was already removing her coat and gloves and sitting down.

"Neither do we," Uriah said, lowering his bulky weight to the settee beside his wife. "That's why we're here."

"And we don't plan to leave until this foolishness between you and my son is settled!" Sally added.

"Oh, that," Temerity said with a disgusted snort. "I

should have known he would resort to sending the two of you to plead his case for him."

"He didn't send us," Uriah said with his own retaliating snort. He pulled his pipe from his pocket and stabbed it into his mouth. "He don't know we're here. We came because we're sick of watchin' two young people we care about do this to each other—and to themselves!"

"Well, it's very kind of you, but you needn't have bothered on my account. I'm fine. And I'm sure your son is also faring well. He got what he wanted from our association, and I did too."

"Fine, are you?" Sally harrumphed. "When was the last time you looked in a mirror, child?"

Bristling under Sally's sharp criticism, Temerity straightened her back. "I was putting up wallpaper, Sally! Do you expect me to do that kind of work in a ballgown? Perhaps if you'd sent word you were coming, I could have been more properly dressed!"

Sally smiled knowingly. "And have you send us back a note saying you weren't up to having visitors and asking us to come another time?"

"Don't you think we can see what you're up to?" Uriah growled. "Locking yourself in this house all alone, not goin' anywhere or seein' anyone."

"I'm not 'up to' anything. I just needed to be alone for a while after Papa's death."

"Alone so you could work yourself to death fixin' this place up—doin' six months' worth of work in six weeks?"

"It needed to be done, Uriah. When you were here for Papa's funeral, you saw how rundown everything had gotten since Mama died. Besides, it hasn't been work. I've enjoyed it. I love this house and like fixing it up!"

"Is that why you had to paint and paper it from top

447

to bottom, inside and out, all by yourself? Ladies hire folks to do that kind of work for them. They don't do it themselves."

"Maybe being a 'lady' isn't all that important to me anymore, Uriah. Besides, I get a great deal of satisfaction out of doing creative things like painting and sewing and—"

"Reupholstering," Sally said, giving the velvet-covered settee an appreciative pat. "Very nice. Is that why you haven't been sleeping at night, Temerity?" she asked with her usual bluntness, which under other circumstances might have been appreciated by Temerity Kincade. However, today it was quite irritating.

"Who told you I've had trouble sleeping?" Temerity asked, her expression incensed.

"No one had to tell me. I'm not blind. Those shadows under your eyes are a dead giveaway."

Temerity's hands flew to her face to touch the dark hollows she knew were beneath her eyes. "My father's only been dead for six weeks. What do you expect?"

"We expect you to fix yourself up and come with us to face what's really tearin' you apart."

"Oh, and what is that?"

Sally joined in. "You love Steele and you miss him. You know you've made a mistake by sending him away, but you're so damned stubborn you won't admit it—even to yourself."

"I do not miss him. I loathe him. He lied to me."

Sally went on as though Temerity hadn't spoken. "And to make matters worse, Steele's just as obstinate. He's doing the same thing you are, trying to kill himself with work."

Temerity's head jerked up, her eyes wide with alarm. "What's wrong with him? He's not sick, is he?"

Uriah and Sally exchanged knowing smiles. "For someone who hates him, you seem mighty interested in

448

his health, girl."

The guilty expression that skittered across Temerity's face was all the answer they needed.

"I am not interested. I only asked out of politeness. For all I care, he can drop—"

"For someone who's so het up about lyin', you're doin' plenty of it yourself. Only you're lyin' to yourself; and you'd better stop it! Or you're goin' to wind up a lonely old woman livin' all by yourself in this house you've gone and fixed up so nice."

"Uriah, I think you've overstepped the bounds of our friendship," she said, standing up and walking toward the parlor door.

"We need to be going anyway," Sally said, picking up her things and following Temerity to the front door. "I do hope you remember what we've said, dear. He won't come to you. It's up to you. If you want him, you'll have to go to him. But I would advise you not to wait too long. He's already receiving invitations from every socialite mother in St. Louis who has an eligible daughter. If you're not careful, he may just start accepting them."

"Let him. What he does makes no difference to me."

"There's nothing more lonely than growing old alone and having no one to love and share your life with. Believe me, I know," she said, leaning forward to kiss Temerity on the cheek.

Uriah gave her a long silent hug and followed his wife down the newly laid brick sidewalk.

"That does it!" Temerity snatched the bandanna from her head. "I'll show them! Call me a lonely old woman, will they! Mrs. Winters!" she hollered, running toward the kitchen.

"What is it, Miss Temerity?" the housekeeper asked, stepping into the entry so quickly, it was as if she'd anticipated being called.

Temerity narrowed her eyes suspiciously at the smiling woman and then looked over her shoulder at the front door. Surely they hadn't gotten together and planned . . .

She shook her head and turned back to Mrs. Winters. "Will you ask Jesse from next door to come over? I want him to take a message to Mr. Rawson's hotel for me. Then I'm going to take a nice leisurely bath before I dress for dinner. I'm going out."

When the door knocker announced Charles Rawson's arrival several hours later, Temerity still wasn't dressed. She shot a frantic look at the stack of discarded dresses that covered her bed. "Damn! What am I going to do? Everything's too tight!"

As well as she could figure, she was a bit past four months along; and except for her slightly swollen breasts and rounded belly, she'd been certain she hadn't gained any weight. In fact, looking at her face in the mirror, she could have sworn she'd lost some. But that didn't change the facts: every decent dress she owned was too tight in the waist and bordered on being that way in the bust.

Remembering the armoire full of her mother's dresses that neither she nor her father had been able to part with, she scurried into the master bedroom. Maybe, just maybe, something of her mother's would fit.

As she closed the door to her parents' room behind her, she heard Mrs. Winters downstairs telling Charles Rawson that Temerity would be right down.

Thirty minutes later, her glistening ebony hair styled up in what she hoped was a glamorous coiffure that made her look sophisticated, Temerity swept down the staircase. "Mr. Rawson, it was so good of you to come

450

on such short notice. I'm sorry I've kept you waiting."

His gaze appreciatively raked the length of her, lingering unduly where the low-cut green velvet bodice displayed her cleavage and full breasts. "I assure you it was worth the wait, my dear. And please call me Charles."

"All right . . . Charles," she said with a nervous little laugh as she turned away from him to take her cape from the coat tree in the hallway. She wished now she'd found a less revealing dress among her mother's things. Unfortunately, everything with a more modest neckline that fit in the waist was too tight across her bosom. She'd had no choice."

"I'm so glad you've finally decided it's time to start living again. I've made arrangements for us to have dinner at the Chez Orleans. Will that be all right?"

"It sounds wonderful!" she said, wishing she'd never done anything so rash as to tell Charles Rawson she'd go out with him. Right now, she wanted nothing more than to tell him she was suddenly ill and ask him to leave. She just wanted to go back upstairs and go to bed early. But she couldn't very well do that. Not when he'd been so kind to her since her father's death. She would just have to go through with it.

By the time the carriage drew up in front of the elegant Chez Orleans, Temerity was sick with the need to escape. All the way from her house, Charles had carried on a cheerful conversation, to which she had responded with inane comments and forced smiles. Her eyes focused on the restaurant and the exquisitely dressed men and women who were walking up its red-carpeted walkway under the protection of a gold-trimmed canopy.

Another wave of insecurity rocked through her. What was she doing here with these people? She, who was very comfortable cooking on an open fire, or sleeping under a wagon, or steering the *Intrepid,* or papering walls dressed in her father's old shirts, or laying a brick sidewalk rather than hiring someone to do it for her.

Not only was she out of place here, but she realized for the first time that she didn't have the slightest desire to be like these people or to have anything to do with them. "Charles, I'd rath—"

The door to the cab ahead of theirs opened and a particularly handsome couple stepped out. Tall and statuesque, the woman's blonde hair glimmered like gold, and her skin glowed peaches-and-cream perfect in the yellow light of the gas street lamps. The woman's shoulders were draped in what Temerity believed to be ermine, though she'd never seen real ermine. And Temerity was more certain than ever that she didn't belong here with her out-of-style dress and her self-arranged hair and her velvet cloak.

Then her gaze focused on the beautiful woman's escort, and her heart dropped to the pit of her already restless stomach. "Oh!" she gasped, covering her mouth with her gloved hand.

It's Steele.

"What is it, Temerity? Aren't you feeling well? Would you prefer someplace less lively?"

"What?" she asked, looking at Charles Rawson as though she'd just realized he was with her. "Someplace else?" she said absently.

"Perhaps we're rushing things—"

"No, this is fine." She stole another hasty glance toward the red-carpet walkway, just as Steele and his lady friend disappeared through the double doors being held by two uniformed doormen. "In fact, this is perfect!"

When a third doorman opened the door to her carriage, she took his hand and stepped out with all the grace and confidence of royalty. She'd show Steele Cameron. He wasn't going to send her running back to her house like a scared little girl.

Tucking her arm in Rawson's, she held her head high and entered the restaurant through the same double doors Steele and his companion had disappeared through only minutes before.

Inside, strains of soft violin music wafted through the air, and the exotic scents of French food permeated the subtly lit rooms. Gigantic, gas-burning crystal chandeliers swayed and sparkled over lavishly clothed diners who sat at white cloth-covered tables eating dishes Temerity had never heard of with gleaming silver forks and knives.

Any other time, the beautiful display of opulence would have thrilled Temerity; but she was unable to appreciate any of the magnificent atmosphere that surrounded her. Nor was she aware that many of the diners turned toward her and Charles as they stood at the top of the three wide stairs leading down into the main dining room, all of them wondering who the handsome pair were.

Her eyes darted from table to table, searching for Steele. But she couldn't find him and finally assumed he had chosen to share a more intimate dinner with his companion in one of the small private dining cubicles that circled the balcony overlooking the dining room.

Throughout the luxurious dinner Charles ordered for her, which could have been lima beans and cornbread for all she knew, Temerity's attention was on the balcony doors. Though she told herself it didn't matter to her where Steele was eating, every time one of the concealing doors opened or closed for a neatly dressed waiter to serve dinner or remove dishes, her gaze flew up to see if she could determine who was inside. And each time she could see nothing, she would

453

promise herself she wouldn't look. But no sooner did she make the vow than another waiter would appear at the top of the stairs with a tray of covered dishes, and her attention would again be drawn to the balcony.

"I would like to take you to places even more wonderful than this," Charles said silkily, taking her hand and lifting it to his lips. "There's a place in Paris you will adore."

"Mmm?" she hummed, her eyes darting along the line of balcony doors, then down to her hand, which she was surprised to find in Rawson's. How long had he been holding it? She pulled back on it, but Charles caught the tips of her fingers in his and bent to kiss them one at a time. "Charles, please," she whispered, her face turning red as she glanced nervously around her.

"I want to put diamonds on every one of these sweet fingers. Diamonds at your throat, diamonds on your wrists and on your ears. And furs. You should wear ermine or white fox."

Shocked by his behavior, she was unable to do anything without causing a scene. "Charles, please, I know you're just trying to boost my spirits—and I've had a lovely time. But I would really like to go home now, if you don't mind. I'm feeling a little tired."

When he didn't release her hand but leaned forward to kiss her behind her ear, she jerked her head back, adding, "And I have the most dreadful headache. Please take me home."

It was another ten minutes before Temerity and Charles stepped into the carriage the doorman had brought around; and by that time, her headache was no longer a lie. In fact, it was accompanied by nausea. And when the cab pulled up in front of her house, she wasn't certain she could make it into the house before she became quite ill.

"Really, it was wonderful, Mr. Rawson . . ." she said, turning to face him at the door and offer her hand.

"Charles," he corrected. "And the evening isn't over, Temerity." He leaned forward, trapping her against the door.

"Charles," she said, "I'm awfully tired. My headache is getting worse," she added, doing her best to keep the rich French dinner in her stomach.

"Perhaps this will help you feel better," he said, reaching in his pocket and bringing out a small box.

"What is it?" she asked, afraid to know.

"Let's go inside and open it and see," he said with a secretive smile. He took the key from her hand and inserted it in her front door. "You'll be able to see better in here." He backed her through the front door and closed it behind him once they were inside. "Go on and open it," he coaxed.

Temerity did as he asked, opening the velvet box to reveal a large diamond solitaire ring.

"What's this?"

"Haven't you seen a diamond ring before?"

"Not this big. Why are you showing it to me?"

"I'm not 'showing' it to you, love. I'm giving it to you as a pledge of my love for you."

"Your love for me? But I never—"

"I want to marry you, Temerity," he said, taking the ring from the box and starting to put it on her left hand.

"Stop!" she cried, drawing her hand back in horror. "I can't marry you, Charles!"

A flicker of irritation twitched across his face, but was quickly disguised. "Why not? Is there someone else?"

Steele's dimpled smile floated across her memory, but she shook her head. "No, it's not someone else. It's just that . . ."

"What?"

455

"I just never thought of you that way. We're friends and I care a great deal for you. But I can't marry you. I don't love you."

"It's that first mate of yours, isn't it?"

Temerity shot Charles a trapped look. "No!" she protested adamantly. "It's no one. I just can't marry a man I'm not in love with! Please understand!"

"Oh, I understand, all right. You've been leading me on for weeks now, letting me visit you every day, giving me those teasing smiles of yours to make me think maybe tomorrow! I should have just taken you on the *Intrepid*. Women like you prefer that, don't you? Instead, I thought you would like being treated like a lady and courted. I should have known a daughter of a man like Tim Kincade wouldn't appreciate the finer things."

Shrinking back from the force of his tirade, Temerity held her hand to her mouth. "Please, Charles. Don't do this!"

"Do what?" He took a menacing step toward her. "This?" With surprising speed that took Temerity off guard, he reached out and grabbed the low bodice of her gown and gave it a jerk, ripping it and her underthings open to her waist in one violent motion. "I have a right to see what I've waited so long for!"

Inhaling a sharp gasp, Temerity's arms flew up to cover her bared breasts. "Charles, stop!" she shrieked, backing away from him.

"Move your hands, whore!" he said, advancing on her retreating figure. He grabbed her wrists and wrenched her arms behind her, then slammed her back against the wall beneath the stairs. "Show me what you've given that common bastard you chose over me!"

"No, Charles, please!"

"I've waited too long for you. You're going to know what you're missing by rejecting me!" He buried his

456

face in the curve of her neck and pushed his hips hard against hers.

"Stop right there, Rawson!" a woman's voice shouted.

Temerity and Charles both looked up to see Mrs. Winters standing in the kitchen doorway. She had a rifle aimed at them.

"You don't have the nerve to use that, old woman," Charles sneered. "Now get on out of here before I lose my temper."

"Just you try me, mister!" Mrs. Winters said, pulling down on the lever of her Henry .44 rifle to slide a cartridge into place. "I didn't like the looks of your face from the first minute I saw it, and I wouldn't mind rearrangin' it in the least!"

Charles looked from the old woman's face to Temerity's and back to Mrs. Winters again. He dropped his hold on Temerity's hands and stepped away from her. "Don't think you've seen the last of me, ladies!" he said, opening the front door and leaving.

"Oh, Mrs. Winters," Temerity wept, sagging back against the wall. "Thank God, you came!"

Keeping her rifle aimed at the front door, the fat little woman ran with surprising speed toward it, not relaxing until it was locked. "Are you all right, missy?"

"Yes, I'm all right now," she said, the tears streaming down her cheeks as she clutched the torn edges of her bodice together. "Why would he act like that, Mrs. Winters? I've never encouraged him to believe I considered him anything other than a friend."

"Well, you just forget about that scoundrel. I bet he won't be comin' around here anymore. His type's too worried about his pretty face to chance gettin' his nose blown off."

Mrs. Winters wrapped her arms around Temerity and guided her away from the wall and up the stairs.

"You just get your nightgown on and go to sleep. In the mornin' we'll see about havin' the police come out here and give us a little extra protection for a while."

"What about tonight? What if he comes back tonight?"

"He ain't goin' to. But if he does, I'm goin' to shoot off more than his nose!"

Temerity managed a weak laugh.

"Don't you laugh, girl. I could do it in a minute if I had to. Mr. Winters bought me that rifle before he died and he made sure I knew how to use it. You don't worry. Nobody's goin' to come up here and bother you! Unless it's over my dead body. I'll be sleepin' at the foot of the stairs just to make certain. And my ol' Henry rifle will be right there with me!"

Suddenly feeling very foolish, Temerity prodded the housekeeper toward the bedroom door. "That's not necessary. You go on and sleep in your own bed. I'll be fine."

"I'll sleep where I said I would, and that's all we're goin' to say about it. Now go on to sleep." Mrs. Winters gave Temerity a motherly kiss on the cheek. "Tomorrow's another day!"

Steele shoved his hands into his pockets and strolled along the riverfront. "Damn! If I just hadn't seen her tonight!" He kicked an empty can and listened as it clacked over the brick levee and disappeared into the darkness. *I might have known she'd turn to that son-of-a-bitch Rawson the first chance she got.*

What difference does it make to me? She can see whoever she wants to see. I'm through with her. She had her chance, but she was too stubborn to even speak to me at her father's funeral.

"To hell with her!" he yelled. *All she ever cared*

about was the money anyway! Let her spend the rest of her life with him, for all I care.

But no matter how Steele tried to convince himself, he couldn't believe that it was truly over between him and Temerity. He thought about how beautiful she'd been tonight when he'd seen her in the dining room of the Chez Orleans, and renewed anguish tore at his heart.

Poor Marian Peabody had no idea what she'd done wrong. He hadn't wanted to take her out in the first place, but his grandmother had arranged it and he'd been unable to gracefully get out of having dinner with the girl. Then when he'd spotted Temerity and Rawson together, every ounce of the good manners he'd tried to show had disappeared. He'd gulped his food down, quaffed down too much wine, then hurried the girl out of the restaurant and home so quickly that he knew he would hear about it in the morning from his grandmother.

Maybe if I went to talk to Temerity one more time, he mused dejectedly.

"No, goddammit! If she wants me, she knows where to find me!"

She'll never come. Temerity Kincade would shrivel up and die before she'd admit she was wrong!

"Dammit! I ought to just go to her right this minute and make her admit she still loves me no matter who I am!"

What have I got to lose?

"Not a goddamn thing!" he shouted in answer to himself. "Not a goddamn thing!"

Chapter Twenty-Eight

It was useless. She wasn't going to be able to sleep. Too much had happened today, and her mind kept jumping from thought to thought.

Temerity tossed off the sheet and swung her feet to the floor. She lit the gas lamp on the wall, then crawled back into bed and leaned against her headboard, her arms folded across her midriff.

She had no one to blame but herself for what had happened with Charles Rawson. If only she'd listened to Steele. He had tried to warn her about what kind of man Charles was, but she'd been too stubborn to listen.

In fact, she thought with the rancid taste of self-disgust in her mouth, she'd been too obstinate to listen to lots of things. She hadn't listened when Steele had tried to explain why he'd helped her. She hadn't given him a chance. Oh, she had heard him say the words, but she hadn't really listened to them. She'd been too worried about protecting her own stupid pride.

"Oh, Steele, I've been such a fool!" she cried, burying her face in her hands. "I'm so sorry. I turned my back on you when you needed me most."

Everything he did, he did for me, and I was too blind

to see it. Never once did he turn away from me when I needed him. He was always there. I never could have made that trip without him. But I threw it all back in his face because of my pride. And now I've lost him.

Temerity sobbed into her hands for a long time before her instinctive determination for survival exploded to the surface of her conscience.

Are you giving up, Temerity? Is that why you're sitting here crying and feeling sorry for yourself?

"No, dammit! I'm not giving up! I've never before let anything stop me from going after what I want! And I want Steele Cameron! I want my baby to know his father! And I don't want to sleep in this bed alone anymore!"

She leaped off the bed and began sorting through her clothes for something she could put on that would fit in the waist yet look acceptable for an early morning call. Because she *was* going to go calling today. And she was going to get Steele to take her back if she had to get down on her knees and beg him. *Begging as a last resort, of course!*

Locating a skirt with a drawstring waist and a loose-shaped jacket that fell to her hips, she lay her clothes out on the bed and went to the washstand.

As she began to pour tepid water from the pitcher into the washbowl, a loud thud suddenly sounded from downstairs, as if something very heavy had hit the floor.

Cocking her head toward her door, she listened. But all she heard was silence.

Just as she was about to shrug off the noise as her imagination and lean over the washbowl to clean her face, she heard the familiar creak the seventh step made when someone stepped on it.

Her head jerked up. Someone was coming up the stairs. Dropping her washcloth into the water, she ran to the bedroom door and yanked it open.

462

"Mrs. Winters, is that you?" she called out.

A large hand clapped over her mouth, rendering her silent as an arm swooped under her knees and lifted her off the ground. "Mrs. Winters is out for a while," a gruff, unfamiliar voice barked.

Temerity's startled eyes opened wide to stare at the dark bearded face looming next to hers. She kicked her feet and reached up to rake her nails down the ugly scowling face, narrowly missing his eye with the four bloody trails left by her fingers.

"You bitch!" he screamed, tightening his hold on her face and making it nearly impossible for her to breathe. "If I wasn't gittin' paid so good to deliver you in good shape, I'd give you plenty for that! Now you be still or I'll forgit myself."

Minutes later, her vision blurring and her ears ringing from the lack of sufficient air, Temerity was tossed into a carriage waiting in the alley beside her house.

"You owe me extra for this," her captor hissed at a man who sat in the far corner of the carriage.

The second man didn't answer, but he pulled a pouch from his pocket and pitched it toward the other, who scrambled to catch it. Reaching over where Temerity lay semiconscious on the carriage floor, the man shut the door and tapped the roof with his cane. The carriage immediately lurched forward, jostling Temerity's face up against the man's booted leg.

"Let this be a lesson to you, my dear," he said softly, lifting his other foot and placing the heel of it against her shoulder, then rolling her over onto her back and pinning her to the floor. "Saying no to me is very dangerous."

"Charles?" she choked, her chest bursting with fear and pain from the pressing weight of his boot.

*   *   *

Before the powerful horse could achieve a complete halt, its rider had dismounted and was covering the sidewalk to Temerity's house at a run.

"Help!" he heard a short, bulky woman in a white nightgown scream as she came running out onto the porch, a rifle in her hands. "They've took Miss Kincade!"

Steele mounted the steps to the porch in one aggressive leap. Unmindful of the rifle, he grabbed the housekeeper's meaty upper arms and shook her. "What are you talking about, woman?"

"Someone hit me and stole her! Please, mister, you've got to help her!"

Fear and rage exploded in equal proportions in Steele's brain. "When?" he yelled. "Who?"

"There!" the old woman shouted, pointing an arthritic finger at the carriage speeding down the street away from the house. "That's the same carriage that scoundrel Rawson was in earlier!" she shrieked. "I'm sure he's got her in there!"

Steele became aware of the clatter of horses' hooves and carriage wheels on brick pavement sounding through the silence of the night just before a team of horses and carriage disappeared around the corner.

"Are you sure?" he asked, taking a moment to assimilate what the woman was suggesting.

"It's him all right. He threatened to come back after her. I know it's him!"

Not waiting to hear more, Steele released the hysterical woman and ran back to his horse, leaping into the saddle and kicking the sorrel up to a full gallop.

"Why are you doing this, Charles?" Temerity asked tremulously, not even trying to disguise her fear as she lay on the floor of the carriage.

464

"Because you're mine! And after tonight no man will have the right to say otherwise!"

"What's going to happen tonight?" she asked, moving slightly in an effort to ease some of the pressure on her chest.

Charles laughed, a vicious mad sound that tore through Temerity with jagged chills. He pressed his foot down harder on her. "Did you really think I'd let you go, Temerity? When your mother left me and married that ill-bred Scot, I—"

"My mother? What's she got to do with this?"

"I'm the man her parents chose for her. It was me she jilted to run away with Tim Kincade. I'm the man she made a fool of in front of all of Philadelphia's society."

"You knew my parents?"

"But despite all she did to me, I loved her. And when she died, I swore to get even with Tim Kincade for what he'd done. I set out to destroy him where it would hurt him most. Because of a series of 'unfortunate accidents' orchestrated by me, he was forced to witness the slow ruin of his business before he died, the business he'd spent all his life building."

"Are you saying it was you who—"

"I had nearly done it last year when I convinced his partner to let me sell all his goods for him. Then the profits mysteriously disappeared. But Kincade was more determined than I expected. So he mortgaged his boat to finance another trip this year. Oh, it was such fun to watch him stock his packet so carefully in a last effort to save himself. That's when I arranged his — 'accident.'"

A sinking feeling of disbelief hit Temerity in her stomach. "You caused his accident?"

"Of course I did. You don't think I was going to give up until he was completely destroyed, do you? Then you came home and announced you were going to take

465

the *Intrepid* upriver. At first I thought I'd just burn the *Intrepid* to the water line and be done with you and your father for good."

She lifted her head and tried to see him. "You set the fire in the hold when we were in St. Charles, didn't you?"

"Not exactly. I don't like the smell of kerosene. Yeager set the fire—under my orders."

"Yeager? But he worked for the Cameron Line!"

"And for me. That was why I couldn't afford to let him live after I realized that marrying you would be the greatest revenge of all against Tim Kincade. That way, everything he spent his life working for would be mine! A just reward for the man who destroyed my life when he stole my fiancée from me, wouldn't you say?"

"It was you who killed Mr. Yeager?"

"Of course, and the Rigby sisters, and the two guards who 'deserted' at the Indian agency."

"You killed all of them? But why?"

"The Rigby sisters knew too much, and the guards were simply in the way when I arranged to have the Indian agent and his friend take you off the *Intrepid*."

"You arranged my kidnapping?"

"I hoped that if I saved you, it would make you grateful to me. You see, by then I'd begun to care for you and wanted you to come to me willingly."

"And you put the bloody handkerchief in the hold and arranged for me to find Rosalie Rigby and Steele together, didn't you? Steele tried to tell me, but I didn't believe him."

"The handkerchief in the hold *and* the ribbon from Rosalie's dress in his drawer. It's too bad you refused to believe my 'evidence.' If you had, you could have spared us all this unpleasantness."

"It was you on the deck watching me that last night in St. Charles!" Temerity said with an accusing glare.

466

"Of course it was. And I was the fourth man on the levee that night. Your deckhand lover saw me, but he didn't know who I was," he bragged with a smile.

"When you outwitted the fools I hired to steal your profits in Montana, I was very angry. I wanted you to be completely broken so you'd be forced to turn to me to save your beloved riverboat. But your bastard lover kept getting in the way . . ."

"You were in Virginia City?"

Charles curled his fist in absolute loathing. "I was there and I was in Helena to witness your disgusting display with Cameron. It all would have been so much easier if I'd killed him when I shot him! And I would have if that damned nosy woman hadn't bumped my arm. That and the fact that he stole your virginity from me are my two regrets in all this.

"But none of that matters now, does it? I have you and that's what is important. Would you like to get up now?" he asked, his voice smooth with pleasantness as he removed his foot from her chest and offered her his hand.

Refusing to take it, Temerity scrambled to the opposite seat and cowered in the corner. "You won't get away with this. I'll have you arrested the first chance I get."

"But you'll be my wife by then and won't be able to testify against me, so it will do you no good."

"I'll never be your wife."

"Yes, you will," he said, reaching across the carriage and jerking her over beside him. "Before the night is out, you will be Mrs. Charles Rawson and we will be on a boat for New Orleans. There we'll board an ocean liner for our wedding trip to Europe."

"You're crazy! You can't *make* me marry you! I'll refuse. I'll get away from you."

"No, you won't, my love. I had hoped it would not

come to this; but if necessary, I have made arrangements to keep you locked in our cabin on the steamer. I've told them my wife is quite mad and that I have to keep you drugged and in restraints most of the time. Because I'm such an adoring husband and can't bear to lock my darling wife away in a mad house, I'm taking her to Europe for special treatment. The captains both feel quite sorry for me."

"Please, Charles, don't do this," Temerity pleaded.

"Call me darling," he said. "I like the sound of that!"

Temerity choked back her frightened tears and said, "Darling."

"Yes, that's much better," he said.

"I'm sorry for the misery my parents caused you, Char—darling—but I'm not at fault. Just let me go, and I'll never tell a soul."

Charles chuckled and kissed the top of her head. "Don't you see? It wouldn't be the same without you at my side to share my greatest victory. My revenge against Tim Kincade."

"But he's not even alive to know. What satisfaction are you going to get out of revenge against a man who doesn't even know what you've done?"

"Your father knows. I told him how I had destroyed him the day I informed him that you and I were going to be married."

"You told him what?"

"You should have seen him. He was livid! And of course he was quite adamant about his refusal to allow it. You can see I had no choice but to get rid of him permanently"

"You killed my father?" she gasped, the memory of a pillow on the table beside her father's chair exploding in her mind.

"Of course. I would have preferred to have him witness our wedding. It would have been the perfect

468

ending. But I couldn't take the chance he would find a way to stop me from marrying you. I love you, Millie. I've always loved you! You've always been mine and I couldn't let him take you away from me again."

"Millie? Millie was my mother's name. Not mine. I'm Temerity! You don't love me, Charles. You love Millie!"

He looked at her for a moment, his expression confused, then laughed. "And I love you. I've waited over twenty years to have you for my wife!"

"No, not me! It was Millie you wanted! Not me!"

The carriage pulled to a halt and the driver jerked open the door.

Charles bounded out of the carriage, dragging her behind him.

"What is this place?" Temerity protested, fighting with every shred of strength she could muster.

Rawson's fingers dug painfully into her upper arm, and he slapped her across the face, sending her head snapping backward. "Behave yourself," he warned in a low, threatening hiss, "or I'll be forced to have Winston tie your hands. Not a very pleasurable way to be married."

The driver ran ahead and opened the door to the ramshackle building before them. "Here they are, preacher! Get up off your drunken ass and get this wedding started."

Her vision blurring from the force of the blow to her head, Temerity tried to focus her eyes. The inside of the one-room building was filthy, filled with what looked like old horse gear. Dressed in a tattered black suit, the lone occupant was an old man who crawled to his feet from a pile of rags in the corner where he'd been sleeping.

"Come in," he mumbled, his unshaven face old and filthy. He lifted a bottle to his lips and took a long swig

469

of the cheap whiskey. "Where's the happy couple?" he asked, whipping a ragged prayer book from his pocket.

Temerity shot Rawson a frantic look of appeal. "Please, Charles, you can't do this. I can't marry you. It won't even be legal!"

"Oh, it'll be legal!" he said, giving her a shove toward the swaying preacher.

"He's drunk!"

"Go on, Reverend," he said, positioning Temerity between himself and Winston and facing the old man. "Let's get on with it."

"Dearly beloved," the reverend started, "we are gathered—"

"Skip that part!" Charles ordered.

The man turned the pages in the book and ran his bleary-eyed gaze downward until he came to the part he was looking for. "Do you take this woman to be your bride? To have and to—"

"I do," Charles interrupted impatiently.

The preacher looked at Rawson and frowned, then shrugged his shoulders and went on. "Do you take this man for your lawful wedded husband?" he said to Temerity.

"No! I don't!" She struggled against the hold Winston and Charles had on each of her arms.

"She does," Charles offered with a vicious jerk on her hair that left her eyes watering.

"Then by the powers vested in me, I—"

Without warning, the door to the tiny shack came crashing into the room, followed by the large bulk of a man who loomed in the shattered doorway like an avenging angel.

"Oh, my Lord!" the preacher cried, quailing back into the corner. He tripped over a broken chair and was sent sprawling.

Charles and Winston dropped their holds on Temerity and spun to face the intruder. "This is a private ceremony, mister," Winston snarled, whipping a revolver from his holster.

Too fast for his opponent to see it coming, Steele's boot rose from the floor and kicked the gun from the driver's hand. A fist planted dead center in Winston's face immediately followed the boot.

Winston's entire body lifted off the ground and flew back into the pile of rubbish where the preacher lay mumbling his prayers of forgiveness.

Temerity's heart jerked in her chest as she saw Charles hurl himself parallel to the floor and come up with Winston's revolver pointed at Steele. "He has the gun!" she shouted.

"So, the deckhand won't give up!" Charles said with an evil sneer as he signaled for Steele to raise his hands. "I was sure we'd seen the last of you! But it's just as well you came. I don't like the idea of having unfinished business. And you're definitely unfinished business!" He cocked the hammer on the revolver.

"No!" Acting instinctively, Temerity grabbed a broken chair leg from the floor and brought it down on Charles's arm, sending the gun clattering to the floor.

"You bitch!" he yowled. "You've broken my arm!" Whipping a pistol from inside his coat, he aimed it at her. "I should have known you were no better than your mother!"

But before he could fire it, the sound of a shot reverberated through the tiny building, and an instant later a bullet in the chest propelled Charles back against the wall.

The expression on his face stunned, he watched in horror as the red stain on the front of his shirt spread. The fact of his own death registered in his eyes just before they glossed over in a blank stare, and he slid down the wall into a heap of filth and discarded harnesses.

"Oh, Steele!" Temerity cried, running across the

room and wrapping her arms around the man who held the smoking gun. "You were right about him all along! He killed them all! Mr. Yeager, the Rigby sisters, the missing guards, my . . . father! Steele! He killed my father!"

"Hush, Temerity," he whispered, gathering her trembling body into his embrace. "It's all over now."

"I was so wrong," she wept against his shirt, her words coming between great racking sobs. "About Rawson, about you, about the Cameron Line. Can you ever forgive me for all the terrible things I said to you?"

"Ssh, Temerity, let's not talk about it now." He smoothed his hand over the back of her hair and buried his face in its thick black silk.

"But we have to. I've made so many mistakes, I can't bear the thought of going another minute without telling you how sorry I am and how much I love you."

"I love you too."

"I know I don't deserve your forgiveness, Steele, but—" She stopped speaking and looked up at him, not daring to believe her ears. "What did you say?"

"I told you I love you, too! I always have," he repeated with a helpless, dimpled grin.

"Oh, my sweet, sweet love!" she sighed, catching his cheeks in the palms of her hands and bringing his face down to hers. "If you only knew how afraid I was I'd never hear those words again." She touched his lips softly with hers. "I love you so much, Steele. To think I almost let my stubborn pride destroy us!"

Steele tightened his hold on her and grinned sheepishly. "It wasn't all your fault. My stupidity did a pretty fair job of messing things up on its own."

"You weren't stupid! You were only trying to help. I was the one who did everything wrong!" she insisted. "I'm the one who's to blame."

"Tem . . ." Steele said with a light kiss on the tip of

her nose.

"Mmm?"

"Let's not argue about whose fault it was. I just want to go home."

"But what about—"

"Temerity, shut up," he said, silencing her with his mouth on hers in the life-sustaining kiss they both had been longing for.

"Oh, Steele, I do love you!" she sighed when the kiss finally ended. All thoughts of the past were unimportant compared to the magnitude of the glorious happiness splintering through her heart. "I'll never question you again."

"I find that a bit hard to believe. Let's get out of here," he said, scooping her up into his arms and stepping outside the shack in time to witness the first pink rays of a dawning new day. "We're going to get married today."

Snuggling deep into his embrace, she smiled through her tears. "Aren't you taking a lot for granted, Mr. Cameron? Suppose I've already made plans for today?"

"Then you'll cancel them!"

"Even if I was planning to finish papering our baby's nursery today?" she asked with an innocent expression on her face.

"Even if you were planning on having lunch with Queen Victoria of Eng—What did you say?" he stuttered, putting her on his horse and staring up at her.

"About papering the walls?"

"Temerity! Stop it!" His expression was confused, hopeful. "What did you say about a baby?"

She giggled. "You mean this baby?" she asked, taking his hand and placing it on her belly.

As if on cue, the baby in her womb did a fluttery somersault against its father's hand.

473

"What's that?"

She lay her hands over Steele's. "That's your son, Papa."

"A baby? We're going to have a baby? Are you sure? When?"

Temerity nodded her head and pressed his hand harder to her stomach. "The doctor estimates he'll be born in late March—just in time not to interfere with our first trip to Fort Benton in the spring."

"Hold on now. Your days of operating a riverboat are over! I'm putting my foot down this time. From now on, you're going to stay home and let someone else do it!" he said sternly, mounting the horse behind her.

"Oh, I am, am I?" She glanced back over her shoulder and gave him a knowing grin. "Surely that's negotiable."

"Now, look, Temerity . . ." he started, then rolled his eyes heavenward, with an exaggerated groan. "What the hell am I going to do with you?"

"You could try kissing me and telling me you love me again!" she said, twisting her upper body to wrap her arms around his neck. "We have plenty of time to decide about next spring."

"It's already decided, Temerity! I mean it! This time you don't have any choice."

"I don't?" she said with a knowing smile, accenting each word with a teasing kiss. "We'll see. After all, a lot can happen between now and next spring."

"That's what I'm afraid of!"

Epilogue

"I can too be a train engineer if I want to!" the petite seven-year-old girl yelled, pushing her angry face up to her brother's and balling her fists on her curveless hips.

Copying her determined stance, the chestnut-haired six-year-old brought his face within inches of his sister's. "Can not!"

"Can too! I can be anything I want," she said with a haughty lift of her freckled nose. "I can be a doctor, or a sheriff, or even the president of the United States if I want to be. But I don't. Cause I'm going to be an engineer when I grow up!"

"Nuh-uh. You're a girl! Everyone knows girls can't be the engineers. Boys have to be the engineers," he said with a smug nod of his head. "Girls are supposed to be the teachers and the mamas. So there!"

"Well, I'm going to be one, and you can't stop me!" she vowed, sweeping her dark braids up on top of her head and striking what she was sure was a glamorous pose. "I'll be the most beautiful engineer in the world! And people will come from all over to ride on my train."

"You're so dumb!"

"What's going on in here? I could hear you all the way downstairs in my office," Temerity scolded, rushing into the large playroom above the offices of the Cameron-Kincade Packet Company.

"Timmy says girls can't be engineers," the girl tattled with a righteous sneer in her brother's direction. "He thinks only boys are engineers! He's wrong, isn't he?"

Temerity smiled at her oldest child and stooped down to bring both of her children into her arms. "Well, Trish, I don't imagine there's even been a woman engineer, so it would be awfully difficult."

The boy flashed his inherited dimples and a smug grin at his sister with a self-satisfied, "I told you."

Trish stared at her mother, her expression hurt and betrayed.

"On the other hand, Timmy, just because no one's ever done it before, is that a reason not to do what you know is right for you? Besides, wouldn't you be proud to have a sister who was the first woman engineer in the country? I know I certainly would."

Timmy shrugged his shoulders and made a face.

"The important thing for you both to remember is that boys *and* girls must follow their dreams and do their best at whatever their hearts guide them to do when they grow up. Even if it's something no one else believes you can do—because you're the wrong size, or the wrong color or the wrong sex. If you believe in yourself and are willing to work hard, there's nothing you can't do."

"Better listen to your mama, kids," Steele said, coming up the stairs behind Temerity. "How do you think she turned out to be the first woman to earn a master pilot's license? Seems to me, I remember more than one or two nonbelievers who insisted she couldn't be a river pilot when she went down to St. Louis to take

476

her test three years ago. There was even an editorial in the newspaper asking what the world was coming to when wives and mothers were allowed to leave their homes to do men's work. But none of those dissenters stopped your mother. She just followed her dream and went into that test and made the highest grade the board gave that day."

Temerity tossed a happy grin over her shoulder at her husband of nearly eight years. Still, after all this time, the sight of his mischievously dimpled face set her heart fluttering like a schoolgirl's. *"Those* dissenters? Seems to me I remember a time when you—"

Steele shrugged his shoulders and grinned with pretended sheepishness. "So I didn't always believe in the equality of the fairer sex," he admitted. "But about eight years ago a stubborn riverboat owner showed me the truth. There's nothing a determined woman can't do if she sets her mind to it."

Standing up, Temerity walked to Steele and wrapped her arms around his neck. "And about eight years ago a domineering first mate taught me that there's nothing a stubborn woman can't do if she has the love and support of a good man."

Trish and Timmy looked at each other, the smiles on their young faces turning to expressions of mutual disgust. "Let's go, Timmy," the girl said, taking her brother's hand. "They're going to get all mushy again."

"Yeah, all mushy," Timmy agreed with a grimace as they disappeared down the stairs. "Want to play sheriffs and robbers?"

"I get to be the sheriff!"

"You always get to be the sheriff. Girls aren't supposed to be the sheriff . . ."

Temerity smiled up at Steele, her blue eyes sparkling. "I think our little talk went over a certain male-superiority believer's head."

"He'll learn," Steele said, burying his face in the curve of her neck and taking a nip of the sensitive flesh. "I did, didn't I?"

"Yes, you did. We both did!"

"Then why don't you quit talking about it and get down to something important—like getting 'mushy'?"

Historical Note

Though Frank and Jesse James committed their first robbery—and the first bank robbery in the United States—when they robbed the Clay County Savings Association in Liberty, Missouri, on February 14, 1866, it was four years—and six bank robberies—later before it was known that the James brothers were leaders of the brazen outlaw gang that would ride over the Midwest for the next fifteen years.

During the first years following the Civil War and the start of their career as outlaws, Frank and Jesse stayed with their mother, Mrs. Zerald Samuel, at her farm in Kearney, only ten miles north of Liberty, Missouri. And while there, no one ever suspected they were criminals. Jesse, who'd shown a strong interest in religion even as a child, attended church services regularly with his mother, and Frank became known as a young man who was an enthusiastic admirer of Shakespeare and Francis Bacon and always had his nose in a book.

Though the James gang specialized in stealing from banks, they also robbed individuals, trains, stores, and stagecoaches, but emphatically drew the line at taking from widows, Southerners, preachers, and friends! In fact, to the people of the Missouri Ozarks, Jesse was considered a kind of hero who had been driven to a life of crime by the authorities, who continued to hold his loyalty to the Confederacy against him.

In 1881, when the governor of Missouri offered a $10,000 reward for the capture of Jesse and Frank James, dead or alive, the temptation was too great for gang member Robert Ford. He shot Jesse, who was unarmed at the time and in his own house in St. Joseph, Missouri, in the back of the head for the reward. Frank turned himself in but was acquitted, twice, and spent the rest of his life living quietly on his farm in Missouri.

Special Thanks

To the Montana Historical Society for their generous and valuable assistance, to the North Texas Romance Writers for their constant and sustaining support, and to all of you who read *Untamed Surrender* and *Captive Surrender*. Your letters and kind words have meant more to me than I can possibly express. I love hearing from you and will continue to do my best to answer your letters, as well as write the kind of romantic adventure stories you've told me you like.

Michalann "Micki" Perry